GW01607465

To Peter Terry,
with best wishes,
Joe Milner
July 96

To Blazes With Glory

A Chindit's War

JOE MILNER

EDWARD GASKELL
The Lazarus Press
DEVON

To Blazes With Glory: A Chindit's War
First Published 1995
by Edward Gaskell
The Lazarus Press
Cranford House
6 Grenville street
Bideford Devon EX39 2EA

Typeset Printed and Bound in Great Britain by The Lazarus Press.
Jacket Design and Artwork By Norma Fynn

British Library Cataloguing in Publication Data.
A catalogue record for this book is available from the British Library

ISBN 1 898546 11 8

For Scottie
and
His Laddies

Acknowledgements

Much of the factual content of this book derives from the recollections of old Chindit 'muckers' and myself. I am particularly indebted to Jack Lindo, Fred Holliday, Harry Winstanley, Bob Campion, George Jones, Tom Pickering and Steve Vasey, for their recollections and their corroboration of my own.

R. Rourke of 'The Chequers', Thompson, Norfolk spent a precious part of a family holiday reading my draft MS. I am grateful to him for his constructive criticism and for his persistent urgings to get the work published.

In the mid 1980s a group of pensioners – mostly ex-service like myself – styling ourselves 'The Old Codgers' yarned away Wednesday afternoons in the 'Waggon & Horses', Griston, Norfolk. Inexorably mortality took its toll, and their stories went with them. These losses initiated this book in the hope that my tales of the Chindits would not be lost to posterity. I am indebted to Mr J Woodhams for hosting the 'Old Codgers' – often beyond the constraints of the (then) licensing laws.

Mrs Lydia Sampson – a very busy family woman – checked and corrected the grammar and other mistakes in the original manuscript with commendable thoroughness. I am most grateful for her help.

Most of the verses I quote were indelibly committed to memory in my school days or during my early soldiering. Nevertheless, to validate my memory I consulted *The Definitive Edition of Rudyard Kipling's Verse* published by Hodder & Stoughton, *Siegfried Sassoon: Collected Poems, 1908-1956* published by Faber & Faber, *The Complete Poems of WH Davies* published by Jonathan Cape and *Longfellow's Poetical Works* published by Oxford University Press. The sources of *Break the News to Mother* and the parody *Fred Karno's Army* are not easily determined but in *British Soldiers' Songs* by Roy Palmer published by Michael Joseph a version of the latter is credited to a Frank Richards (1883-1961) of the Royal Welch Fusiliers. In the same book *Break the News to Mother* is credited to a Charles Russell Harris in 1897. I believe *O'Reilly's Daughter* dates back to at least the first World War – the only printed version I have been able to find is in *The World's Best Dirty Songs* by Don Laycock published by Angus Robertson.

Acknowledgements

Researching, drafting and re-drafting my Ms took several years, throughout which time almost the entire burden of household duties and maintenance fell upon my wife, Anne. I gratefully acknowledge and appreciate her 'behind the scenes' contribution to the completion of this book.

J.M.
Caston, Norfolk.

The author and the publisher of this book would like to express their appreciation for the kind permission of the following authors and publishers to quote from and reproduce where necessary extracts from the below listed editions of their books.

Prisoners of Hope by Michael Calvert
Transworld Publishers Ltd. Corgi Edition 1973 ISBN 0 552 09179 0

Chindits : Long Range Penetration by Michael Calvert
Ballantine Books Inc. Pan/Ballantine Edition 1974 ISBN 0 330 24103 6

Chindit by Richard Rhodes James
Published by John Murray (Publishers) Ltd 1980 ISBN 0 7195 3746 0

The Chindit War by Shelford Bidwell
Published by Hodder & Stoughton London 1979 ISBN 0 340 22213 1

Maps and Illustrations

Contents

South East Asia Command Order of Battle and Chain of Command

- Supreme Allied Commander, South-East Asia (Mountbatten)
  - Deputy Supreme Allied Commander, South-East Asia (Stilwell)
    - Eastern Fleet (Somerville)
    - 11 Army Group (Giffard)
      - Ceylon Army Command
      - XIV Army (Slim)
        - XV Corps (Christison)
        - IV Corps (Scoones)
        - 3rd Indian Division (Special Forces; Wingate)
          - 3W.African Bde
            - 6 Nigerian
            - 7 Nigerian
            - 12 Nigerian
          - 14 Bde
            - 1 Beds & Herts
            - 7 Leicester
            - 2 Black Watch
            - 2 Yorks & Lancs
          - 16 Bde
            - 2 Queen's Royal Regt.
            - 2 Leicester
            - 45 Recce Regt.
          - 23 Bde
            - 2 Duke of Wellington's
            - 4 Border
            - 1 Essex
          - 77 Bde
            - 1 King's (Liverpool)
            - 1 Lancs. Fus.
            - 1 South Staffs
            - 3/6 Gurkha R.
            - 3/9 Gurkha R.*
          - 111 Bde
            - 2 King's Own Royal Lancasters
            - 1 Cameronians
            - 3/4 Gurkha R.
            - 4/9 Gurkha R.
      - Indian Ocean Garrisons
        - XIII Corps (Stopford)
    - Air C-in-C (Peirse)

* Attached as an infantry battalion to garrison Broadway.

Notes for Non-Military Readers

The British army ranks in descending orders :

Officers	Other Ranks	
Field Marshal	Regimental Sergeant Major	Warrant Officers
General	Quartermaster Sergeant Major	Warrant Officers
Lieutenant General	Company Sergeant Major	Warrant Officers
Major General	Colour Sergeant/Quartermaster Sergeant	Non Commissioned Officers
Brigadier	Sergeant	Non Commissioned Officers
Colonel *	Lance Sergeant	Non Commissioned Officers
Lieutenant Colonel	Corporal (Bombadier in Royal Artillery)	Non Commissioned Officers
Major		
Captain	Lance-Corporal (Lance-Bombadier Royal Artillery)	Non Commissioned Officers
Lieutenant		
Second Lieutenant	Private †	

* Colonels are usually General Staff Officers, or commanders of specialist echelons, e.g. Engineering, Medical Services, Artillery etc.

† Privates in the artillery are known as Gunners; In the Royal Engineers they are Sappers; In Light Infantry (Rifle) Regiments they are known as Riflemen; In armoured and cavalry units they are known as Troopers. In the King's (Liverpool) Regiment they are known as Kingsmen. In Fusilier Regiments they are known as Fusiliers.

At the time of the 1939/45 War, each British infantry regiment had a number of battalions, usually two regular and several Territorial army battalions.

Battalions were normally 800* men, made up as follows :

Battalion H.Q.	–	Commanding Officer (a Lieut. Colonel), Adjutant (a Major or Captain), Medical Officer (usually a Captain) Captain Quartermaster, Regimental Sergeant Major, a Quartermaster Sergeant Major, Orderly Room Sergeant, and other rank clerks and orderlies.
4 Companies	–	About 130 men, usually commanded by a Captain, assisted by a Company Sergeant Major, and divided into 3 Platoons, plus specialists, e.g. quartermaster, stores orderlies and signallers.
Platoons	–	Were usuallycommanded by a Lieutenant, (but sometimes by a Captain) assisted by a Sergeant, and divided into 3 sections consisting of a Corporal, Lance Corporal and 8 to 10 men.

Chindit Battalions – except the 3/9th Gurkha Rifles who were assigned to garrison Broadway – were split into two columns of about 400 men. Each column was composed of an infantry company of four platoons : a commando platoon of especially trained infantry men and Royal Engineers; a reconnaissance platoon including Burma Rifle men; a support platoon with two Vickers machine guns and two 3inch mortars; and Column H.Q. with its own defence platoon.

* Not including the battalion Band Officers and other ranks.

Preface

This is a soldier's tale of war and love.

In 1942/43 when the morale of the British 14th. Army had been badly shaken, if not shattered, by the Japanese conquest of Burma, Brigadier Orde Wingate conceived the idea of a Long Range Penetration Force (LRPs) to operate in seven columns, deep in enemy territory. Columns would rely solely on radio for communication with Army HQ in India and on air drops for supplies.

Wingate's novel proposal clashed with the Army's entrenched doctrines of fixed lines of advance and earthbound supply lines, and he was grudgingly allocated only troops that, hitherto, had been regarded as second, even third rate units. The British element was the 13th. Battalion King's (Liverpool) Regiment, a Territorial unit shipped to India for garrison duties. The other principal component was the 3/2 Gurkha Rifles, a battalion raised in wartime that had no combat experience – only two of its British officers were proficient in Gurkhali. A sprinkling of Burma Rifles as linguists and guides, and a few demolition and wireless specialists were drafted into the brigade.

Wingate forged these 'nondescript' troops – as Shelford Bidwell describes them in his book *The Chindit War* – into seven columns of tough, enthusiastic jungle fighters. This achievement was all the more remarkable in that by and large the British Gurkha officers, steeped in the tenets of conventional warfare, started out with little if any faith in Wingate's tactics. Indeed, WD Lentaigne, a Gurkha brigadier – then raising another Long Range Penetration force – made no bones about his loathing of Wingate and his disdain of Wingate's ideas.

This force, known as the 77 Independent Infantry Brigade became the first Chindits – a name derived from *Chinthe* the mythical lion of Budhism, whose stone statues are the guardians of Burmese temples. Wingate, himself, became known throughout Northern Burma as the 'Lord Protector of the Pagodas'.

In mid-February 1943, Wingate's columns infiltrated hundreds of miles into Japanese occupied Burma. For about three months they throttled the Japanese lines of communications, demolishing bridges and blowing up supply dumps.

They returned to India towards the end of April having lost over 800 of their 3,000 men and for what it strategically achieved the expedition was condemned as a dismal failure by the orthodox army hierarchy. However, after the long demoralising defeats by the Japanese, the British propaganda machine turned it into a spectacular epic of British and Gurkha commandoes raiding and rampaging for three months behind enemy lines. The press and radio eulogised Wingate as a modern day Lawrence of Arabia or Clive of India.

The expedition captured Churchill's imagination. In August he summoned Wingate to England and took him to the Allies Summit Conference in Quebec. There, Wingate's dynamism and ideas won him the authority to raise a Chindit Division for a long range expedition into Burma the following year, 1944. Moreover, the division would have the exclusive use of No.1 Air Commando, U.S. Army Air Force. This meant strike aircraft, Dakotas for air supply, Waco gliders, and above all, since many wounded had to be left in the jungle in the 1943 expedition, the Air Commando would include a light plane fleet to evacuate casualties.

Wingate, promoted to Major General for this campaign, was assured of direct access to Churchill – a privilege he was never backward in threatening to invoke whenever there was opposition to his plans. This 'blackmail' won him many concessions, and not unnaturally, more enemies than friends in Command circles, for which, after his untimely death his troops were to suffer grievously.

The British ground troops assigned to this second Chindit campaign were not an elite force of volunteers. With the exception of a few men – notably officers like Brigadiers Mike Calvert and Bernard Fergusson; and Lieutenant Colonel Walter Scott from the 1943 expedition – they were ordinary, run of the mill infantry battalions toughened and inspired by six to nine months of Wingatian training in the jungles of central India. The United States also fielded three battalions of Rangers to operate on

Chindit lines under the command of U.S. General Joseph Stilwell, with the code name 'Galahad'. These battalions, under U.S. Brigadier-General F. Merrill, officially entitled the 5307th Composite Unit, were soon dubbed Merrill's Marauders.

As already stated, this is a soldier's tale of the second Chindit campaign. The military historians, and commanders have had their say. In scholarly language, sometimes with only third hand information, they have variously condemned the campaign as a futile enterprise, or commended it as an invaluable contribution to the defeat of the Japanese in Burma. Some have narrated self justifying accounts of the punishing, ruthless, demands they imposed on their troops.

Whether the campaign was futile or invaluable – the purgatory, the inhuman privations of this latter day Flanders are beyond overstatement. No other units throughout World War II were kept in the field, deprived of any relief or recuperation, for any length of time approaching that of the Chindits. They went into Burma in high spirits and superbly fit believing they would be behind enemy lines for a maximum of 90 days. It was 5 months before the survivors, debilitated by malnutrition and disease, were pulled back to India.

For them, there were no safe billets between battles. No week-end passes, let alone lengthy furloughs. No cookhouses. No canteens. No village shops. Nor – some would say thankfully – any ENSA concerts. Their lives were a nightmare of brutal terrain, brutal climate and a brutal foe.

Chindit commanders, with some exceptions— notably Colonel Scott, but for whom few of the King's (Liverpool) men would have retained their sanity, if not their physical health – have published their memoirs of the campaign. The soldier's, the poor bloody infantryman's, has not so far been told for a variety of reasons. Chief among these must be that the plodding 'Tommie' was denied the privilege of a war diary. At the time, this was no hardship, nor grievance. In that world of tropical rain and eternal mud, writing materials, their preservation and use, were superfluous baggage to the footsloggers. Even the rare opportunity to write home could generally only be accomplished on scraps of paper – ration packages and toilet 'coggage' were at times resorted to –

and to the writer's knowledge few of the missives reached Britain. So, not for the rank and file the benefit of war diaries to substantiate their narrations and prod their memories. They, including the writer, have only unchronicled reminiscences to shriek through their sleep, and embellish re-union *bonhomie*.

The grand strategy and tactics that spawned those reminiscences were only vaguely – if at all – known to the Tommies. Thus there can be no clinically accurate account of the Chindits from a footslogger's pen. Much of this 'factionalised' narrative is based on the recollections of ex-Chindits, including myself, and the passage of time – over 50 years – may among other things have distorted the chronology of those recollections.

Badger does not exist – he never existed. He is a composite of many men who slogged through five months of hell. His experiences and attitudes are a microcosm of the thoughts of such men.

Wherever it may have given offence, or caused anguish to surviving comrades – or the kin of deceased Chindits – the names of characters have been disguised. Otherwise actual names have been used.

Finally, this is a story of passions and jealousy. In World War II – perhaps more than in any other war – combatants were not the only casualties. Apart from the aerial destruction of cities, concentration camp massacres and the like, marriages were mutilated by long separation. Couples had rushed into marriage in the heady emotion of a lad's embarkation leave, or even imminent posting beyond workaday commuting distance. Badger's was but one of those marriages, typical possibly of many thousands, that were the unrecorded casualties of war.

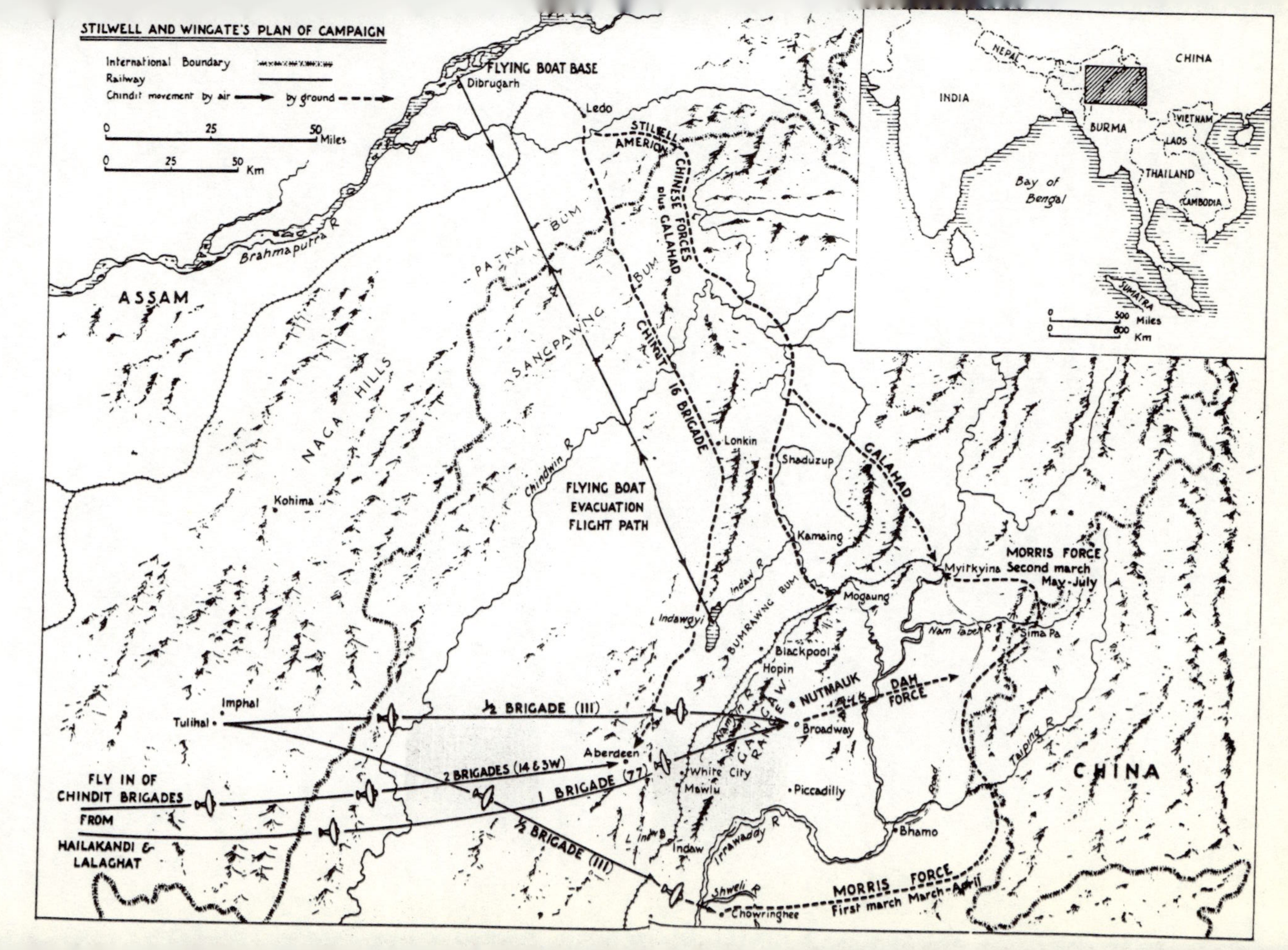

STILWELL AND WINGATE'S PLAN OF CAMPAIGN
International Boundary
Railway
Chindit movement by air
by ground
0
25
50 Miles
0
25
50 Km
FLYING BOAT BASE
Dibrugarh
Ledo
STILWELL
AMERICAN
CHINESE FORCES
plus GALAHAD
Brahmaputra R
ASSAM
PATKAI BUM
SANGPAWNG BUM
CHINDIT 16 BRIGADE
NAGA HILLS
Kohima
Chindwin R
FLYING BOAT
EVACUATION
FLIGHT PATH
Lonkin
Shaduzup
GALAHAD
Kamaing
Indaw R
BUMRAWNG BUM
Mogaung
Myitkyina
MORRIS FORCE
Second march
May-July
Indawgyi
Nam Tabet R
Sima Pa
Blackpool
Hopin
NUTMAUK
DAH
FORCE
Imphal
Tulihal
½ BRIGADE (111)
Broadway
Aberdeen
2 BRIGADES (14 & 3W)
1 BRIGADE (77)
White City
Mawlu
Piccadilly
GANGAW RANGE
Namyin R
Taiping R
CHINA
FLY IN OF
CHINDIT BRIGADES
FROM
HAILAKANDI &
LALAGHAT
½ BRIGADE (111)
Indaw
Irrawaddy R
Bhamo
Road
Shweli R
Chowringhee
MORRIS FORCE
First march March-April
NEPAL
CHINA
INDIA
BURMA
VIETNAM
LAOS
THAILAND
CAMBODIA
Bay of
Bengal
SUMATRA
0
500 Miles
0
800 Km

PART 1

Kachin Hills, Northern Burma: July 1944

'All Roads Lead To Dehra Dun'

On the shapes of the slain in their crumpled disgrace,
I stared for a while through the thin cold rain,
O'lad that I loved there is rain on your face,
And your eyes are blurred and sick like the plain

Siegfried Sassoon

'All Roads Lead To Dehra Dun'

Chapter One

Dawn was cold. Colder than the night had been. Colder, it seemed to Badger, than the ice-rimed country platform had been when Barbara, his bride of one night, had blown that last tearful kiss from the carriage window as her train chugged out of the station. Yet in a couple of hours this jungle chaung would be steaming. The sun was already distilling the mist and the dawn cacophony of screaming monkeys, shrill cicadas and shrieking brain-fever birds was drowning out the croaking frogs.

Up and downstream of him, spread along both banks of the narrow ravine weary men were squatting on rocky outcrops, calf deep in the chill mountain water. Hollow eyed men. Dazed by the days of futile fighting to take and hold Point 2171, and by weeks of remorseless monsoon storms and mud.

Point 2171. A mere pimple in the Kachin hills. A pimple that probably no human had trod, except some diligent, long dead ordnance surveyor, until the Japanese invaders occupied it. A cartographical triviality, but a crucifying mountain to the worn out column that had grappled to dislodge the invaders, and had fought off their savage counter attacks.

Emaciated men. Hunched under sodden blankets or dripping ground-sheets. Spent men. Six months ago, they had been vigorous, cocky youths. Toilworn, footsore men. 2171 was an eternity of 24 hours behind them, and they still had 15 miles to go to the security of Moguang. 15 crow flight miles, nearer 25 by meandering jungle and mountain tracks. Mountain and jungle to traverse and a brutal foe to elude.

The chaung was cold. Polar cold around Badger's feet. The column – remnants of 1st. King's (L/pools); a few Gurkhas and Signallers – had been huddled in the gorge since last night's cloudburst made further progress impossible. Stinging hail and chilling rain obliterated the moon. For hours the waters had roared downhill in a knee high torrent. He shuddered. Not only with the cold, but also with the prospect of the arduous trek ahead. The gruelling climbs up numberless false crests, the slithering descents down the reverse slopes. The raw, omnipresent fear of ambush at every zig and zag of the tracks. The impossibility of concentrating the straggling, single file column for a cohesive counter attack. In his condition he'd no chance of outliving a skirmish. Worse, he couldn't quell the faithless conviction that the column would scatter and flee at the first hint of an ambush.

Weeks ago as Chindits – Long Range Penetration troops – deep in enemy territory, they would have been the hunters thirsting for Jap blood, boldly harrying them and seeking opportunities to attack. They had been trained and armed only as 'hit and run' raiders, but the higher powers had flung them, willynilly, into set-piece battles. The three-month campaign had stretched to over five. Now, devitalized by months with rarely a full night's sleep, and by weeks of malnutrition they were physical and spiritual wrecks. Whatever traces of offensive spirit they had left were being expended in vituperate mutterings against their new enemies – their own commanders back in India. Whatever traces of stamina they could muster would hardly be enough to get them out of Burma. They were not prepared to sacrifice those final traces battling the Japs.

Nor, Badger thought, peering beneath his soggy bush hat brim at the hollow eyed men around him, could they be spurred into battle by threats of courts-martial. With the end of the of the campaign in sight, no military retribution could match the terror of being pipped at the post.

Reaching down through the chill water to rub his ankles he saw olive green slivers from his torn off trouser legs that now bound his feet quivering around his loosely tied boots. His ankles were blue-black. His galled feet numb. There was a creeping tenderness up his legs and a throbbing ache in his groins. Gangrene. Please,

Jesus, no!

Across the chaung, two bearded officers were wringing out the hems of their sodden blankets. Their packs, with rolled up jungle hammocks strapped to them, were standing in the stream. Staring at them, the irony of their privileged acquisitions distracted his attention from his feet.

Badger had never envied the recent issue of U.S. Army hammocks to some officers and specialist NCOs. The contraptions, with their zipped-around mosquito curtaining, were perilous traps in a night alarm. They were also prone to capsize and dump their occupants in the mud. Then again, Nature's tree spacings seldom coincided with the lengths of their sling ropes. Here in this wretched ravine hammocks were useless. No, Badger told himself, their benefits were not worth their encumbrances and weight. Weight was critical when men had to carry everything — weapons, ammunition, bedding and – when available – their rations.[1] Like many others, Badger had long since dumped even his groundsheet to lighten his pack.

The Army, he ruminated glumly, was climatically blind. Centuries of bitter Imperial campaigning had taught it nothing about the morale value of good personal weather protection. Heedless of operational topography, or climate, or Tommy's discomfort, it issued inadequate groundsheets to double as equally inadequate rain capes. As groundsheets they collected chilling pools under sleeping men's bodies. As for rain capes, well... Tommies shivered under them in cold, wet climes and were lathered in sweat under them in monsoon rain. He visualised his rain sodden forebears, sloshing to Ypres and Ladysmith, blaspheming under identical groundsheets. Any idiot knows a rectangle makes a farcical cape. The skewed, slanting hem saturates wearers from hip to shin. The hump of their packs tugs the back up to shed water precisely on to the backs of knees and calves. And no sod can fight in them!

The bearded officers, sharing a sachet of bouillon powder into their mess-tins and pouring in water from their water-bottles, reminded Badger that the only thing he had left from his 'K' rations,[2] was a sachet of lime juice powder. Leaning back to tug the powder and his mess-tin from his pack, he paused to watch the mist thinning out along the top of the gorge.

'Fucking hell, we're vulnerable!'

A month ago they would have had picquets atop the 20ft. high banks. Now, in their sodden apathy, there was neither the will to scale the banks, nor concern for the risks to which they were exposed. Half a dozen Japs with grenades and mortar bombs could annihilate the column without risk to themselves.

Trying to stifle his mounting fears, he told himself that, if the column had to come down into the chaung because they found the jungle up there impassable, then it would be just as impassable for the Japs.

The chaung gouged through thick jungle. Dense, razor sharp undergrowth and bamboo. Thick, impenetrable bamboo that latticed overhead, veiling out the sun and clamping in the stifling, enervating humidity. Typical 'Boy's Own' jungle. Fetid, malevolent, spiky bamboo that snagged clothes and pierced unwary eyes. If a track seemed to be going roughly in your direction, you stuck to it. However circuitous it might be, it was invariably quicker than hacking through a more direct route.

Pursuing Japs, Badger speculated, would have to follow in the column's footsteps to get at them, and we must have a rear-picquet somewhere across the chaung. Weary as he was, his professional wariness gnawed at his brain. He was too good a soldier to underrate an enemy – especially the Japanese – by wishful rationalisation. If the Japs knew where they were, they would get through to them, jungle or no jungle, just as they would have gotten through to attack the Japs. Until a few weeks ago.

Forget it! Leave the sodding jungle to the chattering monkeys. Leave it to the '...gotyerrifle...gotyerrifle...gotyerrifle...' of the screeching brainfever birds and the foraging, squealing wild boar. The column would be all right with Scottie in command. Scottie knew what was necessary – he'd not even ordered a dawn 'stand-to'. It would have been a futile gesture. Men standing, weapons and ears cocked, their bleary eyes scanning the overburden of foliage instead of recuperating as best as they could lolling on the rocks.

No 'stand-to' and no brewing up. Even if anyone had the stuff to make tea, there was nowhere to make a fire. Tugging out the top half of his mess-tin, he bent to dip it in the water and tried to recall when he'd last had any hot tea. He wondered when he would next have any.

Upstream, towards the rear of the column, a Scouse voice he dimly recognised, was softly groaning out an up-dated ditty from his father's war, to the barely recognisable hymn tune 'The Church is one foundation'.

"We are Fred Karno's army
The Chindit infantreee,
We cannot fuck, we cannot fight,
No bleeding use are we,
And when we get to Nippon,
Old Togo he will say,
Ah so. Ah so.
What a bloody lotten show,
Are the Chindit infantlee..."

As Badger dipped his mess-tin in the chaung, faint pink tinges were trickling from his boots. Yesterday's coagulated blood was dissolving from his bandaged feet. Pausing to watch, he was about to pour the lime juice powder into his mess-tin when he remembered Tony lolling, semi-conscious, to his left.

Tony, the wavy haired Scouse barber, who'd learned his craft in HMP Walton, improved it in Strangeways, and then migrated to the Bolton slums to go 'straight'. The normally dapper rogue who would have been a 'conchie' but for his prison record, was now a crumpled, wheezing scarecrow.

The rain had ceased, but rivulets draining down from the rocks were washing excrement from Tony's trousers into the chaung. The stained water awakened residual vestiges of Badger's field hygiene discipline, and he cursed himself for supping his water bottle dry last night. Clicking his tongue in despair, he dropped his half mess-tin and watched it sink to the river bed.

Like Tony, and most of the column, Badger's guts were churning and squittering, draining his last ounces of stamina and sapping at his final traces of morale. But it was his raw and rotting feet, not the endemic diarrhoea, that had relegated him to the sick and wounded section in the middle of the column. His feet were lifeless now, but when they quit the chaung, the marching would quicken the agonising throb and smarting galls. Shuddering, he cast around in his mind for something to distract him from the awful prospects of the march.

One of the bearded officers vigorously scratching his beard reminded him of his own wispy, three day growth. Other Chindit columns might grow beards, but The King's kept themselves as clean shaven as they could.

Taking his razor from one of his ammunition pouches, he sneaked a steel mirror from the left breast pocket of the semi-comatose Tony. Like many soldiers Tony religiously carried the mirror as a sort of heart shield. Ironically, Tony was now dying from, among other things, heart failure. How the hell did he get graded 'A1' by the medical board when he was called up, or before embarking for India?

Dabbing the razor in the chaung and splashing his cheeks, he looked into the mirror and winced. Pissholes in the snow! He'd known that prolonged dosage of *Atebrin* had yellowed his naturally fresh complexion, and that his lips would be mottled with malaria scabs. What shocked him was the leadenness of his grey eyes, sunk deep in ebony sockets. His normally lean cheeks and cleft chin were fleshless, gaunt. He barely noticed the thickened bridge of his nose broken months ago by the arse end of a mule when their glider had made a violent, bumpy landing. With his crumpled felt hat, dark hair straggling around his prominent ears, and bushy brows over the black eye sockets, he looked like the consumptive villain in a silent movie. He grinned wryly at his reflection.

Face smarting from the cold, latherless shave, he slipped the mirror back into Tony's pocket, and dropped the razor among the rocks. If he survived to Mogaung he'd get another. If he didn't survive, well.....

"Don't know about you, Dick," one of the bearded officers was saying to the other, "but I haven't fired a shot in this campaign."

"Nor me John, and I don't suppose we will now." Dick replied, dashing the dregs of his bouillon into the chaung.

"Christ! Did you hear that?" Badger hissed to the man to his right.

The man, a muleteer, could only painfully nod in reply. His face was a hideous coalescence of bruises and congealed gashes from a three day old mule kick. His eyes were hidden by swollen cheekbones, his nose a blackened pulp, and his lips a laceration of corrugated tissue.

Bleeding mules! Badger fingered his thickened nose. During his two years as a battalion heavyweight boxer, although his 5ft.8in. frame had been outreached by most opponents, he'd never even suffered a thick lip. Now, he had a bent nose. He grimaced as he remembered the bumpy landing. The explosion of stars before his eyes, as the terrified mule lost her balance, and collapsed on to him. Poor Daisy. She'd really made a good meal for them when, starving, they'd slaughtered her at the Indawgyi Lake.

Selfconsciously he clenched his fist, flexed his biceps beneath his threadbare sleeves and glanced at his scrawny legs. Heavyweight? He'd scarcely make featherweight now.

Giving the muleteer a comradely pat on the shoulder, he glared at the officers with a contemptuous sneer that, in other circumstances, would have landed him in the guard-room for 'dumb insolence'.

For the first time in six years soldiering he was consumed with contempt. Like many of his fellow regulars he had little reverence for ex-ranker officers but – as a class – he had always admired the dedication of the hereditary officers. They were generous patriarchs. Their fulsome, if sometimes eccentric participation in regimental activities, forged good *esprit de corps.*They would defer to the experience of their N.C.O.s, deal compassionately with their Tommies' problems, and knew when to treat his peccadillos with a Nelsonic eye. Ex-rankers were bullshitting, bumptious upstarts; wise to all barrack dodges, and tyrannical disciplinarians. At least, so Badger had believed until now.

What was it about these two bearded Sandhurst types that was threatening his deeply entrenched beliefs? What was it about them that filled him with foreboding? It wasn't just that they hadn't fired a shot at the enemy. Whatever it was, it was something more fundamental than that. Who were they? Certainly not Kingsmen with beards like that, and where had they been skulking through all the fighting?.

Badger's mind was a disorder of despondency, taunted by a nagging notion just beyond reach of his comprehension. He was harassed by something more than the column's vulnerability, or the prospect of gangrene, or the agonising throb that would awaken in his feet when he started marching again. These things would pass into history with the campaign. Somehow he knew that if he survived the war, whatever his mind was trying to bring in focus would permanently influence the rest of his life.

Tony coughed, and spluttered mucus down his chin.

"Tony! Sit up you silly sod! You'll drown in your own vomit."

As Badger struggled to pull the ex-con. upright, a heavily pregnant Kachin woman moaned. A few yards downstream she was lying on an open bamboo palanquin almost as big as a double bed. Lop-sided, its legs raising her above water level, the litter was surrounded by a score of Kachins. Men, women and children, in soggy black, red and yellow longyis and headscarves; necklaces and bracelets dangling with silver coins. Pro-British hill people, they had infiltrated themselves into the column yesterday to escape Japanese retribution. He marvelled that the Kachins could have forced their way through the dense jungle with the unwieldy litter without tipping the woman off. They were certainly resourceful and hardy people these Kachins, but as he hugged Tony to his shoulder the mournfulness of the woman's tones surprised him. He had always thought that only pampered burra memsahibs, in labour, would whine as melodramatically as she was doing.

As he wiped Tony's mouth with the hem of the barber's blanket, Scottie, with a Burma Rifles interpreter, waded up to the Kachins, spoke a few words to them and, leaving the Burrif behind, strode over to Doc. Pritchard, the column's M.O.

The Medical Officer, who had just finished dressing the bamboo pierced eye of a man next to the muleteer, greeted Lt. Colonel Scott D.S.O., M.C. with a sad shrug that epitomised the impossibility of properly treating the wounded .

The two men spoke softly and the M.O. nodded pointedly to each man in the pitiful group. The despair, evident on their weary faces as they looked towards Tony, confirmed that his survival could be measured in hours. For most of the night the M.O. and an orderly had been fighting for Tony's life with what meagre resources they had. It was a hopeless battle, and now they had to bow to the inevitable.

"Buck up, Laddie!" The lean, care-worn C.O. to whom everyone one of his soldiers was a 'Laddie', smiled at Badger.

"I'd light up if I had any tobacco. If I had a match. If my pipe wasn't broken." Badger managed a grin.

It was a daft, inane, attempt at mocking at their privations, and the C.O. grinned, tossing him a stick of chewing gum. As Scottie turned away to speak to the bearded officers Badger abruptly let Tony slip back against the rocks. Now he *knew* what was tormenting him! The valorous Scottie was not one of the hereditary officer class. None of the King's officers were! Scottie, the slaughtered Coulthard and Thomas and the rest were ex-rankers or at best only Emergency Commissioned Officers. Hostilities only officers. Some of them had only been 'Saturday afternoon soldiers' – Territorials – in peace-time. Yet these 'amateurs', even the column's supercilious adjutant, were all more competent, caring officers than any professional he'd ever served under.

Other columns may still have some professionals but those in the King's had, at the eleventh hour, been scrubbed from the order of battle. Ostensibly they were physically unfit; or due for promotion; or their administrative genius was needed at some staff office. To Badger, in his broody recriminations, that seemed pure bullshit. They had been commissioned and salaried for years to discharge the ultimate duty of leading their units in battle. The vainglorious sods had dodged that crucifying ordeal. Probably Wingate had decided they were battle-shy, for he certainly got rid of them.

More likely they were too regimental. They were regular sahibs, when what was needed was irregular leaders. They had been regimented too long to doctrines of earthbound lines of supply. They couldn't, or wouldn't, adapt themselves to campaigning that relied solely on parachuted supplies. Their initiative had been shorn by indoctrination with the canons of fixed lines of advance and retreat, with supporting convoys of artillery, engineer and signal troops, and armoured and field ambulance units. As L.R.P. officers deprived of all the panoply of war – except that which men and mules could carry – and entirely dependent on the vagaries of the weather for air supplies, and the fickleness of radio for contact with rear echelons, they were flounderers....

Badger scoured his mind for an aphorism. That was it. They were procrustean disciples, kneaded and moulded by the inflexible, stereotype precepts of the Army pharisees. The rigorous months of jungle training had exposed both their incompetence – when operating outside those precepts – and their ingrained antipathy to Wingate's novel warfare.

Tony was feebly pulling at Badger's water bottle but he was too deep in thought to notice it. Yes they were failures but the officer corps had, as usual, closed ranks. The Army's brahmins had drafted those pukka sahibs to sinecure billets, preserving their careers, and concealing the shallowness of their own Regular Army tutelage.

With mounting resentment he mentally scoffed at the absurdity of it all. Their dedication to orthodoxy mis-fitted them for Chindit operations, yet many of them were now in control of the Chindits' vital rear echelons in India. He could see them now, petty nabobs in freshly dhobied khaki drill, supping burra pegs of whisky in their comfortable messes. Sleeping every night in dry, clean charpoys. The crawling bastards would be damning Wingate with feint praise, bantering about his eccentricities, blurring his genius, and camouflaging the reasons they were scrubbed from the columns. Their duty was to support the columns, to plead the Chindit cause in the continual wrangling over supply priorities, but it was an open secret that they fuelled the whispering antipathy towards Chindit operations, embellishing the rumour that Bill Slim, the G.O.C. 14th. Army, himself deprecated the L.R.P. concepts.

Still oblivious that Tony was pulling at his water bottle, Badger scanned the lines of hollow eyed men. Those smarmy staff buggers had a lot to answer for....What was that bit of Shakespeare? Something about 'a heavy reckoning to make... when all those legs, and arms, and heads chopped off in battle shall join together at the judgement day and say we died at such a place...' With the Army breeding spiteful, professional Blimps like them, it was no wonder that L.R.P. principles were butchered when the 'Lord Protector of the Pagodas' was killed.

The revenge of the Wingate bashers had been swift, and cataclysmic. Remote from the monstrous terrain, heedless of the pitiless weather and indifferent to the limits of human endurance, these Staff College disciples had thrust the columns into set piece battles. Battles for which they were neither armed nor trained. Breaking promise after promise they had committed the Chindits to one 'final' effort after another, and then denigrated their prodigious efforts to fulfil impossible tasks.

Badger swiped viciously at the mosquitoes hovering around his bare knees. No, they weren't broken promises! They were false promises, never intended to be honoured. Only Wingate's were genuine. He'd have got the columns out before the rains, as he'd promised. He'd have got all the casualties out, as he'd promised. And it wouldn't have been necessary to shoot some poor sods to put them out of their misery. But messianic as Wingate was, if he hadn't been such a bloody intemperate, egocentric professional, he'd have left far less hostility behind him, and his devotees would have had more friends in the corridors of power.

The Calverts and Scotties of this Army would have done better for them than the Lord Protector. Devoid of arrogance they would, by tactful persuasion and patient importuning, have moderated the antagonism of the orthodox professionals. That was too humbling an approach for Wingate. His paranoiac, acrimonious obduracy, his scornful treatment of his peers, his blatant *lèse-majesté* towards his superiors, had only multiplied and inflamed opposition to his ideas. His aggressiveness had breathed life into the fight against the Japs, but his abrasiveness had been the kiss of death for his Chindits.

Bleeding so-called professionals! Wingate must be churning in his grave because Lentaigne, and not one of his disciples like Calvert, had been put in command of his columns. Joe Lentaigne, another Staff College apostle past his fitness peak, who openly denigrated the L.R.P. concept. Everyone knew he had prophesied that 'the rest of the Army' was out for Chindit blood. Then he immediately put his protégé, John Masters, in command of a brigade. A major, with several valiant Lt.Cols. under his orders. Masters was another Staff College devotee, the virtuoso *par excellence* of conventional warfare.

Lentaigne and Masters were battle-hardened professionals

wedded to the concept that wars must be won by set-piece battles. Honest men who couldn't stifle this conviction sufficiently to convince their seniors that surrendering the Chindits to Vinegar Joe Stilwell's pitched battle fanaticism, was a murderous folly.

Tony, having given up the struggle for Badger's water bottle was croaking with thirst, but Badger was lost to anything but his venomous thoughts.

Bleeding General Joseph W. Stilwell! The viciously anglophobic U.S. Army commander of Northern Burma and Chiang Kai-shek's chief of staff. It was common knowledge that Chiang was dominated by his power mad wife. Bloody Vinegar Joe had sacrificed Mike Calvert's superb brigade at Moguang for Madam Chiang's ambitions, on the altar of his Chinese troops' indolence. To cap this, he'd lied to the world that his Chinese divisions had captured the town. And months ago he had bragged that his American troops had captured Myitkina, but it was still in Japanese hands.

Stilwell – another egocentric, profligate professional murderer!

Badger struggled to constrain from shrieking to the heavens. He believed he must be going doolally – going barmy. Huddled up there, stoking up hatred on rumour and speculation. This is sedition, he told himself. I could be shot if I broadcast what I'm thinking. Well, I wouldn't be alone. The iniquities of the hierarchy had milked the last ounce of morale and loyalty from the columns except – perhaps – from the gallant Gurkhas. They had been as ill-used as the rest, but lacking English, had not been contaminated by the tales of rear echelon knavery. Knavery which had driven British other ranks perilously close to mutiny. And the other ranks were not alone in their disaffection. Revelations of the knavery could not have reached so extensively and powerfully the other ranks' ears, unless the fidelity of the usually tight mouthed officers had been fractured.

Well, that's it, Badger vowed. No more soldiering for me if I get out of this lot. His obsession since infancy was shattered. He'd never hankered for anything grander than to retire as a Regimental Sergeant Major. But even that modest ambition would mean unwavering fidelity to a professional officer caste he could no longer respect. After hostilities, the war time officers would be returned to civvy street. The old pretentious, time-serving clique would be back with their battalions. Back with their studied, haughty nonchalance. 'Squiring it' over the rank and file and flaunting their privilege.

In his near delirium, Badger's forelock-pulling subordination, inculcated by infinite ancestral pride in military service, seemed irreparably shattered. Shattered as the most devout cardinal's faith would be by some irrebuttable revelation of papal fallibility. It had been the longest running con-trick in military history. Generations of Tommies, his forebears included, had taken the Sovereign's shilling and sworn their allegiance for the privilege of being shot at by the sovereign's enemies. Or being shot by his, or her, underlings if they did not! They'd all been deceived by the creed that only born patricians could officer the Army. Lesser men were, at best, 'jolly good' yeomen, at worst a rabble of scoundrels. Yet here they were, in this God-forsaken gorge, and not a patrician within hundreds of miles.

A couple of months ago he'd been a model soldier, never questioning an order. Loving every minute of his service. His loyalty to superiors had been beyond doubt. True, he'd grumbled and groused like most soldiers do. That was more by way of letting off steam, and cementing the 'one-ness' with his mates. There'd never been any shadow of hate, or subversion in it. He would have fiercely challenged even the merest criticism of his allegiance and furiously chastised the slightest display of insubordination. Now it was as if the 'scales had fallen from his eyes.' His pacifist, alcoholic maternal grandfather had been right. That boozy old man's perpetual denunciation of the supposed superiority of upper class leaders had got him ostracized as a Bolshie by his jingoistic in-laws.

What would Badger do if he survived the war? He had no industrial or commercial skills. The only trade he'd known since leaving school was soldiering. Heaping despair upon despondency, he brooded about the long pre-war dole queues, and the hunger marchers. They were mostly skilled workers. He remembered bosses putting men on short time instead of laying them off, so they they couldn't claim the dole. He recalled men going cap in hand to their doctors, shamming illnesses, and the doctors perjuring themselves by certifying 'illnesses' so that the shortfall in a man's wages would be partly made up by 'friendly society' payments. For crying out loud, six years soldiering instead of learning a peacetime trade. What a waste of six youthful years......

Tony's hand pulling on his bare knee, and croaking something, cut short Badger's brooding. What did the silly sod want now?

"...for Jesus sake let's have your water bottle wacker... thought you'd gone bleeding deaf!"

Badger wanted to continue wallowing in his orgy of self-pity, but looking down at the dying man reminded him that others were worse off than him. Compassion conspiring with guilt forced the selfish, perverse forebodings from his mind.

"Sorry Tony, its empty but I'll fill yours for you."

Unhooking Tony's bottle, he hobbled a yard or two upstream and filled it from the chaung. No matter how polluted the water was, it couldn't harm the poor devil any more. He gently lifted the dying man's head, and poured a drop or two of water into the gasping mouth. Tony coughed it back and pulling the bottle out of Badger's hand took a long gulp, coughed, splattered most of it out, and then settled back to sip it slowly.

The sun was now shimmering through the overhanging bamboo and mosquitoes were swarming about his face and arms. A leech was clamped to one of his ankles. Badger viciously squashed it between his fingers until it spurted blood, threw it on the rocks, and crushed it with his rifle butt. There'd be an ulcer now on his ankle, but he had neither a match, nor a pinch of salt, to remove it without leaving a sore. It had been ticks in the hot dry teak forests and lantana scrub. Now it was sodding leeches. Downstream there was a stirring of men accompanied by an outburst of monkey chatter, and he instinctively started to pull on his pack.

"Stay where youse are," Tony croaked, "it's not 'packs on' yet."

Dropping the pack Badger looked quizzically at the little barber.

"Just heard Scottie tell the M.O..." the barber wheezed and panted, "...he's sending commando section to recce... way out... You must've been bloody unconscious not to hear him... be a bit before we move again..." Tony took another sip from the bottle and again wheezed, "...Scottie said all roads lead to Dehra Dun..."

He collapsed back against the rocks in a paroxysm of coughing.

Commando section? His old section. It used to be Commando platoon until casualties whittled it down from 30 to 10 men. His remaining muckers, Smudge, Ginger Slater, Terry Nelson, and Jack Ryan – no, Jack would not be with them, hadn't been with them a month or more – would be scouting a way out. They'd surely have taken a Kachin along to 'scout' for them.

It was ignominious! He should be leading them. He'd shepherded them through jungle training. Jollied them along when they were weary. Joshed with them in bivouac. Cringed with them under bombardment. He'd chided them during week-long training marches when they had hobbled along, crippled by blistered feet and he had bragged that his feet were too tough to be crippled by any marathon marches. Above all, he'd endlessly boasted he'd outmarch any of them. Now here he was – a lame, demoralised wreck – with trench feet, feeling as dishonoured by them as if they were self-inflicted wounds. Would Ginger, good old Ginger – the lanky, droll Lancastrian – be in charge of them now? Was it only yesterday they quit 2171? Where were the Japs? On our heels? Lying in ambush ahead of the column?

Refilling Tony's water bottle he poured his lime juice powder into it, and shook it vigorously. Gently cradling the dying man on one arm, he slowly fed the liquid to him in short swallows. As they sat hunched together, Badger's thoughts drifted back to yesterday's punishing eternity.

Footnotes to Chapter One

Page 5 Note No.1

When fully equipped each Chindit carried 60 to 70lbs. of personal weapons, ammunition, bedding and rations; in many cases, particularly Gurkhas, men were carrying half their own weight. Heavier weapons (machine guns and mortars) ammunition reserves, medical stores, radio transceivers and demolition explosives were carried by mules.

Page 5 Note No. 2

A day's 'K' Rations comprised 3 heavily waxed cartons, about 4" x 7" x 1½" of chewing gum, several sheets of toilet paper, and a book of matches. The breakfast pack contained a small tin of processed meat, a compressed fruit bar and a sachet of coffee. The dinner pack also included processed meat but in lieu of the fruit bar and coffee, it contained a packet of Dextrose tablets and a sachet of lime juice powder. The supper pack, instead of meat, coffee, lime juice, fruit bar or Dextrose, contained a tin of processed cheese, a chocolate bar and a sachet of bouillon powder. K Rations were supplemented by tea bags, sugar and powdered milk, and occasionally by tinned fruit, bread and corned beef. Master's calculated that, even full rations resulted in a daily deficiency of about 800 calories a day. But, particularly in the last months of the campaign, since they relied almost exclusively on supply drops, the foul weather and the demands of other forces, drastically curtailed air sorties to the Chindits, and they were often on the threshold of starvation. In the incessant rain, Chindits became experts in brewing tea by using only a single waxed K packet to boil a mess-tin of water.

Chapter Two

After the column had disengaged from enemy contact on 2171 before dawn yesterday, good old Ginger had half dragged, half carried Badger for hours.

Hours that seemed as long as days. In torrential rain they had plodded down into stream beds and up and down hills. Bordering the chaungs it was bamboo thickets, between these it had been lantana scrub, thorny bushes, interspersed with plots of shoulder high elephant grass.

Together, lathered in sweat and sodden with rain, they had squelched, stumbled and slithered through the mud. The going must have been bad enough for the leaders of the column, but the couple of hundred boots that had squelched through it ahead of Badger had churned the glutinous red mud into an ankle deep slurry.

They had dropped further behind with each pace, and it seemed that the distance covered by each painful step grew shorter. At each of the hourly halts the column already had their packs back on and were again beginning to move by the time the two of them caught up with the tail end.

Ginger had scoffed at Badger's infirmity, cajoled and cursed him to keep him on his feet. But comradeship, like physical endurance, has its limits. At the foot of a bamboo forested escarpment Ginger had dropped him. It would have seemed steep to fit men, but to the exhausted Chindits it was precipitous. Men, almost on all fours, were clawing up through the saturated undergrowth. Their sodden packs and weapons repeatedly snagged by bamboo spears. During the final ten minutes, before they parted, as the track rose towards the escarpment, they had trudged in silence except for their laboured breathing. They had parted without a word. One hand on the other's shoulder, a firm, brief hand clasp – a fleeting, affectionate meeting of their eyes – and Ginger was gone.

Breathless he had watched Ginger straining almost full length to pull himself, yard by yard, up towards the rear files of the column until he was out of sight. He had been relieved rather than grieved, to be on his own. Relieved of feeling responsible for jeopardising his comrade's survival. Relieved that he could take his own time and rest when he wanted without feeling guilty.

Slumping down in the mud Badger had lain for a timeless span, dimly conscious that it had stopped raining. Head propped on his pack and eyes watering in the thinly clouded sunshine, he had been vaguely aware of other stragglers trudging past him and cared naught if he was the last to climb the escarpment. He had hardly cared that the men still coming up might not be stragglers but Japs, and half expected they were. He just couldn't believe that the Japs, for a second time, would let them off the hook.

Two months ago, at the height of a bloody battle they had broken off the action, and quit their 'Blackpool' citadel. Yet despite the Japs' overwhelming numbers, the column had not been pursued. On a smaller scale, the withdrawal from 2171 had been a repetition of 'Blackpool'. It seemed improbable that such a fanatical enemy could let them escape a second time. It couldn't be that the Japs were too exhausted, or that their casualties were too high. They were fresh troops, and had plenty of locally based replacements to call on. Had they leap-frogged ahead to cut them off from Moguang?

He dozed for a while, and when he awoke the sun was blazing directly overhead in a sky dotted with small white clouds. The last of the stragglers were well up the escarpment. Somewhere above them a man's scream, as a bamboo spike pierced his eye, had startled the monkeys into a crescendo of chatter, and roused flocks of birds into hysterical flight.

Sitting on his pack, he had taken off his boots and scraped off the drying mud with his jack knife. His toes were sticking through holes in his socks. Gingerly, he had eased them off, and sloshed his smarting feet with the contents of his water bottle.

His insteps and arches were a bloodless pulp. The balls and toes were shrivelled, weeping tissue, and raw bone. Damned Indian issue socks! The grey woollens had shrunk to toddler size, and the grubby white cotton legs were as abrasive as sand paper. Throwing the socks down in disgust, he had then cut both legs from his threadbare trousers at the thigh, slit them into strips and bound his feet.

From then on most of yesterday was a misty kaleidoscope of recollection. With difficulty he had pulled on his boots, but was able only to tie them loosely over his bandaged feet. Somehow he had clambered up the escarpment to the top... only it wasn't the top, just a false crest. He had nearly screamed when he saw yet another valley.

Slithering down arse first he'd bumped into Tony. Sweltered by the sun and their exertions, sweat stinging their eyes and pouring from their armpits, shirts under their packs like soggy chamois leather, they had staggered along the column's tracks. At each stream they'd drunk their water bottles dry, refilled them, rested briefly, and trudged on again. Then there were no more streams. Sweat dried on them, starching their shirts with salt. Dehydrated, faces flushed, bone and muscle feverish, they dared not stop for more than an occasional sip from their bottles.

Somewhere they'd fallen and rolled in acrid ashes. The lower slopes of a valley, burnt by the Kachins to clear for cultivation, had been a blackened, charred stubble. Arms around each other, streaked with soot like drunken coal miners they'd limped up the next crest, crossed one valley, over another and into another, until at dusk Scottie had materialised.

"What's your trouble laddies?" Their indefatigable colonel had strolled back to shepherd stragglers into the chaung.

"Bad squitters, sir." Badger, ashamed to admit to crippled feet, had blamed his incapacity for marching on diarrhoea which was no dishonour when everyone else had it.

Tony could only groan, ".. am knackered, sir."

"Right, laddies, join the M.O.s walking wounded down-stream. We'll be moving on again in about 15 minutes."

His bandages had by then been stiff with congealed blood. Stepping into the chaung he had yelped aloud as the water almost sucked his loosely tied boots off. 'Walking wounded' – that was a laugh. There were no other kind of wounded on this march. Whether fit or crippled, you marched – or you died.

The M.O. had given him a dose of something for the squitters and he'd drained his water bottle dry, cleansing the horrible taste from his mouth. The M.O. had also handed him a few ounces of gentian violet for his feet, but it would be useless to apply it – as the Doc. had told him – whilst they were trekking through the chaung.

Then there'd been the slow trudge along the chaung, until that cloudburst brought the column to a shivering halt....

Chapter Three

With Tony's head in the crook of his arm, Badger put the water bottle down and wiped the feverish sweat from the dying man's face.

"Wonder how many more days we'll have like that before we get to Dehra Dun ?" he asked Tony, as though he had been discussing yesterday with him, and not just thinking about it.

Tony could only reply with a puzzled, " Eh, what..?"

"Forget it, just thinking aloud."

How long had the Commando section been gone? 10, 20 minutes? Certainly not half an hour. Still feeling shivery, though sweat was beginning to drip from his armpits, Badger prayed that the section would not be too much longer finding a way out of the gorge. Then all roads would '...lead to Dehra Dun' – the long promised rest and recuperative camp in the Himalayan foothills. They'd been promised it so many times it had almost become a myth. This time it was different. It was Scottie who had told them. Whenever they'd been told before there'd always been a sting in the tail.

"Yes, you're going to Dehra Dun for a rest... but there's just one final job for you before that..." Scottie had never promised them that before, never jollied them along with false promises – not like the other prevaricating sods. If Scottie said they were going anywhere, then it would be true beyond a shadow of doubt.

At the moment Badger had no longing for the hill station. A stint in that cool, invigorating rest camp, might be paradise to the garrisons sweltering on India's plains, but it was no El Dorado to Badger that morning. He was yearning for a warm dry charpoy on any fly ridden, sun baked maidan. He could die peacefully and warm there. Robert Service's *Sam McGee* was his type of man, 't'aint being dead, it's my awful dread of the icy grave that pains'. He might not make it out of Burma, but sore feet or not, he was damn well not going to cash in his chips in this ravine. Somehow he'd stick to the column's tail and if he had to die, find a warm dry spot for his bones.

The quiet jabbering of the Kachins suddenly became noisy and argumentative. The Thugyi was chastising a young girl bouncing on the litter, and the pregnant woman was remonstrating with him. She had obviously bested the headman in the slanging match for, turning his back on her, he spat into the chaung and walked a few yards down stream leaving the girl still playing on the litter.

Watching the girl Badger wondered what Barbara's child would be. The irony of it. Her last overdue letter had been a gut-twisting 'Dear John'. That was over a month ago, and she was three or four months pregnant then. Her flat belly must be gone by now. Her infidelity hadn't shocked him. He'd been overseas two years and she was vivacious – devilishly attractive – and constantly surrounded by amiable fly boys when on duty. What surprised him was that, with her medical connections and training, she had not only been caught but had been unable to get an abortion (a 'cute appendicitis' was supposed to be the cover name). That, and the fact that she had delayed telling him so long.

He felt a warm stirring in his loins – nothing to do with his inflamed lymph glands – as he recalled their wedding night. The first time he had ever really lain with a naked, thrusting woman. Their only night together, and she'd insisted on a sheath for him and a pessary for herself. Yet, she gets caught on what the letter said "...was truly my one and only indiscretion..." with a nameless man after drinking too much at an Air Force Officers' Mess party. He knew her too well to accept that story. For one thing, she could never be persuaded to have more than a couple of drinks and, for another well...

She was far from modest, but too proud of her body to yield it to a stranger's impulsive, fumbling titillation. It had taken Badger a year to gain anything more than a chaste embrace. No fumbling under her dress, no probing beneath her bra – not until the week before their wedding.

He clasped his head in his hands, recalling the first glimpse of her exquisite body. They'd schemed to get his family out of the house. On the sofa their usual closed lips kisses turned to breathless, feverish tongue probing. Then, tantalisingly, in that sensually husky voice, she had told him to sit on the other side of the room to, '...see what you're getting first. Don't be so impatient..' Slowly, oh so gracefully slowly she had stripped naked. With her tormenting eyes relishing his desire for her, she'd stretched out on the sofa, and beckoned him to her. Too late! Too bloody late! His family were already walking up the path.

Yes, she would have recoiled from an impetuous, hole in the corner, edge of a desk, inebriated copulation. Only when her body had enjoyed the pleasure of a man's eyes, would anyone have the pleasure of her body. That meant it had to have been a mutually premeditated tryst.

Tormented by jealousy, he conjured up a picture of her on an elegant hotel bed. Her arched back thrusting her flat bellied nakedness to a shadowy figure. Her delicate rib cage quivering under caressing hands. She was drawing the shadow's head on to her full breasts. She would not be taken any other way, and only a persevering, suavely flattering relationship could have succeeded.

His mind flashed back two years, to when he had scoffed at a pestering Bombay soothsayer who had impudently predicted Barbara's adultery. Then there was the bizarre vision he'd had of her adultery, at the height of the Blackpool battle. Apprehensive of the clairvoyant implications, he swiftly dismissed both incidents as co-incidences, and turned his thoughts to the 'Dear John'.

'....can you ever forgive this one stupid loveless sin...' Loveless? Perhaps. But would she, of all women, let any man go so far without there being some deep mutual affection. Forgive her? Maybe. But not until they were eyeball to eyeball. He needed to see the truth – whatever it was – behind the words, in those polar green eyes. That would be a long time coming, if ever. There were no compassionate postings home from here. He couldn't even write to her.

His bitterness was more envy of the other man's opportunities, than of her infidelity. He was sorry too, for her. Sentenced to unnatural celibacy, she'd been condemned by her natural libido to be a target of gossip. Disgraced from the service, she would be fretting for his reply. Dreading, yet praying for every mail delivery to bring his letter. All she would get would be a cyclostyled aerogram from Base H.Q. 'Dear Madam, ...you will not hear from your husband for some time.... the operations he is taking part in make it impossible for him to write to you.....'

Her anguish, one of the unchronicled malignancies of war.

Tony was now quietly croaking a sentimental chorus. He was married and had two kids, but his song was a tear jerking message to his mother. How were they faring without him? How would they fare when he was dead? How many thousands, like them and Barbara, had been so callously condemned to years of agonised separation from loved ones. Fathers, husbands, brothers and sweethearts – all had been summarily exiled by Imperial rescript to remote battlegrounds for a minimum four year tour. A tour? That's what the powers that be euphemistically called their exile. Shades of Thomas bleeding Cook! Dying parents, and bereaved relatives were denied the comforting presence of sons and brothers. Lonely widows were deprived of their supportive sons. Distraught mothers were obliged, single handedly, to tend and protect their children, cope with their illnesses and heartbreaks, and wrestle with shortages and rationing. Faithful wives thrashed on their spouseless mattresses until either the incessant frustration lured faithless gratification between their sheets, or transformed them into frigid, guilt ridden, melancholics. A row of kisses on an infrequent air letter was no antidote for pent-up sexual hunger. Babes were growing to infants without the joy of Daddie's cuddles. Dad was just a name for a photograph on the sideboard, like the piggies and doggies in the picture books. Schoolchildren were blossoming into adolescence without the benefit of their dad's bantering indulgences and moral restraints.

"Yes," Badger muttered, so audibly that the bearded officers shot questioning looks at him, "those are the silenced malignancies of war."

Embarrassed, Badger gently patted Tony's shoulder. The little barber, his eyes in a fixed stare, continued with his song.

"...break the news to mother and tell her that I love her..."

Yeah, Badger told himself, as he glanced around the M.O.'s pathetic group, before lapsing back into his ruminations, those back home are just as much casualties of war, if not more, as this lot are. They are disabled at the moment of that last farewell hug at the end of embarkation leave. Yet their letters are studiously free of self pity, invariably jaunty, full of optimism and sprinkled with dotty sentiments. They were blasé about air raids. Made light of their rationing problems. But the lines on their war weary faces, in the snapshots they sent, belied the lines of their letters. They would be fearful of air-raids all right, but they were plagued by more personal, terrifying omnipresent fears. They prayed for news from their exiled kin. Yet dreaded that every knock on the door might be the War Office telegram '...regret to inform you...'

Then there were the exiles themselves. Young, virile and fit. They had to be fit to be exiled. You could be assured that these exiles, from other nations, drafted into your homeland were fit to slip into your bed! Lusty, robust men, pressed into unnatural celibacy. And there were women exiles too. Pleasant, vibrant, dutiful nurses and service-women, but they were too grossly outnumbered, and assiduously courted by officers, for there to be any lower rank socialising between sexes.

The only relief for the other ranks would be the occasional recreational leave in Bombay or Calcutta. *Privilege leave* they called it. Some Privilege! Recreation? Aimless elbowing through teeming, stinking streets and bazaars. Tea and rock hard buns, served by sanctimonious memsahibs doing their bit in temperance canteens, between chota pegs at their clubs. Stifling matinées in third-rate cinemas. Then boredom would erupt into hooliganism. The Tommies would cheat and harass gharry wallahs, pushing them from the driving seats of their carriages and, taking the reins, whip the skin and bone ponies into a reckless gallop. In rowdy, raucous groups they'd rampage through bazaars and markets, turning over stalls, pilfering, trampling on fruit and vegetables. But, despite the risks of disease and punishment, rowdyism was no substitute for the out of bounds attraction of the Grants' and Forests' Roads. And the Army knew it!

The Army knew what the desperately frustrated soldiery needed, and that they would risk their health and pockets in the disease ridden brothels. Why hadn't it re-instituted medically supervised 'regimental brothels'? Without them it forced men to break its 'commandments', riddle them with guilt and probably disease, by surreptitious dalliances. It drove those more fearful of disease or army punishments – as well as perverts – to the young, almost infant 'gobble-wallahs' around the arch of the Gateway to India, under the shadows of the 'out of bounds to other ranks' Taj Mahal Hotel. It was bloody inhuman! Catching a packet was bad enough and, if you did, the Army added insult to injury by reducing your pay! It was all so bloody unfair... The hypocritical commanders who prohibited brothels, spent their furloughs with their wives – or other men's – in Simla, Rawalpindi, or other hill stations.

Badger's morbidity was curtailed by a bustling downstream, and a renewed screeching of monkeys as men struggled into their equipment. The order 'Packs on!' was being passed along the column from mouth to mouth.

Ah well! Barbara and himself had less justification for bitterness than most. The majority had been pressed into service. He was a professional. He had enlisted expecting – hoping for – overseas service. Barbara knew that before she agreed to marry him. He squared his shoulders and vowed to stop whining but, as he pulled his pack on, he knew deep down that it was a forlorn vow. His dejection was too deeply entrenched to be banished by shrugging his shoulders.

Tony, still softly crooning '...break the news to mother...' made no effort to get up. Passing Tony's rifle to the muleteer, Badger stripped him of his webbing equipment, dumped it on a rock, and started to drag him to his feet. As he was doing so, the two bearded officers waded over and each taking one of Tony's arms over their shoulders pulled the ex-con into the file of men forming up in the chaung. With Tony's almost dead-weight dragging on their shoulders, his legs buckled at the knees and his feet barely scraping the stream bed, the officers stumbled along with the column. He was still crooning,

> '...just break the news to mother, and tell her that I love
> her, and tell her not to wait for me, for I'm not coming

home. Just say there is no other can take the place of mother and kiss her two sweet lips for me for I'm not coming home..."

Hobbling behind Tony, forcing his toes to curl to prevent his boots being sucked off, and thankful that the column could only move at a snail's pace, it suddenly struck Badger as foolish to have the sick and wounded in the middle of the column. After all, they were a burden that could be dispensed with to the benefit of the remainder. If the wounded were at the front of the column, the going would be better for not having been churned up by hundreds of boots ahead. They could set the pace to suit their capabilities, and not have to be either, constantly spurting to close gaps, or dropping further behind. Any soldier knows, he told himself, that no matter how leisurely the leaders of a column stroll, gaps persistently appear and the further back you are the faster you have to move to close up, until those at the rear are consistently trotting. It wasn't selfishness to put the wounded with the leading sections, it was common sense. In return for having the best of the going and setting the pace, the brunt of the casualties in an ambush would probably be those already sick or wounded, thereby reducing the totality of casualties, and the overall burden on the rest.

Even as his mind toyed with this grim, callous idea, his soul told him that theorising was specious. Seasoned troops like the Japs wouldn't spring an ambush until the bulk of the column were within their sights. In that case his feverish mind countered, the leading elements had the best chance of slipping through an ambush. 'Jesus! Now I'm destroying my own arguments, and I've not got the bleeding strength to hobble, let alone sprint from an ambush.'

Anyway, wherever he was in the column made no difference whilst they were in the chaung. Even the fittest could only creep along over the stony river bed, and the ravine was too narrow for anyone to overtake weaker men in front of them.

In front of Tony and his bearers, the M.O. was shouldering along a Kingsman with a bandaged leg, and the muleteer in front of them, half blind, was clinging to the bayonet scabbard of the man in front of him. Men were bunching and bumping each other as they stumbled over boulders.

Tony's crooning suddenly changed to a long rattling gasp, and he was silent. Except for the splashing of feet, the occasional clatter of weapons against rocks, the muffled blasphemies as men stumbled over submerged boulders, and the rustling of bamboo overhead, the gorge was quiet. Even the monkeys and the birds were silent.

Badger's pack contained only half a mess-tin and his blanket, but the sodden weight bit into his shoulders, and abraded his back. The two ammunition pouches hooked to his belt and pack straps, each carrying only a single grenade, were persistently tugged up to his armpits by the weight of his pack, and repeatedly dislodged the rifle slung over his shoulder.

His feet were beginning to throb.

Can't be much further to a track out of the chaung. Like most rivers in Burma the water was flowing generally from north to south, and they were going with the flow, but Moguang was to the north east. Around the tops of the bamboo thickets, the last of the morning mist was swirling in steamy patches.

Can't be much further. The Commando section could not have taken an hour to find it and report back.

Head hunched on his chest with thumbs tugging on his shoulder straps, Badger stumbled into Tony's back as the whole column concertina'd to an abrupt halt, and the man behind him toppled him into the water. Squatting on the river bed, too exhausted to even curse, he dumbly held out an arm to the man behind him.

"At bleeding last!" The man blurted.

Helping Badger to his feet, he nodded pointedly towards the head of the column. Over the heads of the tightly packed files Badger could see the Kachins manhandling the palanquin up one of the banks where the bamboo swept down almost to water level. Behind the Kachins soldiers were scrambling out of the chaung, each man helping the man in front with a push up his rear on to the bank.When they shuffled up to the exit point, willing but feeble hands helped the M.O. drag his wounded and sick on to the bank. Between them the bearded officers and Badger hoisted Tony clear of the water, on to a narrow track spiralling up through the bamboo spine where the gorge took a sharp westerly turn.

It was obviously a well used, dry season track, beaten free of undergrowth by the leathery feet of the women water carriers of a nearby village. Now, with its dense bamboo overburden shielding it from the sun, it was a Stygian tunnel, furrowed with rivulets of slurry. A steep, glutinous zig zag of slimy clay. At each step, even the fittest men gained less than half a pace. Ankle deep in brick-red sludge men cursed, slithered and slipped.

Sweat streamed into Badger's eyes, and down his spine. First one boot then the other was sucked from his feet. Groping through the slush he recovered them, laced them together, and slung them around his neck.

Twice, almost within arm's length of the crest, the bearded officers slipped full length. Face down and feet first they slid, gouging and clutching through the mud to arrest their descent. With Tony between them they slithered into Badger and all four piled down on to men below them.

When they reached the crest they found themselves at the apex of a roughly triangular sunlit plateau. The sides to the left and right descended steeply into the bamboo gorge they had just left. The other side, half a mile or so away, was a long gently-sloping hill clothed in tall teak trees. Far beyond the hill, hazed in purple and gold thunder clouds, were the towering peaks overlooking the Moguang valley.

Gasping and heaving, Badger stumbled a few yards clear of the track and, without removing his pack, slumped down near the stump of a banana tree. As the heaving of his chest subsided and the yo-yoing of his head eased down, he saw on the other side of the track Tony stretched flat on his back. The bearded officers still with their packs on were prostrate, one on either side of Tony, arms outspread like supplicants for ordination.

Perspiration was now giving way to dry, burning fever. Despite this – and the hot sun – he felt shivery and the back of his pack, sodden with sweat, was chilling through his shirt. Standing up to shrug off his pack and to cast his blanket over a bush to dry, his eyes wandered over the plateau.

For a hundred yards or so, the track cleaved through waist high scrub and patches of elephant grass. Beyond that, swerving three or four times to bypass a plantain tree or a clutch of banana bushes, it ran straight, almost due north to the hills. On both sides of the track, beyond the scrub, the ground was yellow and ocherous with decaying corn. Maize, disciplined neatly into acre plots by intersecting paths, was trampled and prematurely stripped of its cob by marauding soldiery.

At the centre of the plateau just west of the track, surrounded by the corn plots and raised on stilts, was a cluster of deserted bashas. Their neglected banana leaf thatches, agape at their ridges and eaves, rustled in the gentle breeze. Children from the palanquin group were gleefully swinging around a basha's sturdy stilts. The litter had been set down in the shade of a broad-boughed tree, the only one in the village. The Thugyi, squatting against its bole, had gathered the grown ups around him.

The rear elements of the column, backs bent under their packs, each man's eyes seemingly transfixed on the heels of the man in front of him, were passing Badger as, shielding his eyes from the sun with his hands, he focused towards the hill. As they moved along the track, men were slicing through banana trees, with bayonets or dahs,[3] and stuffing portions into their packs for a future meal. Close to the foot of the hill small groups were crouching, water bottles in their hands, at what was obviously a spring or stream. Others were squatting along the lower slope, while the leading sections were already nearing the top. He could just make out the indefatigable Scottie, upright as ever, among the tall teak halfway up the hill, coaxing and jollying men on.

On the other side of the track, the bearded officers had rolled on to their backs. With heads pillowed on their packs and bush hats tilted over their eyes, they seemed to be peacefully asleep.

Parched and dehydrated as he was, Badger decided he couldn't make it to the spring without resting for a while and lying down he savoured the warm sun on his face for a few moments before sleep became irresistible.

§

"On your feet, you dozy shirker!"

Ginger woke him with a gentle kick at his rump and grinning down at him, pushed a water bottle into his hands.

"Thought I'd better come back and remind you that you

were the big-head who was going to march us off our feet. You were going to see we got out of Burma safely, and here you are skiving with the sick, lame and lazy!"

Squinting up, his eyes dazzled by the sun and smiling wryly at Ginger, Badger took a long drink, wiped the drips from his mouth, and offered the bottle back to him.

"Keep mine, I'll take yours. Sorry mucker – can't stay with you – Commando section's got to keep up with Column H.Q."

"Thanks Ginger, you're a Godsend. Smudge, Terry, OK?"

"Sure – except for squitters." Ginger nodded towards the hills, "Scottie thinks just one more hill after that one, and its all downhill to Moguang."

Glancing briefly towards the inert Tony and the sleeping officers, Ginger picked up Badger's bottle.

"Those three alright?"

"Think so...Tony's in a bad way, but they are looking after him."

"Well, ta-rah mucker. We'll have a brew ready for you at Moguang."

"Ta-rah Ginge. Be seeing you."

No pretentious bonhomie. No false optimism about his chances of reaching Moguang. They'd been through too much together – too much for there to be any euphemistic chat about his prospects of survival. He watched Ginger amble off towards the hills and then dropped his head back into a doze.

He was awakened by the bearded officers talking loudly, trying to arouse Tony. Badger must have slept for over an hour. The sun was overhead when Ginger had left, and was now casting short diagonal shadows. His face and legs were stiff with baked on mud. Not bothering to put on his boots he looked to the hills, and hobbled over to Tony. Through a gap in the teak he could just see the MO's group, with the Kachins in tow, breasting the first crest. Even the tail enders were more than half way up the hill.

"Afraid he's dead" Dick said as Badger reached them.

"Does the MO know?" Badger cocked his head towards the hills.

"No...he was well ahead of us when we topped the ridge. I

suppose one of us should have tried to catch up with him..."

"Nowt to sound so guilty about," Badger interrupted, unable to bring himself to add the customary 'sir', "the M.O. couldn't have done anything. The poor sod's been dead for hours..."

"Not at all! He grunted as we dragged him up the ridge, didn't he Dick?"

"That's right," John nodded, adding firmly, "and when we first laid him here."

"I'm telling you he's been dead for hours. The grunts were just residual air in his lungs being expelled as you moved him. Just look at his legs."

Tony's face was the colour of putty, his eyes wide open and his left cheek pitted where it had lain against rough ground. His ankles were swollen, and mottled blue with the gravitation of blood.

"Got to bury him. Can't leave the poor little bugger here for the shite hawks. Have either of you got an entrenching tool?"

Dick nodded and pulled the tool, one half a miniature spade – the other a short spike, from under his pack. He had lost its wooden handle.

"We'll have to make do with that and my bayonet." Badger had been about to curse Dick's carelessness when he remembered that he – and others – thinking the campaign was over, had rashly jettisoned their entrenching tools before 2171. He had never received a replacement dah for the one he presented to the Thugyi at Nutmauk, "Use the spike as a handle... like a garden trowel."

With his bayonet, and the other two taking turns with the entrenching tool, or scraping away with a mess-tin, they hollowed through the soft topsoil before striking hard, stony ground. Desperately they hacked and chipped, anxious to get Tony buried and be over the hill before dusk. The ground seemed to get harder with each inch of depth. Sweat was pouring from the officers, soaking their shirts and streaming down their arms into the grave. Badger was smouldering with fever. His eyes felt peppery, his joints burning, and his skin aflame.

At barely eighteen inches down, the exertion and earth beat them.

Sipping off his remaining water, and leaving the officers panting at the grave side, Badger bent over Tony and snipped off one of his identity discs before emptying the dead man's pockets. A rusty army jack knife; a soggy packet of Camel cigarettes; a tattered air-mail letter signed 'Mum'; a sodden field dressing; the mirror; and a heavy chrome lighter with a Blackpool Tower motif. The flint sparked as he abstractedly flicked the lighter, but the wick did not ignite.

Going over to his own kit, he stuffed Tony's earthly possessions, except the disc, into his own pouches and called to the officers.

"Be putting him in while I make a marker."

As he walked back to the top of the ridge, and chopped off two canes of bamboo, it suddenly occurred to him that he had been giving the orders. Him, a lowly corporal, taking charge of officers. He had no rank markings. Maybe they took him for one of them. Perhaps he had some natural air of authority, some latent charisma. He didn't really believe that, but the thought of taking 'command' over them gave his spirits a little boost.

Death had cast Tony with his mouth and eyes open, his trunk twisted, right hand under left armpit, left forearm across his left thigh, and his legs bent at the knees. No matter how they tried to push and turn him, the shallow grave provided scant top cover. Kneeling over the grave to remove Tony's boot laces, Badger silently prayed they could gather enough earth for a substantial mound.

"Either of you remember the words?" he asked, lashing the canes into a cross with the boot laces.

Both of them shook their heads, and looked hopefully at him.

"Sorry Tony – nor do I, but I'll do the best I can."

Motioning to the others, he moved with them to the head of the grave and with heads bowed, they stood silently for a moment.

"Dear Father... we commit this, the earthly body of our departed brother to Thy bountiful earth, and beseech Thee to take his soul into Thy gracious keeping. Grant eternal peace unto him O Lord, Amen."

With mess-tins and the entrenching tool, they filled the grave in and scraped together sufficient soil from the surrounding earth to pad it over it with a good mound.

'FAREWELL MUCKER'

Putting on his hat, Badger pushed the cross into the mound, stiffened himself to parade ground erectness, smartly stepped one pace back and saluted. Standing there in a rigid salute he silently counted to sixty, oblivious that the officers behind him were following his example. His face was caked with mud, shirt tatty, trouser legs tattered, crumpled hat on his head, feet in ragged bandages, and aching in every joint. Still, his salute would not have disgraced a sovereign's parade. He was back on the barrack square at the Regimental depot – in full ceremonials, brasses and buttons gleaming, boots burnished, scarlet banded cap square on his cropped head, at the peak of youthful fitness. He was saluting to a silent 'Last Post' which was as real to him as if a bugler had been at the grave-side.

§

"Give this to the adjutant," Badger handed Tony's identity disc to John as they started off towards the hills, "and a map reference of the grave." Now that they were back on the column's route, he seemed to revert to a subordinate being, and found it difficult not to say 'sir'.

Before the grave fell from sight behind the scrub, he stopped for one last look imprinting the position and the ground features firmly in his mind.

"You'd never make a good soldier, Scouse, but for a conscript, you were a bloody good jungle fighter. If I get out of this I'll come back for you... when the fighting's over."

His boots were slung around his neck, but the going along the track was good. A little squelchy at first, but firming up as they passed between the cornfields and he couldn't distinguish the throb in his feet from the feverish rigors besetting his entire body. Instinctively he tried to keep pace with the officers, and vainly scanned the banana trees for one that had not already been sliced to a stump by other hungry men to make a stringy, indigestible stew.

When he reached the infant stream at the foot of the hill, the sun was beginning to dapple the track with shadows of the basha roofs, and grey cloud was crawling over the distant hills. John and

Dick were already there, stripped to the waist and sponging themselves. As he filled his bottle, he was struck with guilt. Dick had a dark bloodstained shell dressing under one armpit, and John was adjusting a similar dressing over his navel. He'd certainly done them an injustice. He had casually wondered from time to time, why they were in the M.O.'s group. Nevertheless the wounds failed to moderate his newborn antipathy to their class.

Filling his mess tin from the stream, he greedily drank it dry, refilled it, and settled down against a tree stump. Slowly sipping the cool water, he debated whether to bathe his feet, and decided against it. The bandages were dry and stiff with mud, and he could stride over the stream without getting them wet. Disturbing them might pull off any scabs and start the bleeding again. Better wait till he kipped for the night. The officers, anxious to be off, were pulling on their equipment and John called over to him.

"Are you ready? The wind's freshening and we want to make it to the column before it rains." He pointed to the tree tops, stirring in the breeze, under thickening clouds.

"One minute... got to put my boots on."

He was relieved that, as he gingerly eased them on and tied them loosely, the pain was not half as bad as he expected. Perhaps the mud had some curative properties. His relief was short lived. Within a few minutes of leaving the stream, the throbbing returned and he was back to a hobbling gait.

The officers, freed from the burden of Tony, quickly left Badger behind and by the time they had topped the crest, he was barely half way up. His legs ached, feet smarted and eyes burned. The water he'd recently drank churned his bowels and forced him to stop within a few yards of the summit to defecate. He was sorely tempted to bed down there for the night. Limping over the crest, he shrieked with despair. Before him was a steep reverse slope and the opposite side of the valley was a teak-forested mountain. Dick and John were already near the valley floor. There was no sign of the main body but near the summit of the mountain he caught a fleeting glance of a few stragglers.

There can be no more demoralising isolation, even for a fit man, than the prospect of a long, lonely trek in the footsteps of comrades who have long passed out of sight and sound. For Badger it seemed the ultimate abandonment.

"God help me!" he cried dropping to his knees, and the hills faintly echoed, '....help me'ee.'

Well, this is it. He had prayed for a warm dry spot. This would have to do, he told himself, crawling to the base of a tree and shedding his equipment.

"You alright?" John was coming back up the hill to him.

"This is as far as I go."

"You sure?"

"Of course I'm bloody sure... sir!" The subordinate 'sir' added emphasis to his insubordinate tone.

"We're too beat to carry you far... and I've got to support Dick."

"Forget it! If you could put me in a wheelbarrow I wouldn't move from here. Leave me here, I know the drill. I'm not being gallant... only selfish... just want to rest."

"Got any ammo?"

"About ten rounds and a couple of grenades. It's enough. You got any matches?"

John shook his head.

"Go on, you two push on. I've told you I know the drill." March or die, he silently added. It sounded so melodramatic, but it was what it amounted to.

"I'll leave you this." John dropped his hammock at Badger's feet, "If you can't sling it, use it for a tent. You'd better have my bottle and these salt tablets, sorry they're all I have."

"Thanks very much, sir." He was betraying his newly born contempt for the officer class, but was too dispirited to reject the offerings.

"We'll send someone back for you. Good luck."

Badger, watching him walking back down, thought how naive John must be. It would be a miracle if there were any men fit and willing enough to backtrack in the darkness, to search for and pick up casualties. In the Column's present state it was virtually every man for himself. If you fell behind, and could not stagger along to the next rendezvous before the Column moved on it was your tough luck.

Although the clouds were thickening, the sinking sun was still warming the earth, but it was that sultry, humid warmth that presaged a storm. When it came he would be chilled. He must have a fire. Tinder and kindling would be no problem, but without matches...

Dick and John re-appeared, slowly climbing up the opposite side of the valley. He returned their wave and watching them disappear behind the teak, unrolled the hammock.

A rustling in the undergrowth, an outburst of monkey chatter, and the distant barking of a dog ape, agitated his desire for a fire. With wild boar or other predators about he daren't sleep without a fire. With his bayonet, he hacked four sprigs from the trees. Stretching out the hammock he propped up the four corners of the canopy with the sprigs, and unzipped the mosquito netting sufficiently for him to crawl through when the rain came. In the gathering twilight he could see the distant glow of the column's fires. Envious though he was, the glow was reassuring. They must be pretty sure there were no Japs about to have fires as big as that, and at this time of night. Dawn and dusk were the safest times, when the smoke mingled with the mists, and then only small fires were usually allowed.

Could he get a fire going like the Kachins, or Boy Scouts were supposed to do, with the friction of sticks? He doubted it, and toyed with the idea of starting one with a grenade primer, but quite apart from the danger, he only had two and they might not be clear of Japs yet... The lighter! It was worth a try.

Excitedly forgetting the pain in his feet, he scrambled around the trees gathering twigs and leaves and piled the tinder a couple of yards from his hammock. Rooting out the lighter he flicked it close to the tinder. There was a spark, then nothing. He flicked again, and frenziedly again, and again, but the wick remained dead. Hands trembling with anxiety and fever, he pulled off the base and took out the wadding. It seemed dry, but still smelt faintly of petrol. Stripping the cotton pugaree from his hat, he shredded it with his jack knife. Then frantically gathering together a small heap of the twigs, he covered it with shreds of the pugaree.

Giving an imploring look to the heavens, he squeezed the wadding furiously. His fingers blanched with exertion as spits of petrol dripped on to the pugree shreds. With childish glee, he forced a few more drops from the wadding, and then placed it on the shreds. Pushing the lighter close against the wadding, he flicked the flint. It sparked, but there was no flame. Again he did it. No flame. Again he flicked the flint. The wadding and shreds sprang ito fire, scorching his fingers. Gently breathing on the flames, he spread them to the twigs, scooping them into his mess tin and placing them on his original pile of tinder. Now he had a fire it was no problem keeping it going. Feverishly, he gathered armfuls of wood until he had a stockpile for the night. Then, praising himself for having had the foresight to dry out his blanket, he sat with it around his shoulders, as he stoked up the fire.

By now twilight had retreated into night, but there was a tawny afterglow, tinged with black and crimson, to the west.

With his knife, he removed the khaki flannel cover from one of the water bottles, took off the stopper and stood it in the fire. By the time he had gingerly removed the mud caked bandages from his feet, halved Tony's field dressing and swallowed the salt pills, steam was rising from the bottle. Using his hat to protect his fingers, he lifted the bottle and poured some of the water into his mess-tin, sponging his feet with half a dressing, and daubing them with gentian violet.

Flames and fever were simmering him and his groins were burning with pain. Simultaneously, he was shivering from scalp to toes. His teeth chattered uncontrollably. He re-heated the water, soaked both halves of the dressing with it and, biting back a cry, pressed one of the hot pads into each groin.

Stretching out alongside the fire, Badger dropped off to sleep watching familiar faces in the flames. He awoke shuddering, cold rain splattering his face and hissing in the flames. Hurriedly piling more wood on the fire, he clumsily scrambled into the hammock, dislodging the supporting sprigs, and the canopy collapsed about him like a mackintosh shroud. Twisting on his elbow opened a gap in the side of the hammock and with eyes that were smouldering coals, he watched the fire blazing away.

"Blaze on, you bugger!" he shouted deliriously, "Even if the rain doesn't put you out, we'll probably both be dead by morning... We'll make a bonfire of our troubles and watch them bla'a'ze awayyy...."

A military band was playing 'Blaze Away' and he was back in

infancy. He was clutching his father's hand, stumbling over the words on a cenotaph, 'To Our Glorious Dead'. The rain, hammering on the hammock, drummed out the band and he slid on his back muttering.

"To blazes with glory... to blazes with glory... "

As Corporal Archibald (Badger) Dixon, 1st Battalion, King's Regiment lay down to die, phantom bugles were blaring 'The Alarm' in his ears. 'There's a stranger in the camp! There's a stranger in the camp! There's a ..' Star shells were flaming the heavens. Mortar bombs were lacerating ghostly de-brayed mules. He was lying in a waterlogged slit trench, being shaved by a nappy wallah, and the char wallah was plying him with hot, super-sweet tea. Now Jack was alongside him, a leaking chagaul,[4] pressed against his blood soaked shirt, was washing blood down his legs. And he was singing 'Rose's of Picardy'. Now little Billy was lying on the parapet, pleading to be put out of his misery. In the canyons of his mind, Carbine shots were thudding into dying men. Cracking and echoing in his skull. Then Barbara was waltzing with him, both of them in uniform. Then it was not Barbara in his arms but a Kachin maiden, the child bride of the geriatric Thugyi of Nutmauk. In that deep throated voice of Barbara's she was singing, 'Let the Great Big World Keep on Turning', but then she wasn't with him. She was naked in brilliant sunlight, jitterbugging 'Under the Apple Tree' with a scruffy Indian fakir. Now Barbara was lying in a copse, blouse open, being fondled by an airman in goggles and helmet. Through all his delirium, his mother was hushing him with poems, all ending in the misquotation,

'O'lad that I love there is rain on your face, and you lie in the mud in your crumpled disgrace'.

The spluttering fire died with his groans, and Badger slipped into limbo, with only the rain and moaning trees for company.

Footnotes to Chapter Three

Page 31 Note No.3 Dahs – Burmese machete; some men carried kukris in lieu of dahs.

Page 41 Note No.4 Chagauls are semi-porous canvas water bags of about one gallon capacity: evaporation of the surface water helps keep the contents cool. They were only used when columns were in bivouac or in static operations.

PART 2

England : March to October 1942

'Sealed With a Loving Kiss'

Ah, such as thou, at last,
Wilt take a false man's hand:
Think kindly then of me,
When thou'rt forsaken, and
The shame sits on thy knee.

WH Davies

'Sealed With A Loving Kiss'

Chapter Four

As Barbara hurried out of King's Cross tube station towards the main line platforms, a turbulent late March wind snatched at the hem of her knee length coat, swirled grimy litter around her ankles and whirled it into the still grimier corners of the vestibule. Her train was not due to leave for half an hour, but she wanted to be sure of a seat. War-time trains were always dreadfully overcrowded. Men and women were bound for – or from – leaves or changing postings, and she dreaded standing, cramped in a corridor until she changed trains at Doncaster.

It wasn't just the passengers. There was also their bulky naval and military paraphernalia. The sea bags and cumbersome rolled hammocks of sailors, the packs, kit bags and rifles of soldiers who were obliged to travel in full 'Field Service Marching Order'.

She'd had more than enough of that, two nights ago, coming down from Manchester and to-day she was without Badger to deter 'accidental' gropers. They had endured four hours packed like sardines in a draughty, dimly lit corridor strewn with military accoutrements, their legs straddling Badger's kit bag and her case. What a way to spend a honeymoon night!

The train had not yet pulled in, but the platform was already thronging with passengers and well wishers. Icy shards of rain were showering through the bomb shattered roof, splattering her shoulders and ankles. The dampness was already seeping through her grey gaberdine coat, and she wished she had her WRAAF greatcoat with her.

Putting her overnight bag on the ground, she numbly played with the brassy new ring on her finger. She'd felt numb since leaving Westerham station. But it wasn't winter's iciness that benumbed her body and soul. She felt drained of emotion. Yet simultaneously, there was a trembling fullness in her stomach. She felt engulfed in nebulous, obscure guilt and remorse.

Not since her last term at school when she had briefly forsaken Miss Steiner, her petite art teacher, and her idolatry of Barbara's pubescent body for the more robust libido of her gym mistress had she felt quite so uncomfortably guilty. Her schoolgirl crush had then solely been for the gym mistress but Miss Steiner had spied them intimately soaping each other in the shower. For the remaining weeks of the term she'd had to surrender herself, with partly feigned willingness and partly honest relish, exclusively to Steiner's orgiastic fondling to escape expulsion.

But why did she feel guilty about Badger and herself? Throughout the journey to Charing Cross, she'd absently played with the pages of a magazine, left it on the train and couldn't even remember its title. On the cross London tube, she'd hardly noticed the passengers squashed around her, and only vaguely taken in the bunks and bedding, stacked along the platforms against a return of the Blitz.

Badger! How she loathed his nick name. But she could never think of him as Archie, and Archibald smacked of highland lairds and their scions, and of being too pretentious for a working class Mancunian. He'd been 'Badger' since his schooldays when almost every week he would badger his father – his mother being no needlewoman – to sew another new badge on to his Boy Scout uniform. The nickname was now as much a part of him as his Manchester dialect.

Like his wildlife counterpart he was intensely faithful to his kin and friends. His love for Barbara so near to reverence, so inherently trusting. Her love for him – or was it of him? – suddenly seemed naggingly negative. Had it ever been there? It was only two hours since she'd left him but some consoling amnesia was clouding her mind and already he seemed as dim and distant as Bettina Steiner.

A couple of platforms away, an engine hissed and clanked, steam wooshing from its pistons as the wheels momentarily slipped and

Field Service
Marching order

then gained traction. Behind her, squatting on over-stuffed kit bags, a bunch of dishevelled cockney soldiers were drunkenly chorussing about '...a luverly week-end...'.

Two day's ago she was a maiden, a 'spinster of this parish', a virgin. Now she was a married woman. They'd had so very little time together. Certainly not enough to really become a married couple. But was she sad, or thankful, that the 'honeymoon' had been so fleeting? Did its very brevity generate the guilt she felt?

Was the truth that she really wasn't ready for marriage. Not to Badger, nor anyone else for that matter?

Her thoughts were interrupted by the crowd shuffling back from the platform edge as a locomotive, steam spewing around its wheels, slowly drew its carriages into the bay. As the crowd surged towards it, a short, stiffly built, bearded petty officer picked up Barbara's case and elbowed his way through the scrambling passengers. He ushered her courteously into the carriage and followed her along the corridor. The compartments were filling up rapidly from both ends, passengers hurriedly staking claims to seats with uniform caps, haversacks, kitbags, then jostling back to the the platform to make their final farewells.

Barbara, just pipping a moustachioed corporal to a forward facing window seat, smiled her thanks at the petty officer as he put her case on the rack. Giving her a knightly salute, he staked a corridor seat with his cap, and shouldered his way back to the platform. With a resigned shrug the corporal settled himself opposite her, his feet almost brushing her ankles, and stared saucily at her.

His black, bristling moustache looked incongruous on his chubby baby face and there was a puffiness around his eyes as if he had been crying.

"If you are not Rita Hayworth, you must be her twin."

"Yes." Her stiff, dismissive tone made it clear she wanted to be left alone with her thoughts, "So people tell me."

At first glance she was a mirror image of the star. Yet striking though the immediate resemblance was, on closer scrutiny the likeness was harder to define, mystifying, like that of an infant to its parents. In detail she thought only her fine nose, squarish cheekbones and complexion matched the film star's. Her jaw always seemed more rounded, oval, rather than angular like Rita

Hayworth's. Her lower lip was overfull, pouting and sensuous, whereas the star's lips were symmetrically proportioned, calculatingly cool. There was a close similarity in their hair lines and eyebrows, but these were artificial. Since the likeness first struck her, she had cultivated high arching brows and copied the star's off screen 'casually' wayward coiffures.Through the window, fretted with crystallised frost, she absently watched the last lingering farewells.

The petty officer, self consciously shifting from one foot to another, was clasping the hand of his stooping elderly father. Their resemblance put the relationship beyond doubt. The D.S.M. and other medal ribbons on the father's overcoat testified to his past courage but there was dread in his moistened eyes as his lad, bound perhaps for another Murmansk convoy, Alantic submarine, or other hazardous sea duty, returned to the carriage.

The platform was a mass of embracing groups. There were the abandoned caresses of the young, the self-conscious hugs of old married couples, and the restrained embraces of dads and mums, sons and daughters. Near her window a swarthy airman and a black haired, pale faced girl were locked in a passionate kiss, their arms elbow deep under each others' coats.

Above the clamour of farewells, the mixture of forced humour and melancholy good-byes, the cockney soldiers, now cramped in the corridor, were for the umpteenth time chanting

'.. the smile on yer fice as yer stepped orf the tryne...
the look in yer eye like the san arter rine.."

A whistle shrilled, there were frantic hugs, mad scrambles into the carriages, doors slamming and a melee at each window, yelling and waving farewells.

The engine hissed and the clashing couplings took up the strain, and the swarthy airman lurched into the compartment, roughly crushing against Barbara's legs, and pressed his face against the window shouting to the girl,

"See you Thursday Marie, usual time!"

The girl's sobbed reply was inaudible above clanking wheels and swish of steam.

"Blimey mate, thought you were going away for years, with all that fussing. Didn't you, miss?"

Barbara ignored the corporal's sarcasm as the airman, squeezing out of the compartment, responded with a vigorous two figure gesture that could not be mistaken for Churchill's victory sign.

"Those Raf blokes must get home every week-end." The corporal was leaning forward to her, offering her a choice of three magazines. Was the bitterness of parting greater with repetition? Probably those two would suffer no less daily anguish than if they were parting for years. The years are short; it is the minutes, the hours and the days that make absence eternal.

Barbara didn't feel like reading, but his sorrowful brown eyes looked as though they would fill with tears any moment. Anyway it would be an excuse for not talking to anyone. Smiling her thanks, she took the 'John Bull' leaving him with 'Men Only' and 'Lilliput'.

As he lit a cigarette, she mentally cringed. The backs of his hands were ingrained with oil. His ragged nails were ringed with what looked like black polish residue. His fingers ochred with nicotine. Dropping out of nursing hadn't blunted her hospital indoctrinated fastidiousness, and her years in R.A.F. medical units had instilled the diagnostic importance of instinctively registering physical appearances. There was a shadow of dark stubble around his chin, and a greyish 'tide mark' below his hairline, but his Royal Artillery cap badge and boots were highly polished, his hair close-ly cropped. She guessed that he was some sort of mechanic who for some reason had been roughing it for a few days and had made a hasty attempt to make himself more presentable to return to duty.

Wedged tightly against the window, she hunched up her collar against a knife like draught and covertly surveyed the other seven passengers in the compartment. Between the petty officer, now snuggled up in a topcoat and the corporal, two Scots in tartan trews and greatcoats were dozing on each others' shoulder. Squashed as she was, all she could see of those on her side of the compartment without boldly leaning forward was that the man next to her was an Army sergeant and that the other two pairs of legs were in khaki trousers.

Still not clear of the Edwardian tenements ramped along the rail cuttings the train juddered to a halt, stood for a few minutes, jud-dered slowly forward for half a mile, and stopped again. The rain had stopped. The sky was clearing. Along the embankment the afternoon sun was casting sharp edged shadows of the carriages. Frost on the roof of a plate-layers hut, was glistening like quartz. It would be a hunter's moon to-night.

A bomber's moon.

Suddenly she felt released from regrets. She was going back to the convivial camaraderie of her Driffield base, free from the cloying chaperonage of the past week. The only guilt she now felt was that she *didn't* feel sorrowful about being away from Badger. For all practical purposes she was single again, back in her pre-marriage independence. It would be months, perhaps years, before Badger returned.

She would she vowed, keep herself for him. She would not, however, put herself in absolute purdah. No one – not even her husband – could expect that, though being married could be a useful foil against unwelcome advances.

Smiling as she turned these thoughts over, the moustachioed corporal took it to be at him. As he grinned back at her, she swiftly looked out of the window

They were still in the suburbs of London and she wondered how she could get back for her engagement ring. Whether or not she wanted to, she really ought to try and get back soon to recover it. Could she trust it in the post? As she was mulling over the idea, the engine whistled, couplings clanged and the train rolled and rattled forward. The slow, distinct didi.. didi.. tap.. didi.. tap of the wheels quickly accelerated into didididitapdiditap, and London fell behind them.

Fancy having to use an engagement ring as surety for honeymoon lodgings! She stifled a grin. It was as much her fault as Badger's, if not more. When he'd arrived on embarkation leave last Tuesday – was it only 6 days ago? – she should have been firm, sensible. Instead she had been soft-hearted, foolish, and agreed to marrying him by special licence. He was going overseas for God-knows how long, to God-knows where, and was desperate for her. His pleadings had touched her like a child's prayer and she could not – would not – surrender her virginity elsewhere than in the marriage bed. Her chapel-dedicated mother had drilled that morality into her, threatened her since puberty with the dire consequences of ever daring '...to bring your trouble across this threshold...'

Was that it? Was that why she had agreed to Saturday's wedding? Was it that she wanted legitimate release from virginity? Her mother firmly believed that copulation was solely for procreation, and would have been outraged by the contraceptive precautions her grammar schooled daughter knew about and had insisted upon last night.

Legitimate release? From what? Being married didn't remove the risks from fornication. Grass widows could still '...bring trouble...' home. Had she given herself to Badger merely as a consoling farewell gift to a dutiful soldier, and not for love of him? Or was it for a morally acceptable excuse to experience the thrills other Waafs extolled in conspiratorial whispers? She could not convince herself that surrendering herself to Badger was for the right and proper reasons. Deep down inside her, there was a feeling of being cheated of some ultimate rapture. 'It' surely should have been a more – much more – satisfying experience. Resentment was quickening a hunger for that obscure, ultimate rapture. How long could she withstand that hunger? Pleasurable as the final hours with Badger had been, some primeval instinct told her that they'd not reached the summit of rapture. At least she hadn't. She felt deprived of some elusive Elysian contentment. In those hours she'd abandoned every shred of innocence, and still felt left in suspense like a tantalising, cliffhanging serial, when the climax and denouement are promised in some future, indefinite episode. Now that her primitive urges had been stimulated, her craving for that denouement would be hard to control.

At the airfield there were temptations enough to demonize a saint. Even the plainest girls were never short of presentable suitors. With her looks and figure she had to effect aloofnesss. Marriage would not have changed that. She might now be Mrs. Dixon, but she'd still be that 'gorgeous' Dixon to them.

The co-incidence of their family names had first brought them together. Without that, she probably would not have looked twice at Badger. Compared to the devil-may-care, debonair aircrews back in Driffield, Badger was a callow, gauche youth, but he was a thoughtful, indulgent and protective companion. She lingered over the word. *Companion* didn't seem right – wasn't right – but she could think of no other. He was a lithe, agile and tireless dancing partner. She loved dancing, but too many other men ruined that pleasure with their roving hands, thrusting genitals and crude propositions. With Badger it was different. They danced together for the sheer joy of the rhythm, she felt feather-like in his arms. He didn't squeeze or crush her, she could relax, completely free of any sensual clinching.

That apart, what else did they have in common? Poetry? Yes, they both loved that. They had spent days roaming the East Yorkshire wolds reciting to each other. She'd been at a school renowned for its English scholarship, and had been repeatedly astonished that Badger, an elementary schoolboy, could so often 'out-quote' her. He'd never had an elocution lesson in his life but when he recited, his distinct Mancunian accent vanished. His intonation, timbre and metre, wondrously captured the poets' moods.

Were those simple, mutual pleasures enough? Enough for marital bliss? Fidelity?

It was almost a year to the day since they'd first met. She was only a corporal when, with six men, he had marched into the M.I. room. They'd volunteered for the newly formed Glider Regiment, and had to have a medical check up as preliminary measure. She had collected their A.B.64s, passed them to the MO and told the soldiers to strip to the waist.[5]

In her tiny office they had shyly bunched together, the paleness of their sun starved torsos accentuated by their weather reddened necks. As, one by one, the M.O. had called them into his room, she'd studiously avoided any scrutiny of them, ostensibly concentrating on the documents on her desk, partly to save them further embarrassment, but mainly to choke back her mirth. They had looked so comical. Their battle dress trousers, suspended by broad webbing braces over their bare, pale chests. No matter how well pressed their trousers were, they still had a Charlie Chaplin bagginess.

When the M.O. called for 'Corporal Dixon', she and Badger had simultaneously made for the door, and collided into each other. He had gashed his forehead on the door plate, and the M.O. had to put a stitch in it. After that, they'd chuckled and chatted about their identical ranks and surnames. He'd arranged a date with her that ordinarily he'd have been too shy to ask for, and she'd have been too affectedly aloof to take seriously. She'd often teased him that he had deliberately tripped, and played on his injury to coerce her into a date.

A week later he'd been posted to Kent, but had written to her almost every day. Long letters, full of adoring, youthful sentiment. In return, she replied with a few chatty lines each Sunday after church. Since then they'd only spent three weeks together. Two, ten day furloughs, and an odd week-end. Twenty one chaste days at one or other of their parents' homes. Jolly, carefree days, free of worries about housekeeping finances, domestic chores and routines that would have explored the depth of their compatibility.

How would they fare later, when they had all the time in the world together, when there were no more joyous re-unions, no bitter sweet partings, when domestic priorities kept them indoors. When nights out dancing – or theatres trips – were very special rare treats instead of common pursuits? And what about a family? They'd never really discussed their respective wishes about children.

She really had been daft to go ahead with the wedding. She'd twice had opportunities to at least postpone it, but flunked them. She could, should, have done it last Wednesday when they went from her home in Yorkshire to his in Manchester, and found the telegram ordering him back to his unit. Half heartedly, she had suggested postponing the wedding until he found out why he'd been recalled. It would give them time to plan a proper wedding, to save a little towards a home of their own. She'd been so sure that dedication to duty would scurry him back to his base, that she'd steeled herself to letting him have 'It' to sweeten his disappointment. She had even conspired with his family, who saw the sense of a postponement, to leave them alone in the house to 'work on' him.

Her loins trembled fleetingly, recalling the raw desire in Badger's eyes when she had undressed and draped herself on the sofa. Reflected in the mirror behind him, she'd seen herself as he was seeing her – legs, stretching up the sofa arm, toes and ankles flexed, tautening her calves and thighs. Her shoulders, overhanging the sofa edge almost brushing the floor, pulling every muscle of her torso into exquisite relief. The firelight had softened the alabaster starkness of her upthrusting breasts, emphasising the auburn of her hair. Its flickering shadows accentuating the delicate contours of her loins and navel. Then, as Badger moved nervously towards her, they'd heard the garden gate click.

Hurriedly she had slipped on her dress.

She now stifled a giggle, and winked at her reflection in the carriage window, as she recalled hurriedly stuffing her lingerie under the sofa cushions. Why, oh why, did the pub have to run out of beer? That night of all nights. If his family had not returned so prematurely she might well have gained a marriage postponement, in return for her maidenhead. As it was, Badger had uncharacteristically ignored the telegram. A second one, more imperative, had arrived on Friday.

So absolutely convinced was she that no one as regimental as Badger would dare to ignore its unequivocal command that she again hinted at calling off the wedding. To her astonishment – and his parents chagrin – he insisted he would not return until his leave had run its term, even if it meant a courts-martial, and had telegraphed for an extension 'to get married'.

Poor Badger, he was not to know then that his failure to return to duty, cost him his third stripe and a Home posting. They were leaving for the church when another telegram, refusing him an extension, had arrived. Petulantly he had ripped it to shreds.

Barbara felt more than a twinge of resentment about the austerity of the wedding. There was no solemn glide down the aisle on the arm of her proud father. Instead she'd walked down the aisle on his father's arm. Instead of a white gown, a light grey suit and pill-box hat that had taken almost all her savings and all her clothing coupons. No music, no hymns. None of her kin present, only his parents, sister and a couple of his uncles and aunts. Badger's father in Home Guard battledress. Badger in pre-war blue patrols with gold braid chevrons. Both of them stern faced and erect as Prussians. No photographers, no banquet. Only high tea in the parlour – John West salmon and pineapple chunks with custard.

When later that evening they were washing the dishes, Badger's resolve crumpled. Shamefacedly he told them he would catch the last train to London, and the family had clubbed together to find the fare for Barbara to go with him.

With only sixpence to their names, Sunday morning had found them in a Salvation Army canteen near Charing Cross station sipping tea and waiting for the 7.30 am train to Westerham.

At Westerham, the bleary-eyed but kindly landlord of the Royal Standard pub had let them in for breakfast and given them a single bedded room for one night, against the deposit of her engagement ring.

When Badger, after reporting to his orderly officer, had returned to the pub she'd not known whether to laugh with relief or cry with disappointment. He had originally been recalled for posting as a sergeant, to the Glider Regiment on Salisbury Plain, but a 'standby' corporal had taken his place. Now his overseas posting was irrevocable.

At seven in the evening they'd had a bar supper, and were longing to go to bed, but the locals intuitively sussed they were newly weds. So, partly to be polite, but mainly to avoid any ribaldry that would accompany an early retirement, they had lingered over a couple of complimentary drinks until closing time.

In the cold bedroom Badger, with mock nonchalance, had undressed before switching off the light. It struck her, that since the day of the medical examinations, she'd only once seen him without his shirt. That was at an Army boxing tournament. Even then he'd been wearing the mandatory Amateur Boxing Association singlet, and from her seat behind the privileged rows of officers she hadn't seen much more than his weaving head when he was in the ring.

Last night she'd been relieved to see that even though he was a fitness fanatic, he was no muscle-bound Adonis. There was something sickeningly effeminate about the meticulously nurtured symmetry of body culturists, and their displays of pumped-up muscle. Except for his weather reddened neck, Badger's body was maidenly pale. Hairless. Yet there was nothing feminine about the muscle that lightly corrugated his tapering abdomen and fleshed out his powerful shoulders. His physique was the natural evolution of the arduous regimen of an infantryman – not consciously developed nor preserved for oil-glistening poses.

He had come to her in trembling haste. His vice-like hug under her shoulders, nails biting into her flesh, almost blanked out the exquisite pain of his first, rupturing penetration. Crushing their lips with dry kisses, he'd lunged at her thrusting crotch until breathless and sweat lathered, they slid apart in an anticlimax of truncated consummation. If they'd got to that frustrated communion – and no further – last Wednesday night, she'd certainly have cancelled the wedding. There must be more to it than they'd achieved.

For a few minutes she'd lain there, fretting with disillusion, and listening to Badger's laboured breathing. Her whetted passion would not be checked. Switching on the light, she had gently guided his hands in an exploration of her body, as Steiner had so many times explored it before. When they next kissed it was with open mouths and probing tongues. There was brief bewilderment in his eyes, but she had parried any suspicion of past experience by teasingly questioning how he was so practised in quickening a woman's nipples. Then, pressing his mouth to her breasts, she had taunted him that he must have done this many times before with other women. With gestures and submissive sighs, she quickly had him believing he was inspiring her in their love making. In each of their voraciously repeated couplings, she had vainly expected, striven for, some sublime satiety. Desperate for ultimate ecstasy, oblivious of time, they had missed breakfast.

Racing into the station, breathless, no time for even a quick kiss as the guard's whistle shrilled through the sharp, frosty air she had stumbled into a compartment and mechanically blown kisses from the window until Badger's forlorn figure was out of sight.

Strange how, on the train to Charing Cross just this morning, she had felt so lost without him. And now, a few hours later, she felt blissfully free. One of her mother's favourite adages for once did not apply – She *had* made her bed – but she didn't have to lie in it.

§

"Tickets please!".

The guards voice along the corridor as he stumbled over rifles, kit bags, rolled hammocks and squatting passengers, roused her from a doze. The train, rattling and swaying through the

Huntingdonshire twilight, was rocking her against the sergeant. Ostensibly he was searching through his pockets, and Barbara realised with a start that it wasn't just the guard's voice that had roused her. The sergeant's right hand, under his greatcoat, was pressing against her thigh. She gave him her most withering, haughty look, but with a disclaiming flourish and a lecherous grin he pulled out his rail warrant.

The corporal nudged her ankle with his foot, and looked as though he was about to chide the sergeant. With a swift knitting of her brows, and a barely perceptible shake of her head, she signalled him to stay silent.

Steadying himself against the compartment's door frame and reaching for their tickets, the guard officiously reminded them of the black-out requirements, and curtly directed the corporal to pull down the window blind. Putting her ticket back in her handbag, Barbara jammed it between her hips and the sergeant's, winked at the corporal and heard with relief, the guard tell the sergeant to change at Peterborough, the next stop.

"I bet plenty of men have told you've got a beautiful pair of big..." the sergeant was impudently staring at her bustline, and provocatively pausing, "....green eyes."

The corporal, scowling, opened his mouth to say something but, again with her eyes, she signalled him not to interfere.

"Yes, scores of men," she smiled sweetly at the sergeant, "but you are the first moron to do so."

There was a chorus of appreciative chuckles and the sergeant, red-faced, muttered something about just a bit of a joke, and turned his attention to filling his pipe.

Footnote to Chapter 4

Page 53 Note No.5 A.B. 64s are soldiers' personal pay and record books.

Chapter Five

At Peterborough the train was nearly an hour late, and the sergeant's seat was taken by a willowy young mother and her infant daughter. Their ears and noses were tinged blue with cold, and the mother, her waist swollen by a new pregnancy, was clearly wearied by long wait on the frosty platform. She pulled the girl on to her knee, and vainly admonished her to keep still 'or else' while she chafed some warmth into the child's fingers and ears. Before the train had pulled out of Peterborough, the girl had wriggled free from her mother's lap, and stumbled across to the drowsing petty officer.

"Veronica! Come back here! Let the man be, he's tired."

"She's all right, dear." The petty officer sat up, parted his knees so the girl could stand between his legs, and asked her how old she was.

She was going to be six next week, and wished Daddy would send her a card. He didn't send her one last year 'cause mam said he couldn't get stamps in the 'spacific', and this year he was in a Japanese camp, and mam said the postman might not know where they lived now. They 'ust' to live with gran and grandad until they got 'blissed'.

Veronica's chatter brought smiles all around. By the time the train reached Doncaster, she had broken the the reserve of the passengers. Under the girl's questioning, everyone soon knew Barbara and Albert, the corporal, were bound for Driffield. The petty officer, who had a hat 'just like my daddy's' was a submariner going to Scapa Flow. The two 'Scots' were in fact Londoners, going to Catterick along with the other two soldiers.

At Doncaster Albert carried Barbara's case and, after leading the way into an empty compartment on the Hull train, hurried over to a refreshment trolley, returning with two mugs of watery tea.

Unlike the train from London, there were few passengers on board, and Barbara felt decidedly apprehensive when the doors slammed, and the train chugged out of the station. Not only were they the only two occupants of the compartment but it was an old, non corridor carriage. If Albert 'got funny' what could, should, she do?

She settled herself facing forward and as she sipped the tea Albert slipped his greatcoat over her lap and sat down beside her. She wanted to refuse the overcoat, so as not to feel under any obligation but accepted it with murmured thanks to avoid giving offence.

The gloom of the compartment, with its drawn black-out blinds and dim blue war time lights, sharpened her trepidation. Albert was pressing his shoulder against hers, and she had to fight hard to stop herself trembling. Was it fear? Or incipient arousal?

The train, slowly rolling and swaying, was rocking them gently against each other. Albert, slipping his arm around her waist, told her he was in the transport section of the aerodrome defence battery.

He had always looked out for her when he was on sentry, at the main gate.

"You always looked as if you had stepped out of band box. All the blokes said that. You have a smashing pair of legs."

The M.I. room was well within wolf whistling distance of the main gate, and she seldom went in or out without attracting shrill acclaim.

His voice was becoming sensually husky and as the train pulled into a station she gently removed his arm from her waist and leaned away from him to peep through the blinds.

"I thought we'd be further along than this," making believe she recognised the deserted rural station. She felt suddenly uncertain whether to be pleased, or fearful, that no one else had got into the compartment.

The train rolled forward again, and she realised now that she was not so much fearful of what Albert might attempt but how far, in her lingering frustration, she might want him to succeed. Before last night's unappeased arousal, that would never have entered her head.

She leant back in her seat as Albert, lighting another cigarette, started telling her about his model airplanes, then his pre-war job as an apprentice bricklayer, and then went boringly on about the cups he'd won for billiards and darts. The swaying carriage was soporific, and she'd hardly any sleep for 48 hrs.

"Sorry, Albert," she said as she twitched upright from a micro-moment's doze.

"That's all right, love, its still more than half an hour to Hull. You have a kip. You'll be safe with me. And don't worry, I'll wake you in good time."

Letting herself relax into a doze, she was dimly aware that her head was slumped on to his chest, and that his right arm was comfortingly around her shoulders.

§

A sudden lurch, as the train left another station partly stirred her from sleep, and she was vaguely conscious of his hand pressing her left breast. Through her thin coat, his fingers were on her nipple. He was arousing more than wakefulness in her, and she dreamily wanted to draw his hand through to her bare flesh, but resisted the temptation. She could have the pleasure, without revealing her receptiveness. Shamming sleep, she snuggled deeper into the hollow of his shoulder as his hand slipped through her coat lapels on to her thin dress.

Albert momentarily twisted away from her. She thought he was leaning over to stub out his cigarette but the greatcoat, over her knees, was being deftly lifted. His right hand was under her skirt, above her stocking top. Hot and moist, stroking her bare thigh. With a simulated start she sat bolt upright, and pushed his hands from her.

"That's enough of that! Thought you said I'd be safe!"

She was angry and disgusted with herself, both for letting him go so far, and then having to stop him before his fingers reached into her crotch. But for the coarseness of his hand on her smooth skin, reminding her of his grubby fingers and broken nails, she might not have stopped him. If he'd been a well groomed, well manicured man, she might have let him go a little further. It would've been little more than pleasant titillation, and she was sure she would not have let any man, go too far! In any case, they'd have been in Hull before titillation could become passion.

For a few minutes they sat in silence. Albert, drooping his head on his chest, idly twisted his beret in his hands. Barbara, haughtily upright, stared blankly at the framed picture of Scarborough's seafront above the seat opposite. The train juddered into another deserted station and, as it rolled foward again, their eyes met.

"What's your husband do?" His voice was ingratiating, like that of a repentant child. "Is he in the RAF?"

"Badger? No, he's a sergeant major in the King's Regiment." She waved away the cigarette he was offering her. It niggled her that she had married someone of the same lowly rank as Albert, and would have said Badger was an officer, but then he might have asked why she was not travelling First Class.

"King's Liverpools?" He was lighting his cigarette, and dropped his match in astonishment, "That's a rough mob!"

"Yes. His father tells everyone he has two sons in the Army, and the other is in the King's." They exchanged cynical smiles, and she went on, "His battalion were on airfield defence for two years, before your mob took over. Their turn out was smarter than your lot."

"Didn't mean to run them down its just that I thought a person like you would have married someone from... a man... you know..."

"You mean," she interrupted as he floundered around for the right words, "someone as stuck up as me would not lower themselves to be seen with a ranker, let alone marry one from the King's."

"No, I don't mean that. Its not that you are... stuck up... I just thought you'd be married to an officer."

"Look Albert, I don't come from an upper class family. If I am well spoken it is because I had a scholarship to a grammar school, and not because I was born into the aristocracy. After all,

I'm a ranker myself."

"Sorry, meant it as a compliment." Then, trying to change the drift of things, he asked, " Is Badger his real name? Sounds unusual."

"No of course not, it's his nickname."

"R.S.M. or a C.S.M?"

"Er... C.S.M." She'd nearly said R.S.M. but remembered that there is only one Regimental Sergeant Major in each battalion and if Albert gossiped around the base, he would soon find out she was lying. Company Sergeant Major was a little safer, there were half a dozen or so in each battalion. Nevertheless she now regretted saying that he was a sergeant major in the first place and hoping to cloud the issue added, "Acting C.S.M. really... he's just finished embarkation leave so I suppose he'll have to drop down to Sergeant if he's posted abroad."

"He will if he's not war substantive. When's he going?"

"No idea. You should know everyone's very close-lipped about those things. Careless talk costs lives, and all that stuff."

"What did you do before you joined up?" There seemed to be a growing buoyancy in his voice, as if Badger's posting made her fairer game for future assignations.

"I was nursing at St. James's, Leeds."

"Couldn't you have got a commission in Queen Alexandra's, or Princess Mary's nursing services?"

"No. Failed my S.R.N. finals, and in any case I hated nursing."

It was not entirely true. She'd enjoyed casualty and surgical duties but found chronic and infectious wards unrewarding. She detested the skivvying of bedmaking, sluicing bedpans and spoon feeding geriatrics. Barbara had set her heart on being an anthropologist, but that required years at university which her parents could not afford, and they'd pushed her into nursing. She'd sailed through the surgical, and anatomy and physiology papers, and had been referred in materia medica and chronic diseases.

With a few crocodile tears, she'd lied to her parents about failing abysmally, and not being able to face the humiliation of continuing at St. James's. Reluctantly, they gave their blessing to her joining the WRAAF.

"So naturally they put you in the medics branch," they exchanged wry smiles, "and after the war, it will be housewife and nappies."

"Good God no! At least not for a long time. Badger's set on staying in the Army, and I'm set on being an anthropologist. That means years of university ..."

She could only recall having told Badger of her plans once, and that was during their first leave together.

"I hope he realises how determined I am..." The words were an inaudible whisper, and Albert, puzzled, knit his brows.

"Sorry, its nothing, just thinking aloud."

The train, its brakes squeaking and couplings clashing, was pulling into Hull's Paragon Station, and a burly woman porter was yelling "Hull! All change for Hell!"

As they hurried towards the ticket barrier, the wail of air raid sirens gave meaning to the porter's words. Hull was a frequent target for German bombers, and it looked as though it was in for another 'blitzing' to-night.

At the barrier the ticket inspector, anxious to get away to his bomb shelter, brusquely told them to get a move on. The last train to Driffield had long since gone. The next would be the milk train, in five hours.

"Let's get to Maxi's Club first, Barbara, we might get a lift from there."

Chapter Six

As they dashed across Feren's Way, vermilion flashes lit the night. Bombs were crumping around the dock area. Searchlights probed the sky. Ack-ack guns were splotching the heavens with cotton ball detonations.

She wasn't due back on duty for another two days, and her first thought had been to see if she could book into a bed and breakfast place till then. Badger had stuffed two borrowed pounds into her bag at Westerham. The twenty five shillings she had left wouldn't get her a room, even for the night, in the plush Broadway Hotel adjacent to the station.

Maxi's Club turned out to be a tarted up Victorian lodging house. The patchy green and red colour wash of its crumbling exterior, and the corrugated sheeting blinkering its bomb damaged windows gave it a derelict, deserted appearance, belying the clamorous crowded interior.

"What'll you have if there's no gin and tonic?" Albert hung his greatcoat on the newel post, and propped his rifle against his pack on the cracked linoleum of Maxi's dingy, chocolate and cream lobby.

"Oh... a glass of any beer they've got."

The lobby and narrow staircase was a mass of uniformed revellers singing 'There'll be blue birds over the white cliffs of Dover', their voices almost drowning out a piano, somewhere beyond Barbara's vision. The two bars, through double arches at the foot of the staircase were seething throngs that allowed little room for elbow bending without nudging other drinkers.

The crowd packing the tobacco hazed lobby and staircase was comprised predominantly of airmen and Waafs, presumably also waiting for the milk train. Here and there, up the staircase and in the lobby, couples were ardently nestling each other.

On the lower stairs just behind Barbara, a busty Land Army girl was cooing over a youthful Squadron Leader's medal ribbons and drawing his mouth to hers by pulling on his tie. Near the top of the stairs a shoe-less Waaf and a crew-cropped marine were in a pulsating kiss. Her skirt was rucked up above her suspenders, his knees tight between her thighs, with her calves wrapped around his. A few steps below, another marine was fast asleep, neck cricked against a baluster, hugging her shoes to his chest.

But for the most part, the crowd were just asexual boisterous comrades in arms, their improbity extending only to unbuttoned tunics and bawdy parodies of popular songs.

The service-womens' youthfulness and sexless carousing, contrasted with the desperate coquetry of the sprinkling of care-worn strumpets. Their bosoms bulging provocatively beneath skimpy bodices, or tight jumpers, as they touted their 'wares'.

As Albert fought his way to the bar, Barbara's eye caught that of a tall, bulky shouldered Flying Officer. In the dark blue of the Royal Australian Air Force, he stood out like a sore thumb from the lighter blue of the R.A.F. as he lolled against one of the arches. Even without the differences in uniform or his giant frame, his leathery, outback complexion that had long lost the bloom of youth, would have set him apart from the crowd. The paler skin above his hat band line, was finely furrowed. His heavily lidded eyes were deeply set below dark woolly brows, as though nature was giving them refuge from the sun that had etched the squint wrinkles around them. The harsh creases, curling from his puggish nostrils, down each side of his lantern jaw, like a Mexican bandit's drooping moustache, gave a knavish emphasis to his thin lips.

A tall blonde in a deceptively simple black dress, long elegant legs sheathed in sheer black stockings, had his cap on her head. On the tips of her black patent court shoes, she was stretching to ruffle his thick black hair as she pressed him against the archway. In one hand he had a half bottle of gin. His other arm was around the waist of a Wren officer, whose classic features put her aristocratic ancestry beyond question.

Over the blonde's head he stripped Barbara, from thigh to shoulder, with half hooded eyes that even in this dim light, glinted with fascinating arrogance. She felt her face flushing and, when he grinned at her discomfiture, there seemed to be a brutish satisfaction about his lips. To break the spell, she turned with exaggerated disdain towards the staircase, and wished she hadn't. The Land Army girl was passionately nibbling the squadron leader's ear. One of his hands was under her green jumper and she was rocking on his other which was down inside the rump of her corduroy breeches.

Seeing them through the banister rails, Barbara felt as if she was spying on the obscene antics of caged orang-utangs. Embarrassed, she turned quickly from the pair, and was relieved to see the Flying Officer now too occupied embracing the Wren to look her way.

Feeling terribly alone, and vulnerable, she pressed her back hard against the newel as a tipsy soldier tried to squeeze past.

"Give us a feel 'til pay day love," he said, swiftly squeezing both her breasts, and attempting to kiss her.

"Beat it, you drunken bum!" The Aussie pushed through the crowd, and elbowed the soldier across the neck. As the soldier meekly slunk off, her rescuer gave a dismissive salute to the Wren and the blonde. As they sulked towards the bars, he pressed himself against her.

"Have a drop of this sweetheart, heard you ask that corporal bloke for gin." His cultured baritone voice muted his 'stryne' and reminded Barbara of an imperious theatrical barrister. "Sorry, no tonic."

"Thanks no! Can't stand it neat."

"Suit yourself." Taking a quick drink himself, he passed the bottle to the squadron leader, bowed his head over hers, and brushed her brow with his lips.

"Name's Leslie Brodie. What's yours, and what's a beaut sheila like you doing with that pommy corporal? Ditch him and I'll show you a really good time."

"Barbara, and he's...he's my brother."

"Aw! Come off it. Him your brother." He nodded at Albert carrying two glasses of beer, pushing through to them. Through those half hooded lids, his cool grey eyes flitted to Albert and bored back into hers.

"You are nothing like each other."

"Thanks, Albert." She took one of the glasses. "I was just telling this officer that I'm your sister." To avert her eyes from Leslie's sceptical gaze, she took a sip of the beer and put the glass through the balustrade on to a stair. "He doesn't believe me."

"Sister-in-law actually, sir." Albert darted a conspiratorial wink at her, clearly indicating she now owed him a favour. "Her sister's my wife."

"If that's true, all the better." The disbelief was obvious in Leslie's tone. "There's nothing to stop us getting together for a night or two..."

"Look sir, Barbara's married..."

"Not only that," Barbara interrupted, "I'm a WAAF sergeant and I've met your type before, *sir*."

Oh! How she hated calling officers 'sir'. She forced a distinctly insubordinate tartness as she said it.

"So. What does that matter? We Aussies don't give a toss for class distinctions." Glancing scornfully at Albert, he half turned his back on him and rested his left elbow on the newel close to her neck. Cutting off Albert from her sight he said, "I'm at Leconfield but I don't remember ever seeing you there..."

"You wouldn't have. I'm at Driffield."

"Good O! I'm being posted there next week."

His right hand was now firmly spanning the nape of her neck and as his fingers gently pressed beneath one ear she noticed the half wing 'Navigator' insignia and D.F.C. ribbon over his left breast pocket. She noticed something else too. Almost every other man she'd been this close too, if he didn't smell of carbolic or cheap talc, smelled of stale sweat. Leslie didn't. He had a pleasant aromatic scent with only a trace of musk, and his hands, hard as they were, were well groomed and scrubbed.

"Look, Barbara, I'd better go and rustle up that lift, or your old man will think I've run off with you."

"Yes, but don't leave me here alone too long with this

Don Juan."

"Yes, run along corporal, Barbara and me can get to know each other." His tone was as contemptuous as a Nazi chastising a Jew and when Albert mumbled something, he followed up with, "Go on sonny, don't waste our time!"

"Are you naturally arrogant, or do you only bully people smaller than yourself?"

"What was he mumbling about?" He gave a supercilious grin but otherwise ignored her taunt.

"He was only trying to tell you he's a bombardier not a corporal."

"Ah yes! Your Artillery. Sorry, Royal Artillery."

Strange, poor Albert had not tried to correct her when she called him corporal, and she should have known better. He was obviously trying to get back at Leslie. His cavalier treatment of Albert vexed her, but uppermost in her mind was the elation. Without lifting a finger, the handsomest man in the place had forsaken two lovely women for her.

Without being in the least surprised by it, she felt his left arm slip under her coat, and snake round her back until his hand rested on the side of her left breast. With his other hand still spanning her neck so she couldn't turn her face away, he kissed her full and long, on the lips. For only a split second did he try to force his tongue into her mouth and, when he found her teeth tightly clamped, gentled her lips with his tongue.

Self hatred welled up in her at what she was allowing this domineering stranger to do. The more so because she knew that, by her trembling, he could tell that any resistance would only be a sop to convention. They both knew that only time and place were curtailing his conquest and her submission. Her arms were pinioned over her breasts, but it would not have required any great effort to push him away.

With supreme confidence, that simultaneously vexed and bewitched her, his hand released her neck and slid down the ridge of her spine to her buttocks.

"That's far enough!" She hissed sharply, and instantly he returned the hand to her neck.

"If you expect me to drop you off be at the car in five

minutes!" The Wren officer was tugging at his tunic hem, "I've got to be back in town before reveille." She clearly meant London, but spoke as if it were just down the road, and not a couple of hundred miles away.

"I'll be there in a mo, Joyce!" he called as she made for the door.

He effortlessly lifted Barbara, with the arm around her back, until her feet were clear of the floor and their eyes were level. Her elbows shifted to his shoulders to balance herself, and with practiced ease his right hand slipped down the neckline of her dress into her brassiere.

"Your tits are as ready for me as your eyes" he whispered, his hand deftly cupping her right breast, his fingers teasing the erect nipple.

"Put me down!" His cocksureness incensed her to break from him, and she struggled all the more fiercely because she knew he was right, "You're hurting my ribs, you... you bloody brute!"

"Sorry darling. You'll just have simmer for me, until next time."

He let her down slowly, and was plainly not sorry for her, but only sorry for himself that he had to leave.

"There won't be a next time" She snapped, pushing his hands away as he calmly smoothed the bodice of her dress.

"I... I could have you on a discipline charge ...indecent assault."

"But you won't." Seizing the lapels of her coat, he drew their faces together, and kissed her forehead. "Bye! See you at Driffield." Trembling with mixed emotions – humiliation, elation, and yes, randiness – she watched him push through the crowd to retrieve his cap from the blonde. As he made for the exit he salaamed her with his cap and called, "Keep it simmering!".

Dry mouthed she picked up her beer from the stair and was relieved that no one seemed to have noticed what had been going on. If they did, they were concealing their awareness. Between intervals of singing, the crowd were laughing loudly and shouting requests to an invisible pianist. Now they burst out 'There'll always be an England' and a Taffy somewhere was yelling 'What about pluddy Wales?" with each chorus.

What had got into her? Less than 24 hours out of her bridal bed and she'd allowed – if not surreptitiously encouraged – both Leslie and Albert, complete strangers, to fondle her more than any other man she'd known, excluding Badger.

"You're shivering! Its not that cold in here." Albert had pushed his way back into the lobby, and was staring quizzically at her.

"No, I'm not cold, its just that insolent bastard annoyed me."

"Yeah, thinks he's God's gift to women."

"No. He's the Devil's gift of a god to women." Her husky voice had a trembling throatiness and, as Albert hesitantly put a consoling hand on her shoulder, she piously whispered, "Jesus help me keep clear of him."

"Don't let him frighten you. If he harasses you again, report him."

"It's me, not him, I'm frightened of."

Albert looked curiously at her for a few moments but, when she offered no further explanation, he put his greatcoat around her shoulders, and picked up his rifle and pack.

"Well, we've got a lift to Pocklington, if you're game to sit in the back of a utility. I warn you it'll be a bit cold and uncomfortable, there's a load of boots in the back."

"I'll put up with the discomfort." A 'utility' was a small two seater pick up, with a canvas hood at the back, "But Pocklington is about ten miles from Driffield. How do we get from there?"

"Mary – she's an A.T.S sergeant, with Jock Ferguson who's taking us – reckons she can charm a certain officer to run us to Driffield."

"At this time of night?" There was deep suspicion of Albert's intentions in her tone. "They'll all be fast asleep."

"Not this one. He's battery orderly officer to-night and dead regimental. He'll be dossed down in the officer's mess, until he makes the rounds of gun sites, and he's got to go to those at Driffield. He fancies Mary. She's the battery clerk, and I think she's got something on him."

Still suspicious and apprehensive, Barbara followed him out to where a small camouflaged Hillman pick-up was parked. Searchlights were still sweeping the sky, but there was no sound of guns and she wondered whether the 'All Clear' had gone. As if in answer, there was a distant hum of aircraft and a burst of ack-ack fire, as Albert introduced her to Mary O'Connor and Sergeant Ferguson.

The two men had taken it for granted that Jock would drive, and Mary would sit in front with him. Mary, raging with indignation, had other ideas and would 'Not at all, at all,' have Barbara riding in the back. Jock Ferguson might be in charge of the van, but 'no heathen Scottish non-conformist was going to sit in comfort, alongside her, whilst a good Christian woman froze to death in the back.' She would hear no argument. She would drive, Barbara would sit with her. The two men could sit on the boots in the back.

Chapter Seven

"Another cup of tea, Mary?" Mary nodded and handed her mug to Barbara. They were in Barbara's room, the main bedroom of a pre-war married quarter. A soot blackened kettle was precariously balanced on the newly lit fire.

There had been an almost instant rapport between the two women. True to her word Mary had got the orderly officer, Captain Wilson, to drive them to the Driffield airdrome where he had dropped them at her quarters, before driving Albert off to his billet.

"You shouldn't have done this," Barbara admonished as she refilled Mary's mug, "he'll expect ..."

"Jaysus, and don't Oi know it, but he's going to be disappointed. Oi've got my period." She winked at Barbara, "Not really, but it's astonishing what the mere mention of the word does to a man's ardour."

They both giggled. Mary, lounging on the bed, lifted up her legs to expose her issue bloomers. Even in the khaki lisle stockings, she had the most attractive thighs and elegant ankles Barbara had seen – at least since Bettina Steiner's.

"Don't fret Barbara, Oi can handle old Wilson and he's very useful"

Barbara pulled off her dress, and took a dressing gown from her locker. Over the rim of her mug, Mary's blue Irish eyes roamed over every inch of her hostess.

"No wonder Brodie made a bee-line for you. You've got lovely Bristols."

"Oh! You know him do you?" Blushing, and striving to conceal her embarrassment, Barbara picked up the fire tongs and placed a lump of coal on the fire.

"Oi've seen him about a few times, so Oi have. He's a divil incarnate. He's only been at Leconfield a few weeks, but he's put his mark on ony number girls in that time, so he has. Always grabs the best looking at any dance, and puts a lot of fellers noses out of joint. He's not made a pass at me, and God forgive me Oi wouldn't mind him putting his shoes under my bed at any time, so Oi wouldn't."

"Mary Connor! And you, a convent- bred girl!" Spinning on her haunches she stood up, arms akimbo, shaking her head in mock astonishment, "Anyway, come off it, you weren't at the back of the queue when good looks were being rationed."

"Sure, and Oi'd be a liar if Oi disputed that, so Oi would. And you would be too, if you denied you were good looking – beautiful in fact."

There was neither false modesty, nor envy, between them as they ran their eyes admiringly over each other's slim form.

Mary was not the archetypal red haired, Hollywood colleen. Like so many of her compatriots, she had the creamy Latin complexion and thick, Guinness black hair of their Armada ancestry. Her hair was swept back, behind small delicate ears, into a tight French roll. Her wide brow, with its pronounced widow's peak, and finely curved eyebrows was unblemished by any creases. Her high boned, hollow cheeks, exquisitely flared nostrils and pouting lips, were the loveliness that beauty photographers' dreams were made of. Even in the drab, mass produced A.T.S. uniform, the full bust, taut flat flanks and shapely calves were the stuff that men's fantasies were made of.

"Why is he coming to Driffield anyway, do you know?"

"Old 'Ant-dim' says he'd done well over thirty bomber ops. without a break....."

"Ant-dim?"

"Jim Wilson. The first thing he checks at kit inspections, is whether the gunners' respirator lenses have been ant-dimmed, and he flies into a rage if they aren't." Mary shook her head in affectionate disparagement of Wilson, "He's a bit dim for an officer – a Blimp, a flanneller. Everyone knows he couldn't run a piss-up in a brewery"

"Speaking of breweries, what about a drop of this." Barbara produced a half empty bottle of rum and two tumblers, "Got it off one of the flyers.... Cheers"

"Cheers... Phwat was Oi saying?" Mary sipped the rum, coughed involuntarily and grimaced. "Bit fiery... Yes, Wilson's a bit dim, but Oi string him along because Oi can always wangle transport out of him. Like today. By rights, Jock should have been back with the boot repairs before 1600, but Jim let me go with him and have a night in Hull. "

"But what about Brodie?" Barbara asked, trying to sound only triflingly interested, as she shared out the last of the rum.

"According to Anti-dim, he was posted here as Intelligence Officer for a break from ops. after he got his D.F.C." Mary sighed wistfully and, with humorous irreverence, crossed herself. "Ah! The divil is irresistible, to be sure he is." But there was no irreverence when she added "Jaysus Christ, help us."

"Amen to that." Barbara added with priest-like solemnity. For a moment she stared thoughtfully at the fire, "Mary, do you think," she asked hesitantly, "that losing your virginity makes you more vulnerable?"

"Oi wouldn't call it vulnerable, so Oi wouldn't." She gave Barbara a knowing look. "Its a release, so it is. You've nothing to protect onymore – and once you've found out it's so good, you can't resist wanting more. That's what you mean, isn't it?"

"Something like that...yes. And I suppose its because once it's gone, and the temptation's there..."

"Stop being bashful. Oi know phwat you're thinking, so Oi do. You're thinking that if Badger's away ony length of time, and you need it badly enough, he'll never know if you do it with Brodie, or ony other man."

"Don't bring Brodie into this!" Tartly, then more amiably, "I wouldn't put rape past that brute. But you're right, of course, Mary. That *is* what I was thinking. I feel so bloody guilty, but I know I won't be able go for long without it."

"O.K., sorry Oi mentioned Brodie. Forget the guilt. Enjoy life while you can. You know what they say, 'no one ever misses a slice off a cut loaf'. But for Jaysus sake, take precautions."

"Oh I will, I will." There was gratefulness in barbara's eyes. Her new found friend was no hypocrite and understood her feelings, even though she had not expressed her own very well. Intuitively, she knew she could confide her innermost feelings and transgressions to her without the slightest fear of Mary blabbing them to others. Somehow, she felt paroled from marital constraints.

"The officers at the Carnaby airstrip are having a dance on Saturday, it's near Bridlington, and the Waafs here are getting a bus load with the nurses from Driffield Base Hospital, I do wish you would come with me, Mary."

"Sure. Love to, but can you get me a ticket ?"

"Not necessary – and there'll be plenty of room on the bus. The nurses are a flirty crowd, lead the men on something awful."

"The wicked sods, so they are." There was no malice in the Irish girl's voice, only humour tinged with trace of envy. "They've got less to worry about than we have. If they get into trouble 'a cute appendicitis' solves their worries."

"Yes, but if there are less on the bus coming home, its usually Waafs or ATS that are missing."

"Phwat time?"

"Be here about seven – we'll have a quiet noggin before we go. Can you manage that?"

"Jim'll run me over. Oi'm on duty early on Sunday. Oi'll get him to pick me up at Carnaby. He'll jump at the chance, so he will. It'll boost his ego if he thinks Oi won't let any other bloke take me home"

"You're a crafty one, so you are." With a grin Barbara wagged a finger reprovingly at Mary. "Look, now you've got me using your Irish idioms."

With exaggerated Irish inflexion, and smiling broadly, Mary retorted, "Oi'll thank you not to mock my lovely brogue, so Oi will..." Two blasts of a car horn interrupted her, "That's typical of Jim observing the proprieties, so it is," she shook her head despairingly, "he won't risk compromising us by sneaking up and tapping on your door, so wakes up the whole block! Oi'll have to go before the idjit does it again. Bye, see you Saturday love."

From the door Mary blew a kiss, and flew down the stairs.

For a few moments Barbara pensively stared at her wedding ring then, with a decisive shrug, wrenched it off and slipped it on to her identity discs cord around her neck.

Chapter Eight

As the last notes of the jive session faded and the four bandsmen set down their instruments for the refreshment interval, Mary nudged Barbara and cocked a knowing grin at her.

"You really fancy Yorkie, so you do." She nodded towards the slightly built, blond Group Captain making his way towards them through the dispersing, perspiring couples.

The Group Captain had arrived when the second dance was being announced, and made straight for Barbara. Since then, except for excusing himself for sitting out the jitter-bugging, and for a 'duty dance' with a WRAAF officer, he had claimed Barbara for every dance.

"No I do not!" The adamance of her denial gave the lie to her words, and studiously avoiding Mary's perceptive eyes, she clicked open her compact, and concentrated on dabbing her glowing cheeks.

As Yorkie, carrying three glasses, approached them Barbara and Mary – unable to find seats – hitched their bottoms on to the stage edge which was really an assemblage of trestle tables.

"Gin and tonic for you Barbara, whisky soda for Mary."

He had a bluff, gravelly Northern accent that seemed out of character for such a senior officer. All the others she'd met had had public school accents.

"Barbara? Mary?" He held out a silver cigarette case to them. Barbara had been surprised – and flattered – that he had used her Christian name when first he'd asked for a dance. He'd obviously been interested in her enough – before this evening – to find out who she was, and his genial familiarity earned her envious looks from nearby women, especially a couple of WRAAF officers.

"Thank you, Bill." Taking a cigarette, she looked smugly at an eavesdropping nurse, who had been at nursing school with her and was now a staff nurse at the local Base Hospital. Lingering over the lighter flame, one hand seductively on his wrist, she peered, through winsomely lowered lashes, into his golden brown eyes, savouring his attentiveness, drinking in the desire in them. Taking a long draw at the cigarette, she blew smoke rings towards the roof, and smiled conspiratorially at Mary.

"Is Captain Wilson coming here to collect you, Mary?" She had not the slightest doubt that Bill would eventually offer to drive her back to Driffield. Mary had confirmed earlier that Antidim was picking her up, but she wanted to tip Bill off that she wasn't travelling home with Mary.

"Sure and didn't Oi tell you he'd be here for the last waltz?" Obviously divining her friend's motive, she flashed an intuitive smile at Barbara. "We'll run you back as well... "

"No need for that. It'll tack thee miles out of your way. I'll be delighted to run Barbara home." Bill's eyes caught Barbara's, and fixed on them with a mischievous, dominating stare.

"That's kind of you Bill, but I really think I should go back with the rest of the girls..."

The swiftness of his interruption, the eagerness in his tone and boldness of his eyes, promised more than just a chaste drive back to Driffield. Scouring her mind for some plausible, innocent excuse to accept his offer, she took a long draw on her cigarette, exhaled, and taking a sip from her glass, smiled diffidently over its rim at Bill.

"I don't want to cause any gossip... you know... a Group Captain consorting with a ranker. On the other hand I wouldn't want you thinking I prefer a bus load of inebriated chattering women to you."

A twinge of innate morality stabbed her mind, damping but not extinguishing, the thrill of what she thought – hoped – he was expecting from her. The warmth of his thighs as they had danced had whetted the yearning that Badger had left her with. She'd been impatient for him to make his offer. Connived with Mary to prompt him. Now she was floundering between fidelity to Badger, and incipient yearning for Bill's embraces. Pensively gnawing her bottom lip, she looked wryly at Mary.

"Jaysus sorr! Will you listen to the woman. Playing hard to get, so she is." Mary plopped her glass down on the stage and casting her eyes with mock exasperation to the heavens, thrust out her hands, palms upwards beseeching Divine intervention, "Stop wavering – carpe diem and all that. Seize the opportunity. Life's too short these days to worry about gossips. Stop dithering and put him out of his misery." Brazenly outstaring two onlooking, whispering couples, she raised her voice a pitch, "Sure, their tongues will wag whatever you two do now, so they will. You might as well be hung for a sheep as a lamb."

Bill chuckled, and winked amiably at Mary.

"It's matterless to me what spiteful conclusions folk jump to." There was a fascinating, almost mesmeric, appeal in his eyes as he fixed them on Barbara's. "Any rowad, tittle tattle is a pittance to pay for a lovely woman's company."

His North Riding inflexion flowed easily, naturally, but his occasional colloquialisms were inconsistent – a little too contrived, theatrical and spurious. She had the impression he resorted to idioms to foster his popular image as a blunt, no nonsense, man who'd come up the hard way. An affable mannerism to set himself apart, and above, the conventional, old school tie, air force hierarchy.

"Yes, of course I'll go back with you. It's the least I can do to repay your company..." Smiling alluringly at him she watched the onlookers sheepishly edge out of earshot as, slipping down from the stage and stamping out her cigarette on the floor, she linked an arm possessively through his.

"Best sup up!"

He drained off his drink in one, as the band leader announced that the next dance would be a 'quick step', and led Barbara on to the floor.

§

"Have you known Mary long?" They'd managed to find two unoccupied chairs between dances.

"No, only since last Monday – we hit it off together from the first moment."

"I'd 'ave bet a pound to a pinch of sh... salt – that you'd been pals, for years."

"Really? Why?"

"You seem so close, able to read in each other's mind. You know I didn't need any cue to offer you a lift." The reproof in his tone was softened by an impish gleam in his eyes.

"I don't know what you mean, Bill..." Her eyebrows shot up in a fabricated guileless, bewildered expression.

"You can drop t'wide eyed innocence, tha' knows what a'm getting at." Chuckling, he playfully ruffled her hair.

"But, Bill..."

"Nuff said. Think no more on't." Slipping an arm around her shoulder, he softly brushed her cheek with the back of of his other hand, "Blushing becomes you, but if you doan't stop it quickly, those busy bodies over there will think I'm making improper suggestions"

Smiling wanly, Barbara took hold of his hand and they sat in silence for an eternity of minutes. She should've have waited for Bill to make the first move, and have accepted without false demur. Frowning, she probed her mind for something to break the silence, something to change the subject.

"Doan't look so worried luv." Smiling, he gently pulled her shoulder closer to his.

"I'm not worried, just..." She couldn't think what to say next, and desperately wished the band would start the next dance.

"Just what? Tha's a puzzled frown."

"Yes. That's it I *am* puzzled." Bill's words triggered off a new thought, and her frown gave way to the ghost of a smile.

"Oh?"

"Do you mind if I ask how you found out my Christian

name?"

"The M.O., Squadron Leader Thomas." His eyes twinkled as if lit by some pleasant recollection.

"Oh! Him." So he hadn't looked up her personal records. She masked her relief with wide eyed, querying, smile and whispered, "When?"

"In the airman's dining room, when the officers and sergeants were serving Christmas dinner to the erks."

"And?"

"And nothing... Oh, he did say 'you mean her with the elegant ankles' and..." Bill paused, obviously considering whether to complete the M.O.'s words.

"Don't be bashful, I bet he said 'gorgeous bouncers'. He's always on about them. But, to you, I bet he used a cruder word for them. Anyway, why me? There were more than a few good lookers there."

"You're right, of course." His arm slid under her armpit and pressed the side of her breast. "And, he's right. Why did I pick you out? Well, you stood out from the rest. You walk tall, upright, proud shouldered. A lot of women seem to mince along, knees buckled, torsos tilted half a pace afront of their feet, bums pushed backwards. You've seen 'em, like Groucho Marx. Frightened of shoving out their breasts, shrinking with bashfulness."

"Oh Bill! You make them sound like crippled apes...."

"Ladies and gentlemen!" The band leader, cutting her off in mid-sentence, announced that the next dance would be a 'Paul Jones'

"Can't we sit this one out, Bill?" An imploring pout.

"Sorry. Got to show I'm not too besotted to let you out of my reach." Abstractedly tugging at the hem of his tunic, he added mockingly, "Got to give other wenches the honour of partnering me. "

When the music stopped, halting the counter-flowing circles of men and women, Barbara found herself partnered by a tubby, flabby faced officer.

"Had my eye on your buffers all night, darling." Reeking of rum, right hand groping under her armpit, left hand beneath her shoulder blades, fumbling through her blouse material for her bra strap, he tried to nibble the tip of her ear.

"Stop it, or I'll walk off the floor!"

He stumbled over her foot as she pushed the hand from her armpit to the small of her back, and tried to grasp the other hand.

"Aw, c'mon, les ge' close." With his fingers straining into her skirt waist, the other hand still fiddling with her bra strap, he crushed her to him, "Don't be such bloody prude...Aaagh!"

Her knee thumped into his crutch, leaving him doubled up in agony, eyes bulging. She stalked haughtily from the dance floor and out into the adjacent ablutions hut.

The dank, corrugated hut, reeked of coal-tar disinfectant. The wooden framed, zinc trough, running down the centre, was slimed with with soap residue, and stained with razor blade rust. The mirrors above the row of corroding, dripping taps were discoloured and peeling. Mary was the only other person in the hut.

"Heavens Mary! What's happened to you?"

The Irish girl, combing her hair, a couple of hair grips in her mouth, was peering into a peeling mirror. It was a calm night, but her normally neat hair looked storm swept. Her blouse was open from neck to waist, her tie askew, and there was an angry flush on her face.

"Frustrated is the word. Frustrated, is phwat Oi am. Bloody frustrated!" Mary poked the grips into her hair. and stared questioningly at Barbara, who was smoothing her own disarranged blouse into her waist-band. "You too? Not Bill?"

"No, not Bill! A damned drunken slob!" Slipping a hand inside her blouse she adjusted her shoulder straps. "Bloody lecher ...one hand inside the back of my skirt..." She paused to straighten Mary's tie. "...the other trying to unhook my bra. Too sodding puerile to know a Kestos fastens at the front, thank Christ!"

"Don't fuss yourself." Mary playfully tweaked one of Barbara's breasts. "Bill won't need any help finding the fasteners, so he won't."

"Don't be so sure he'll get the chance!" Stooping to brush specks of blanket fluff from Mary's skirt, she gave her friend an admonishing grin. "So, what happened to you, you naughty girl."

"Here's me, lying on this lovely boy's bunk, one leg out of my knickers, his pants round his ankles, and he's not got a French letter!"

"Mary! You didn't?"

"No fear! Phwat, bare backed with a stranger!" Mary made it sound as if using a sheath would have sanctified the act.

Chapter Nine

"You're not still upset about that drunken groper are you?" Bill nudged her gently with his elbow as, changing gear, he eased the Humber station wagon out of the dirt lane from the airstrip, on to the Driffield road. Ahead of them, there were occasional glimpses of the rear lights of Jim Wilson's utility, and the bus, slowly moving along the unlit rural road.

"No, he'll have a monumental hangover to-morrow, and be wondering why his testicles are bruised." She stifled a giggle as she recalled the man's tear filled, bulging eyes, and explosive gasp.

Bill gestured to the road ahead. The overcast sky had blacked out the moon and stars, and the masked headlamps barely illuminated the road for more than twenty yards ahead. Even the verges, on each side of the carriageway, were hardly discernible.

"Look at yon two." Slowing down, he nodded to a long, brick cowshed along the right side of the road. A special constable, notebook in hand, was officiously remonstrating with a soldier who was leaning on his bicycle. "Must be serious," he chortled. "He's having his name t'aen! Watch." Lowering his door window he called, "no lamp on his bike, constable?"

"Aye, sir. Second this week."

"Good Lord, what next? Crime wave in Burton Agnes! Keep it up, they'll mack thee a sergeant time the war is over!"

Emphasising his sarcasm with a two finger gesture, he drove on.

"What a bluudy paradox! Merest glimpse of a light from a window and you're a criminal, no lights on a bike ditto! Necessary of course, but yon constable's over zealous be half. Lurks behind t'cowshed most nights to catch some poor bluudy squaddie."

As he wound up his window he nodded towards the grounds of a mansion lying a little way from the road.

"Yon's Burton Agnes Hall. Dids't thee know it's haunted?" Again those forced Yorkshire idioms.

"So they say. Something to do with two sisters, donkey's years ago. Apparently another sister wanted to be buried in the grounds, but she was buried in the churchyard. But later, her sisters disinterred her and buried her skull in the walls of the Hall." She didn't want to talk about ghosts – she wanted to hear more about his life, especially now she new he was a widower. During the drive he'd mentioned that his wife and daughter, a nurse, had been killed in an air raid, and that his son was training as a pilot in Canada, "Bill, doesn't the M.M. mean you were once a private soldier or NCO?"

"Aye. Joined the Army in 1916. Falsified my age of course." He slewed his head briefly towards her, and she guessed rather than saw his puckish grin. "Just in time for t'fust battle of t'Somme..." Barbara's sharp intake of breath, and slight shudder, cut him short.

They were passing 'Betty's Cafe' where Badger had taken her for a meal on their first date. Egg and chips before going on to the cinema! The recollection reminded her of the letter from him this morning, still unopened on her mantlepiece. Why did it have a Liverpool post mark?

"...You all right luv?" Taking one hand off the wheel, Bill pulled her head against his shoulder.

"Yes. I'm all right, sorry Bill, its just that.." Leaving the sentence unfinished, and banishing the letter from her mind, she stroked the back of his hand against her cheek.

He pulled the Humber to a halt at the main gate, and the sentry, with a cursory glance through the windscreen, raised the barrier and waved them through.

"Shall I drop you at your quarters, or are game for us to park somewhere?"

"Well, I'm not really tired, and tomorrow is Sunday. But won't it be a bit risky?"

"No, we'll be perfectly safe at the spot I have in mind."

"Well... if you are sure. But you'll have drop me off to spend a penny first." They were passing between the parade ground and a barrack block, and Barbara shuddered.

"What's up? That's second time you've done that to-night."

"Nothing, Bill." So he *had* read something into her shiver as they'd passed 'Betty's Cafe', "Just a ghost walking over my grave. My..." about to say 'husband' she swallowed back the word. "Just that a squaddie I knew used to be in that block. He's overseas now."

"89 Block?" Bill gave her what instinct told her was a penetrating, enquiring glance. "Aye, a detachment of the King's were there before they took over the perimeter posts. Must 'ave been a close friend, to make thee shudder like that, or a bad experience."

"Something like that." Her intonation begged him not to spoil the rest of the evening by prying.

Chapter Ten

Rushing into her room, humming 'I'm in the mood for love', she kicked off her shoes, stripped off her stockings, suspenders and close fitting pants. Hastily rummaging in her locker, she pulled out her favourite French knickers. They were ivory satin, and fastened up both legs with tiny pearl buttons from hem to waist. As she hitched up her skirt, and pulled on the knickers, her eye caught Badger's letter on the mantlepiece.

Her humming changed to loud "Damn! Damn!" For a moment or two her promise to Badger harassed her tempting her to tell Bill she had changed her mind about going out again. Picking up the letter, she tapped a corner of the envelope against her teeth, puzzling about the Liverpool postmark. What difference did it make? If the letter hadn't been there, she'd not have changed her mind. Her intention had been as faithless as its consummation would be. Infatuation or not, going with Bill was the opportunity that might discreetly, thrillingly, prove the climax to the desire Badger had awakened in her, and had left her unfulfilled.

Shrugging off her vacillation, she dropped the unopened letter on her bed. She was in the mood for love, and wasn't going to spoil it by reading Badger's missive. Back to humming, she smoothed down her skirt, and made for the door hopping into her shoes she did so.

Almost through the door she abruptly doubled back, slipped off her discs and ring, dropped them in her locker, and fished a Gynomin pessary from her case under the bed.

Hurrying down the stairs, worrying about keeping Bill waiting, she reached the hall before remembering to use the lavatory. Dashing back up to the first floor w.c. she 'spent her penny' and inserted the pessary.

Resisting the urge to hurry, and striving to appear relaxed, she had difficulty concealing her surprise that Bill was holding the driver's door open for her.

"It's best if you drive," he said, handing her into the cab.

It was normal for a Group Captain, making official trips, to be driven by a Waaf, and she knew he meant it would look less suspicious.

With her nerves still tingling from her brazen preparations, and breathless from the scramble making them, she settled herself behind the wheel of the Humber.

Bill looked thoughtfully at her, his eyes on her gently heaving chest.

"You're not nervous of driving this are you?" Bill, climbing into the passenger seat offered her a cigarette.

"No thanks Bill. Not when I'm posing as your chauffeuse." Tut tutting saucily, she turned on the ignition. "No, I'm not a bit nervous about driving. I used to drive RAF ambulances. Where to?"

"Out of the Main Gate and turn left."

As she drove towards the Main Gate, he mentioned that whilst she was 'spending a penny', he had told the orderly officer, via the field telephone in her hallway, that he was going see what the new runway extension would look like at night.

"Don't want any trigger happy perimeter posts, mistaking us for saboteurs!'

Changing gear, her bare calf brushed the edge of her seat, and she guiltily wondered what Bill's reaction would be, if he'd known what she'd been doing whilst he was telephoning. 'A nymphomaniac? A tart?'

The sentry waved them out of the main gate and about a quarter mile along the road Bill told her to take a left turn into a dirt lane.

"Are you sure?" She knew that a little way along, the lane petered into a rustic footpath to the back of Driffield. "It's a dead end as far as vehicles are concerned."

"Just drive a little way along. I'll show you where to pull off."

Less than 100 yards into the lane he directed her through a gap in the hedge on the left of the lane, to park behind a dilapidated larch-lap fence. In the masked headlights, the condition of the ground was barely discernible but as the car crawled forward, she sensed the earth was getting softer,

"This is far enough!" He tapped her knee. "Don't go any further it's a bit swampy."

"You're a dirty old rascal Bill!" she chided as, for the first time, she noticed a grey blanket over the back of his seat. "How many women have you ha..." swiftly swallowing the word, she went on, "brought here?"

"You're first, and that's the truth. Came here when the engineers were surveying for the runway extension. Mind you, I'll not deny I marked it as a likely spot to bring a lass."

"I'll believe you – thousands wouldn't." Tittering, she playfully poked him in the ribs then, unbuttoning her tunic, she turned her back to him so he could help take it off.

Dropping the tunic behind the seat, he put his arm around her waist.

"You know my pet, we could sit here for hours, wasting time making small talk, angling for the right moment." He slid one hand under her skirt and stroked her bare thigh. "Let's not waste precious moments. We both know why we're here..."

"Why Bill! What wickedness is in your mind? As if I didn't know."

Defensively crossing her arms over her bust, she comically shrank against the door, "What makes you think you can have your wicked way with *this* poor maiden?"

"It'd be wicked to take any maiden, poor or not, against her will," he briefly chuckled. Then, with a seriousness that surprised her, went on, "I want to give not take, and that's too blessed natural for melodrama. Come on. This no time for modesty."

His fingers on her bare thigh were hinting at the significance of her stockingless legs, "Let's have no shyness. Don't be coy – you must *say it*."

"To make love?" Her femoral artery, under his fingers, throbbed as he traced the muscular furrow inside her thigh. Half heartedly she attempted to push his hand down.

Bill shook his head. "*To make love* is too prosaic for the beautiful thing we came here for." His hand, under hers, was now stroking the hollow of her trembling groin. "Try again."

Dry mouthed and seized by an unaccustomed girlishness, the words she knew he wanted her to say, stuck in her throat.

"To have me?" She temporized, but Bill shook his head.

"To take me?"

Again he shook his head. Through tremoring lips she tried again.

"To screw me? As our American cousins would say."

Again his head shook.

The Anglo-Saxon word froze on her tongue. "A bunk-up?"

"RAF slang. Too coarse for something so wonderful. I brought you here hoping you wanted what I wanted. Not to *take* thee, but to *give* each other some pleasure. Making love should be more giving than taking, that's what *fucking* should be."

The natural, prosaic way, he said it conferred a respectability of everyday usage, that would not have been out of place at a vicarage.

"Isn't what I said the same as..." The sensuous warmth of his hands under her arm pit and on her thigh, whetted the impatience of her loins. With tremulous lips she added, "...fucking?"

Saying it to a man for the first time in her life, gave the word a sophisticated, aphrodisiac piquancy. She pressed herself closer to him as his tunic buttons dug through her shirt and into her ribs.

"Not always, darling! That's why so many marriages fall apart in bitterness and frustration. Writers of tuppeny dreadfuls say 'he took her' or 'he had his way with her' or 'he ravished her'. That's one sided, taking pleasure, leaving t'other one feeling robbed." His lips brushed her ear lobe, and he went on. "You must *fuck* – not just *take* – to satisfy each other."

His words seemed a little too implausible, a little too glib, yet they stimulated her libido. This verbal foreplay was delectable. It fired her every cell with wantonness. Her every sinew was inflamed yet her limbs felt icy. Cold beads of sweat trickled from her armpits.

"You mean..." She moistened her lips with her tongue. "Really mean, if I only want a..." Hesitating, she drew his hand down from her groin to her knee and, incited by its lewdness, strove vainly to mouth the Anglo Saxon word, "...because I only want to *give* myself to you, we'll finish up dissatisfied, unfulfilled, so we should stop now?" She wished she could sound worldly, sophisticated, not damned ingenuous.

Bill nodded and, to her chagrin, pushed her from him. Surely he wasn't going spurn her now.

"But I do *want* you, to give..." As she leant to kiss him, he flipped the blanket into the back of the car, and switched on the interior light.

"Come on my lass, we'll be more comfortable in the back."

Humming again, she tip-toed round to the tail-board to keep her heels out of the swampy earth. Bill dropped the tail-board, and helped her into the back of the station wagon. Straightening out the blanket, it struck her that – dubious as it seemed – his verbal foreplay had been delightfully effective. Her loins were quivering for his touch. There was a fullness in her breasts. Her belly was taut, constricted. Her nipples were prickling. Her heart was racing. Pressure points in her ankles were throbbing.

Bill, crawling in after her, knelt astride her legs, his knees touching hers. Slowly, methodically, he unknotted her tie. With fumbling fingers, she undid his tunic belt and buttons. Laying the tie neatly over the seat, he reached for the light switch.

"Lets keep it on please, darling," she whispered, and pulling his lapels she drew his lips to hers for a brief kiss.

"Oh! Want to see what you're going to get, eh?" Smiling, he shrugged off his tunic. His haunches pressed on her calves. Her legs were trembling as his warm genitals stiffened against her knees.

"No! I want you to see what I've got!" Could that husky, brazen voice be hers? She was in an tartish haste to show off her body.

Bill was casually unbuttoning her collar and shirt front. Her fingers seemed to be childish thumbs, fumbling to open her cuff buttons.

When he bent to unfasten her skirt waist-band, she caressed his shoulders and strained to smother the nape of his neck with kisses. Unhurriedly and with practised ease he unclipped the fastener and eased the band down her hips.

"No Bill!" Her every fibre was pulsating with the most powerful urge she'd ever known. Aflame with impatient, bridled lust she wanted to yell that the skirt was no hindrance. She wanted no fumbling, no dallying. No inelegant tugging of the skirt past her rump. But he didn't attempt to tug the skirt down. Instead, he gently pulled her shirt free from the skirt waist-band.

Slowly – maddeningly slowly – he opened her shirt, from neck to waist. His hands slipped under the shirt, baring her shoulders. His warm palms tenderly, deliciously, slid down her naked arms, tumbling the sleeves from her wrists.

For a few moments he wrapped his arms around her shoulders. Her trembling fingers, locked behind his neck, crushed their lips together. His tongue skimmed the sensitive inner flesh of her lips. Their teeth scraped. Wildly, ravenously, their darting tongues teased each other. The rasp of his, on her soft palate, sent a tingle down her spine, and a searing spasm to her very core.

Bill's hands, firmly, almost brutally, tracked down her back. His fingers seemed be stripping every vertebral nerve to raw ultra-sensitivity. When he reached into the fissure of her buttocks, she nibbled her lips to restrain a shudder, a whimper of impatience. Then, hastily breaking the embrace, and sitting back on his heels, his moist palms slipped under the waist of her knickers.

"Bill. Oh Bill!" His fingers, caressing the tremulous concavity of her navel, were so near, and yet a continent away from her pulsating core. Desperately pushing up her pelvis, she vainly tried to lure his hand into her throbbing crotch, "Come on! Stop torturing me!" But it was a rapturous torture and, dropping her hands from his neck, she reached for his flies.

"Soon, my love, soon." Squatting back, he brushed aside her hands, and unfastened her brassiere. The full, freed breasts drooped only slightly. Her nipples, delicately pink, were proudly erect in the duskier pigment of their exquisitely pimpled areola.

"Christ! They are beautiful! Perfect!"

Her shoulders quivered as he slipped off bra straps, and cupped a pulsing breast in each hand.

"Perfect!" Back on his heels, his hands crept down her torso. Tantalisingly smooth as satin, yet firm as a sculptor molding clay, his fingers inched down her gently heaving rib cage, until his thumbs pressed her navel. With her narrow waist almost completely spanned by his hands, he held her at arm's length, his lips pursing with admiration.

"A Titian Aphrodite!" His erection was an iron brand against her knees. His warm, swollen scrotum was pressed into her bare shins.

The relish, the gloating, in his golden eyes, intensified the thrill of his touch. Putting her hands on her head, she watched his eyes devour every inch of her nakedness. Sitting there, her breasts uplifted, her stomach tautened by the pose, she wished he was seeing her completely naked on black satin sheets.

"You're Helen, Venus, Pandora all in one."

Murmuring huskily into her soft flesh, his head slipped down from her neck to her breast. Shivering as he kissed each tingling nipple, the pressure of his lips shot convulsions through her loins.

"You're shivering. Want my coat around your shoulders?"

He had her breasts in his hands again.

"No! We're both shivering, and you know its not with cold."

Her nipples were hardening between his thumbs and forefinger. The tips of his other fingers were teasing the pimpled areola. Down-casting her eyes, she watched the pink teats respond to his touch. Erect, hard and smooth as sea washed pebbles, they spurred a primitive, maternal, desire.

With her left hand on his neck, she drew his head down, and clamped it to her right breast. Wincing with joy as he suckled the nipple, she steered his left hand towards the buttons of knickers. But his fingers went into her damp crotch. Instantly her buttocks tensed. Her thighs parted. Opening herself, giving herself to his exploring, lubricating fingers, her nails dug into his shoulder blades.

Then he was tenderly lifting her, and she clung to him as he slewed her diagonally on to the floor.

His mouth slipped to kiss her navel, her thighs, her shins. She kicked off her shoes, and he kissed each ankle. Then his thighs were between her bent knees. Her hands locked behind his neck. His shoulders, wet from her perspiring armpits, chilled her flesh. She gave a short sharp cry as his rock hard dome, slowly, devilishly slowly, pushed just inside the tight, moist entrance of her throbbing vagina. For a purgatory of moments, he held the head of his engorged penis motionless.

"For God's sake, Bill!" Almost panicking that he was going to frustrate her with a premature ejaculation, she screamed, "Jesus! Don't leave me now!"

Gradually, tormentingly pausing between each jab, he inched further inside her, until she felt he would rupture her hot, foaming membranes. Then, kneading her breasts in rhythm with his hips, he taunted her with slow, deep thrusts and retractions. With darting tongue he teased her ear from tip to lobe.

Baited to the threshold of dementia, her upthrusting buttocks drove her shoulders and soles of her feet hard into the floor. With frantically summoned strength she contracted her abdominal muscles, jolting their pelvic bones together. The entire vitality of her being seemed to be convulsing in her womb. Biting into his collar-bone, she forced a vaginal contraction, and fleetingly gripped his erection like a vice.

"Bitch! Bitch!" It was a curse of marvel. A voracious gasp for more. Then he was serving her with swift, powerful strokes that gave her no respite for muscular concentration.

"Come on, darling! Harder!" Her knuckles beat his shoulder blades. She wanted to scream obscenities, but could only gasp, "Give you lovely bastard, give!"

His hands went under her raised buttocks. Ravenous for the utmost penetration of his every stroke, she savagely hooked her ankles around his calfs. With every atom of energy, she desperately crushed her crotch against his. Their loins buffeted in a paroxysm of bruising, ecstatic lunging. Frantic to give him the impossible fusion of their bodies, boosting his strength with hers, she forced him deeper inside her with every thrust. Perspiration was beginning to stream down from her labouring belly to her buttocks.

"More, darling, more!" Shrieking, she plucked at her own

nipples. "Don't stop yet!"

His nails gouged into the flesh of her buttocks. Deliriously she pulled his head to hers. Simultaneously, they spent themselves in frenzied, gasping kisses, thrashing loins and incoherent mutterings. Breathless, clamping his panting body to hers, instinctively she willed her climaxing cervix to briefly grip his faltering erection.

"Beautiful bitch!" His spine arched, his thumbs dug into the small of her back. "Again!"

"Lie still! You'll slip out." Entranced by her newly discovered ability, she greedily, repeatedly, clenched and relaxed the muscles of her womb, milking him of every dreg of fluid, until he shrank lifelessly from her.

Delightedly satiated, her head rocking gently on his heaving chest, she purred like a cat that had stolen the cream. Ephemeral recollections of her marriage vows, flitting through her adulterous bliss, stirred no remorse or guilt. An adulteress? No, she felt like a worldly-wise victorious courtesan. The lingering elation of her first true orgasm, was too exquisite to be even faintly smudged by repentance. Deep down she knew that, after tonight's ecstasy, any penitence would be brief and false. All week she'd wondered how long she could live with the disillusion of her bridal bed. Now it was how soon she'd have another opportunity like to-night.

If only she'd met Bill before she married Badger. Nuzzling her cheek against his neck, dreamily fantasising about a future as Bill's mistress, she sighed as the mingling vapours of their sweat began to chill her spine.

"Penny for 'em." Bill squeezed the side of her right breast, eased her upright, and reached to pick up her bra.

"What I'm thinking is priceless, but it won't cost you a penny." Waving away the bra, she slipped on her shirt.

"Don't say you're not satisfied!"

"No, darling. It was beautiful. You were beautifully satisfying. More beautiful than..." Pondering her next words, she reached for her tie as an excuse for pausing. Bill obviously knew she was no virgin, but if she let on that she was married, and a newly wed at that, it would lead to more embarrassing revelations. On the other hand, if he believed she was single, he might think she was every officers' floozy. As she knotted her tie, she decided to risk the floozy image. "...More beautiful than anyone I've ever known. Money couldn't buy that, and I was thinking I wanted to give it to you again soon."

He put her tunic around her shoulders and taking her face between his hand, he kissed her forehead.

"I hope that doesn't make you think I've known many men."

"Don't worry about that, darling." Kissing each of her eye-lids, he took her hands gently in his, "I could tell that from the start." Then settling himself alongside her, their backs resting against the rear of the front seat, Bill lit two cigarettes and handed her one. "My guess is I'm the first since you lost your virginity."

"Was it that obvious?" Her hair brushed his cheek as she puffed at the cigarette. "Wasn't I all right?"

"You were fantastic. It was your impatience that gave the game away. Great as it was, it was only the frontiers of paradise. Next time, in the proper surroundings, we'll push each other beyond them."

"Oh Bill! Make it soon."

The thought that they could surpass to-night's ecstasy, seemed incredible, and the promise of a 'next time', sent her ego and dreams soaring. This adorable man, wanted her for more than just a one time fling. She would become his mistress. Love or lust, all she wanted at this moment, was the exclusive possession of this man's ardour.

"You were right, my darling Bill. About giving, I mean."

"Yes, it does seem to work, love."

The scepticism in his tone, jarred a nerve and jerking herself bolt upright, she flashed him a reproachful frown.

"Do you mean all that talk about giving was flannel?" Tears of wrath misted her vision, "That you were just shooting me a line?"

"Yes, if you like, you sensitive, naive little poppet."

Taking her face tenderly in his hands, he gave her an indulgent, paternal smile, "You women are a little gullible, when you want seducing."

Flabbergasted – lost for words – Barbara indignantly brushed aside his hands. Swift as the speed of light, she felt she'd plummeted from from an exultant paramour to a cheap harlot. All the joy of the evening, the erotic anticipation of becoming his mistress, was turning to humiliation and anguish, plaguing the pit of her stomach with leaden nausea. Hurling her cigarette out of the car, she aimed a slap at his face, but he grabbed her wrist, and arrested it in mid-air.

"Hold on, love!" Throwing out his own cigarette, he seized her other wrist and, forcing her hands down, held them firm on her lap, "No need to get steamed up. Shooting a line as you call it didn't stop us enjoying each other." Releasing her hands, he gently took hold of her shoulders and, as she dabbed her eyes, went on, "Darling, think for a moment. I've wanted you desperately since I saw you at Christmas. I couldn't wait a moment longer tonight so, instead of beating about the bush, I plunged straight in. Your bare legs were a 'come on' but..."

Pushing his hands from her shoulders, and pulling on her tunic, she tartly interrupted, "Jesus Christ! Why shoot me a line then?"

She wanted to believe him. Wanted to recapture the enchantment of his seduction. He sounded so earnest and sincere, but how many times to-night, had her gullibility tranquillised her suspicions?

"Cool down! Let me finish love, please, before you say any more." His hands were back on her shoulders, and he kissed the crown of her head as she sulkily bowed it to do up her buttons.

"I couldn't then just say 'let's get down to it' – could I now?"

"Suppose not," she said huffily, and fixed her eyes belligerently on his. Her anger had almost ebbed away, but her mind was still too ruffled to give him any hint of forgiveness.

"Look at me, darling. I've got a confession to make." Lifting her chin up so their eyes met, he gave her a crooked, entreating smile.

"I was having a quick noggin with the M.O. in the mess to-night, and I casually asked about you, and he said you'd gone to Carnaby. I was due at a 'dining out' at Leconfield mess, but I sent an excuse, and followed thee. Now, doesn't that show you how much I think of you?"

The earnestness of his confession dispelled her last vestiges of anger and dejection. Brimming with elation, she kissed his cheeks and, simultaneously, their arms were around each other in a warm, reconciling hug.

§

In the doorway of her quarters he kissed the backs of her hands, and then gently embraced her.

"Believe me, the hours will seem like years until I come back. Apart from making my number with the Yanks, there's a whisper that the RAF are planning something big towards the end of May, and I want to be in on it..."

"A big raid?" Surely, as a Group Captain, he wasn't being sent on a bombing mission.

"Shush!" He put a forefinger across her lips. "Mum's the word. I've probably said too much already, and don't know much more than I've told thee. Anyroad I'll be back in about six weeks, then we can go away together for a few days, if you agree."

"Oh, yes Bill!" Her green eyes sparkling with delight, she gave him a swift hug. "I'd like that."

"Good, but before that you'll get an invitation, as my guest, for the Officers' Mess Summer Dance on the first Saturday in June. It used to be called the Summer Ball. War-time austerity's downgraded it. Not many war-time officers have mess dress. Mind you it's still pretty formal. The ladies think long dresses definitely *di rigueer*. Is that all right?"

"Of course, darling." The ghost of a frown wrinkled her brow. What she could wear?

"Have you got something elegant and strapless?" With a roguish smile he playfully pushed her bosom up. "I want 'em all to envy me. If you want to buy a special dress, I can let you have some clothing coupons."

"No, that's all right, Bill." She'd remembered her long strapless, black taffeta dress, with a front split to the knee. She'd only worn it once, for her 21st. party. It was still in her mother's wardrobe, but there would be plenty of time to pop home for it before the dance, "I've got just the thing," with a saucy grin she said, "and it needs more than just pride to keep it up."

Giving her a fierce hug and a lingering goodnight kiss he hurried towards the Humber then, darting back, he handed her his gold braided cap.

"I'll keep your bra, you keep my hat, until next time. Now you know I'm earnest about you."

Starting up the Humber he, called to her in a voice just loud enough to to be audible above the engine purr.

"Wish I could take you along, my darling." He picked up her bra from the back of the seat, and crushed it to his mouth before stuffing it into his breast pocket. "Got to take a staff officer with me. It's his dining out I was supposed to be at to-night. An arrogant sod, and a womaniser to boot, but the best damned navigator the allies have got..." Blowing each other kisses, as the Humber moved away, his barely audible words froze Barbara's hand to her lips, "...you'll be seeing him here soon. Australian, name of Brodie."

§

In just a pyjama top, Barbara, sitting on her bed, chin on bent knees, arms clasped around her shins, drowsily mused about last night's rapture, and where and what her intrigue with Bill might lead to.

After he'd driven away last night, she had lain awake until daybreak, alternately savouring the lingering ecstasy, and fretting whether he would speak to Brodie about her. If he did, would he be discreet, or brag and tell all. He didn't seem the kiss and tell type. But she was still unsure of his character, hadn't completely swallowed a lot of what he'd told her. It would be hard enough facing Brodie again, without the suspicion that Bill might have implied she was an 'easy lay'.

Promising herself an early night, she'd bathed and yawned through the ritual of listening to the BBC's nine o'clock news on her old, crackling wireless. The news was as depressing as ever. The propaganda euphemisms of 'strategic withdrawals to prepared defence lines' no longer fooled anyone. General Alexander's forces in Burma were in headlong retreat. Rangoon had long since fallen. The seemingly invincible Japanese were thrusting northward, through the Burmese mountains and jungles, towards India's frontiers. In the Middle East, Rommel's Afrika Korps were dominating General Auchinleck's 8th Army. Hitler's Panzers were overrunning Russia. The only shred of optimism was the hint that Atlantic shipping losses were declining.

The fire had died to a smouldering ember and, though the night was already chilling her bare legs, she was too pre-occupied by sleepy reveries to slip under the blankets.

Bill's cap was resting in the crook of her thighs and waist. All through last night, she'd hugged it to her chest and probably would do the same to-night.

Badger, with boyish idealism, gushing with regimental pride, had once given her a brooch replica of his cap badge. It must have cost him nearly a month's pay. 'Where it with pride, my darling,' he had told her. 'Not only for me, but also in memory of all the men, down the centuries who have won the Battle Honours on the Regimental Colours.' She'd worn it only the day he gave it to her, and had forgotten where she put it. Maybe it had been stolen. Whenever Badger asked why she wasn't wearing it, she'd made up some excuse, 'not allowed to wear it on her uniform,' or 'don't need a reminder of you when we are together.'

Although compared to Bill's cap, the brooch for Badger's pocket, was probably the equivalent of the 'widow's mite', she'd never really prized it. In fact, on the rare occasions it came into her mind, she'd resented the implication behind the white metal and enamel brooch. It proclaimed she was someone's possession – it branded her as Badger's chattel.

Bill's cap didn't debase her individuality, didn't mark her as some man's possession. It was an impetuous, romantic, earnest symbol of his intention. The faint essence of his hair cream, tinged with male muskness from the cap band, added substance to her flights of fancy. Pressing the cap to her breast, she thought of it as a knightly favour, the gage of a modern warrior lover. Lover. The word lingered deliciously in her mind. That's what they were going to be, lovers. Despite her doubts about him, after only one short night she felt a deeper affinity, a more intimate communion, with Bill than after a year with Badger. Where would it all end? She brushed aside the instinct that hinted someone's fingers might get burned.

Damn! She ignored the rat-a-tat on her door. Who the hell was that? Probably the scatter-brain girl downstairs, wanting to cadge a brew of tea.

Holding her breath, and cocking an ear to the door, she silently cursed the caller. Musing about the future with Bill was too enthralling to be aroused to full wakefulness, and side-tracked, by some prattling girl. She wanted to be left alone, to resolve her doubts, and then drift into sleep building on her fantasies.

There wasn't another knock, but with dismay she watched the door knob being turned.

"Oh, all right, damn you, come in!" Why didn't they put locks on the doors!

Her scowl became a welcoming grin as Mary, waving half a bottle of gin and two bottles of tonic, pirouetted into the room.

"That's a foine way to greet a friend bearing gifts, so it is!"

"Mary, sorry, I thought you were someone else. Glasses are in the locker."

"Were you asleep? At this time of night?"

"No, just about to nod off. Anyway, what brings you around, at this time of night? And don't try and tell me its just to share a drink."

Mary giggled, and returned a wide-eyed, tongue in cheek look of innocence, as Barbara wagged an admonishing finger at her.

"Ah! Sure Oi could tell you Oi came to invite you to a dance at Beverley," She gave a wry smile as she handed a glass to Barbara, "but Oi wouldn't kid you with that excuse. You know damn well Oi'm dying to hear phwat happened last night..."

"I thought so, you old nosey parker."

"Seeing that." Mary nodded at Bill's cap. It slid to the floor when Barbara swung her legs down from the bed, "And this, still unopened." She picked up Badger's letter from the mantle-piece, and tapped it rebukingly on her friend's head, "And that enchanted look on your face, it doesn't take a genius to guess you've done nothing but dream about it all day. It must have been good."

"It was. Stoke up the fire, and I'll tell all."

Barbara pulled on her dressing gown and, with Mary sitting in the only arm chair, she sat on the floor with her back resting against the Irish girl's legs.

§

"That's the last of the tonic." Replenishing their drinks for the umpteenth time, Barbara settled herself on the floor, cross legged, facing her engrossed listener.

Her eyes, that were passive with sleepy introspection when Mary arrived, were now sparkling, and her cheeks were glowing. Confiding everything Bill and she had said to each other, and almost all they'd done together, sharpened the focus of her earlier musings, whetted her anticipation of Bill's promise of a few days away together. Being his mistress, she silently mused, could be her stepping stone to high society. But she'd be mistress to no man. When, and if, she took up with any man, she'd be mistress of and over him.

Taking Mary's hands in hers, her eyes begged for the Irish girl's empathy, "There were moments when I thought I hated him. I told you, I could have clouted him, almost did once. Didn't want him to touch me. The next moment I'd be throwing myself at him, terrified he'd snub me."

"So, phwat's the problem?"

Struck by a sudden thought, Mary flashed a penetrating glance at Barbara, "Is it the thought of adultery? Can't pacify your conscience?.."

"Gosh no! That doesn't perturb me..." A flicker of loyalty to Badger, prompted her to soften the denial by adding "...well, I suppose it does a bit, but not enough to drop Bill."

Gripping Mary's hands, she pulled herself to her feet, ruefully shook her head, picked up Bill's cap, and sat on her bed with it in her lap.

"I suppose, in a way, it is Badger that's making me uneasy about Bill. Oh, not the infidelity." She plucked nervously at loose strands of the gold wire round the cap peak, "Marrying him showed me how weak willed I really am. I was too spineless to break it off with a boy like him, before it was too late, and Bill's far more worldly and forceful. It could turn out to be a Jekyll and Hyde existence, me balancing on a love-hate knife edge that I hadn't the will to break from."

"O.K., it may turn out badly, but not you're not marrying him. You can walk out anytime it gets rough, so you can. Jaysus, Oi'm not trying to persuade you to do it." Getting up from the chair, she stretched and leaning with an elbow on the mantlepiece, an exasperated edge in her voice, she continued, "You don't need any persuading one way or another. You've already made up your mind to do it. So stop faffing around for some justification, or encouragement. Forget his flaws, have your fling with him."

"Yes, if it was love, I suppose I'd be blind to his flaws."

"Then you would be shackled to him, for good or ill!"

"All right love, let me make one more point, then we'll have an Ovaltine, and change the subject, before you blow your top."

Putting Bill's cap on her head at a rakish angle, she put the kettle on the fire, " I'm randy for him. Oh, Mary, I do wish I was sure it was love that made me hanker for him, and not prostituting myself for pure vanity. Ouch!"

Mary, impatiently drumming her fingers on the mantelpiece, aimed a playful kick at Barbara's bottom as she stooped over the fire.

"You know what I mean... the kudos of being a VIP's woman... moving in high society and all that."

"For heaven's sake, Barbara, stop making a rags-to-riches Hollywood spectacular of it. Accept things for what they are. You're now a hot-arsed bitch, he's an available cock – to mix metaphors – and you're playing while the cat's away. Now Oi've got to dash. Anti-dim will be reporting the Utility stolen. He doesn't know Oi sneaked out with it."

As she made for the door, Mary tossed Badger's letter on to the bed, "Get reading it!"

"As soon as as you've gone, I promise."

§

It was a glorious, golden hazy morning. One of those rare April days, when only a feeble breeze stirs the trees, and the dew on the grass twinkles like thousands of heliographs. One of those days that deceives the English with its false promise of a sultry, halcyon summer. The sort of day that, to expatriates in the nostalgic delusions of their sun-downers in the sweltering outposts of empire, were typical of an English spring.

Strolling back from breakfast in the Mess, Barbara had watched thrushes tugging earthworms from the grass verges. Between the croaking of crows, and the joyful song of a hovering skylark she was sure she'd heard a cuckoo.

Looking through her window, she paused in the act of opening Badger's letter. Richtofen, one of the squadron's cats, was rolling in the overspill of dust from a coal bunker. The wily, black and white Tom was camouflaging himself, preparing to stalk hedge sparrows, scavenging the flower beds for worms.

After Mary left last night, she was still too horny for Bill to be bothered with reminders of Badger. Now she wished she'd read the letter yesterday. She wasn't due on duty for a couple of hours and wanted to cycle into Driffield for a new Kestos. Until Bill returned with the other, she only had one spare one. The service issue bra's were ill-fitting, matronly armour. She'd have to answer the letter straight away, or she'd never get round to it. Then, damn him, there'd not be time for shopping, and they'd be closed before she came off duty. With a resigned sigh, she sat down to read the letter.

She could not repress a derisive smirk when she read his address, ' Somewhere in England'. How dramatically regimental, when the postmark proclaimed he was in Liverpool. Maybe there would be time for shopping after all. She certainly couldn't reply to an address like that.

> *My dearest Angel,*
> *Officially we are not allowed to send any letters until we reach our destination, wherever that is. However, a docker who happens to be a friend of a friend of Tiger Lyons has promised to post this for me. You remember Tiger, my darling, he's my slightly chubby mucker on the group photo, when we were at the Guards' depot last year. You noticed he*

had a chip out of one of his front teeth.
Oh, darling, this will be the last uncensored letter I will be able to send to you. From now on, all our intimacies will have to be shared with the censoring officer, and I have so little time – the docker knocks off in half an hour – to try to tell you how much I love and miss you.
Darling you are so good for me. Never in my wildest dreams did I envisage having a wife as beautiful and thoughtful as you. Just thinking of you fills me with a warm glow in my —you know what — that cheats the distance between us.
Did you have a pleasant journey to Driffield? What a stupid question. You must have felt as bitterly lonely as I did. We had a miserable journey to the port of embarkation, slow, boring and cold. [Why didn't he say 'Liverpool'].
The train spent at least 4 hours in some rural siding. All 800 of us were de-trained, and had to doss down on a frosty station platform. But I bet not even the officers, cramped round the coke stove in the waiting room, were as warm as I was thinking of your shiny chestnut hair [Wish he wouldn't call it 'chestnut'. I've told him a dozen times – I'm not a horse.] *spreading over the pillows, and your firm beautiful body, squeezed against mine in that creaking single bed. It was a wonderful honeymoon, even though it was only 24 hours – wasn't it my dearest wife.*[Heavens, it sounds as if he's got other wives and I'm the dearest of them.] *I can picture you now. Standing in front of me, your delightful bosom* [He's still too callow to call them breasts.] *swelling above your brassiere. I have that so etched in my mind I'll never need a photo to remind me of you. After the war we'll have a second, real, honeymoon in Westerham.*
I am writing this on a crowded open deck. This is a Union Castle ship – dare not tell you its name – it must have been wonderful to sail in before the war. I started to write this in an elegant, beautifully furnished writing room, but I was thrown out of there – politely of course – because it's reserved for Q.A. nurses and officers.
You would laugh. When they gave us our boarding cards, Tiger's had the odd number next to my even number. Good Oh! We thought we'd be in a cabin together. The joke was on us. We are berthed in what looks like the Grand

Ballroom. Its filled from floor to ceiling with hundreds of bunks, with only about 2ft. between each tier. Mine's the third one up, and Tiger's above me. As well as sleeping in them we have to stow our kitbags, and all our equipment, except our tropical kit, which they've put in a store some where.

I don't know when you will hear from me again, but I promise I will write a few lines every day and send you a mammoth letter when we get wherever we are going. Naturally they won't tell us but all the cargo they are loading has Indian addresses, so my guess is we are heading for the 1st. Battalion in India.

Write to me often, my love, to the RNHFK Army Post Office number I gave you. They have told us that mail will be sent by air, and be waiting for us when we reach our destination.

Take good care of yourself, my darling wife. Chin up and keep those lovely eyes smiling.

Au revoir, Ma Chère,
Your ever faithful husband,
Badger.

'Ever faithful' she thought cynically. He'd no opportunity to be anything else.

Well, that was that. She could get over to Driffield now. Plenty of time later to dash off a reply. How long would it take them to sail to India? Three weeks? More like six. They'd have to zig zag down the Alantic to evade 'U' boats. Couldn't go through the Mediterranean and via the Suez Canal. They'd have to go the long way, around South Africa. Air mail shouldn't take more than a week. Promising herself she'd write to him within a fortnight, she folded up the letter and saw there was a 'P.S.' on the back of the last page.

P.S. Darling if my future letters seem a little cool and impersonal, please remember its because I have to have them censored. [Foolish boy, there's no military embargo on the words of love and endearment wives and kinfolk

want to hear, even if it was misplaced, withering love.]
Dearest Barbara, remember I do not expect you to cut yourself off from male companions all the time I am away. Have as happy a time as you can, go to your usual dances and so on. I know and trust you so much I know you will always be faithful and never misbehave.

Through misty eyes she watched a tear blotch the ink. "Dear Lord," she sobbed, "I wish my tears could be because I sincerely long for him, and not because the letter rouses only pity for him." She'd been bitchy, sarcastic, when reading the poor deluded lad's adoring words. She was truly sorry for that, but her consuming remorse was that she could muster no guilt, let alone penitence, for her adultery with Bill.

Chapter Eleven

Head down against the drizzle, holding her greatcoat, cape like, over her head and shoulders, Barbara half ran into the Officers' Mess. The dozen or so couples in the lobby, were piling coats and umbrellas on the arms of stewards. Bill was nowhere in sight, but as she shook the rain from her greatcoat, Brodie made straight for her.

"There you are, I promised Yorkie I'd look after you." His courtly, solicitous tone, surprised her, "You look especially chic and glamorous to-night." His eyes, sweeping over the black shoulder-less gown, lingered admiringly on her cleavage, "Here let me get rid of your coat."

As he turned to hand the coat to a Mess steward, disappointment that Bill was not there to welcome her, suddenly became an ominous premonition, parching her throat, "Thank you. Where is he?"

"Let's go in here." Handing her a schooner of sherry, and tenderly holding her elbow, he squired her to a sofa in a deserted ante-room, and sat beside her.

"I was hoping to get over to your quarters to see you before you came, but I only got back here twenty minutes ago. Cigarette?" Without waiting for an answer he put two in his mouth, lit them, and handed one to her, "Bad news I'm afraid. You knew Bill was going on this 1000 bomber raid last Saturday?"

"Oh God! Not Bill!" Stumbling to her feet, sherry spilling over her trembling hands, she ran to the window. She didn't want to hear what instinct – and his funereal tone – told her he was going to say. With a fist to her mouth, biting her knuckles, she leant against the window frame.

The blackout curtains had not been closed, and the ante-room lights against gloomy background of early twilight, reflected Brodie's image in the rain spattered window as he came behind her.

"Why, Leslie? Why?" Damn! She could have bit her tongue. Ever since Bill had said he was taking Brodie with him, she'd been steeling herself to be coolly formal with him if ever they met, and here she was using his Christian name, "He was too old for ops. He'd done more than his bit."

"Whoa! Steady on. He was only a few years older than me," his hands were warm and avuncular on her bare shoulders, "anyway he wasn't supposed to be on the op. He made some excuse to leave me up-dating my control tower gen. Didn't realise he'd gone, until I heard him radio that he was ditching on the home run. He ordered the crew to bale out, stayed with the plane until they were all clear of it.

He took the quivering sherry glass from her, and placed it on the window ledge.

"Yorkie had this recurrent dream, a nightmare. Told me about it, whenever he was in his cups. He saw himself ditching in a flaming Spitfire, clothes alight and screaming..."

"But Bill is – was – a bomber pilot." For a heart beat, she thought she might be jumping to the wrong conclusion. Her mother had always insisted dreams go by opposites. Brodie hadn't actually said Bill was dead, only that he'd ditched. He might be alive, just wounded or missing. But intuition, and the compassion in his deep set grey eyes, told her this was wishful thinking.

"...That's just it. When they were burying him, in this nightmare, Bill himself was standing over the grave, crying over the grotesque remains of his son. Makes me wonder if he had a death wish by going on that raid. You know he lost his wife and daughter... thought he'd keep some heavenly audit balanced by sacrificing himself to preserve his son – if you follow me."

"Oh my God!" Unable to constrain her sobs, clutching blindly at his lapels, she pressed her forehead into the hollow of his shoulder. For the moment he was no longer Brodie, the arrogant lecher, but just a sympathetic, commiserating shoulder to cry on.

Moments later, as she brought her sobs under control, she realised he had his arms firmly around her, and was tenderly brushing his cheeks over her hair.

"Sorry about that, it's not just Bill."

Once again her conscience pricked her. She forced herself to mentally confess she was grieving as much for her own shattered ambition, as for Bill's death.

"Bill didn't know you were married did he?"

Astonished by the question, she glared angrily at him as he sat beside her.

"None of your business! How do you know I'm married?"

"Well, apart from you telling me at Maxi's, I made it my business to check your file." His arm around her shoulders gave her a conciliatory squeeze, "I'm not criticising you. I'm just confirming my judgement of Bill. He was a fair dinkum bloke for a Pommy. It wasn't in his nature to take advantage of a lonely soldier's wife. Now me, I'm different. As you've obviously guessed, given half a chance I'll shack up with any sheila, married or single." He peered brazenly down her cleavage, "Especially when they've got what you've got to offer."

Her eyes blazed disdainfully, as Barbara jumped to her feet. There was a discreet cough as, behind them, in the half-opened doorway a waiter, sherry decanter in hand, deferentially motioned to their glasses still on the window ledge.

"Come on, sit down." Gently taking her wrist, Leslie pulled her back on to the sofa. Imperiously dismissing the waiter with, "Chalky, not now, and knock in future!" He waited until the door clicked shut before he spoke again.

"I may be an arrogant bastard, but beaut that you are, I'm not so bloody insensitive as to make a pass at you to-night."

The ring of sincerity in his deep voice subdued her antagonism, but she sat out of his arm's reach, waiting for him to continue.

"Let me finish about Yorkie, and then you can decide whether to go or stay." Bringing their drinks from the window, he perched himself on the sofa arm, "The crew were picked up, within an hour by an RAF launch. They're all recovering well. He was picked up by trawler nearly twelve hours later. Any other bloke would've been dead. Legs full of shrapnel. He held out until this morning. I spent most of the last five days with him. Most of the time he didn't know I was there. Mumbled about you quite a bit. Was fairly lucid for his last hour."

"Oh?"

"Don't look so worried." His strong, even teeth, seemed bleached white against his tanned cheeks, as he smiled down at her. "He didn't blubber anything that would've shocked your ma."

"We did nothing together that would have." Her green eyes narrowed to challenging slits, but she felt the lie bring a flush to her cheeks, "No matter what you think."

"Whatever I think doesn't matter. Yorkie obviously found you fascinating. Now, I don't suppose you feel like staying here and dancing, do you?"

Smiling wanly, she shook her head.

"Then let me take you for supper to Driffied's Savoy."

Barbara shook her head again and her brow furrowed, "Where..?"

"I mean The Bell Hotel. Promise we'll have a quiet, no-strings meal, mourn over Yorkie together, and I'll drop you at your door afterwards, with no more than a brotherly peck on the cheek."

"Thank you, I'd rather not." Despite her antipathy towards him, there was a diffidence in her voice that encouraged persuasion.

"Come on, if you go back to your quarters you'll only sit and mope all night. I wouldn't enjoy dancing tonight, and I did promise Bill I'd look after you." With his hand under her chin, he gently raised her head, and there was an amiable appeal in his eyes, "I promise you just a chaste tête-à-tête. After to-night, I'll be all out to bed you."

"What makes you think there'll be a next time?" The blandness of her response betrayed the equivocation of her resistance, "Anyway I couldn't go The Bell dressed like this."

"That settles it. I'll run you over to change into something suitable." Draining his sherry, he took her hand, "Right, off we go then."

§

"That was good, as usual. Now, landlord we'll have two tots of my special. Tea for me. Coffee, for my sergeant friend here."

The landlord, a plump jolly Yorkshire man, winked broadly at Brodie, as the waitress cleared the plates from the table.

The meal had been wholesome country fare. A saucer sized Yorkshire pudding starter, a top and bottom and 'nowt' between, swimming in rich gravy. Then rare roast beef, crisp roast potatoes, carrots and cauliflower, followed by rhubarb and apple pie, and custard.

Throughout the evening, both of them had studiously avoided mentioning Bill. Despite herself, from the moment they left the Mess, she'd succumbed to calling Brodie by his first name, as he had waxed lyrical about the Aussie outback. As a Government surveyor, he'd spent most of his adult life in 'the bluey'. He'd listened politely to her family background and probed her cautiously – but vainly – about her husband.

When the landlord returned with two wine goblets of amber liquid, he again winked broadly at them.

"What's this..?" She took an exploratory sip of the liquid, "How did you know he had this..." Dubious of her palate, she took another sip. "Cognac! Remy?"

"Too right! Pilot mate of mine brought me a couple of bottles from Lisbon." Leslie chinked his glass against hers, "Sold one bottle to the landlord. He keeps the other for me. Puts it in wine glasses, instead of brandy bowls, to fool envious eyes."

"Leslie, your wife's a Wren isn't she?"

"Wren?" He looked perplexed for an instant as he warmed the cognac in cupped hands, "Ah! You saw me with the snotty Lady Joyce. She's just a good..." he winked impudently "very close friend."

"But you are married?"

"In name only. Both decided to go our own way. She's not a Wren, but a fair dinkum FANY, shacked up with some..."

"There's no need to be crude about her!" Looking him straight in the eyes, she felt her cheeks colouring.

"Spare your blushes. Evil be to him... honi soi qui mal y pense." Grinning broadly, he wagged a finger under her nose, "I was speaking in capitals. FANY – First Aid Nursing Yeomanry, not *fanny,* as pertaining to that delectable part of female anatomy. Although *that* too would apply to her. Anyway, as I was saying, she's shacked up with some bloke in London."

Then as if pronouncing that matter finally closed, he remained silent until they were in his car.

"In his last moments Bill made me promise to take you down to his cottage, and let you choose any keepsake you liked."

Neither of them spoke for the rest of the journey back to her quarters. Barbara sat half dreading he might force more than 'a brotherly peck on the cheek' from her, and half wishing that he would pull into some quiet spot, and was both relieved and despondent when he did not do so.

"I'll see you again as soon as I can." Pulling up outside, he reached across her to open the passenger door, and kissed her chastely on the cheek. "Remember, my little beaut, next time I'll be out to bed you."

"Thanks for the meal," she said starchily as she climbed out of the car. "and you won't get the opportunity for that." He let in the gear and roared off.

Chapter Twelve

Barbara paused in her writing, yet again, to admire the maroon vanity case. The beautiful calf leather case with solid brass fittings, would be a most useful piece of luggage for weekend leaves.

As he had promised Bill, Leslie had taken her over to the cottage in order that she should choose a keepsake. She had refused to take any jewellery, trinkets or objets d'art. She'd only accepted the vanity case, on the condition that Bill's son had no objection. Brodie had written to him about it, and only yesterday had she received the reply. Now the case was truly hers. The son had written, in amiable terms, that he was pleased for her to have it.

It had been a bleak day for mid-August. The thunder had rolled around the indigo sky all afternoon. Sitting at her card table, looking at the rain-swept runways through the rattling, wind lashed windows, she was glad she'd set this Sunday evening aside to write some letters, instead of agreeing to meet Mary for high tea at Betty's Cafe. Storm or no storm, Mary would no doubt be around later, dying to hear about her date last night with Leslie.

Better get back to her letter writing. She'd written a thank you note to Bill's son, and was half way through one to Badger. What a boon these one and a half page air-letter forms and single page aerograms were. It took only minutes to fill one of them, and with an aerogram she could even stretch out her script, on the grounds that the recipient got only a much reduced photo-stat, which might render her naturally fine hand writing illegible.

She usually sent aerograms to Badger. To-day she felt it wouldn't be too difficult to fill a flimsy air-letter. Describing the vanity box, 'a bequest from a deceased friend' had already taken up half a page.

Badger's first letter from overseas, had arrived about six weeks after her night with Bill. His aerogram form from their first port of call was a forlorn note. All his mates had received letters, but he hadn't. He 'knew' she must have written to him and blamed the Field Post office. Although the postmark had been censored, it was obviously posted in South Africa. He'd cutely said 'by the way Joe Dixon' [his great uncle who lived in Johannesburg] 'is not in our draft.'

Guiltily, she'd dashed off an air-letter to him a few days later, the first since he left Britain. He'd still not heard from her when, nearly a month later, his next letter arrived. His boyish pledges of love had been interspersed with equally boyish impressions of India, and bemoaning the fact that he'd not heard from her. 'Please, my darling wife, make sure you are using this Field Post Office address.'

Since that letter she'd received at least one air-letter a week.

'Wish I could write more often, but they restrict us to one air-letter per week.' Even so, he sometimes sent two letters a week, having scrounged the second form from a mate.

Badger's immense relief and delight, when he finally received her first letter, prompted him to cable a rapturous reply. According to his next letter, the cable cost more in bribes, than it had for transmission. After that, stricken by conscience, she'd dutifully written to him once a once a week. As a bonus – it took no more effort than the initial form filling – she'd arranged for a company to send him a monthly supply of pipe tobacco.

Sealing the air-letter, she neatly printed SWALK on the back, and imprinted it with her lipstick. 'Sealed with a loving kiss' was such a childish thing, and it always gave her an uncomfortable, fraudulent feeling in the pit of her stomach. It reminded her that when she'd married Badger, she must have been a sentimental fool – in love with the idea of love and not the man. But they'd agreed it would be their 'special thing' and he would put BOLTOP, 'Better on lips than paper' on the back of his letters. If she didn't reciprocate, suspicion would gnaw at his soul.

§

"...and that's all we did, last night." Barbara, perched on the edge of her bed, smiled down at Mary squatting by the unlit fire.

"Are you sure that's all that happened?" Mary glared at Barbara, in disbelief and disappointment.

"Yes, after the theatre we parked on the way home, kissed and cuddled a bit, that's all." She fixed Mary with a wide eyed smile of innocence. "I am menstruating, remember.

"But, I'll be honest Mary, if it hadn't been for that I couldn't have stopped him..." She flopped back on to her pillow, and sighed dolefully, "...even if I'd wanted to."

Staring idly at the ceiling, she was tempted to tell Mary how sensitive, yet firmly masculine, his fingers were as they had opened her shirt, and freed her breasts from her bra. She could still feel his lips squeezing her erect nipples. Her satin dressing gown had slipped open and dreamily, one hand stroked the top of her thigh. Her fingers lingered where his rigid, impatient, trousered penis had pressed into her skirt in the cramped two seater roadster. Her other hand traced the dimple of her navel, where his kisses had made their parting obeisance to their thwarted ardour.

"Jaysus, Barbara, you're a horny bitch!"

Mary had quietly undressed, and was standing by the bed, naked except for her shirt round her shoulders. Her breasts sagged only slightly with their own fullness. Her creamy stomach was taut, almost muscular. Her hips had a boyish slimness. She let down her French roll and with her black hair brushing her shoulders, her eyes swept sensuously over Barbara's breasts and loins.

When their eyes met, each held the other's in silent, embarrassed questioning. "Shall we? Should we?"

It was Mary who first broke the spell.

"A beautiful, beautiful, tempting bitch, so you are." Leaning down, she squeezed one of Barbara's breasts. Barbara's hands were almost on Mary's, when the Irish girl hastily straightened up, "Jaysus, its infectious so it is. Make yourself daycent."

Impulsively pulling the satin material over Barbara's nakedness, Mary stretched her arms to the ceiling, and yawned.

"I only wanted to borrow your other dressing gown, so I did, for a luxurious soak in your bath."

The ablutions at Mary's camp were primitive, and she had a standing invitation to use the bath at Barbara's place.

With mixed feelings, Barbara watched her friend take the spare gown from her locker, slip it on, and head for the bathroom.

§

"What a bloody awful show. You Poms – for once – have a real grouse to whine about." With a supercilious grimace, Leslie pulled the M.G. on to the verge of the dirt road, and switched off the engine.

"Oh?"

It was a pleasantly cool September evening, and they'd been driving with the top down. Save for one or two cotton bud clouds, the heavens were a mass of glittering stars, the reflection of the full harvest moon had danced on the roadster bonnet most of the way from the Forces concert party at Leconfield.

"Yes, ENSA – Every night something awful."

"It wasn't that bad. Give them their due Leslie." She thumbed her nose merrily at the silvery, frowning moon spying on them from a pond alongside the road, "Their transport from Hull was late, they'd lost their costumes and props, and had no time for rehearsal. The chorus line brought thunderous applause... "

"Chorus line! Three consumptive hags!"

"What did you expect, the Folies Bergere? Anyway you spent most of the time propping up the officer's bar."

"Some people will put up with any rot." He said huffily, as, pulling her head and shoulders across his lap, he flicked their cigarettes into the pond.

"Ouch!" The gear stick dug into the small of her back. She wriggled around until she was face-on to his chest, her hip dipping in the gap between the bucket seats and her heels cutting into the door trim. The gear stick now dug into her buttocks and she pulled herself back on to her own seat.

To-night, unlike last month, there was no menstrual barrier. Still it seemed the car would thwart them more than any monthly period. She tried to convince herself she was glad about that. He was too sure of her attraction to him. Serve him right for being so cocky. His arrogance dominated her, overwhelmed her will to resist him. Being putty in his hands was demoralising and degrading.

He hadn't even have the manners to invite her to these night's out. Just told her he'd arrange this or that, and would pick her up at such and such a time. Only once had she summoned the will power to turn him down. Then, seeing him drive out, that same night, with a WAAF officer she'd been consumed with envy and fretted for weeks that he might never date her again.

Stealing a glance from the corner of her eye at his rugged profile, she knew that however much she hated this arrogant giant her desire for him was irresistible. She was beginning to see what bullied wives meant by 'love and hate being close bed-fellows'.

"Well, we can't sit here all night. Can we?" His question was clearly rhetorical. Walking round to the passenger side, he reached over the door and tenderly pushed her shoulders back on to his seat. With her heels resting on the door, he knelt between the seats and dashboard.

To-night she was in mufti, and her grey coat had fallen open. Deftly he unbuttoned her cream cardigan as she locked her fingers around his close-cropped neck. The seemingly practised hands, laying her breasts bare, fired a jolt of jealousy through her. How many others had he bewitched. Her nails scored into his neck as their lips met.

With tongue furiously rasping tongue, one of his hands was fiercely, almost barbarously, clamping her head to his. The other hand was softly stealing down her belly. His huge fingers, soft and nimble as a seamstress, zipped open her skirt waist. Undoing the buttons down the legs of her French knickers, he laid bare her loins, and unclipped her scanty suspender belt.

Momentarily he reached deep into her warm, damp crotch. The agonisingly delicious spasm of her womb, arched her spine. Tensing to capture the tormenting fingers, her legs levered her pelvis from the seat. But the hand was already creeping up her quivering abdomen.

As the hand cupped a heaving breast, fingers plucking the erect nipple, she forced their heads apart. Her fingers clutching his hair, she dragged his mouth to the other nipple. His tunic buttons were bruising her flesh, but she was conscious only of the torturing tongue suckling her nipple.

Panting, Leslie released the nipples and, against the savage pressure of her hands, rested his forehead in the valley of her breasts. His hands were now easing her waist-band below her hips. Still cradling his head between her breasts, she tensed her buttocks until the skirt slipped down her thighs.

Now his hands were grasping her wrists, forcing them above her head. His tongue found her navel as she broke free. One massive hand crept under her buttocks. The other hand parted her thighs. Her fumbling fingers reached into his bulging flies.

"You bastard! That hurts!" But his hand kept up its slow, sadistically ecstatic rhythm. He was thrusting, with more than one of those huge fingers, deep into her, his knuckles thumping and thrilling her aroused cervix.

With every grain of strength she could muster, her fingers closed around his immense erection. With almost brutal force, their pistoning hands moved in accelerating unison.

"You cruel sod! I hate you!" she gasped. Then, pounding his shoulder with her free hand, she heard herself breathlessly blurt, "Leslie, I hate you! Bastard I love you! I love you!"

Abruptly he pulled his hand from her, planted a kiss in her navel and stretching back from her, he roughly pulled her knickers back over her loins.

"What..." Astonished, she angrily pushed her breasts back into her bra, and started fastening her knickers.

"No good here... I can't take you here... in a car like .."

Barbara slapped him with a force that rocked his head. The violence of her blow was a mixture of frustration and disgust. Disgust that Bill, after all, may have told Leslie about that night in the Humber. The insinuation that she would do it in any man's car.

"Don't be so bloody impulsive. If you'd waited a second you'd have seen I was complimenting you." As he looked down at her, even in the moonlight, she could clearly see the wealed imprint of her hand on his cheek, "I still want you bloody desperately, as you can see." He patted his still bulging flies, "But I want it to be in the right place. A snatched bunk up is for bungling kids, not a beaut sheila like you."

Getting out of the car, he leaned over and effortlessly lifted her back on to her own seat. She tugged her skirt back into place and defensively clutching her cardigan and coat across her chest, stared blindly through the windscreen.

"When I have a sheila with a body as divine as yours, its got to be in the right surroundings. Somewhere fit for a full unhurried night with her."

She dumbly let him button up her cardigan.

"I want you, but desperate as I am, I'm not going to spoil the pleasure... taking you with a swift bash here. We'll go away together next week-end. Come prepared." He ruffled her hair, and laughed.

"You are so bloody cocksure of yourself!" It was typical of him. When he has a sheila! He wants! He'll take! No thought of giving like Bill. Go away together!

"I certainly will not be going anywhere with you next week-end, or any other time!"

"Oh, but you will my beaut." Tilting her chin, he chastely kissed her, and switched on the engine, "When you've stopped sulking about being frustrated, you'll find the invitation irresistible."

"So, it was an invitation!" She almost screamed the words as he quirked that eye-brow again, "It sounds more like an Imperial command! And what did you mean by 'come prepared'? Is that the real reason you stopped to-night? The big-headed, man-o-the-world, Leslie Brodie has run out of sheaths?" It was childish sarcasm but, in her frustration, it was all she could think of to hit him below the belt, and it lifted her self respect a little. She felt she'd shown she wasn't just a meek, worshipping slave.

"You know bloody well that wouldn't have stopped me. I only meant come prepared for two or three nights." Easing slowly on to the main road, he laughed loudly, and the mildness of his tone seemed to devalue the venom of Barbara's remarks, "But you won't need much more than a toothbrush."

She made no attempt to reply and for a while they drove along in silence.

Heaven's above! Thwarted as I am, she told herself, I'm weakening already. It had been stupid to ask what he meant. Well, I suppose I ought to be glad. Fool that I am, I wasn't prepared either. The Gynomin pessary was still in her purse, forgotten in the anticipated ecstasy. He still has not screwed me, and the devil won't ever, ever, get me into bed with him. Even as she vowed this, another part of her mind was wondering where he had it mind to take her.

To curtail her weakening resolve, she dismissed her duelling thoughts by breaking the silence.

"May I have a cigarette?" She was pleased. She managed to sound cool and haughty, rather than frustrated and humiliated.

Chapter Thirteen

Leslie, cap over his eyes, his long legs sprawling across the floor, was dozing in the opposite corner of the compartment. He'd been like that from the moment the train had left Driffield.

It had been a glorious October day, and the early evening was just chilly enough for her to need the classic Burberry.

As they rumbled towards Hull, Barbara drank in the sunset. The afterglow of which was streaking the azure horizon with blood red and amber slashes. Late harvesters were ladening wagons with golden corn stooks. The draft horses in the shafts, munching at the corn gleanings in the yellow stubble, touched something deep inside her. Somehow, the sight of the horses' shiny, powerful flanks and hind-quarters, always quickened her sensual yearnings.

She glanced furtively at Leslie. Her stallion. That's what he was, and stallions were there to serve, not to be served. The thought made her feel less a bondswoman, less beholden to him for the expensive trench coat.

She had resolutely refused to spend the week-end with him last month. The adamance of her refusal had, increasingly, tinged his repeated 'invitations' with sheepish civility. Instead of going with him, she'd spent a happy week-end at her parents with Mary. Like loving sisters they had passionlessly shared Barbara's bed. She didn't, couldn't, hide the truth from Mary. The strength of her rejection of Leslie's 'invitation' lay in the imminence of her period, not in her immunity to his hypnotic personality.

Now, looking at him across the compartment, she couldn't resist feeling smug. Her persistent refusals had pricked his vanity, softened his arrogance, and had him almost begging her favour.

Last week, after a trip to London, the gift of the Burberry, and the promise of 'only a brotherly goodnight kiss', he had inveigled her to supper at The Bell. A reflective frown creased the bridge of her nose, and she stifled a wistful sigh.

If he had been her brother, their good-night embraces that night would have been damn close to incest. At their first kiss, his hand had slipped inside her blouse. She had pulled aside her bra, to hasten the long fingers to her nipples. His other hand, inside her skirt waist, had found the cleft of her buttocks, clamping their pelvises together. Her loins had shuddered as his granite erection dug through their clothes and into her crotch. But there, in the overlooked doorway, they dared not go further.

So now, here she was, in the luxury of a first class compartment for the first in her life; bound for a first class hotel for the first time in her life; and wearing the most expensive coat she'd ever had in her life.

Fingering the fine quality of the material, her face softened into a smile of child-like pleasure. Except for being a mite too long it was a perfect fit. With her broad-brimmed navy velour jauntily over one eye, she *was* Garbo. A *femme fatale* on a continental express to Lisbon, for an assignation crucial to the Allies' war plans.

Breaking the spell, Leslie yawned. Again she was just an errant wife on a slow train to adultery, in grimy Hull.

"Didn't mind me dropping off. Did you?" He stretched and peered at her through those deep set hooded eyes. That was his old style. Presuming her answer before putting the question.

With an indulgent smile, she shook her head, and wondered how long it would be after they'd made love, before his inherent arrogance re-asserted itself. She desperately wanted to assert herself, and tell him it had been rude and ungallant of him – but her will-power faltered, and she temporised.

"As ops kept you up most of the night, you're excused." The condescending tone made the point. Operational duties had also kept her up most of the night, and his raised his eyebrows signalled *touché*.

§

The grey haired receptionist welcomed Leslie with a familiarity that stung Barbara's pride.

"Ah, Flying Officer Brodie, nice to see you again. A double, wasn't it?" She gave Barbara a knowing 'you can't fool me' look, and as Leslie signed the register, she added, a little louder, "As usual?"

Barbara felt more a whore than a *femme fatale*.

"Thank you, yes, and..." he tapped the newly sewn ring on his cuff, "...it's Flight Lieutenant now."

"Oh! Congratulations, sir." Giving him an ingratiating grin, she fixed her eyes impudently on Barbara.

Haughtily outstaring the woman, Barbara handed her vanity case – her only luggage – and Leslie's holdall to the wizened hall porter. Would she have to register? Did they need to see identity cards? She presumed she would be booked in as Mrs. Brodie. What about ration cards? There had been so much she'd wanted to ask Leslie on the journey but anxious not to expose her inexperience, she hadn't done so.

"All fixed, Mrs. Brodie," the porter said to her over his shoulder, "we've got a nice honeymoon room."

Barbara surmised, rather than saw his wink at the receptionist, as the woman smirked knowingly.

§

To Barbara the room was large and sumptuous. Complimenting the dusky blue, Paisley patterned carpet, pale blue walls and white frescoed ceiling, there were two cream hide, deeply buttoned arm chairs, a matching dressing table stool, and an octagonal mahogany, glass topped coffee table.

Walking over to the ornate mahogany dressing table, as Leslie tipped the porter and ushered him out, she flung her hat on to the pale pink candlewick bedspread, and combed her fingers through her hair.

When she turned to face him, holding her arms out expectantly for his embrace, he lounged back against the door.

"Take off your coat!"

His voice thrilled and constricted her diaphragm. The dominant, husky tone was like a slave trader's command to bare everything. Slowly, burlesque-like, she unknotted her belt, undid each button and theatrically dropped the coat at her feet.

Through those hooded, penetrating eyes, Leslie savoured every contour as, mannequin-like, she revolved before him. The navy crepe de Chine dress revealed every line, every delectable curve of her body. She was beautiful and she knew it, and the transfixation of his eyes proclaimed that she was desirable. Her hands reached behind her spine for the zip.

"Don't be so impatient. We've got all night, and tomorrow." He walked over and kissed her forehead, "Too late for dinner. I'm going down to the bar. You don't want to come, do you?" Without waiting for a reply, he gestured at his new rank markings and added, "I've got to wet these. The blokes expect it."

Pouting, she watched him stride over to the phone beside the huge double bed. The bar had been full of officers as the porter had led them past it. His promotion had been confirmed only a few days ago, and he had been outwardly nonchalant, blasé, about it. But as she had suspected, his indifference was purely pseudo. He was hungry for the back slapping approbation of his fellow officers in the bar.

"Damn! No answer." Impatient to be off, he slammed down the phone and made for the door, " I'll get them to send up some sandwiches as soon as I get down there. Freshen yourself up. Won't be long."

One of Barbara's shoes flew at him, but struck only the door as it closed behind him.

"You conceited, selfish bastard!" She screamed to the empty room. How dare he presume that she had not wanted to go down to the bar! How dare he leave her like this. Just a peck on the forehead, and off he goes to drink with the boys! No thought for her preferences. Freshen herself up, indeed!' She told her reflections in the triple mirrors of the dressing table, "I'll show him. I'll go down there and ignore him, chat to another bloke."

Stripping to her bra and knickers, she hurried into the bathroom.

A bathroom *en-suite* was a luxury she'd always dreamed about. This one was beyond her most fantastic imaginings. Not since the first moment she'd seen the nurses' bathroom at St. James's, had she felt so pampered. Until then it had been a zinc tub in front of the fire at home, or communal showers at school. At home there'd only been the Elsonal privy behind the cottage. Even at the hospital it had been water closets remote from the bathrooms. Of course the village council houses had water closets, but even these were outside the back doors.

This one had everything. Warm grey tiles, matching bath, vanity unit and w.c. – there were even matching towels on a heated, chromium towel rail, and expensive looking tablets of soap.

In her delight, as she drank in the luxury, Leslie's behaviour all but faded from her mind. Forgetting completely that the object of hurrying after him had been to spite him, she now told herself, "He can just wait until I've had a bath."

§

"Excuse me, miss, but I did knock miss."

Barbara, absently towelling her back whilst admiring herself in the vanity unit mirror, hastily pulled the towel over her bosom.

A young waitress, was peering apprehensively round the half open bathroom door.

"The gentleman sent up a gin and tonic." Pushing the drinks tray round the door, she added with awe, "It's a double, miss."

Letting the towel drop, she reached for the drink, and then changed her mind.

"Put it by the bed, dear, please."

The skinny teenager's eyes swept Barbara with a mixture of envy and adoration.

"I'll bring bring up the sandwiches right away, miss," she called as she left the room.

§

With her hands on her head, standing naked in front of the triple mirrors, Barbara scrutinised her reflected figure. No, she thought, I don't think I've put on any weight. Her rib cage was only lightly fleshed. Her waist still sharply defined, and her thighs smooth and lean. Weighting her breasts in cupped hands, a frown of doubt creased her brow. Taking a pencil from her purse, she placed it under each breast in turn, as she'd done many times before. If the droop of a breast held the pencil, the muscles were losing the battle against gravity. The frown vanished, the mirror reflecting the self-applause in her eyes. Twice she tried, and each time the pencil instantly fell to the floor.

She changed her mind about following Leslie down. Chatting up other men could be cutting off her nose to spite her face. She didn't want any acrimony to-night. "I'll just sit here," she told her reflection, "in my nightie, quietly sipping my drink until he returns."

Arranging an armchair to face the door, so that Leslie would see her the instant he came in, she shrugged into the flimsy nightie. She wished it was black, but the ivory-silk was the daintiest the Driffield shops could offer. The bodice, with its trivial shoulder ribbons, scarcely covered her bust. As she tied the first ribbon with a bow, there was a knock at the door.

"Come in!" Brodie had a key, this must be the waitress with the sandwiches.

It was the sandwiches, but not the waitress. The tall, scrawny boy, carrying a tray laden with two cups and a silver coffee jug as well as sandwiches, all but swallowed his prominent Adam's apple.

Normally, Barbara would instinctively have turned her back to him, but at that moment a narcissus devil dominated her. Still with only one ribbon tied, she perched herself cross legged, on the chair arm.

"I thought it was the waitress." With her fingers laced behind her neck, she leaned back a little, and watched the lad's eyes fasten on to her bosom. They were wide set and grey like Badger's, and their adulation delighted her.

"Er... she's gone off, miss." Blushing, his eyes met hers fleetingly, and he stared down at the tray, "I'm the night porter."

"You don't look old enough for that job." Leaning forward, hands around her knee, she watched him ogling the view of her cleavage.

"How old are you? Fifteen, sixteen?"

"Oh, no miss, I'm 18." A spark of indignity flashed in his eyes, "Joining the Army next month." Swallowing his Adam's apple twice, he nervously glanced at the ceiling.

"Eighteen. Really? I can't believe that."

The lad fidgeted his feet. His eyes stared back at bosom.

"Er... well eighteen next month, miss." Mesmerised by the untied side of her bodice, the tray was beginning quiver in his hands.

"Why are you so embarrassed?" Her eye-lashes fluttered mischievously. Her husky voice was an erotic whisper, "Surely in your job you've seen a lady in a nightie before?"

Was he hoping – or fearing – that a breast would slip out? She was tempted to arrange it, and wondered what his reaction would have been if he'd come in moments earlier, when she was naked. Probably he'd have turned and run.

"No, miss, er... it's not that. It's er... that you're so lov..." The tray began to tilt as he stammered. "...it's just that, at first I thought you must be Rita Hayworth..."

One plate of sandwiches slid from the tray, and the cups slipped precariously close to its rim. As the flustered lad looked hastily at the debris on the carpet, coffee and milk dripped from the tray on to his trousers.

"Here, give me that!"

Barbara took the tray, placed it on the coffee table, and hurried into the bathroom. When she returned carrying a damp towel, the porter was on his knees scraping up the debris.

"Let me help you." On her knees, in front of him, any blame she felt for the mess, was all but obscured by the perverse pleasure of his eyes. She knew he could see, and was relishing her nipples. For a satanical instant, she wished he would reach out and touch them.

As they stood up, Barbara picked up the towel and pointed to the stain on his trousers. With one hand on his shoulder – playing the big sister – she gently sponged the stain.

"I'm sorry about the mess." He put his hands timidly on

her shoulders, and looked down at her hand, "Very sorry. I'll bring some more up. Don't worry about the stains, miss, please."

When she made no move to shrug off his hands, he pressed his fingers firmly into her flesh. There was no mistaking the rigid mound at his groin, and his knee was trembling as she sponged his thigh. She took a step back from him, and his hands dropped to his sides.

"That's best I can do," she said, scrutinising the stains and smiling ruefully at his bewitched, yearning eyes, "Shouldn't be much of a mark when they dry. What's your name by the way?"

"Leonard Brown miss... are you going to report me?"

"Report you? No, of course not. What for? It was a simple accident." She bent forward and planted a quick, sisterly kiss on his brow.

"But miss, er..." The Adam's apple oscillated, and he was gesturing diffidently at the stains down the skirt of her nightie.

Part of the skirt was transparent with dampness. For an instant, she was tempted to ask him to wipe off the stains. "Heavens above," she told herself, "I'm taking leave of my senses, tempting a callow lad".

"It'll it be all right. I'll rinse it later." She turned away from him, consumed with self reproach, and hastily tied the remaining shoulder ribbon, "You better go now, Leonard. They'll be wondering what you're up to."

She threw the towel into the bathroom and as she did, the telephone rang.

"Hello... Yes... Who?" She glanced across at Leonard, picking up the tray. "Oh, yes. He's er... just come back to collect the tray. I'll tell him. Thank you." Putting down the phone, she jerked her chin towards the door, "They want you downstairs. You'd better hurry."

"Shall I bring you another tray? Coffee's cold." Leonard asked hopefully, his hand on the doorknob.

"Er... No! Just leave the other plate of sandwiches for my husband." She waved him unceremoniously out of the room.

"I'm sorry about the mess, honestly. I won't put a charge on the bill for any of it. Goodnight Miss."

After Leonard left, Barbara dismissed the idea of rinsing her nightie and, putting a Gynomin on the bedside table, she climbed into bed.

The sirens, wailing out their awesome alarms, had driven the notion of sitting in the carefully arranged chair from her mind. Oh, God! Not to-night. Instinctively she looked at the window. Yes, the blackout curtains were in place.

The room was warm but she felt chilled, and yet sweat was dripping from her armpits. Her tummy seemed to be alternately freezing and scalding. Remorse, for teasing Leonard, fought to subdue the thrill it had given her. Impatient desire for Leslie, wrestled with her abhorrence of his domineering manner. Grief for Bill, mingled with pity for Badger's delusions about their love. The sirens added physical fear to her confused emotions.

With her arms about her bent knees, the rivulets of sweat dripping from her elbows suddenly blotted everything from her mind except vanity. She should have shaved the unsightly hair from her armpits before leaving Driffield. Too late now. Damn! She hadn't brought her razor. Daren't rummage in Leslie's holdall, he might get the wrong idea – think she'd been prying among the letters he'd hurriedly, guiltily, stuffed in the holdall when they had met at the main gate.

Falling back on the pillows, she dabbed her armpits with a corner of the sheet, and listened intently for any sound of approaching aircraft. A hair-grip pricked her scalp. No sound, except a car pulling away from the forecourt. Good, the bar must be closed. Only inebriated servicemen would be stupid enough to go out in an air-raid. Leslie couldn't be long now.

She pulled the grips from her page-boy bob, combed her fingers through her hair, settling it about her neck, and turned on the Rediffusion speaker above the bed.

A nasal voiced woman was singing a bitter sweet verse, in what sounded like a cavernous, echoing studio. Her wistful intonation gave the simple words a tear jerking sentiment. Millions, separated by war, would be listening to her, yet she made it seem she was singing purely to each lonesome listener.

Barbara's eyes moistened. In thousands of wretched homes, folk would be thinking of their absent loved ones. She felt terribly alone, forsaken. No one, except perhaps dear Mary, would be missing her. Badger's parents clearly cared little for her. They'd not been in contact with her since the wedding. She saw her own family too often to be missed. Poignantly, perversely, as she listened to the sentimental words she wished she was separated by this war from someone she truly loved.

...We'll meet again don't know where, don't know when,
But I know we'll meet again some sunny day.
Keep smiling through just like you always do,
Till the blue skies drive the dark clouds far away...

Hearing the key in the latch, she clicked off the radio and sat bolt upright. Leslie threw his tunic on the chair, and flung his cap after it.

"Well! At last!" It was the reprimand of a shrewish wife. She forced an indulgent smile, and added plaintively, "I'm sorry, I'm so tired. I'm sure I'll be asleep before you're undressed."

Sitting there, in that strange bed, watching him pull off his shirt, she suddenly felt childishly bashful, but resisted the impulse to cover her bosom with the sheet.

"Impatient witch!" His breath was tainted with beer as he cupped his hands about her ears, and fiercely kissed her lips, "I can't have been too long, can I?" Again the rhetorical question. No hint of apology, "You don't begrudge me a drink with the blokes. Do you?" It was a statement not a question, "You've got me all night, and you haven't been in bed long!"

"Oh! How do you know?" Furtively, she slipped the Gynomin into place.

"Experience," he called from the bathroom. He brushed his teeth, gargled and spat, "A long soak in the bath, half an hour tarting yourself up..."

"Quite the boudoir veteran, aren't you?" She shouted above the noise of the flushing w.c.

"Don't be bloody silly," he was back in the bedroom, trousers folded over one arm, "you ought to've realised I'm just jossing. I know because not ten minutes ago, the night porter was here. Heard the barman phone you, and you wouldn't be in bed then."

His casualness, as he stripped to the skin, made her feel like a whore waiting to earn her fee. His massive torso was scarcely paler than his craggy, leathery face. To her dismay, he was almost covered by a bear-like thatch of black hair. His loins, around the dense thicket of his stiffened genitals, were no paler than the rest of him. When he turned to put his socks on the stool, she saw that only his shoulder blades, lean bottom and thighs, were completely free of the black thatch. His perfectly proportioned frame was like a centurion's breast plate, and her revulsion faded to fascination. The hollowed flanks and legs, corded with muscular hawsers, reminded her of a classical Apollo sculpture.

"The sirens have sounded." She whispered, trying to sound blasé and imperturbed, as he climbed in beside her.

"Nothing to worry about. Not heard any planes about. Come here, you little beaut."

One arm went under her armpit, the hand spanning her neck forced their mouths together. Sideways on, as their bodies moulded to each other, Barbara shuddered. His erection pushed the nightie between her tensed thighs as her fingers tenderly teased the hair between his shoulder blades.

Leslie's other hand, gently uncovering her thighs, produced another shudder. Her spine stiffened. Was she really taking part in this? Fornicating with this hairy Goliath? Fornication, premeditated adultery. The words filled her with wantonness, extinguishing all misgivings and demolishing all inhibitions.

Her fingers scored into his flesh. Her tongue darted and whipped at his. Teeth nipped into lips. His forefinger and thumb, spanning her neck, gouged savagely into her skull.

Damn! He was wrestling to drag the nightie clear of her loins. She wished she'd not put it on. No she didn't! She wanted, willed him to tear it off. Just as she'd vainly willed Badger on their wedding night. Silly sod had then ruined the thrill by asking if he could.

Leslie's fingers were now deep inside her gently massaging, teasingly stretching the pulsating membranes. He took the hand from her neck. Their mouths parted and, as he toyed with one of the shoulder ribbons, her teeth nipped into his neck.

"For Christ's sake, Leslie..." Smothered into his neck, her words were inaudible, "Don't waste time! Do it!"

Her soul was crying for violation. The massaging had paced into pumping – teasing into exquisite torment. She rolled on to her back, pulling him astride her waist. His warm scrotum crushed into her navel. Every fevered fibre of her body quivered,

Looking up at his lust-fired, almost negroid face, she screamed, "Christ! Do it, you sodding bastard!" Her nails wildly raked his chest. She knew, willed with every atom of her being, what was coming next. He snatched at her bodice, the knots biting into her shoulders. The ribbons snapped. The intact bodice slid down her ribs as her bared breasts seemed to swell towards him. She gasped for air as the full weight of his body bore down on her. His lips fastened on a nipple, fingers ruthlessly kneading the other breast.

The urge to reciprocate the delicious agony was irresistible. She clamped his head to her breast with one hand. Reaching down she squeezed his scrotum. He winced, and she roughly rubbed his rigid dome.

His knuckles rutted her belly as his free hand, squeezing between their compressed bodies, pulled the throbbing penis from her grasp.

"Now who's bloody impatient." She goaded, as wrenching his head from her grip, he parted her thighs.

He pushed into her with a gasp of delight. Not slowly, not tantalisingly. Not like Bill, but with a single swift, deep thrust that threatened to tear her every membrane. Then it was still, rigid and throbbing inside her.

Her heels dug into the mattress. Her spine arched, striving for the impossible fusion of their bodies. The massive hands under her buttocks, clamped their loins as, motionless, his erection tortured her soul.

Closing her eyes, biting her lips, she willed every grain of energy to fiercely contract her womb.

"You bloody beaut! Again!"

She clenched her fists behind his back. The nails cut into her palms as she forced another, stronger spasm.

"Again you bitch! Again!" But he didn't give her time. He was pumping her with rapidly accelerating strokes. Bouncing into the mattress, oblivious to the creaking springs, her nails cut into his shoulders. She felt the thatch tearing from his skin. All her vigour combined with his, demanding the unattainable one-ness.

Every sinew, every tendon of her body was desperate for fulfilment. Sweat was pooling in her navel.

She wrapped her ankles around his calves but rising from her, he brushed them away. Roughly dragging the nightgown over her head, he flung it to the floor. Still hard inside her, hands caressing her tingling breasts, his eyes devoured every inch of her from nipples to navel.

"No wonder Bill fantasised about you. They're beautiful! Your tits are gorgeous."

He pushed deeper into her. Then, as his eyes ravished her, the granite penis slipped from her.

"God! Don't finish now!" Her fists pummelled his chest.

"Finish? You sadistic cow!" Crooking his elbows behind her knees, grasping her wrists, he spreadeagled her hands on the pillows. "Finish? I'm just starting!"

Doubled up, ankles astride his shoulders, she yelped with each deeper, agonisingly delicious lunge. Her knees were being pressed closer to her breasts. When his hands slipped on to her shoulders, pinning her deeper into the pillow, she savagely tugged at her own nipples.

"Oh Leslie! You cruel bugger, I hate you, I hate you!" The wrenched teats throbbed between frenzied fingers. His sweat was streaming on to her face. Stinging her eyes and salting her lips, "More! Damn you! Harder! I hate you. I love you!"

Bill had promised to take her to the moon. This was beyond it. Leslie was shooting her to the stars. Her jack-knifed thighs, like a tightly compressed spring, recoiled into his chest between each of his powerful thrusts. Every sinew of her buffeted loins was convulsing to a volcanic eruption.

"Go! Go!" Her entire spine twitched violently.

"Ahhh yah!" Simultaneously they screamed, and he collapsed into her clutching hands.

"Stay there... don't move or you will slip out." Breathless, she locked her arms round him. Her heart bursting with the joy of concerted gratification, she cradled his panting head on her bosom. The core of her was exultantly vibrant, pulsing with sublime consummation. With her last vestige of energy she contracted her cervix, and held him until he withered and slipped from her.

"That was heaven beyond words, darling." All hatred of him was eclipsed by the rapture of fulfilment. Her heart was bursting with love for him. Listening to their blissful, harmonised breathing she dreamily stroked the thatch down his back. Her serenity would be absolute if he'd just say, even hint, he loved her.

"I must have fallen in love with you, Leslie. It couldn't be as perfect as that without love, could it, darling?"

"If you think that was perfect, wait till I've recuperated, sweetheart." He tenderly kissed each nipple, and ran his tongue down to her navel, "Next time it'll be Utopia."

"But do you? Think there *must* be love, I mean?" Fearful of a negative reply – or worse, a sardonic retort – she wished she'd held her tongue.

Leslie sat up and cupped his hands gently over her ears.

"Love? So soon?" As always, when prevaricating – or being inquisitive – he quirked his right eyebrow high into his heavily furrowed forehead, and screwed his left eye to a pin-point, " An arrogant, egotistical brute like me?"

For a heartbeat, dismay clouded her serenity. She was a fool to expect any affection in fornication. Then, as he kissed the tip of her nose, she caught an impish twinkle in his eye, "Mmm... I suppose," he teasingly drawled the words, "...there must have to be some mutual attraction for that. Let's have a cigarette." He climbed out of bed and added, over his shoulder, "Even love. Maybe."

He hadn't actually said he loved her. That was typical of him. She convinced herself he would only ever be off-handed about loving her, or anyone. She was sure he feared that, by saying anything more affectionate, he might undermine his masculine superiority. Little though it was, what he had said contented Barbara, as much as if he'd actually vowed undying love for her. As he settled back in bed she took the two cigarettes from him, put them in the ashtray on the bedside table, and hugged him like joy-filled child.

§

The sirens, wailing the 'All Clear' woke Barbara from a deep, tranquil sleep. She raised her head from the crook of Leslie's arm. Stretching, and rotating the stiffness from her neck, she suddenly realised where she was. Waking naked – alongside this naked giant – thrilled all sleepiness from her. Snuggling into his chest, her hands wandered to his loins.

"Eh, what?" Half asleep, Leslie rolled sideways on to her, his hands passively spanning her waist. His genitals were warm and flaccid, but as her hands fondled them, there was a responsive quickening and stiffening rising from their roots to his foreskin.

"Darling, I want you." She whispered in her deepest, most alluring voice. Her tongue flicked into his ear. Sleepily he brushed it away.

"Not now. Later. Don't be so bloody lively."

"Not later! Now!" The sharpness of her voice jolted him on to his elbow. His astonished eyes blinked at her as more imperatively, she demanded, "Leslie, now! Not later. Now!"

"Right, you bitch! Remember you asked for it!"

Swiftly, effortlessly, he rolled her on to her stomach. Once! Twice! Simultaneously he slapped both of her buttocks. The pillow muffled her scream, "Stop! You bastard! That hurt."

Fearfully wanting more, she was both angry and delighted when she felt his tongue between her shoulder blades. Notch, by tender notch, the tongue lapped down her spine. It seemed to be stripping her flesh to the bone. Every nerve in her back seemed raw, tingling. Then his hands were under her midriff, pulling her on to her knees.

With her elbows, pushing through the pillows into the mattress, she strained her head round to scream at him.

"Oh God! No! Not that! Not there!" Terrified by the vile thing she believed he was going to do, she struggled to turn on to her back.

One of those huge hands forced her head into the pillows, smothering her protests. The other arm snaked around her waist, and down her belly. Then the fingers parted the lips of her throbbing vulva. His hard shaft insistently jabbed into her crotch, feverishly seeking and probing for the wet, excited opening.

"Hold still you bitch! It's not going where it's not been before." He fiercely shoved her head deeper into the pillows, "You silly cow, hold still! Let it get in where it belongs."

The smooth dome tantalisingly hovered at the taut brink of the moist cavity. She let out a shrill of delight as he lunged into her. For a tormenting moment he was still. In the ascension of her passion her cervix gripped him, striving to crush the uncrushable erection. Her upthrust buttocks pushed against his pelvis. With his fingers taunting her clitoris, he began slowly pumping back and forth. The hand slipped from her head to her ribs. The fingers pulled and rolled a nipple. Her fingers grasped the headboard, stiffening her arms, bracing her spine against each thrilling thrust.

Every stroke was ruthlessly powered, confidently controlled. Smooth and skilfull, not rash and unbridled like Badger's.

His name triggered flickers of apprehension. Gynomin! She hadn't put a new one in. How long do they last? Would the first one still protect her? In the delirious drumming of her pulses, the flickers vanished. All the sensations of her being merged into one magnificent, core of rapture. From head to toe the energy, the vigour, of her every cell was surging to her loins and breasts. Inflaming their wild cravings. She was not a cow! She was a rampant mare, being served by this ravenous stallion.

"Its lovely! Wonderful! You're wonderful!" She gasped over her shoulder. Every moment of elation in her life, every joy of achievement she'd ever experienced, was being eclipsed by the rapture of their unison, "I love you, love you! Love me, love me!"

"Love you.. I love fucking you!" His huge hands brutally squeezed both breasts.

Barbara bit her lips, stifling a yelp of pain. Nothing mattered now. Not the risk of pregnancy. Not love, nor tenderness. Only the sweet pain of the approaching orgasm. Each gasping thrust, each breathless impact of loins, carried her closer to that exquisite fulfilment. He could do anything to her now. Anything! Anything, however perverted, however vile.

Without a word, in the unison of their carnality, they shifted their positions. Barbara, knees straddling his hips, looked down at the sweat-beaded thatch. Hands on her head, she sculpted her swollen breasts to Amazonian fullness. With her regal erectness emphasising the faultless symmetry of her figure, she gloated down at him. The delicate blue tracery of the veins, lent the upper slopes of her bosom the quality of fine marble.

With his hands fondling the moist delta of her thighs, his eyes ravished her statuesque pose. Her pelvic muscles, firmly clenching his pulsing erection, held him still and deep within her. With a husky reverence she'd believed impossible from one so egocentric, he whispered, "Jesus, you are a beaut cow. From now on you're going to be no other bloke's Sheila."

She took this to be an unexpected pledge of his love. His hands reached for her breasts. Barbara's green eyes flashed with joy and, playfully brushing his hands aside, she felt his loins tense to push deeper into her. With his wrists in her hands, she bent to kiss him but impatiently, he broke free of her grasp. His hands spanned her waist. His pelvis slammed into her, and their loins met and parted in a slow, reciprocating rhythm. Her hands cupped her breasts, steadying the gently bouncing mounds, her fingers and thumbs rolled the reddening, erect nipples.

Each uplifting stroke of his powerful hands, crushed the flesh under her ribs. Beads of sweat speckled his sun-creased brow, and dribbled into the deep, almost Neanderthal, eye sockets. Every fragment of her panting body was nagging for the climax, tingling with the rumblings of suspended orgasm. Riding to his rhythm, the power of her thighs joined forces with his arms, intensifying the momentum of his pivoting elbows. The quickening strokes thumped harder, deeper into her. Momentum sped towards panic.

Instinctively as one, they rolled over in breathless union.

Leslie's heaving, sweating frame, buffeted her into the mattress.

His nails cut into her buttocks. Her ankles, locked about his legs spurred his onslaught. Her fingers clawed into his hairy back. Her teeth bit into his neck.

In a fury of thrashing bodies, they drove themselves beyond demented exhaustion. Beyond terrestrial restraints, to the limitless heavens.

"Now! Now, darling!" The moaned plea came through clenched teeth. Uncontrollable convulsions ravaged every fibre of her being. Joyous agony shuddered her limbs. Rapture contorted her face, stretching her lips, creasing her cheeks, wrinkling her nose and brow.

His thighs viciously stiffened against hers, demanding the

ultimate synchronism of their animalism. With a desperate surge of vigour, their loins simultaneously loosed their pent-up orgasm. Barbara's lips crushed into his shoulder, smothering her jubilant shriek. In triumphant prostration, sweat-drenched chests heaving against each other, the throes of their ecstatic frenzy thumped through their beings from lungs to loins.

Barbara laced her fingers behind the small of his back, bonding their quivering mid-riffs in vice-like compression. Draining the stamina from her every sinew with repeated contractions, she milked the final thrills from his abating lust.

"You wonderful, hot arsed beaut!" With her ears cupped in his hands, he kissed her gently, "I told you we'd get better, darling."

Taking his hands in hers she kissed the backs of them and, as they rolled apart, she nuzzled her head into the hollow of his shoulder. This was the perfect bliss of dreams. She was convinced she was at last truly in love. She was certain, too, that he loved her. Straightforward pledges of love and affection, were too alien to this arrogant giant's nature, too juvenile for his veneer of sophistication. If she asked him now, at this divine moment, to say he loved her, even if he said so, she couldn't be sure that it would be for real, or a placating sop in the after-glow of gratification. No, that would have to await the right moment. To the soporific lub-dub of his heart, she drowsily contented herself with the knowledge that he'd repeatedly run after her. That his expensive, practical gift – the Burberry – was surely an earnest token of affection. Of love?

§

As they entered the dining room, the matronly head waitress greeted Leslie like an old, bosom friend and a spasm of irritated jealousy cramped Barbara's solar plexus. Leslie was obviously a frequent breakfaster at the hotel for, though there were only a few tables occupied, she ushered them unhesitantly to a secluded table, remote from possible eavesdroppers. With a brief mental tussle Barbara vanquished the spasm, telling herself not to fret about the jilted ghosts of his past.

"Tea, or coffee, miss? I know Mr. Brodie would like tea."
Persuading herself that 'miss' instead of 'madam' was an innocent impulse, and not deliberate insolence, Barbara smiled pleasantly at the woman.

"Yes, thank you, dear, I'll have tea too."

"I'll send over the tea straight away. And – if you're not in a hurry..." Pausing, her eyes sweeping the room, she winked conspiratorially, first at Leslie, and then at Barbara, "As soon as most of them have cleared off, I'll bring you a proper breakfast."

"What was all that about? More of your smuggled supplies? Like 'The Bell'?"

"Not this time. Just wait and see."

§

"Did you know this feast was coming?" Only one couple, too far away to see what they were getting, was still in the room when their food was eventually brought in.

"Of course, darling. Why do think I was so patient? Old Ruby always has something special for me."

The breakfast was delicious. A thick slice of York ham, off the bone, and real eggs, not the unpalatable war-time substitute of fried spam and powdered eggs, served to the other guests. The toast was hot, and there was an abundance of real butter and marmalade.

As they relaxed with cigarettes, and a fresh pot of tea, Barbara reached across the table and took one of Leslie's hands in hers.

"Thank you for the most wonderful night of my life darling."

Her eyes were alight with love, her cheeks glowing with pleasure. The rapture of the night had been crowned by Leslie's uncharacteristic deference to her wishes as they had planned their day. Lunch in York, theatre in the evening, followed by late night dancing. Throughout breakfast he'd been uncommonly attentive.

"I haven't really thanked you properly for the Burberry." She felt like a love-giddy, hero worshipping, adolescent as she squeezed his hand.

"Yes you have, at least a dozen times, and anyway your

being here is thanks enough."

He gave her a reassuring smile and, withdrawing his hand, fixed her with that quirked, questioning eye-brow. Wondering what was coming next, her heart sank a little at the penetrating focus, the accentuated Neanderthal crevice. To break the contact of their eyes, she studiously brushed imaginary crumbs from her lap, and prayed he wasn't about to sour the moment.

"Have you heard from what's his name... Badger, lately?"

"Yes, a couple of days ago." She was surprised and pleased by the apparent artlessness of his tone, and by the casualness of her own voice, "He's been on the North West frontier. Loves it apparently. Full of Kipling-esque romanticism about mountain pickets, being sniped at by Pathans and all that."

"Who's he with then? The Bengal Lancers?" The flicker of a smile turned his sarcasm into a waggish jibe.

"1st Battalion King's, Liverpools. He's so proud of it." Her off-hand, slightly disparaging voice would have had a stranger believing Badger was just an acquaintance, not her husband, "Sometimes I feel he prefers being there than being at home. They're somewhere near Lahore – Ferozopore, or someplace like that."

"Aren't his letters censored?"

"Usually. But he gives me clues from time to time, and I put two and two together. You know references to films we've seen; places we've been." A wry smile touched her lips, and she winked at him, "No state secrets of course. They'd probably get through uncensored in plain language, but he thinks he's being clever outsmarting them." She briefly knit her brows, thinking she was being a little too disdainful, "To be fair, I suppose he's quite ingenious. When he uses Roman numerals for his pages it means references to books we both like. Descriptions of the weather, places in southern England etc. are anagrams or cryptic clues. Sometimes it's like working out The Times Crossword."

"Clever boy!" His bushy eye-brows flicked up sharply, and his grey eyes flashed with mock admiration.

"Give the lad his due!" Barbara playfully kicked his ankle, "Sometimes he can send what he calls 'honour' letters. You know, special envelopes with a signed affirmation that the letter contains nothing censurable. Battalion officers don't read them, and there must be only random checking by HQ censors. Anyway," her head shook woefully, "those are the ones that irritate me. They are always too long. Make me feel mean dashing off a short air mail reply..."

"Don't gnaw your pretty lips like that. C'mon, my beaut, what's troubling you?"

"What are we going to do, Leslie?"

"Do? About what?"

"Us. What's going to happen after this?"

He abruptly unclasped her hand and, as he leaned back in his chair, she thought she detected a flicker of apprehension in his eyes. Then, briefly, he gave that quirked, prevaricating frown.

"After last night it must be obvious that my marrying Badger was a dreadful mistake, and that I love you. And I think you love me." Her eyes vainly appealed for his confirmation, "Even if you won't say so."

With his hands behind his head, he leaned further back in his chair, lifting the front legs off the floor.

"Suddenly feeling guilty? Immoral?" Does copulation with every man have to mean love, to ease your conscience? Bill? Albert and whoever?"

"Don't be so damned crude!" Snapping, almost spitting the words, "For crying out loud, Bill and I were only with each other for a few hours. OK, I was infatuated, could have grown to love him, gone the whole hog with him... in time." She swallowed back a sob for the loss of Bill. She'd never given another thought to Albert after the night at Maxi's. Now shame and revulsion sharpened her anger as she remembered his grubby fingers, and the surreptitious pleasure of his initial gropings, "As for Albert, you've got a low opinion of me if you think I'd..."

Barbara's voice trailed into silence as, snatching her handbag from her chair back, she rose to her feet.

"Don't go off like that, darling." His chair dropped back on all four legs, and his long arm gently grasped her elbow, "I'm sorry. That was cruel of me." Contrite, appealing, he eased her back into her chair, "Guess I'm jealous of your being friendly with anyone."

His last sentence took the edge off her anger. If he was so jealous, and he sounded sincere, he must really love her.

"I'd like another pot of tea." A subterfuge whilst she composed her thoughts, "Actually, I don't feel guilty at all, Leslie. Horribly deceitful, cowardly, but certainly not guilty. I love you. You can't expect me to stay married to him after last night."

Pouring fresh cups of tea, she slyly studied his reaction, and once again saw that flicker of apprehension behind his eyes, "I thought maybe you intended to take me back to Australia."

"Yes, for sure. If everything pans out right." For once it was he who averted her eyes. The flesh of his lantern jaw seemed to be taut as piano wire. Concentrating on stirring his tea, he asked, "You've not..." trying to conceal his unease, "...you don't intend to..."

"Tell Badger? No, of course not. How could I? In a letter?"

Leslie gave her a brief askance smile, and his jaw relaxed.

"Well not yet." She wasn't going to let him off the hook that easily, "I've not made my mind up whether it's kinder to send him a 'Dear John', or wait until he comes home."

Leslie looked sharply up at her. His jaw stiffened again. His eyes, trying to penetrate her mind, seemed to flinch as she stared into them.

In that moment the realisation of a woman's power, especially that of a desirable woman, hit her. She was 23 years of age, but felt only in this instant that she had crossed the threshold from adolescence to womanhood. She felt she need never again be subservient to Leslie, nor any other man. Except for rape, no man could have her unless she wanted him. Acquiescence was a gift she could withhold at will. It gave her power over any man. However much they wanted each other, she alone, not Leslie, could dictate the terms.

With a confident, serene smile, she outstared Leslie and he took a sip of tea.

"What did you mean by 'If everything pans out right', darling?" She asked.

"Well, we are both still married, and the war won't be finished for a long time yet." His rich baritone was tinged with childish petulance. Hands on his head, sprawling back in the chair again and trying to re-assert his dominance, he rivetted those hooded eyes on her.

"We don't have to wait for the end of the war." Barbara impulsively tested his sincerity, "I can get a divorce after last night, probably even an annulment. It should be even easier for you – your wife's living with another man."

Leslie jerked upright and, in exasperation, raised his palms towards heaven.

"What is it, Leslie? What are you afraid of?"

"I'm not bloody afraid!" He snapped, "One night with you, and you expect me to change my whole life, make a life-long commitment. I've said I'll take you to Aussie." Glaring at her, he punched a fist into the other palm, "If that's not enough you can shove off now. I've had a bloody bellyful. What do you want? A contract in blood?"

"Oh! I'll go all right!" The confident voice surprised her as much as Brodie, his eyes were wide with amazement, "But before I do, let's have an honest answer. No shilly shallying, do you really want us to settle down together?"

"Bloody hell, I can't promise that!"

"I'm not asking you to promise on a stack of bibles. I'm not naïve Leslie, I accept things may change, feelings change, we could break up. All I'm asking is, now, at this very moment, do you truly want us to settle down together. No more womanising, no more dallying with old flames, including the snobby Lady Joyce. If you can't – or won't – assure me of that, it's over for us now."

"Christ, you come on strong!"

"I mean it, Leslie. I'll catch the next train to Driffield, and that'll be the end of us."

It was a threat she knew she couldn't carry out. She loved him too much. Watching him solemnly stroking his invisible beard, as if calculating the potency of the threat, she desperately hoped he wasn't going to call her bluff.

"Make up your mind." She was poker faced. "It's up to you Leslie."

"Listen, you little beaut." He took her hands in his, "I

daren't be mixed up in one bloody divorce, let alone two. It would ruin my prospects. I might even be cashiered."

"But you're only a wartime officer. This is not your career. What difference would it make to your prospects?"

"Darling, don't you see – the higher the rank, and the more impressive my war record is, the more doors will open for me. For us. The higher my rank, the bigger my war gratuity, the more time I'll have to pick and choose a job."

"Aren't you going back to surveying?"

"Not on your life. At least not in field work. I've had enough of roughing it in the outback, no stable home of my own. I want to be up with the bosses. Aussie is supposed to be classless – and it is compared with this country; Jack's as good as his master and all that balls – but every bloke wants to be master, wants to be wealthier than the next bloke." He laced his fingers into hers, and squeezed gently, "There'll be thousands looking for top jobs, but the higher the rank the thinner the competition. You see that, don't you?"

Ah, she thought, there will also be fewer top jobs, but she simply nodded. She was too anxious for a justification – however fragile – to abandon her threat of leaving him.

"My wife's not short of money, so my marriage allowance is going into a deposit account. It'll be a nice nest-egg for us when this bloody war is over."

"Us?" Suspiciously. "You and her?"

"No, of course not. We've agreed on a divorce when the war is over. Apart from anything else, she refuses to live in Aussie." He paused, a reassurring grin stretching his mouth, his strong teeth gleaming white in the rugged jaw, "I won't pretend I'll never fancy another sheila, but no woman I've ever met can match you. It's not impossible, but I don't believe I'll ever meet one."

His gentle pressure on their interlaced fingers, and the solemnity of his eyes, lent sincerity to his words, "You know, darling, when you were smoking earlier, I thought you had the elegance of a swan, and the dignity of a princess."

It was the entrancing, woman of the world, pose she had striven for. Right elbow on the table, forearm upright, cigarette between fingers extended heavenwards, chin tilted upwards, emphasising the slenderness of her neck, the fingers of her other hand resting lightly in the crook of the right elbow. It had obviously been effective.

"Flatterer. Don't try and butter me on both sides."

"And that alluring deep voice of yours is so bloody sexy. Whenever I've met a woman with a husky voice it's irritated me. Wanted to tell them to have a bloody gargle to clear their throat. But yours is positively erotic, makes me jealous that any other bloke should hear it. So, my beaut little darling, I've no desire for any other woman. Unless the improbable happens, we – you and me – will enjoy that nest egg. Now, are you still going to catch that train?"

It was enough for Barbara. He still hadn't mentioned love, but she was already exultantly visualising the bliss, wealth and sun of Australia. Drawing his hands to her face, she tenderly stroked them against her cheeks. He was hers now, and she had it in her power to keep him.

"Right then, darling." He saucily cast his eyes to the ceiling, "Let us go up to our room. Still plenty of time to seal the bargain, before we go to York."

With extraordinary gentility he squired her towards the lift.

PART 3

The Kachin Hills, March to August 1944 / London 1944

"I Bare you on Eagles' Wings, And Brought you Unto Myself"
Exodus, 19 v.4.

Carved on the Memorial at Broadway (Thora Lwin)
Northern Burma, in tribute to the men of the USAAF
and the British 77th Ind. Brigade who lost their lives
in the initial glider landings there – March 5/6th 1944

§

"When you go home tell them of us
and say
for their tomorrow we gave our today"

War Memorial at Kohima

"I Bare you on Eagles' Wings..."

Chapter Fourteen

It had been another sultry day on the Assam airstrip, but the evening breeze tugging at the distant wind sock, heralded another chilly night on the Imphal Plain. To the south east, grey cumulus clouds, edged pink by the setting sun, were dawdling in over the Burma mountains.

Forty minutes before 'H' hour there had been a last minute hitch. The Tommies lounging around the gliders, ignorant of the cause of the delay, increasingly feared the worst. The worst being that the 'fly in' had been called off, depriving their brigade – the 77th. – of the opportunity to leapfrog over the rival 16 Brigade into the heart of Burma, and be first in to action. The monocled Bernard Ferguson's 16 Brigade, having crossed the Chindwin into Burma a week ago, were the envy of the remaining Chindit brigades languishing in Assam encampments. That brigade's epic march through mountainous jungle, which even the Japanese regarded as impassable, had been rewarded by Wingate's signal, 'Well done... Hannibal eclipsed!'

This had stung the pride of Calvert's 77th, and none more so than his two columns of the 1st. Battalion, King's (Liverpool) Regiment. The King's, after all, felt they had had sound reasons for believing Wingate had personally selected them for a prime role in the campaign. The 77th were the elite brigade, and the King's – the Brigade's senior regiment of foot – had been given the 'honour' of spearheading the glider-borne invasion of Burma. It was their glorious opportunity to throw the High Command's contempt back in their teeth.

§

For decades, the The King's Liverpool – regular battalions – had gone about their duties convinced the Army hierarchy treated them with thinly veiled contempt. That they regarded them as a rabble, a second-rate regiment, fit only for garrison duties. Despite the profusion of battle honours enshrined on their colours, the contempt was not entirely undeserved. The regiment had always enjoyed more than its share of rogues. Generations of Kingsmen were no strangers to 'punishment' stations arising from 'out of barracks' crimes and drunken hooliganism. The war had made little impact on the 1st. Battalion's routines in the Punjab. Except for excursions up the Khyber Pass, for which they proclaimed themselves the 'mountain goats of India', it had not fired a shot in anger in this war. Wingate's expedition last year had changed all that.

Last year the traditionally inculcated staff, sceptical of Wingate's hare brained campaign, had forced him to form the original 77 Brigade from unblooded – and as they considered them – expendable troops, the 13th Territorial Battalion of The King's, and the 3/2 Gurkhas, a war time unit. The 13th, 700 city bred part-time soldiers, drafted to India to relieve regular units from garrison duties, had confounded the sceptics. For more than three months, deep in enemy held jungle, relying solely on air dropped supplies, they had harassed, outmarched and outwitted the hitherto invincible Japanese army.

It had cost the 13th. nearly 400 lives. If nothing else they had demonstrated that, given an inspiring leader, even part-time British soldiers were more than a match for the Japanese. Their example had rallied the flagging morale throughout the 14th Army and the reflected glory of their common cap badges and county origins, had sent the 1st. Battalion's pride soaring.

The 1st. Battalion, now bound for Burma, was no longer a truly regular battalion. Many of its regulars, long overdue, and pining for repatriation to Blighty, had been replaced by wartime volunteers and conscripts, no less city bred than any of the 13th. Nevertheless, its presence in 77 Brigade meant one thing above all to most Kingsmen. Wingate, they bragged, must have reasoned that, if the 13th. – mostly married men with ages averaging 30 – could acquit themselves so well, how superb the 1st., the premier King's battalion, would be. It was specious, but newly boosted regimental pride was blind to any other reasoning.

For their Chindit role the battalion was split into two columns coded 81 and 82 each with, among other elements, a Commando platoon of Kingsmen and Royal Engineer explosives specialists. As far as Badger was concerned, the Commandos were the elite of each column. He was only a lowly leader of one of the three sections of 81's Commando. Section leaders commanded the smallest units in the army, but no general could have been more proud of his position, nor more confident in his ability as a commander.

Six months of intensive training, hard marching, burdened with 60 pounds of arms and victuals, in the fever-infested jungles of central India, had weeded out the weaklings and toughened the strong. Then, with only the sketchiest notion of their whereabouts or destination, beset by rumours, woven of wishful thinking and embellished eavesdropping, 77 Brigade had made the week-long trudge from the Silchar railhead, over the Assam hills to the Imphal Plain.

Eager to get to grips with the Japanese, grousing in their ignorance of the reason, 77 Brigade's eight columns had for what seemed endless weeks, camped around Imphal, deprived of any diverting amenities except the occasional film show or concert party.

Idling away the days, it seemed to Badger that all those months of toughening up, hard marching from dawn to dusk, sweating under monstrous packs, and bone chilling nights under the stars, was going to waste. If they did not move out soon they would be too soft. Instead of roughing it – making do with a blanket and groundsheet – makeshift shelters of tree branches and leaves had began to spring up everywhere.

Men had spent every spare moment out-shining each other, improving their shelters, becoming too conditioned, too attached to the comforts of their 'home from home'. Whatever they were doing – skiving in their bashas, routine weapon cleaning or kit inspections, sporadic lectures or drills – the boredom had nurtured pessimistic 'scuttle butt' and despondency.

"For crying out loud, stop grousing! This is what war is," Badger would officiously admonish, "95% killing time, 5% killing the enemy." He'd read this somewhere and, assuming the mantle of a seasoned soldier, he saw it as his duty to set an example of imperturbability. He wasn't any more seasoned than the rest of his section. Except for pot-shots from Afghan snipers he'd no more combat experience than his 11 men. True, from slit trenches on British airfields, he'd fired at German bombers with obsolete Lewis guns, but so also had others in his section, "Wingate, and the top brass," he would repeatedly affirm, "have not spent all this time and money just for us to picnic here. Churchill will have their guts for garters if they don't get us moving soon."

With more assurance than he felt, he had often opined that they would be in action soon enough, and be wishing their twelve week stint was over, and they were back to lazing about in Assam.

Someone, sometime, had heard that Wingate would have them out of Burma, before the onset of the monsoon rains at the end of May. It had become the 'Gospel truth' that they would be back in India after a twelve week's campaign. It fitted in with the convention that, hitherto, the campaign season in Burma was the dry season, December to June. It was already March.

The weeks of uncertainty had ended with the orders that instead of marching in, 77 Brigade would be flown into Burma. 81 and 82 Columns, in gliders would be the spearhead. The King's were cock-a-hoop.

Wingate had done it again! Last year, towards the end of their jungle training he had got them American 'K' rations, instead of the customary 'dog' biscuits, bully beef and raisins. Now he'd got the 1st. USAAC Air Commandos for them. Not only would they be flown in, but casualties would be flown out in light planes and not left to the mercies of the jungle or Japs like last year. It seemed the ultimate confirmation of the campaign time-scale. You didn't have to be a pilot to know airplanes couldn't operate from muddy jungle clearings, even if it was possible to fly over the mountains in blinding tropical storms.

From then on, there had been little time for idling about. They had moved up to the Lalaghat airstrip, and gazed in awe at their first sight of the Armada of Waco gliders. 80 or more huge, engineless aircraft, paired in six rows, stretching for a mile down the rough grass runway.

In the days that followed, sections were allocated to gliders. Equipment weights and payloads were checked, double checked and triple checked. Bamboo stalls were lashed into those gliders earmarked for carrying a mule as well as men. Dakota planes practiced snatching up two gliders simultaneously, one on a long tow-rope, one on a short.

The King's columns, practiced loading and unloading, coaxing mules in and out of the gliders, emplaning and deplaning themselves and accoutrements. Sappers drummed into the commandos the intricacies of explosives. A US 'G' man schooled them in the art of bursting in on armed men, "...shoot the first man to move, he's the one that thinks fastest..."

In the short time they worked together – the easy going discipline and jaunty confidence of the American crews, in themselves and their aircraft, had won the admiration, adulation almost, of the Chindits. The extrovert Yanks treated every one, however lowly, as as equals. Even their ace fighter pilot commanders, Colonel Phil Cochrane – the model for the legendary cartoon hero Flip Corkin – and Colonel Alison, called everyone 'sport'. Everyone that is except Wingate. Colonel Cochrane always referred to him as 'The Man'.

The Yanks were generous too. They freely shared their 'liberal' amenities – movie shows and superior victuals – with the Chindits. The film star glider pilot, Jackie Coogan titillated them with his Hollywood sexual conquests. His coarse, stock introduction, "Shake the hand that held the cock that fucked Betty Grable" became a sniggering catch phrase, 'Shake the hand that shook the hand....'.

The imminence and importance of the fly-in, had been marked by farewell visits from the top brass. Mountbatten – to the consternation of sergeant majors – had disrupted the formal parade by gathering the troops around the box on which he perched, for his pep talk. General Slim had concluded his inspiring address by saluting them, instead of vice-versa.

Wingate had paraded them, and with solemn voice, told them, "You're going to die," and every Chindit present claimed the piercing eyes were on him alone. Wingate had gone on, "Many of you are going to die, or suffer wounds, or near starvation. All of you will meet hardship worse than anything you have imagined."

Good old Wingate! He didn't try to con the men that they were going on a church picnic. He was endorsing their belief that they were the toughest of the tough. So tough, they believed and bragged to other soldiery, that he had prescribed the harshest discipline code in the Allied Forces. Word of mouth propagation was that the High Command had invested Wingate with exceptional punitive authority. The officers made no attempt to disabuse their men of the belief that he could have them summarily shot or flogged – punishments that had long been abolished.

This unwritten code was so ingrained in Chindit lore that, for desertion or cowardice in the face of the enemy, men were convinced that they could be summarily sentenced to death by a firing squad. For sleeping on sentry, or stealing rations, they could be flogged. For repeated offences of that nature, they could be exiled from their column and, with 5 rounds of ammunition, make their own way back to India to face a courts-martial. Minor offences, so they believed, would be punishable by reduced rations, extra sentry duties, or confiscation of cigarettes.

Brutal as Wingate's supposed powers were, they made sense to the Tommies. When they were hundreds of miles behind enemy lines, conventional punishments – imprisonment, confinement to barracks or stoppages of pay – were absurd. They yarned about Wingate's special powers with perverse pride, and as testimony of their own toughness.

§

Now the great day was here. Chilly dawns had slipped into nameless days. 'D' day had dawned at last. They knew it was a Sunday because their diminutive Burmese padre had held an open air service this morning. Badger, squatting on his bursting back-pack, rifle across his knees under the glider's wing-tip, smiled as he recalled the soldier congregation chanting, "Vouchsafe O Lord, to keep us this day without sin." They didn't need the Lord's help for that. Sin meant only one thing to this congregation – and they hadn't seen a woman for months.

In the late afternoon passwords had been issued, and platoons briefed for one or other of two jungle clearings, code named Piccadilly and Broadway. Itching to overtake 16 Brigade, sections had marched up to their gliders, and now, on the threshold of 'H' hour, they were being held back from emplaning.

800 men, Chindits and Yankee airfield engineers, were killing time. Fretting that some balls-up was about to abort the first Allied airborne invasion of the Far East war. 60 of the 80 gliders were primed, ready to transport men, mules and bulldozers over the distant mountains into Jap occupied Burma.

For what seemed hours, Badger's section had been resting under a wing of their glider. Like those hanging around the dozen gliders ahead, and the scores lined up behind them, they were impatient for some sign from their commanders, grouped around Wingate at the rear of the air Armada.

Even in the fading light, at this great distance, the figures around Wingate, in his battered sun helmet, were unmistakable. There was their stocky idol, Brigadier Calvert in his red-banded service cap. The slight Colonel Alison was hatless in distinctive US khaki. Phil Cochrane in his leather wind-cheater, wore his hat as usual on the back of his head. Tall and lean, there was the King's indomitable Colonel Scott. Earlier, Badger seeing General Slim take Wingate aside, bet himself that their leader was being chastened for some intemperate outburst. Now Wingate, with arms folded across his chest, head bowed, looked gravely troubled as Calvert and Scottie, studying what looked suspiciously like aerial photographs, nodded their heads in unison. Were they agreeing to the abortion, or the 'go-ahead', of the invasion?

If they were going to go they would have to be quick. Dusk was already hazing the flight path. The sun had already dipped below the hills into the distant Bramaphutra valley. Even more important there were only five or six nights of good moon left, and they needed all of these to fly in the three brigades that were to follow the King's spearhead. If they did not go in to-night, Chindit operations could be abolished forever. Wingate's enemies, in the higher planning echelons, could justly argue that a month's wait, for the next moon phase, would be too late in the dry season for the campaign to be mounted.

The eleven men around him, in crumpled jungle greens and felt bush hats, ammunition bandoliers across their chests, dahs on their belts, looked more like scruffy bush-whackers than highly trained soldiers. Regimental as Badger was, the only soldierly neatness he could maintain were his sleeves, rolled tight over his biceps to the exact regulation width of a twenty packet of Players cigarettes. At church parade, that morning, his trousers, sandwiched in ration pack cardboard under his groundsheet each night, had a semblance of a central crease. With the toil and sweat of the day, however, they were as rumpled as everyone else's.

Nearest to him – under the wing – Ryan, Smith, Slater and Nelson, the backbone of the section, were stretched full length alongside each other, heads on their packs, hats tilted over their eyes. Closer to the fuselage, Scofield – his Methodist mucker – squatting on his pack, was studying his New Testament. A little further along, Jones – a recent draftee from the Warwickshires – was cracking jokes with the others.

Another three recent draftees from the Warwickshires, Corporal Oughton, Wyles and Trott – all bearing the stamp of grammar school boys – were lolling against the fuselage. Glancing at them, Badger pitied, rather than envied them, for their middle class upbringing and superior education. Their proper 'English', with no trace of dialect, their references to 'mummie', never 'ma' or 'mam'; letters from their 'nannies', damned them as effeminate snobs, and barred them from close fellowship with the others. Wyles and Trott, with their maidenly frames and comely faces and infantile sulks, were the mirrors of each other. They belonged behind the counter of a bespoke gentlemen's outfitters. If they had to be in the Army, they should be behind the desks of the Pay Corps, not in the rugged and vulgar world of a tough infantry mob. Their ineptness with weapons; having to mothering them through field exercises; and their infantile sulks when they were teased or rebuked, had tried Badger's patience to the limit.

The tall, dark and overly handsome Oughton was a cynical, arrogant and overgrown school prefect. Swotting for his matriculation seemed to have crowded tact and commonsense from his brains.

Loud laughs switched Badger's attention to the Jones' group. He caught the word 'Lottie' and guessed they were yarning about the pranks of Lottie Collins, the battalion's consummate con-artist and scrounger.

The stocky, fair haired Jones, was dabbing laughter tears from his cheeks with the backs of his hands. Why couldn't he have got another three Warwickshire draftees like Jones, instead of the other twirps. Jones was a conscript like them, but was proving a first class soldier. He was quick witted, resourceful and never needed mothering to get a job done.

Near the tailplane, a muleteer was dabbing wound powder on Daisy's right fore-knee. The broad backed mule had cut her knee when, stubbornly resisting initial attempts to coax her into a glider, she had shied and stumbled. The muleteer, a raw boned farmer's lad, was as much a stranger as when he had joined the platoon a couple of weeks ago. Whether on the march or in bivouac, he kept himself to himself, rarely speaking except to Daisy. He spent every moment he was free of other duties alongside Daisy, ceaselessly whispering to the de-brayed creature as he groomed her or cleaned her harness.

"Where do you think you're going, Wyles?"

"Only for a pee, corporal." The slim, fresh faced lad shambling towards the tailplane, stopped in mid-stride, uncertain whether he needed Badger's permission.

"Haven't you forgotten something?"

"Oh, yes." Wyles turned about, picked up his rifle from under the fuselage, and headed again for the tailplane.

"Come back, you bloody idiot!" Badger clapped his hands to his head in despair. "What've you been told a hundred bleeding times?"

"What have I blooming done now corp?" Bewildered and pained by the urging of his bladder, the lad looked imploringly at Badger.

"It's not what you've done you silly bugger, it's what you're not doing." Badger glared at Trott. "Tell him!"

"Tell him what, corp?" Trott stared nonplussed at Badger.

"For Christ's sake tell 'em someone before Wyles pisses himself!" Badger's blasphemy brought a reproving frown from Scofield.

"Don't move a yard without your mucker!" yelled the whole section.

"And who's his mucker, Trott?" Badger glared questioningly at Trott.

"Well I am, but he's only going..."

"No matter where he's going, you stick together like shit to a blanket. If you want to see your mummies again, you two had better get the mucker rules fixed in your minds. Mallum?" Without waiting for a reply Badger dropped his voice to an exasperated whisper, "I've told you umpteen times, and Captain Williams reminded you dozy buggers only this morning, you move nowhere – do nothing – without your mucker. If a Jap catches one of you alone, with your pants down... oh go on, juldee, before Wyles wets himself!"

"Put that fag out!" Partly hidden by Daisy, the muleteer was furtively lighting a cigarette. Badger pointed to two jerricans of petrol in the shadow of the tailplane, "You know what the orders are! But you shouldn't need any orders when that's about."

"What you going to do if I don't, corp?" Smirking over Daisy's withers, the muleteer contemptuously blew smoke rings, "Put me on a fizzer?"

"Don't be so bloody cocky. You know the discipline code – you could get a flogging for that once we're in Burma."

The muleteer, casually flicked the ash from his cigarette, and with a disdainful 'you don't scare me' smirk, took out a curry comb, and started to brush Daisy's rump.

"Flogging is nothing to what you'll get from me, if you don't put out that fag – sharpish."

"Yeah, you and whose army?" The muleteer stood up to his full height, elbows resting on top of the pack saddle.

Slowly, deliberately, Badger laid his rifle on the ground, unhooked his belt, and shrugged out of his webbing equipment.

"Put it out, before you start a fire. Now!"

The soft voiced order carried the icy, silent threat 'before I knock it out!'. The recumbent foursome instantly sat upright. Wyles and

Trott, twenty yards away stood stock still, fingers frozen on their fly buttons. Eleven pairs of eyes see-sawed from Badger's menacingly narrowed eyes, to the muleteer's blanching face.

Out of the corner of his eye, Badger saw Ryan and Smith starting to rise. With an almost imperceptible flick of his hand he signalled them to stay where they were. Jack Ryan and Smudger Smith had soldiered with Badger since the outbreak of war. They knew he had never relied on formal charges to assert his authority, and he had once – undeservedly – been demoted for responding with his fists to the taunts of a bolshie private.

Even the rancorous elements of the section never disputed that, for all his regimental officiousness, Badger was a dedicated and caring NCO. He had mothered the dimmest wits of the section through their training and without vindictiveness, had shouldered any officer's castigation of the section due to their shortcomings. Now a stupid confrontation had the makings of a courts-martial for him.

The whisk of Daisy's tail hissed through the fraught seconds.

The muleteer was a head and shoulders taller than any of them, but whatever the pugilistic outcome, Badger would be on a loser to nothing. If he followed up his threat, the CO would have no alternative but to strip him of his rank, and post him to another platoon. The section would lose a dependable leader, and their lives would be in the hands of some greenhorn, like the uppity Oughton.

Badger held out his hat to Ryan. Ignoring the hat, the stocky bull-necked Lancastrian with the rugged street fighter's features, that belied a keen intellect, started to get up. Smith, Slater and Nelson followed suit. The message was obvious. Private soldiers are not fettered by stripes. One of them, not Badger, would take on the muleteer.

Over Daisy's withers, the muleteer gave a resigned shrug and muttering inaudibly, ground the cigarette into the earth with his boot.

The tension lifted, Badger picked up his webbing and as he buckled his belt, the Captain's batman trotted up to their glider.

"All section leaders report to Captain Williams, sharpish."

§

"That's it, get your gliders loaded as quickly as you can." Capt. Williams, their wiry Welsh platoon commander, dismissed his NCOs from the briefing session with a relieved grin, "With luck we should be airborne in half an hour." He glanced at his watch, "Not bad after all. Only about half an hour behind schedule. Good luck!"

The airstrip was a hubbub of activity as Badger, with his mucker Scofield at his heels, doubled back to the section. Pilots were hurrying from their new flight briefings, waving hasty farewells as they fanned out down the long files of gliders. Ground crews were swiftly checking tow lines. Mike Calvert, Scottie and Alison with the leading elements, were scrambling into the half dozen foremost pairs of gliders.

To the rear of the files of troop carriers, US field engineers were double checking the bulldozers and jeeps in the bellies of the freight gliders. With their top hinged noses swung up, the freighters looked like mammoth open jawed whales.

"Good and bad news, lads." Badger, with forced nonchalance, grinned broadly as the section eagerly gathered round him, "Good news is we're going in any moment now. Bad news is that all gliders are going to Broadway..."

"Why?" the entire section chorused.

"Don't know, officially." Badger paused, debating whether or not to repeat the rumour, "Heard the Yanks saying Piccadilly's been blocked by logs."

"Fucking hell!" someone cried, and there was a stunned silence as the grave implications sank in.

It was Corporal Oughton who broke the silence, voicing their fears, "The Japanese must have got wind of us." Typically, the haughty Oughton believed he, and he alone, had grasped the dreadful portent of the rumour, "They'll be waiting for us at Broadway. We could all be annihilated!"

"Worse than that," Ginger Slater cut in drolly, "It could be bloody dangerous. Can I go home, me mam'll kill me if I'm caught with shitty pants."

"Its no joking matter," Oughton snapped above the forced guffaws, "We're flying into a trap."

"That was my immediate thought," Badger held up a hand to silence the muttering, "but we don't know for certain Piccadilly has been blocked." He looked sagely at Oughton, "And, if it's true, it doesn't mean they are waiting for us at Broadway. It may be a routine precaution, like stakes in fields in England during the invasion scare. Don't forget Piccadilly was used to evacuate casualties last year. There was a photo in Picture Post."

"That's right," came a relieved voice from one of half a dozen nodding heads.

"OK lads, take the worst case. If they're waiting for us, what's going to happen?" Badger paused to marshal a plausible scenario, and looked vainly at each man for some helpful comment, "They're not going to open fire on the first gliders to land, are they? The others would turn back when they saw the gun flashes." A weak point, but most heads nodded agreement, "So they'll plan to wait until they think we are all down."

"I'll go along with that." Ryan interrupted, firmly and confidently.

"What's the first thing we do when we land? We push out patrols and set up defence perimeters."

"The man's a genius. Give him a toffee apple." Ginger Slater playfully elbowed Ryan in the ribs, "Took the words right out of my gob."

"Dead right, Jack." Bolstered by Jack's concurrence, Badger resumed with an air of professorial infallibity, "They can't completely surround the clearing, they'd be shooting at each other." In fact gaps in the Japs encirclement could be mined, but he kept that notion to himself, "So, if our recce patrols bump them, the firing will warn Alison to turn the others back before they land. If our patrols don't bump them, we'll have found a defensible area..."

"But what if..." Oughton interrupted.

"O.K, its not going to be a piece of cake,." Badger cut in swiftly, anxious to prevent any question undermining his pacifying speculation, "but there's a more important inference." An inspired thought attenuated Badger's private dread of the fate that threatened them, "If the Japs had really got wind of us, would they tip us off by blocking one field? Not on your Nelly. They'd set up ambushes at both strips. Any arguments about that?"

Badger could almost feel relief surge through the section.

"Bet Slater didn't think about that." Oughton jibed, trying to redress his initial alarm.

"My name's got a handle, Corporal Oughton." 'Ginger' or 'Tom' was strictly for pals, and the newcomer Oughton had yet to earn that privilege, "Its Private Slater, if you please." Exchanging winks with Badger, he went on, "If you hadn't come up with that one Badger, I'd have asked how to spell resign."

"But it's all supposition..." Wyles glumly muttered, "They could still be waiting for us, couldn't they?"

"They could," Smith – Ryan's phlegmatic and barrel chested mucker – took the words from Badger's lips, "but, you dim wit, if the Japs knew we were coming they wouldn't tip us off by blocking Piccadilly. So they aren't likely to be waiting at Broadway for us."

"Wingate and Calvert must think that, too."

With an approving nod at Smith, Badger shouldered his pack.

"Get a move on, corporal!" Their co-pilot, an RAF officer, was irately beckoning from the glider door, "Cut the chatter and get everything aboard."

"Right away, sir. Come on lads, let's get Daisy and the stores aboard, juldee, juldee now!"

§

The glider had persistently yawed, and sickeningly banked left and right, since they were air-borne. Tail gusts repeatedly slackened the tow-line. Instantly the unburdened tow-plane would spurt forward, jolting the glider occupants as it jerked the line to breaking-strain tension.

Straining his eyes in the gloom of the glider, Badger studied the faces of the men opposite him. Were they as apprehensive as he was? None of them had ever flown in a plane before, let alone one of these frail engine-less crates. His own experience amounted to a brief flight in a two seater biplane, during his aircraft sabotage course.

At Lalaghat, veiling their trepidation with wise-cracks, they'd piled into the glider, 'All aboard the Skylark – once round the Blackpool tower back in time for tea', 'Who nicked the bleeding engine', 'Dear Mam, sell the pig and buy me out', 'Dear Son, pig dead, soldier on'. Trying to out-jest each other they'd jostled for floor space for themselves, their weapons and bulky equipment. 'That's my fucking toe. You'll kill someone with that rifle!', 'Aw, shit in it Smudge!', 'Put a plank across it and we'll all shit in it!' Then the whiplashing jar, as the tow plane snatched them into the air had robbed them of their humour.

Penned by bamboo rails – athwart the forward end – Daisy, eyes wide with fear and ears back with anger, constantly fidgeted for balance on wobbling, quivering legs. At her head the muleteer ceaselessly whispered into her nostrils. By her hindquarters, barely beyond reach of her flicking tail, Badger was frequently afflicted by the poor beast's venting dock.

The twelve men squatted, six each side of the equipment and stores, stacked down the centre of the creaking fuselage. Turbulence thumped them against each other and slapped them into the airframe stanchions. The wind, whipping the fuselage and threatening to rip the canvas walls, whined through the plyboard decking and drowned their curses. Gusts intermittently carried back smatterings of the the calm, matter-of-fact radio exchanges, between glider and tow plane pilot.

Without a watch Badger could only guess how long they'd been airborne. It seemed they'd pitched and juddered along at scarcely more than stalling speed for at least and hour. Each time the glider took a belly-knotting dive he prayed they were not over the 7000ft. Chin peaks. It had seemed obvious since take-off that even with their scheduled 4,500 lbs. untried payloads, they would have been dangerously overloaded. As it was, the Tommies – taking advantage of lax controls – had smuggled unauthorised supplies aboard.

A violent side slip thrust Badger across the stacked equipment, before the swifter reverse slip thumped him back against the airframe. Daisy lurched forward, straightened, and slapped her buckling haunches into the fuselage. Tossed to and fro, the men grasped airframe stanchions, bracing themselves against each lurching roll. For a heart-pounding infinity, the canvas creaked.

Every strut shuddered, the cross bracings creaked. In an eternally brief nightmare, they veered, skewed, dipped and tilted.

"Whoa! Ride 'em cowboy!" someone cried.

Another, more alarmed cried, "Wingate wasn't fucking kidding telling us we all going to die!"

Then they were through turbulence, surging forward, moderately yawing and swaying in gentle degrees back into a balanced roll.

"There they go! Good luck fellahs!" The pilot's calm drawl, focused all eyes on the cock-pit, "Better tell the guys back there, bud."

"Nothing for us to worry about, chaps," the co-pilot slewed round in his seat, and called, "the long-tow pilot has cut loose. Apparently we were swinging across him, threatening to foul his line. They should be able to land safely. Should have a more comfortable ride now. Be there in about half an hour."

Hope the poor buggers don't land in the Jap front line, Badger silently prayed. Alarmed though he was during the worst moments of the flight, the thought that if his glider crashed, none of them might survive never entered Badger's head. His overwhelming worry was they'd not been given Broadway's map reference.

He fingered his silk neckerchief. The bright orange material was both a small scale map of Northern and Central Burma,[6] and a means of signalling to aircraft. One of each man's waist band buttons was a micro compass. But it was little more than a novelty, almost useless for working out a bearing. Even without a compass Badger was confident that, given its grid reference, he'd have no difficulty finding Broadway with the 'panic map' kerchief. He'd drummed into the section half a dozen ways of working out cardinal bearings without a compass or watch. A Watch! That was the most grievous deficiency.

Someone, in the higher regions of the Quartermaster-General's department, had decreed that compasses and watches must only be issued to platoon sergeants and above. A compass was important, but in Badger's view a watch was vital for a section leader. A watch could serve as a compass. How many times had he drilled into the section's dim wits, 'point the hour hand to the sun, bisect the angle the sun and 12 o'clock, and that's south'? And how could he time the changing of sentries, every night for the next three months without a watch? In daytime bivouacs he could probably improvise a sun-dial. But at night? He'd have to think up some rule of thumb reference to the moon or stars.

The Chin ranges must be well behind them now. The wind was still soughing through the fuselage but they were only gently, soporifically rolling now. Heads were beginning to nod drowsily. Even Daisy seemed to be dozing.

The leading elements in the gliders ahead must be there by now. Scottie would be pushing out patrols to secure the landing zone. Only if the Japs were there in overwhelming strength, would he fire the red flare to turn the rest of the armada back. Alison and his men would be marking out the strip with three lines of petroleum flares. That at least was no secret. At the first line across the strip, gliders would cut off their tows, at the second they would touch down. At the third, the gliders would stop, men would pile out and drag their glider clear of the strip.

Why were they so secretive about the grid reference for Broadway? They could, at least, have given out the reference as soon as they were airborne. If a glider crashed, the Japs might wring Broadway's location from any survivors, but then it would be too late for them to muster substantial opposition to the landings. If they didn't already know, they surely would soon. An Armada like this, landing in enemy territory, couldn't remain undetected for very long. The risk of the Japs getting the map reference from captured Chindits, was far less important than the risk of survivors being lost in the jungle through ignorance. Well, the co-pilot probably knew their destination, Badger drowsily consoled himself. He was a stranger to them, and Badger sleepily vowed that one of the first things he'd do if they crashed, would be to demand that every man be told the location of Broadway. The rest would be no problem. They had been toughened to jungle conditions, were as much at home in them as their native cities. If they exhausted the five day's rations, now in their packs, they could live off the land. Burma's mighty rivers were minor obstacles to fit men, they'd swum or rafted scores on exercises in India. If only they'd not been so parsimonious with the watches... can time be judged by the stars? Do they move uniformly?

§

"Right chaps, brace yourselves!" The co-pilot's shout roused Badger from his doze, "We're cutting from the Dakota. Broadway, here we come!"

The glider wobbled roughly and, with a terrifying hiss, dived steeply.

"110, 105." The co-pilot called out their air speed, "100, 95..."

With a ginormous thump they hit the ground, and bounded high into the air. All four of Daisy's hoofs seemed to simultaneously leap from the decking. Badger was heaved, head and shoulders into her hindquarters. The glider thwacked the ground again and Daisy's rump smashed into his face.

Blinded by an explosion of stars, he dabbed the salty taste from his lips as the glider rumbled to a halt. His nose was numb, his kerchief saturated with blood.

"Out you get, chaps, smartly. Wheel this bouncing bitch off the runway!" The co-pilot's order was superfluous. The section were already scrambling out. The buckled undercarriage was embedded in the rutted ground. They heaved and cursed, and heaved again, and again. The glider would not budge.

Through the multi-focus of watering eyes, Badger strove to get his bearings. Behind them the rough runway stretched beyond his vision. The rutted ground obscured all but the flame tips of the touch down line of petroleum flares, five hundred yards behind their glider. A hundred yards ahead lay the third line of flares, and beyond them two gliders were wedged in the trees at the jungle edge.

Excited shouts seemed to be coming from all quarters. Somewhere men were moaning. A few yards off a glider was nose down in a ditch. From close by, clear of the runway, Captain Williams was calling for the 'Commando Platoon'.

With no hope of moving the glider, Badger led the section at the double, towards the platoon commander's voice.

A swish behind them accelerated to a roar. To yells of "Gliders", the section flattened themselves on the ground. In a fusillade of horrendous splintering, the off-course glider ploughed into the jungle.

"Good, that's all the Commando platoon safely down corporal." Captain Williams said with obvious relief, and then gasped when his torch lit Badger's face, "What on earth happened to you, Corporal?"

"Arse end of a mule sir." Nasal, lisping as if hare lipped.

"Poor bloody Daisy," jibed Oughton, as the section saw the swollen face for the first time, "Did you hurt her?"

Scofield tenderly dabbed the bloody face with his field dressing.

"Can you carry on for a while, corporal?"

"I'll be OK sir, ouch!" He winced as Scofield pressed his nostrils.

"Good man. We need every man we've got for the next few hours. Colonel Scott has got patrols out, no sign of Japs. That's the only good news." Grim voiced, "Gliders seem to be crashing everywhere. They're trying to turn the rest back. They're setting up a dressing station over there." He pointed to a cluster of torches at the jungle edge, "We've got to concentrate on hauling out the wounded. Start on the glider nearest yours. Keep a sharp eyed lookout, you can't hear them 'til its too late."

As they dumped their packs and equipment the muleteer, leading Daisy up to them, yelled in horror, "Oh my God! Look at that one dropping!"

High above the approach path, a glider's wing-lights momentarily wobbled. Transfixed with awe, they watched the lights plummet to the ground, too distant for the sound of impact to reach their ears.

Within seconds another glider was swooping down the flight path. Yet another, following fast on its tail, turned abruptly to avoid a collision. Banking sharply over their heads, almost reversing its direction, it vanished into the distant jungle.

When the section reached the wreck to which the Captain had assigned them, a medical officer was trying to ease a blood drenched sergeant out of the distorted airframe.

"Don't move me, please, Doc." He groaned. It was more an instruction than a plea, "This is where I lit, and this is where I die."

The MO carefully rested the almost severed torso back on a stanchion.

"The Yank and his co-pilot are dead." He gestured to the pilot and British officer in the crumpled nose cone, "Leave them. Get any live ones out before another glider hits us. I'm going to the dressing station."

From the jumble of contorted corpses, they dragged out two groaning Kingsmen. Four of the section, almost at a run, carried the casualties to the dressing station. They were hauling out a third man when the look-out yelled, "Gliders! Gliders!"

The warning came too late for them to race from the runway. Stock still they listened to the whine rise to a roar, and the wings seemed to brush their heads. Flinching as the glider thumped the ground beyond them, Badger watched it vault into the air again, and crump into another, fifty yards ahead. Before he could decide whether to send half the section to the new wreck he heard, with relief, shouts and dimly saw shadowy figures scrambling from it.

"Come on lads, let's get the others out of this one sharpish." It was a needless directive, the section were already pulling out more casualties.

The bridge of his nose was throbbing like a steam hammer. His swollen cheeks felt anaesthetized, his eyes had closed to mere slits. His focus was now almost normal, but wing lights of disabled gliders, and petroleum flares were rainbowed haloes. He blinked, and rubbed his eyelids. The haloes were still there. Worried that they might be permanently damaged, he cupped his eyes to shield out wing lights, and squinted across the half mile clearing. In the centre of the strip he could just make out two trees. No haloes. Must be only the lights. With a sigh of relief he saw the pale, three-quarter moon and the few clouds as clearly, distinctly as ever. No haloes.

From an immobilised glider, beyond the last flare line there were yells of "Glider! Glider!" Rescuers scampered from the runway. Someone yelled, "Look out sir!" Badger's stomach turned over. A plunging glider was heading straight at Mike Calvert. With a split second to spare, Mike jumped clear. With thunderous splintering it tore into the jungle, the trees shearing off its wings. The fuselage rumbled on, and halted nose down. For a moment there was silence, and then a crunching of undergrowth.

It seemed a forlorn hope that anyone could survive the crash but, instinctively, Badger joined others running towards it. At the edge of the jungle they stopped dead. It wasn't a forlorn hope. Someone was guffawing, heartily, or hysterically.

It was a bloody miracle. The pilot and co-pilot – a US Lieutenant Brockett – the only men who had been in the glider were jovially, almost exultantly, describing their escape. The trees had stripped the wings clean off, but the fuselage was intact and, a few yards beyond it, stood a bull-dozer. The impact had severed the bull-dozer's anchorage, and it had rushed forward, threatening to crush them in their seats. At that instant, the nose had swung up, carrying the two men with it. The bull-dozer had rolled beneath them, and the nose cone dropped down.

"I planned it just that way." Jested the pilot as he strolled around the wreck.

Minutes sped into hours as gliders roared down into Broadway. With sweat-chilled bodies, survivors toiled through the chaos. Hauling out the injured, manhandling gliders clear of the runway. Others went out with patrols, vainly scouring the jungle for missing gliders.

In the moonlit commotion of crying wounded, shouting rescuers, plunging and scudding gliders, Yanks and Tommies hurried from wreck to wreck. Smothering their grief for dead comrades, they hauled the maimed from the wrecks to the dressing station. They fought off nausea as medical officers amputated limbs by torch light. Their anguished souls erupted with boisterous, childish relief, when missing mates appeared, overcompensating for the current horrors, and the morrow's fears.

In a sort of time warp, they worked with ears constantly attuned for the laboured drone of tow planes. Their nerves stretched taut. Their limbs primed for instant flight from the path of wayward gliders.

§

When the section gathered for breakfast, a few yards inside the jungle, the mist of the incipient dawn was already hazing the landing zone.

"Nearly five o'clock, Corporal." Captain Williams wearily flopped down on his pack alongside Badger. "Keep it to half a mug each lads," he warned the men brewing tea in pairs, on small fires, "and no shaving this morning, we've not found any water source yet. Fires out in ten minutes"

Chindit fires were works of art. Two small teak logs laid lengthwise over a narrow trench, precisely parallel, to safely bear a pair of mess tins. Even when water supplies were abundant, brewing up periods made no allowance for slip shod fire making. If a messtin slopped over, the columns could be on the move again before a second attempt could be made.

"Must be a couple of hours since the last glider came in, sir." Was it eleven hours since they left Lalaghat? The night had flown by, but Badger's limbs were as fatigued as if they had not rested for days, "Thank God, they must have stopped half of the gliders before take off, sir." Hoping he was right, Badger looked at the captain for confirmation. If he wasn't right, dozens of gliders must have crashed before reaching Broadway. The captain nodded uncertainly, and handed his mug to his hovering batman.

Fighting off sleep, munching his 'K' ration breakfast biscuits and meat loaf, Badger scanned the wreckage-strewn clearing. The rough runway was rutted with ditches. Ploughed by elephants hauling teak logs? Around him, like all Tommies down the generations, the section were grousing at the 'balls up' that the nebulous 'they' had made. 'It wasn't the size of the clearing that was at fault, it was easily big enough to take all 60 gliders'. 'Yes. Even if there'd been no last minute switch of all gliders into Broadway, the result would have been the bleeding same.' 'Why hadn't aerial recce shewn the fucking ditches?' 'And that sodding bunch of trees on the runway!' 'What makes you think them pricks bother to do any recce?' 'Practice landings in India, before we'd even seen a sodding glider, are one thing – night landings with loaded gliders in virgin territory are another .' 'Aye and I'll bet they were only single tows.' 'Our pilot was bloody good. Nerves of steel. Just kept chewing his gum. Might have been driving a charabanc...' 'Bloody pilots were not to blame, you pillock! Them in Delhi expected too much of the poor cock-suckers' 'S'right, heard some Yank saying he'd never practiced with a double tow.' 'And the bleeding undercarriages weren't strong enough. Didya see those wheels shear off...' '..Staff Officers, I've shit better than them. Didn't allow enough time between take-offs, didn't give us enough time to wheel them off the runway between landings.' 'Wheel 'em? Some of 'em 'ad no fucking wheels.'

Sitting aside from the rest, studiously charging his pipe, Badger silently added to their tattling. 'Gliders had cut off too bleeding soon... Come in too fast... Too high... Stalled trying to make a second circuit... Wing lights left on to mark wrecks could have confused incoming pilots.'

The condemnations and opining were clearly, deliberately loud enough to tempt comment from their platoon commander. Sipping at his steaming tea, Captain Williams remained silent. He might only be a war-time soldier, but Badger knew Williams was wise to his men's ways. They were not mutinous. Their morale had been dented. They'd survived the debacle, and grousing about the real or imagined blunders of some anonymous 'they' was the salve for their lacerated nerves.

Williams could not know much more about any 'balls up' than they did. In any case, as a loyal officer – regardless of his personal feelings – he'd be obliged to intervene as devil's advocate to preserve higher command integrity. And intervening would imperil the mutual trust and confidence that months of training had built up. Mark him as one of 'them', destroy his reputation as a 'good scout'.

"How do feel corporal?" Williams scanned Badger's bruised face, "Better get the MO to take a look at your face as soon as he's finished at the dressing station. You look as though you've just gone 15 rounds with Joe Louis."

"Will do, sir." Gently palpating his puffy cheeks, Badger forced a wry smile, and dashed the dregs of tea on to the fire embers. "What next, sir?" With querying eyebrows, he peered at Williams through his pipe smoke.

"We'll know soon enough, corporal. The CO will be holding an officers' briefing shortly." Stretching flat out, head pillowed on his pack, the captain added, "See that the fires are put out straight away."

The section stamped out their fires, erased all evidence of their breakfasting and, gathering at the jungle edge, counted and re-counted the gliders. They could see only about thirty. They'd seen two disappear into the jungle, and the long-tow glider of their pair had cut off way back somewhere. That accounted for only thirty three of the sixty scheduled for the mission. Only about 350 men out of 800 could have landed, and at least fifty – Tommies and Yanks – had been killed or injured.

As Badger glanced around the section, eleven pairs of sombre eyes seemed to be asking what their lips dare not utter, seeking an answer their ears dreaded, 'What had happened to the other half of the battalion?'

It was Badger's mucker, Scofield – the devout Methodist – who solemnly voiced their fears, "They can't all be back at Lalaghat, can they?" The question was rhetorical, and the short, lean lad went on, "We were airborne for hours. They wouldn't know about this," he gestured at the wrecks, "before all gliders had taken off. So where are they? Teddy Courtcliffe was only a couple of gliders behind us, and he's not turned up."

"That's right – I haven't seen Kennedy..." someone said.

"...Or Kemp, and they were in P15 ahead of us," another chipped in.

"Or Jack Lindo and his muckers, they were in B18," yet another doleful voice added.

A seemingly endless roll call of missing Kingsmen poured from the section. With each name Badger's mind, muzzy with pain and fatigue, was overlaying images of their faces on those of last night's dead. The gentle blonde features of Sergeant Lenwell, '..here I die..' merged with Bill May's, Lottie Collins' and a dozen other corpses, and took on a foggy likeness of each missing pal. He was on the verge of tears, and was glad his bruise blackened cheeks gave him the excuse to dab his eyes.

"Four hundred men missing," the muleteer glumly muttered, as he joined the group, "Fifty killed or injured. Before we've fired a shot!"

"It's Murphy's law," despairingly Badger shook his head, "If something can go wrong – it will, and hasty planning is an open invitation for it."

"Yes corporal, it *is* Murphy's law!" Captain Williams's stern tone, as he strolled up behind them, was clearly an admonition to cut the grousing, "Leave it at that! If we'd marched in we'd probably have lost a lot more men. I'm going to column HQ. Be ready to move off at a minute's notice."

Watching the platoon commander stride away, Badger wondered and admired, as he had done many times marching behind him, how Williams's short, slightly bandy legs could cover so much ground with each stride. The sure-footed captain as always, seemed to skip over the ground, light footed as a boxer, and reminded Badger of that Irish-Scouse rogue Lottie Collins.

Poor old Corporal Collins, he would be charming the wings off the angels now, just as he'd charmed the money out of rookies' pockets. Lottie, the consummate con man, and middle weight boxer, owed his stripes more to his ring-craft than any soldierly competence. Badger clicked his tongue, knocked the ash out of his pipe and, as they wandered back to their breakfast site, a broad grin replaced the sombre look on his bruised face.

"What's tickling you?" Scofield grabbed Badger's arm.

"Lottie Collins. Remember how he spoofed the Yanks into buying all those drinks, in India, posing as a British aristocrat. His Eton accent was perfect."

"Yes, and what about the time he threw that kukri..."

"What kukri?" The muleteer was the only man neither grinning widely nor chuckling.

Half a dozen tongues vied with each other to enlighten the outsider. Lottie, walking along at Lalaghat had thrown his kukri at a potato ten yards away. Miraculously it had sliced the potato in half. Yank aircrews chatting nearby, were stunned to silence. Lottie had picked up the kukri, wiped the blade and whistling quietly, nonchalantly strolled on, as if the feat was a mere everyday trifle. A Yank had observed, "Jeez, boy, I'd hate to be a Jap with these guys around."

Now Lottie was dead. He'd crawled to the door of his wrecked glider, gasped "Ah, fuck it!" and dropped dead. The 'artful dodger' always was something of a fatalist. Rather than building a shelter, like his muckers, when they were languishing in Assam, he'd slept in the rain. "I was pissed on last night," he would chant, "I was pissed on the night before, and I don't care if I never wake up no more." It was typical for him to give up life that way. And somehow, reminiscing about him dispelled their grief for him.

§

"Settle down, rest easy and pay attention to the platoon commander." The platoon sergeant, Bob Gregory, motioned the chattering sections to squat around Captain Williams, "It's the last rest you're likely to get for the next twelve hours or more."

Nothing ever seemed to ruffle Bob, a volunteer from the Essex Regiment, and a former London fire officer. The lithe, soft spoken sergeant had the most intriguing eyes Badger had ever seen, one blue, one brown. His recent posting to the battalion had quashed Badger's hopes of promotion, but they had swiftly acquired a close rapport.

"Right lads, Colonel Scott wants you all put in the picture as to what's happened and what's in store." Captain Williams glanced quickly at his field service note-book, "Fifty four gliders took off and only thirty seven gliders reached Broadway." A chorus of horrified gasps. "It's not as bad as it sounds. Many of them returned to Lalaghat, and some of those that landed in the jungle are making their way either to us, or back to Assam. Those forced landings could buy us time to consolidate Broadway. Gliders landing all over the place will have the Japs guessing our main objective..." Somewhere in the jungle a heavy duty engine roared. "...if all went well last night, Brigadier Calvert had arranged to radio the signal 'Pork Sausage' back to base, otherwise he would send 'Soya Link'. Last night he sent 'Soya Link' because of the wrecks, and to stop any more take-offs." Williams paused, cocking his ears, like the rest of his platoon, to tune into the sound of a labouring jeep engine.

The 'Soya Link' code brought sardonic grins. The soya flour substitutes for meat sausages, were among the worst evils inflicted on troops in India, whereas pork sausages were heavenly, unobtainable luxuries.

"With first light, things don't seem so bad," the captain resumed, "we've lost the mechanical grader and some heavy earth movers, but two bulldozers and a jeep with a scraper are OK Seven of Lieutenant Brockett's engineers have survived, and he's positive that, with the King's help he can have a strip ready for Dakotas by nightfall. So the Brigadier has now sent 'Pork Sausage'..." He paused again as a passing bulldozer, barging through undergrowth, lumbered out of the trees onto the strip. "...so that's our task for to-day. Patrols are scouting for water, missing gliders and Japs. The Dakotas will bring in the other columns of 77 Brigade, the Lancashire Fusiliers, South Staffords, 3/6th. Gurkhas and all the rest. Field artillery and equipment will be coming in to turn Broadway into a stronghold. Light planes are coming for the wounded, and there'll be a burial service this morning. Any questions?"

"Does that mean we are going to garrison the stronghold, sir?" There was a hint of dismay in Badger's tone. The last thing any of the section wanted was to be cooped up in a defensive perimeter, waiting for the Japs to attack. They wanted to be out harrying the enemy, sabotaging his supply lines. That was what they'd so assiduously trained for.

"No corporal, it does not." Relieved smiles all round, "The 3/9th. Gurkhas are being flown in for that. Both King's columns will be floaters, patrolling from the Irrawaddy to the Kaukwee hills, with one column always close enough to kick the backsides of the Japs if they attack Broadway. Does that ease your minds?"

Someone called "Good ho!"

"Brigadier Calvert will take the rest of the brigade into the Moguang Valley. Colonel Rome will come in to command the Stronghold." Williams turned to Bob Gregory, "Do you want to add anything, sergeant?"

"Only this, sir... It's going to be hard and thirsty work. Take only your weapons, bandoliers and entrenching tools. Right, on your feet!" Gregory pointed to the mules tethered 50 yards further into the jungle, "Dump all your kit over there, the muleteers will keep watch over it... Everything!" Two or three men were preparing to take their water bottles with them, "That includes water bottles!"

In single file, rifles slung over one shoulder and entrenching tools over the other; whistling 'Colonel Bogey' and mimicking worn out navvies, they followed the platoon commander across last night's landing strip.

In the bright sunlight they saw the true extent of the clearing for the first time. In an irregular oval, it had a roughly East-West axis of over a mile and a half, and was more than half a mile at its widest breadth. One bulldozer was already tearing up the two lone trees in the centre of the clearing. The other and the jeep-scraper – shrouded in dust clouds – were ramming away hillocks and filling the ruts.

The prospect of a Gurkha garrison and Colonel Rome – Mike Calvert's second-in-command – turning Broadway into a Stronghold had raised everyone's spirits. Exhilaration banished the exhaustion of the night. Enthusiasm overcame lamentation. All that mattered now was to hack out a 2000 yards runway to receive the Dakotas. Without that there could be no Stronghold. With it Broadway would become an arsenal, a refuge and evacuation base for wounded, a safe harbour between exhausting guerilla operations.

The immutable motto of Strongholds was 'No Surrender' but, given time for consolidation, that motto would be superfluous. Surrounded by mountains, remote from motorable roads, the doughty Claude Rome and dauntless Gurkhas, would put Broadway's impregnability beyond doubt. The Allies had air supremacy. A few Jap bombers, slipping through the net might inflict a few casualties, but would not dislodge a well dug-in garrison. Ground assaults could only be mounted, and sustained, with such weapons and supplies as men and animals could carry via precipitous tracks, vulnerable to ambushes, and harried by floating columns. If Hirohito's honour drove his troops to try that, they would be committing mass hari-kari. The entrenched defenders, and field guns would slaughter them.

Imbued with optimism, almost hoping that the temptation to attack the Stronghold would prove irresistible to the Japs, the King's working parties laboured tirelessly. In the heat and dust, they hacked at the ground with entrenching tools, filling ruts, levelling bumps. Their throats parched, mouths gritty, they tugged up bushes and hauled away disabled gliders.

"Here they come!" A look-out pointed to the distant tree tops as he yelled. With the bright mid-morning sun glistening their windscreens, a line of light planes was skimming the jungle roof. Two hundred aching backs straightened up. With hands easing their stiffened back muscles, they strained back their heads to watch the planes swoop down on to the runway. It seemed incredible to Badger that the pilots of these small unarmed machines, easy meat for Jap fighters, had flown over 200 miles in broad daylight over enemy territory.

"Those Yanks must have nerves of steel," Captain Williams said as he rejoined the platoon, "Take a ten minute break lads. The planes are not the only good news. I've just been over to Column HQ, they've found a good stream. Let's go over for our water bottles and chagauls, and send a squad to fill them."

"Will they take out the wounded straight away, sir?" Badger took a mouthful of water, swilled it round his gritty gums and spat it out.

"I hope so, corporal, but it's asking a lot from them. Jap fighters could've been tipped off and be waiting for them. Even without that, they've got to fly over a couple of hundred miles of wild country with an extra load. Anyway Major Rebori, the Yank light plane commander, is discussing it with Brigade HQ"

The platoon greedily drank their water bottles dry. Bob Gregory and four men gathered up the empty bottles and chagauls and wandered off to refill them.

§

"If Barbara could see your face now Badger! You make Frankenstein look like an angel." Corporal Lyons, strolling over from his own section, settled himself on the ground alongside Sergeant Gregory and Badger, at the fringe of the jungle. Dusk had given way to moonlight. The runway they had laboured on, until an hour ago, was now etched in petroleum flares, "Got a match?"

"Yes, you old skiver, my face and your arse!" Badger tossed over a book of matches. They'd been firm friends since their NCO's course at the Guard's Depot three years ago, and their traded insults were a demonstration of true affection.

As 'Tiger' Lyons lit a cigarette, Badger handed him a packet of 'K' ration Philip Morris, "You might as well have these, you old scrounger. I'll stick to my pipe."

"How does your face feel now, Corporal?"

"Do you have to remind me, Sarge?" Badger, drawing on his pipe, timidly ran his fingers over his cheeks, "Doesn't seem to hurt as much as this morning, except when I touch the bridge of my nose. My muscles are sorest, all that digging to-day has worn out muscles I didn't know I had."

"Well, get along to the MO tomorrow morning, before we march out."

"If the Daks. do come in do you think they'll bring any mail, Sarge?"

"I doubt it, we had a delivery two days before we flew in yesterday. The Field Post Office in India won't re-direct it in dribs and drabs. They'll wait until they've got a worthwhile shipment." Bob looked sympathetically at Badger, "Worried about your wife? When did you last get a letter from her?"

"Him and his mail Sarge! I've spent more time in canteens, waiting for him while he writes to his missus, than a lifer in Dartmoor. And, when he gets no mail from her, he's a pain in the arse."

"Pipe down, Tiger! You know very well she writes every week. The illiterate bugger's only jealous, Sarge. No, I'm not worried!" Defensively, over emphatically, " Sends me tobacco every month. She won't get much time to write in her job."

Some of her letters had London postmarks, and it niggled him that she never mentioned visiting the place. Would he have been suspicious but for that bloody Indian's prophecy?

It had been their first day in India. Swaggering along Hornby Road with Tiger, in their brand new tropical dress, a wizened Indian in filthy sackcloth had sprang from a shop doorway and grabbed Badger's wrist. For a few moments he had curbed his irritation, hardly listening as the man, peering at his palm muttered ingratiating auguries and beseeched 'bakshees'. Then, sickened by the man's foul breath, and lips crimson with betel nut, he had given him a few annas and hurried away. But the man had shambled after them, persistently snatching at Badger's shirt, until they dodged into a photographer's. As they had posed together, sun helmets in the crook of their arms, in true Victorian soldierliness, they had scoffed off the old man's repeated cursing of their paltriness. That was two years ago and whenever Tiger mentioned Barbara it triggered his memory of the soothsayer stuttering her name. He had made some vague prediction about adultery and a child. Funny how he'd hit on her name. Badger was sure the only words he'd said to the man was "Get away!" or "Scram".

"Of course he's worried, Sarge. Thinks she's run off with a Brylcreem boy!" Tiger playfully slapped Badger's hat brim.

"No I'm not! Just a little disappointed I didn't get a letter from her before we flew in." Ashamed of the distrust kinking his stomach, he abruptly changed the subject, "Well, we built an airstrip in a day almost with our bare hands, that'll be something to tell our grandkids – if we live to have any!"

"Yes, and you've got to hand it to the Yanks, risking their necks to fly the wounded out in those L 5's, this morning." Tiger rose to his feet, "Better be getting back to my section. They're going to brief us to guide the incoming units to their overnight bivouacs... if they arrive."

"OK, see you later. We've been detailed as unloading parties."

Tiger disappeared through the trees, and Badger turned to Bob Gregory, "Whose planes do you reckon they were, the ones that came over during the burials this morning – ours or theirs Sarge?"

The dead had been buried together, regardless of rank or nationality, in a shallow grave, heaped over with stones, a sort of protective cairn against predatory beasts. As the survivors stood there, reciting the Lord's Prayer, planes had droned high overhead. Not a man had moved but, defiantly, their voices rose steadily until they almost bellowed the 'Amen'. Then, and only then, did they break ranks, and run for cover.

"God knows – probably ours – they didn't attack us. The Japs might be shortsighted, surely they're not deaf as well." A brief chuckle, "You could have heard that prayer in the stratosphere... Listen!" A faint drone rose to a roar.

"Here they come, Sarge... bloody hell! He's coming in the wrong way!"

The huge Dakota seemed to brush the tree tops as it swooped over their heads. The touchdown point was at the opposite end of the runway. As a man, the platoon raced to the jungle edge. The plane's tyres raised a dust cloud and squealed as they hit the ground. Trailing dust, the plane raced down the runway in a perfect landing.

To a chorus of 'hurrahs!' the plane slewed round at the touch-down flares, and slowly taxied back down the runway.

§

"It's fantastic, in the heart of enemy territory all those planes have landed. The good Lord must've been on our side to-night." Wonder, excitement and reverence, tinged Badger's voice as he lay on the groundsheet alongside Scofield, "I make it over sixty planes landed. Heard an officer saying we took more planes in a few hours than La Guardia takes all night."

"Sixty seven actually, Corporal." Captain Williams called from his blanket a few yards away, "Squadron Leader Thompson says we can take over one hundred a night."

"Christ! We'll be too knackered to fight if we have to unload that many." Someone muttered under his blanket, "Might as well be fucking coolies."

"Write to your MP then," came another voice.

"Complain to your shop steward," another quipped.

"Settle down and get some sleep!" Williams sternly called, "No more unloading for us. We're trekking to the Irrawaddy to-morrow, and we'll need all the rest we can get."

Tired as he was, sleep eluded Badger. For a while he tossed and turned before, in deference to Scofield's reproaches, he pulled his blanket around his shoulders and sat against the bole of a nearby tree. At least he didn't have to worry about sentry changing to-night. Whilst they were at Broadway sentries were a platoon responsibility. Bob Gregory's watch would be used to time their changes. Anyway, it couldn't be more than a couple of hours until the dawn 'stand-to'.

Not daring to light his pipe, for fear of enemy patrols, Badger unwrapped a Hershey bar saved from his 'K' ration supper pack.

Broadway was more a forest than a dense jungle. The crowns of the lofty teaks were indigo blots against ivory clouds. The creaking of branches, and the occasional grunt as a sleeper rolled over to ease a stiffening hip, seemed to emphasise the desertion of the indigenous forest fauna. The noise and bustle of the past few hours must have driven away all wildlife.

Meditatively chewing the chocolate bar, Badger's mind roamed over the day's events. The back-breaking hacking at the rough ground. The gallantry of light plane pilots. The solemn burial service. Poor Bill May. His blanketed body had been one of the last he'd seen as they covered the mass grave. If the truth be known, a virgin soldier had left a virgin widow. They had been married on the same date as he had but on the troopship, the gentle-mannered newly-wed had tearfully confided to Badger that nature's inopportune visitation on his bride had thwarted consummation of their marriage. Thank God no such curse had been upon Barbara on their bridal night.

Absently he heeled a hole in the earth, and buried the chocolate wrapper. It was incredible that so much could be achieved in so few hours. Astounding that the noise of thousands of men – and so much heavy machinery – had not brought the Japs down on them. The Yank Colonel, Alison, and the RAF Squadron Leader, Thompson, had controlled the procession of incoming planes as calmly as if it were a peacetime air display. Survivors from the previous night had shepherded incoming battalions to overnight bivouacs. Other survivors had offloaded ton upon ton of stores, barbed wire, ammunition and rations. Wingate, a RAF Vice-Marshal, and Yankee Brigadier-General Old – the pilot of the first Dakota – had strolled about as if they were back at an Indian airfield, chatting to men and confidently discussing the future with Calvert and Scottie.

Footnote to Chapter Fourteen

Page 166 Note No.6 'Escape' and aircraft recognition scarves were dubbed 'Panic' maps from the moment of issue.

Chapter Fifteen

"You've certainly had a nasty clout, Corporal." The senior MO had gently palpated Badger's nose, and was examining his eyes with an opthalmoscope, "But there's no serious damage done." Putting away the instrument, stroking his chin thoughtfully, he studied the bruised face again for a few moments, "Not much we can do to speed up the healing. Nature will do that in about a week. I'm sure only the cartilage is bruised, but we can get you flown out for X-rays to be absolutely sure."

After dawn 'stand-to', that second morning at Broadway, Capt. Williams had firmly ordered him to see to the Column MO. 'Doc' Pritchard, declaring him unfit for the arduous march to the Irrawaddy, had referred him to the Senior MO at the 'Stronghold' casualty station.

"Can they do any more at base hospital, sir?"

"Not much. Rest and clean sheets won't help it much." The MO's eyes twinkled, "They could splint it, but you may always have a bruiser's conk. It'll be your old war wound to romance the ladies with."

"I'd rather not fly out then, sir." A hopeful grin lit his face. With a bit of luck, he could get back to his section before the column moved out, "Can I go back to my column then, sir?"

"No. Better for you stay here for a few day's. I'll give you some painkillers, and you can attach yourself to Broadway HQ for light duties."

"But Sir," downcast, pleading, "I'll be all right marching..."

"Sorry, Corporal." The senior MO handed him two pills and a mug of water. I agree with Captain Pritchard. There's an outside chance of it becoming septic. Can't risk your developing a fever from it, and becoming a passenger, young fellow. Stay at Broadway, take these now – then two every four hours – and report here to-morrow morning."

§

Badger, waiting his turn to see the Senior MO, watched the smoke and flames from the distant funeral pyre soaring high above the forest roof. A patrol had found a wrecked glider containing the decomposing corpses of American field engineers that morning. Brockett, their officer, had wanted to bring them in for burial at Broadway, but Mike Calvert had tactfully persuaded him to cremate them where they crashed.

"Tik Hai, Johnny!" For a moment, Badger's pensive face broke into a broad smile as he waved to a passing Gurkha. This was his third morning visit to the MO, and he was desperately hoping that this time the medic would relent and return him to full duties.

"Tik Hai, Tommy!" Grinning from ear to ear, the Gurkha held up a brace of screeching hens, their legs bound with rattan strips, destined for the Stronghold's chicken pen.

Mike Calvert had selected a perfect site for the Stronghold. In only four days a wooded peninsula, east of the runway and watered by a good stream, had become a formidable jungle redoubt. Raised slightly on three sides, above the surrounding area, it dominated the clearing.

For three nights scores of Dakotas, some of them making two round trips, had freighted in troops, stock piles of rations, defence materials, trenching tools, ammunition, a battery of 25 pounder field guns, 3 inch mortars and ack-ack guns. The garrison had encircled it with rows of barbed wire. The Gurkhas had surrounded it with a palisade of 'pangis'. These razor sharp bamboo stakes added a medieval touch to the defences. Dense rows of them encircled the outer perimeter wire. Every stake 'planted' at just the right height and slope to pierce the thighs of charging attackers.

From bunkers within the perimeter the rifles, mortars and machine guns, with co-ordinated arcs of fire, would be able to sweep every yard of the territory. Outside the defence perimeter on the fringe of the forest six Spitfires stood at instant readiness to deal with any threats from the air.

Salvage from gliders had been fashioned into housing for the casualty station, a radio centre, the Stronghold command post and – out along the runway – the air controller's shack.

The Stronghold had also become a busy trading post. Stocky, pro-British Kachins bartered local produce for manufactured goods flown in from India, and they brought in information of Japanese activities.

The casualty station had become an outpatient clinic for Kachin villagers, as well as a rudimentary field hospital for troops. Badger, lounging forlornly at the sandbagged entrance, absently watched a grateful Kachin couple paying for their treatment with a squawking chicken. His section – with 81 column – was marching east to Bhamo, hunting Japs and enforcing Calvert's edict that Irrawaddy craft must fly the Union Jack. 82, the other King's column, was roaming west of Broadway, re-establishing the King-Emperor's omnipotence, and ready to maul the rear of any Jap attack on Broadway. Colonel 'Fish' Herring, with another 77 Brigade column – Dah Force – was trekking north east to raise a Kachin force to help Chinese guerillas. One Lancashire Fusilier's column was heading south east to block the 'Waddy' at Shwegu.

Only a hour ago, he'd heard that Mike Calvert with the rest of 77 Brigade were leaving tomorrow, to block road and rail traffic in the Moguang Valley. Six columns, one Lancashire Fusiliers, two South Staffs, two Gurkhas and Brigade HQ, sallying forth to battle. Elsewhere in Northern Burma, four other brigades – 20,000 Chindits – would soon be harrying Japs from bases code-named Aberdeen and Chowringhee.

And here he was, tied to the Stronghold by super cautious medics!

The jossing of some of the garrison was getting under his skin, taunting him for 'dodging the column'. Even he, himself, was beginning to feel he was malingering. An injured nose would not hinder his marching ability and waiting his turn to see the MO, his mind almost frantically clutched for the words to secure his return to full duty. Tomorrow seemed his last hope of getting back into a 77 Brigade column.

"Let's have a look at you, corporal." The MO beckoned him in and scrutinised the bruises, "Swelling's nearly gone. Eyes clear. Your face is yellow as Chinaman's." Chuckling he passed over another supply of pills, "A few days and you'll be back to full duties."

"I'd like to go back today, sir."

"Perhaps tomorrow. Be patient."

"But I'll miss the column, Sir." With a petulant frown, he resisted the impulse to scorn the MO's ruling.

"Tomorrow. Let us see tomorrow, Corporal." Firmly, but there was a glimmer of admiration in the M.O.'s eyes.

"Please, sir. It won't be any harder than what I've been doing here for the last 48 hours – unloading planes, humping ammo, digging bunkers." Badger pointed to the mass of scratches on his arms, "Erecting barbed wire."

"You've a very apt nickname, Corporal." The MO grinned indulgently, "You'll badger me 'til you get your way." With mock exasperation, he waved Badger out of the place, " Go on! Get along then. I'm not going to mark you fit to-day, but if I don't see you here to-morrow morning you won't be missed. Off you go and see if 77 Brigade's Senior MO will have you. Good luck, young fellow!"

With a school-boy skip in his step, and childish elation firing his adrenalin, Badger hurried away from the casualty station. As he passed the Command Post he threw a joyful salute at the Union Flag. At the flag raising parade, the other day, his had not been the only misty eyes, and that had nothing to do with the sun's glare. In the heart of enemy territory, it fluttered defiantly above the tree tops.

Humming 'Land of Hope and Glory' he paused at a notice board to read, for the umpteenth time, Wingate's Order of the Day.

Our first task is fulfilled. We have inflicted a

complete surprise on the enemy.
All our columns are inserted in the enemy's guts.
The time has come to reap the fruits of the advantage we have gained. The enemy will react with violence. We will oppose him with the resolve to reconquer our territory in Northern Burma. Let us thank God for the success He has vouchsafed us and press forward with swords to the enemy's ribs to expel him from our territory.
This is not the moment when such an advantage has been gained to count the cost.
This is a moment to live in history. It is an enterprise in which every man who takes part may feel proud to say one day, 'I was there'.

Mike Calvert's bivouacs were about half a mile south. Trading cheerful 'Tik Hai's!' with an incoming Gurkha patrol, Badger made for the Stronghold's southern exit. Passing the dugouts of Yank engineers, placarded with 'Chew Mukergee's Betel Nut', 'Kilroy's not here' and 'Chuck's Spamburger House', he exchanged thumb's up signs with crews servicing light planes around the perimeter. Within, and around, the Stronghold defences, the 'stick with a mucker' rule had been universally ignored, but now, as he jauntily left its security, he was flagrantly flouting the rule. He knew he should have waited to attach himself to the dusk patrol of outlying bivouacs, but his euphoria outweighed all risks, knowing that before he was out of sight of the perimeter posts he would be in sight of Calvert's outposts.

§

Badger did not take the risk of being rejected by the column MO Instead he went straight to the 77 Brigade's Brigade Major.

"Corporal Dixon, Sir." Saluting smartly, "Stronghold HQ sent me over for attachment to Brigade column, sir."

"Right, Corporal," the slim, aesthetic major, with the finely drawn look of a consumptive, intently studied Badger's face, "What regiment?"

"King's, sir. 81 Column, Commando Platoon." His heart sank. Was he going to be sent to the MO?

"Fine. For the time being you'd better muck in with the Hong Kong Volunteers. They're the Signals Unit's defence platoon." With a wry smile, he pointed to the Oriental soldiers bivouacked around Army and RAF wireless detachments, "Your complexion matches their's."

A jest tinged with sympathy.

§

In the late afternoon of the fifth day, Mike Calvert's column turned off the track into the shade of the teak jungle, and fanned out in platoons. The dispersal was ritualistic, needing only brief, cryptic orders passed from mouth to mouth.

"Fires out in half an hour. Officer's briefing in ten minutes."

With well-drilled precision, platoons formed a perimeter around Brigade HQ. Section leaders posted sentries; muleteers slackened off the mules' girths; signallers offloaded radios from other mules and set up their aerials. Sweat streaming from every pore, men shrugged off their packs and accoutrements.

Badger was grateful he was not a signaller. They marched with monstrous packs like everyone else but, when everyone else settled for a rest, the signallers had to erect aerials, start up generators, and work on their radios. All he knew about the radio network, was that there was no lateral link between columns. The movements and halts of columns could not be synchronised, so signallers had to work directly to Chindit HQ in Assam. Distance, mountain ranges, and weather, made this network tenuous and invariably, signallers spent hours striving to establish and maintain the radio link whilst almost everyone else rested.

Five mornings ago the column had crossed the dry, dusty Broadway plateau and plunged into the steamy, malevolent, bamboo jungle of the Kaukkwe. For the first time since they landed, droves of mosquitoes whined about their ears and startled birds screeched. At times the high pitched hum of the insects rose to a stunning crescendo.

The fast flowing Kaukkwe was only a few yards wide, but its crystal clear water was deceptively deep. Waist high, they waded the icy river and without pause started the gruelling ascent of the Gangaw Range.

With a brief halt every hour, they had trudged in single file. Mike Calvert had boldly kept them to well-beaten tracks. The going underfoot was firm, but each hundred foot ascent would have stretched the stamina of fit, unburdened men. They were superbly fit, but not unburdened. With seven day's rations in their packs, pouches bulging with Bren magazines, grenades clipped to their shoulder straps and a 50 rounds bandolier across chests, they were carrying nearly half their own weight.

Sweat swamped their shirts and hat bands. Salty streams flowed from their foreheads, into their eyes, and poured off their chins. The overstuffed packs abraded their backs. A water-bottle and dah chafed one hip, haversack and bayonet the other. Their entrenching tool slapped against their buttocks. The bulging pouches galled their ribs, the rifle slings dug into their shoulders. Belts raised weals, but the men could not get at the flesh to scratch the offending itch.

Except for the occasional gasped curse at a misplaced foot, or relaying an instruction down the line, men toiled in silence. Even if they had the breath for talk, one of them had to turn round, breaking the automated rhythm of his gait and inviting a stumble.

As they climbed, the jungle became a mixture of wooded glades, scrub and bamboo thickets. Between sentry duties they slept the sleep of the just, woke to crisp, invigorating mornings, and set off light-heartedly in soft, sun dappled shade. Too soon the shadows grew harsh. The sun mounted to a merciless glare, and the air became stifling. The hour between each halt seemed to lengthen as the day wore on.

Bent under under their loads, their horizons were the buttocks and heels of the man – or mule – in front. Left and right, there was nothing but scrub, bamboo or teak forest. Each man plodded through the weariness and tedium in a world of his own. For Badger, it was a world paced by memorised pages of *Barrack Room Ballads*. After months of marching in sweltering Indian jungles, silently reciting Kipling's verse, he could judge almost precisely the point in his repertoire when a halt was due. Bitterness compounded his fatigue if the halt was delayed even half a verse beyond that point.

Now, at this late afternoon halt, they were 4000 feet up, among lofty teak and iron trees. But it had been no straightforward climb. The Kachin hills were a series of dismaying false crests. Time and again, a gruelling climb had been followed by a descent into a valley, and the dismal prospect of another trudge, to gain the same height on the other side.

In less than an hour the brief tropical twilight would be upon them. Well before that, the column had to move on to find a secure overnight bivouac.

As always, when he shrugged off his sweat blackened pack, there was the delight of seemingly floating on air, of being several inches taller. With his pack he shed his fatigue. As he brewed his tea the glow of achievement replaced weariness. Exhilaration superseded boredom. He was back with a column. Even if he wasn't with his own muckers, he was marching towards battle – doing what he'd joined up and trained for.

The Hong Kong Volunteers were a mixed bunch of pure Chinese, Portuguese-Chinese and Anglo-Chinese. For the first few days, although they had adopted western forenames – Willie, Charles, Maxi and the like – Badger found it difficult to distinguish one Oriental face from the other. As an odd number, he teamed up with various pairs of their 'muckers' depending upon on duty details, and persistently pressed them about their exploits.

In bivouacs, and on sentry with one or other of them, he had listened with awe to their modest accounts, mostly in grammatically perfect English, of their flight from Hong Kong. They had been in the thick of the grim, abortive defence of Hong Kong. When the Japs over-ran the Colony, in December 1941, they had escaped into China's vastness. Determined to get back into the fight, they had trekked thousands of miles, living off the land, outwitting enemy pursuits. When eventually they reached India, they had been dumped in Deolali's vast transit camp and ignored until, fortuitously, Mike Calvert had found them.

As they sipped at their steaming tea, Major Taffy Griffiths strolled over to brief the platoon. Badger had never seen him before, but he instantly recognised the bushy moustached Burma Rifle's officer. Most Chindit officers needed no introduction. Their reputations, eccentricities and exploits were popular camp fire topics. Taffy, a former Burma forestry officer, was one of them. He had been through Wingate's campaign the previous year. His jungle lore had become legendary, and he was a trusted confidante of the tribal elders.

"Rest easy whilst I put you in the general picture."

The Japs, he told them, were marshalling their divisions against the 14th Army, at Imphal and Kohima, to invade India. Stilwell's Chinese divisions, with Merrill's Marauders – the Chindit's American counterparts – were pushing south down the Hukawng Valley from Assam, to take Kamaing, Myitkyina and Moguang. US Army engineers, following behind the advance, would drive a road-link to China.

The major laid a map of the local area on the ground. 77 Brigade's tasks, he explained, were to block Jap communication and supply lines. To generally create havoc in this area and to divert Jap reserves from the 14th Army and Stilwell's forces. Brigadier Fergusson's 16 Brigade were making for Indaw to establish a base code-named 'Aberdeen'. Half of Lentaigne's 111 Brigade had landed by gliders and Dakotas in a clearing south of Katha, code named 'Chowringhee', after a Calcutta thoroughfare. Its other 4 columns, having been diverted to Broadway, were marching to join the remainder of 111 Brigade. They would harass the enemy south and west of 77 Brigade.

"Right, now for our task. The single track railway through the Moguang Valley, is the Jap's jugular vein. It's the only all weather supply route. The road alongside is not continuous, motorable only in disconnected stretches – little more than dirt-tracks in the dry season. To-morrow, both South Staffs columns will establish a road and rail block somewhere here." He stabbed a finger at Henu, "There's a couple of hundred Japs at Nansiaung." His tapped the village just north of Henu, "63 Column, the 3/6 Gurkhas, will put a holding attack tonight at Nansiaung. We'll move down into the valley at first light, and be in reserve with 36 Column of 3/6 Gurkhas. If we're dispersed rendezvous will be here, north west of Nathkokyin. Password unchanged. Questions?"

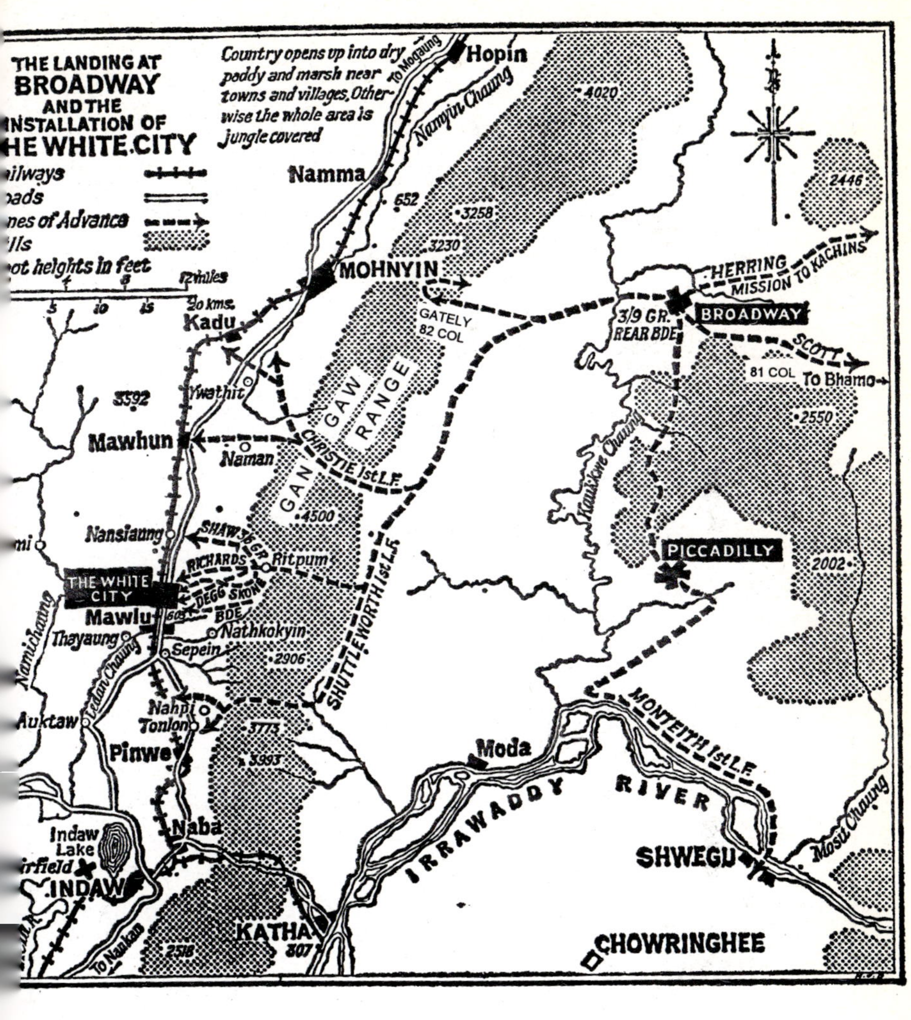

THE LANDING AT
BROADWAY
AND THE
INSTALLATION OF
HE WHITE CITY
ilways
oads
nes of Advance
ills
ot heights in feet
Country opens up into dry paddy and marsh near towns and villages. Otherwise the whole area is jungle covered
Hopin
To Mogaung
Namyin Chaung
Namma
MOHNYIN
GATELY
82 COL
Kadu
Ywathit
Mawhun
Naman
GAN GAW RANGE
CHRISTIE 1st L.F.
SHUTTLEWORTH 1st L.F.
Nansiaung
SHAW 3/GR
RICHARDS
DEGG
SKONE
BDE
Ritpum
THE WHITE CITY
Mawlu
Thayaung
Nathkokyin
Sepein
Ledan Chaung
Namichaung
Auktaw
Nahpi
Tonlon
Pinwe
Naba
Indaw Lake
Airfield
INDAW
To Nankan
KATHA
HERRING
MISSION TO KACHINS
BROADWAY
3/9 GR.
REAR BDE
SCOTT
81 COL
To Bhamo
Kaukkwe Chaung
PICCADILLY
MONTEITH 1st L.F.
Moda
IRRAWADDY RIVER
SHWEGU
Mosit Chaung
CHOWRINGHEE

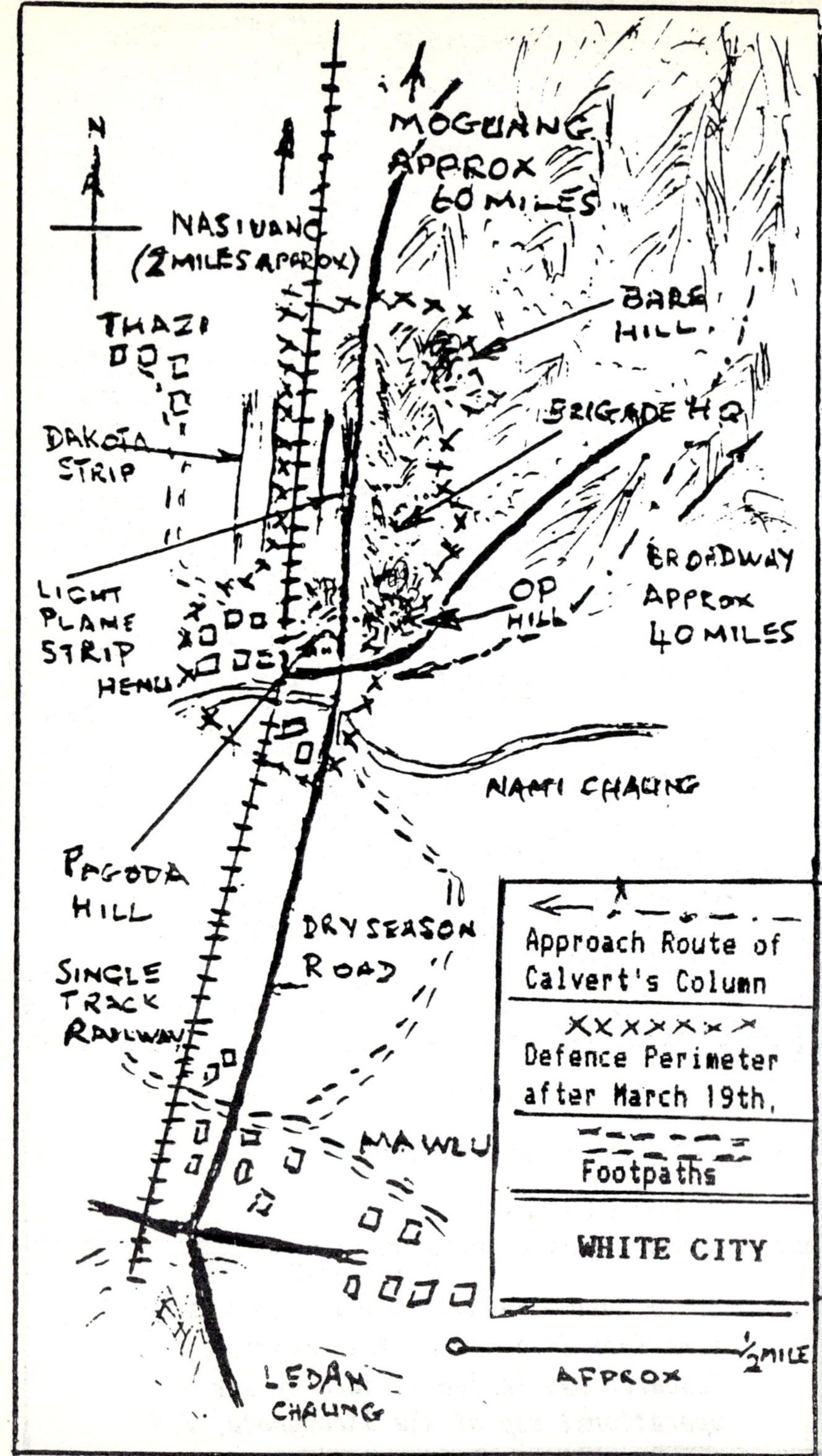
N
MOGUANG
APPROX
60 MILES
NASIUANG
(2 MILES APPROX)
THAZI
BARE
HILL
BRIGADE HQ
DAKOTA
STRIP
BROADWAY
APPROX
40 MILES
LIGHT
PLANE
STRIP
OP
HILL
HENU
NAMI CHAUNG
PAGODA
HILL
DRY SEASON
ROAD
SINGLE
TRACK
RAILWAY
MAWLU
LEDAN
CHAUNG
1/2 MILE
APPROX
Approach Route of
Calvert's Column
Defence Perimeter
after March 19th,
Footpaths
WHITE CITY

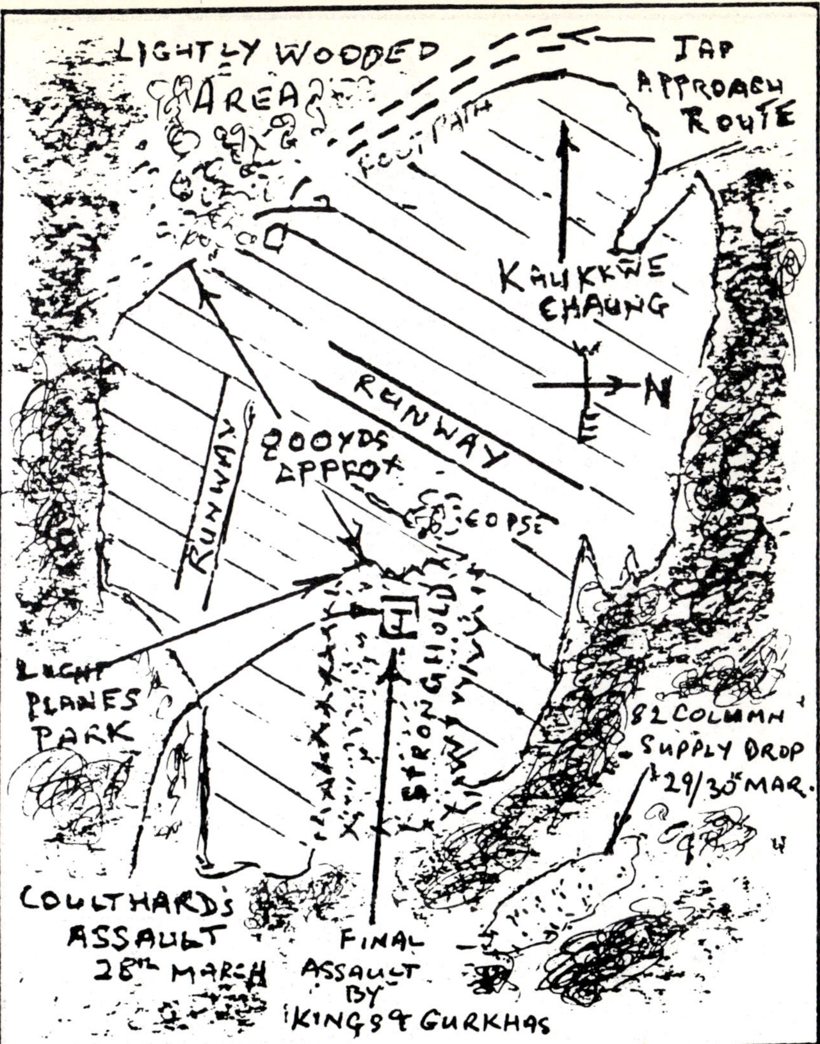

Jungle/Afforestation

Japs Lodged in US Airforce Positions

First Contact with enemy by D Coy. 3/9th, Gurkhas.

Broadway

From memory (after 50 years it might be more from imagination than memory). Research has failed to turn up any operational map of the Stronghold. J.M.

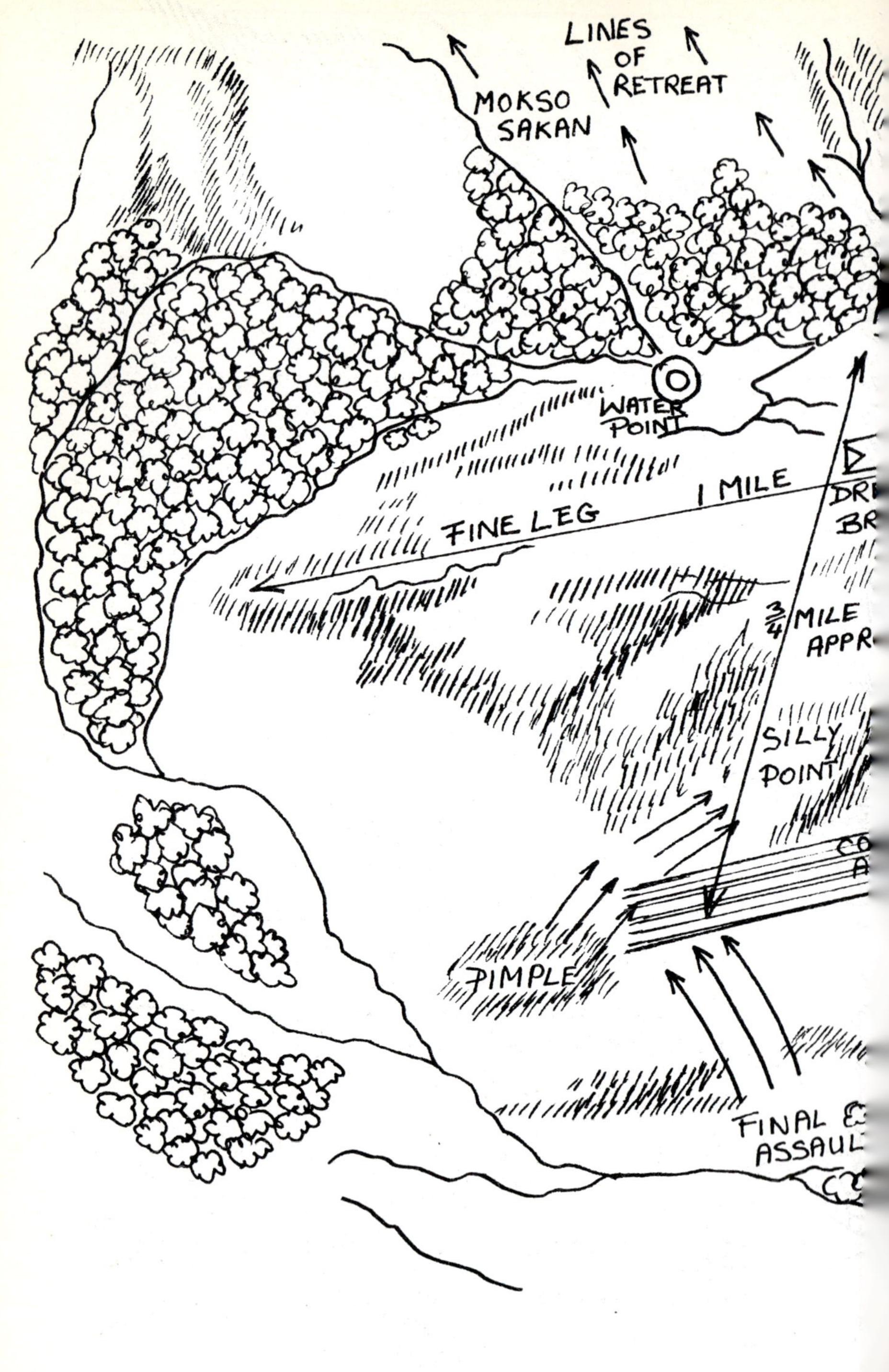

LINES
OF
RETREAT
MOKSO
SAKAN
WATER
POINT
1 MILE
FINE LEG
3/4 MILE
SILLY
POINT
PIMPLE
FINAL
NOT

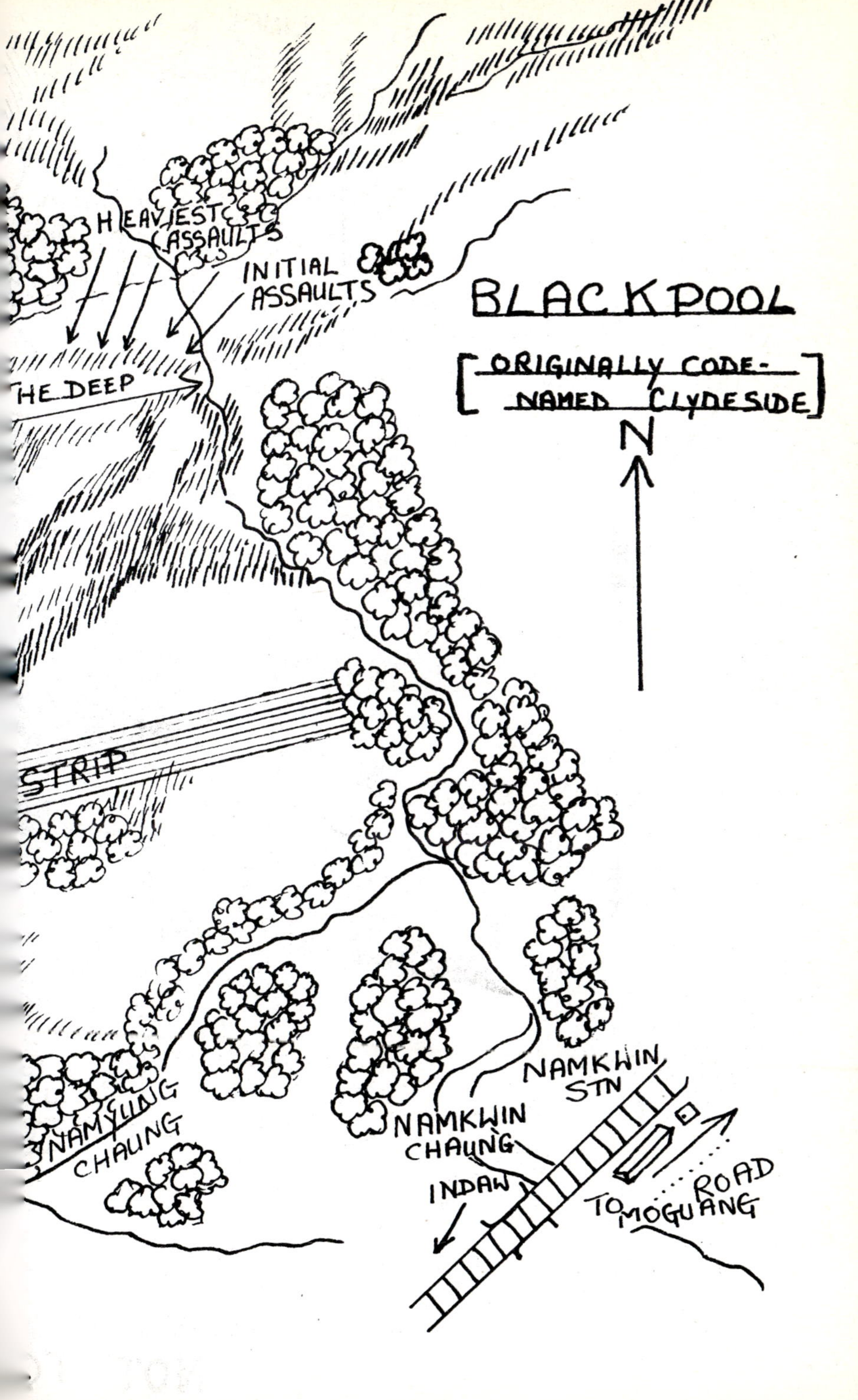
BLACKPOOL
[ORIGINALLY CODE-NAMED CLYDESIDE]
N
HEAVIEST ASSAULTS
INITIAL ASSAULTS
THE DEEP
STRIP
NAMYUNG CHAUNG
NAMKWIN CHAUNG
NAMKWIN STN
INDAW
TO MOGUANG ROAD

① BRIGADE H.Q. SHELF
② DEFILE TO SUMMIT
ROUTE OF MAJ. BAKERS FLANKING ASSAULT

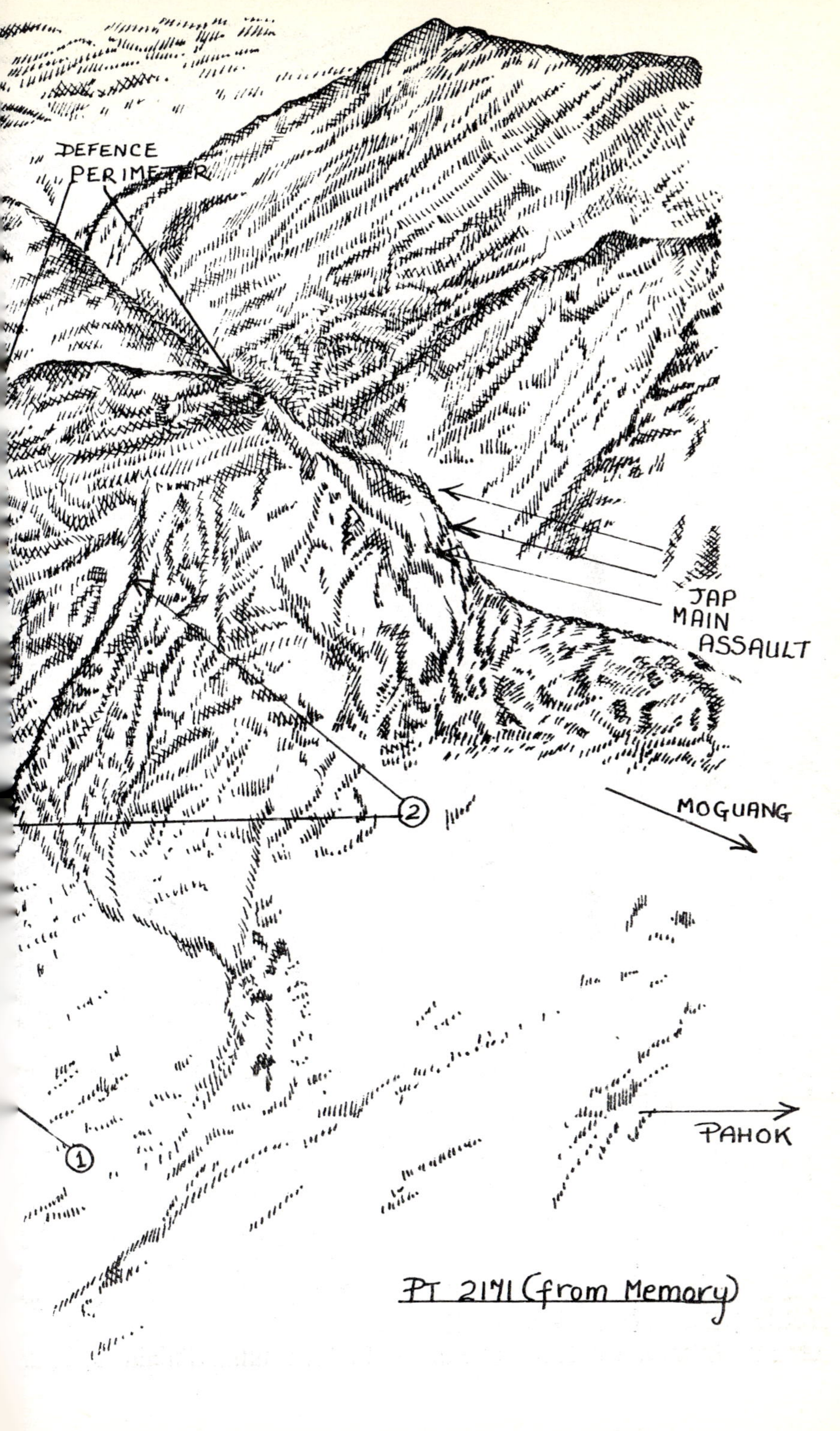

PT 2171 (from Memory)

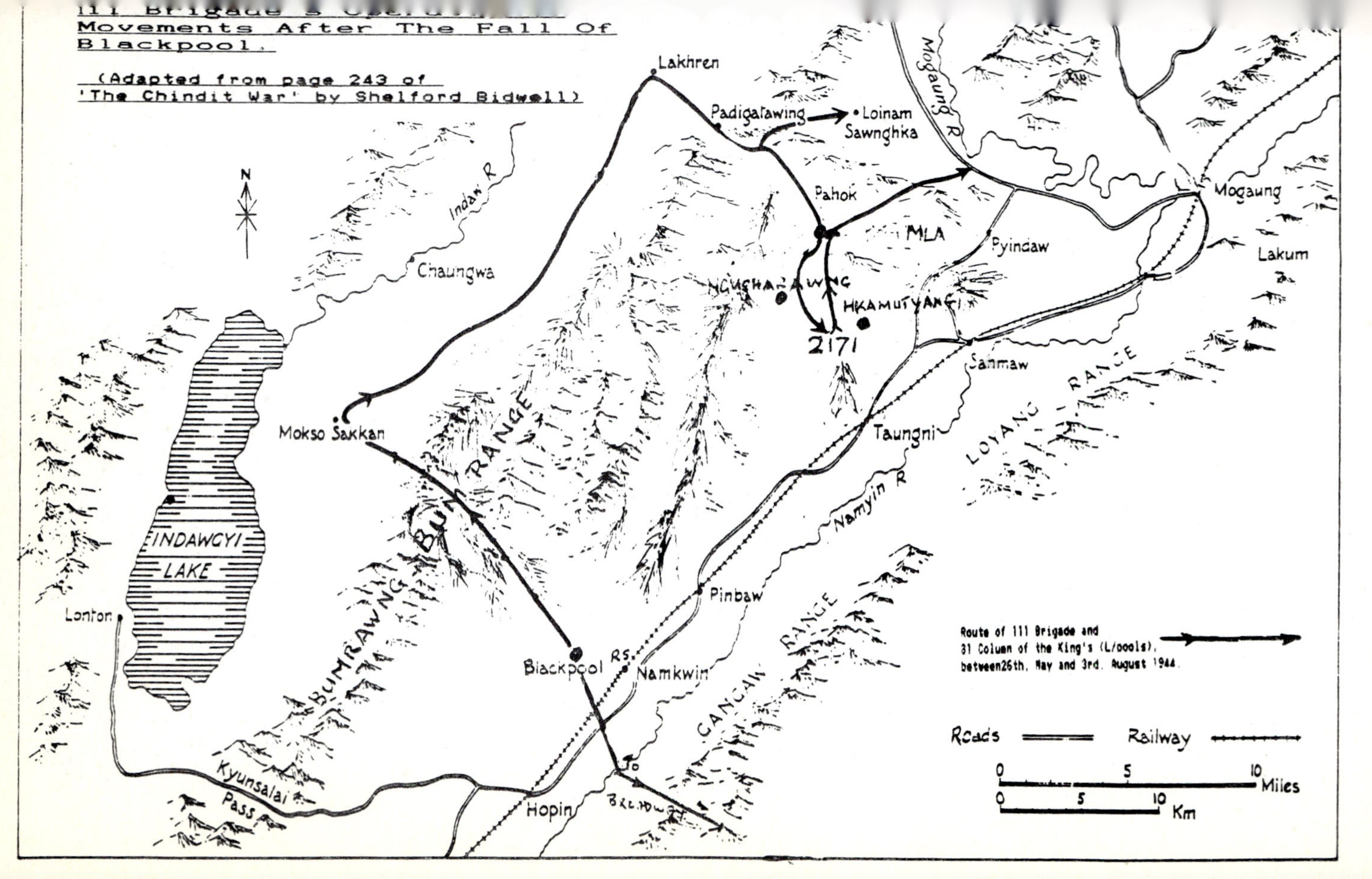
Movements After The Fall Of Blackpool.
(Adapted from page 243 of 'The Chindit War' by Shelford Bidwell)
N
Lakhren
Padigatawing
Loinam
Sawnghka
Mogaung R
Mogaung
Pahok
MLA
Pyindaw
Lakum
Indaw R
Chaungwa
2171
Sahmaw
LOYANG RANGE
Mokso Sakkan
Taungni
Namyin R
INDAWGYI LAKE
Pinbaw
Lonton
BUMRAWNG BUM RANGE
CANGAW RANGE
Blackpool
Rs.
Namkwin
Kyunsalai Pass
Hopin
Route of 111 Brigade and 31 Column of the King's (L/pools), between26th. May and 3rd. August 1944.
Roads
Railway
0 5 10 Miles
0 5 10 Km

Silence for a moment, then Badger asked, "What about the Lancs. Fusiliers, sir, and 14 and 23 Brigades?"

"One Fusilier column, under Colonel Christie, is moving south of Henu to demolish bridges. Major Monteith with the other column, is blocking the Irrawaddy at Shwegu." He paused meditatively, and decided not to divulge the plans for the other two brigades, "14 and 23? They'll be coming in later," he said evasively,. "Your a King's aren't you?"

"Yes, Sir."

"Thought so. You'll be pleased to learn Scottie's got an immediate award of the DSO for the glider landings. Your mob did a damn fine job."

"Thank you, Sir." Pride welled up in his throat, and he could think of nothing better to say.

The drone of aircraft turned all heads to the heavens.

"Nothing to worry about." The major nodded skywards, "That'll be the consolidation drop for the South Staffs. Ammo, wire, tools and the like. That's all. Packs on in five minutes and we'll move a couple of miles to bivouac for the night."

§

"Jesus bloody Christ! They've dropped miles away from the Staffs." In the dawning light, as the column 'stood to' in their hillside bivouac above Henu, Badger nudged the Chinese alongside him. Below them, scattered over acres of trees and the rugged hillside, were scores of parachuted bales and barbed wire coils. It would take days to gather and haul them down to the block. The South Staffs would have to establish, and hold the block, with what they carried on their backs. At least for a few days.

Back in India, the targeting of dropping zones had been practiced to perfection. But this was the first drop 'in anger'. Its inaccuracy stirred forebodings and doubts about absolute dependence on air supply in this mountainous terrain.

"Stand down. Fires out in half an hour." The order passed from man to man. The ritual move to another site for breakfast was abandoned. Expediency was paramount. The Gurkhas' night attack had kept the Japs pinned down. The South Staffs were installing the block, and the Brigadier was anxious to get his Brigade HQ there.

The crack of rifles and machine guns, the crumping of mortars, as the Gurkhas attacked, had woken Badger, and long after the firing had ceased, the thrill of this first close proximity to battle had kept sleep at bay. Nevertheless, as he brewed his tea and consumed his 'K' ration breakfast, he felt fresh and invigorated. The prospect of this baptism of fire quickened his adrenalin. Engrossed in thought, he finished off the 'K' breakfast ration. Absently he tossed the cigarette pack to a Chinese mucker, pocketed the chewing gum, and lit his pipe. Only as he buried the packaging did he notice that the meat loaf had been the rarer, more palatable 'chopped ham and egg yolks' instead of the more common 'chopped pork and egg whites', and he mentally kicked himself. It was his favourite, and he'd not savoured the treat.

"Packs On"

§

Downhill, into the railway valley, was scarcely less strenuous than climbing. To a cacophony of screaming gibbons and shrieking birds, they descended into the steamy bamboo foothills. Humped forward under their packs, their calves and thighs ached with the braking against headlong stumbles. Mules and ponies slithered, threatening to shed their loads, cracking their masters and panniers against bamboo or boulders.

At the valley rendezvous the Gurkhas, from the night attack, were waiting for them. They were uncommonly subdued. No cheery 'Tik Hai's'. No ear to ear grins. Their baptism of fire had clearly shaken their morale.

As the columns rested, bursts of gunfire from the direction of Henu sent conferring officers scurrying back to their platoons. Mike Calvert quickly gathered together six platoons.

"Battle Order!" This meant no packs.

Badger dumped his pack with the rest. Almost at the double, Mike headed towards the firing with the platoons at his heels.

The battle noise intensified as they came upon open ground. Warily they crossed the clearing, splashed through a brook, and mounted the high bank beyond it. Stray bullets and ricochets were sporadically whining overhead. Badger began to experience dry-mouthed fear, and gut-crimping fright. Like most of the others, he ducked unnecessarily at each whine. The temptation to go forward at the crouch was almost irresistible. Mike Calvert was striding ahead, upright, and holding aloft a panic map on a long bamboo, as a recognition signal. Nor was anyone else crouching. Fear of showing fear, was more potent than fear itself. Stiffening his spine, shoulders back, rifle at the high port, he rallied his nerves with the aid of Kipling, and strode on.

When first under fire an' you're wishful to duck
Don't look nor take 'eed at the man that is struck.
Be thankful you're living, and trust to your luck
And march to your front like a soldier...

Moving along a ridge, the leading officers called out loudly to identify themselves, but there was no answering shout. Striding at Mike's heels an officer with a walkie-talkie achieved contact with the South Staffs and received directions.

Suddenly, on a knoll across the paddy of a narrow and shallow valley, there were the Japs. In the mid-afternoon sun, from a cluster of village houses and a pagoda atop the knoll, overlooking the railway, they were pouring mortar, machine-gun and rifle fire on to a nearby hillock.

No orders were needed. Mike's platoons flung themselves down, and opened fire. Their first, furious fusillade caught the Japs unaware.

Scurrying for cover, the Japs dragged their dead or wounded with them. Badger felt elated, not because he was sure he had accounted for some of the Jap casualties, but because of the absence of any nerves. Calmly, swiftly, as if on a rifle range, he had got off 10 well aimed rounds, before the last Jap vanished behind cover. His elation was short lived.

Scoring 'bulls' and 'inners' on rifle ranges was one thing, firing at targets that fired back was another. From behind cover, the Japs raked the ridge with machine-guns and rifles. Badger was convinced he was their lone target. Bullets whined past his ears, or ripped into the the bank, gouging earth inches below his chest. Dry mouthed he squirmed back from the ridge, hugged the earth, and ceased firing. The man alongside, slewing sideways to fill his magazine, gave him a swift accusing glance. Conscience-stricken, pretending he had been searching for a clip of cartridges, he steeled himself back into position and resumed shooting.

§

The embryonic Block had the shape of half an oak leaf. About half a mile of rail track formed what would be the midrib. A dirt road ran adjacent and parallel to the east of the rails, and the scalloped eastern perimeter, about a half a mile wide at its extremes, was formed by the contours of seven wooded hillocks and their intervening valleys.

The South Staffs, deprived of their consolidation supply drop, had worked strenuously through the night, with entrenching tools and dahs, and had encircled the perimeter with shallow slit trenches. At the southern extremity skirting the fringes of Henu – a hamlet astride the road and railway – the Japs and British, unaware of each other, had toiled to fortify adjacent hills overlooking the railway.

Screened by the night, and the undulating scrub land, the Japs had laboured around the crests of Pagoda Hill, and picqueted a neighbouring hillock. The British had dug themselves in on the opposing slopes, only a grenade throw away.

Apparently mistaking each others' strange tongues for those of worried Henu villagers, both sides had feverishly concentrated on their tasks. A mid-morning Chindit recce, bumping into a Jap picquet near the foot of Pagoda Hill, shattered the blissful ignorance. The skirmish detonated a pitched battle.

The Japs, from their dominant hills, rained mortar, machine-gun and rifle fire onto the Staffs' exposed slit trenches.

For over four hours, the lightly armed Staffs in their fledgling defence works, doggedly held their ground expecting, every minute, the superior Jap force to swarm down, overwhelm and dislodge them.

§

From the ridge, the vulnerability of the Stafford detachment was evident to the dumbest of Calvert's men. Under covering fire from the ridge, Calvert, with a bayonetted rifle and a half a dozen men at his heels, raced downhill and across the valley. Impulsively Badger sprinted after them. Dodging, undetected, around intervening Jap dug-outs they scrambled up the opposite slope to the beleaguered Staffords.

British corpses, and groaning wounded, already black with zizzing flies, were strewn around the slit-trenches. Jap machine guns viciously sprayed the earth. As muckers strove to drag the wounded into cover, Calvert, seemingly heedless of the danger, stood alongside a Staffs officer. Then, rifle gesturing at the Japs on Pagoda Hill, like the hero in a Victorian epic, he bellowed, "Charge!" and, without a backward glance, bounded downhill.

The hours of mortar and grenade bombardment had driven the detachment wild for Jap blood. Scores of men chased after Calvert.

Badger's hand trembled as he drew his bayonet. A thousand times, on parades, he'd deftly snapped it on his rifle boss. Now he fumbled. The ring hit the boss, fouling the spring-loaded catch. Then it snapped the catch but missed the boss. A couple of platoons of Gurkhas brandishing their kukris, skeltering from the ridge, swept past him.

At the foot of the hill, as men raced across the sunken road to Pagoda Hill, Mike Calvert looked back, "Bloody well Charge! What the hell do you think you're doing!" he yelled to men lagging behind, some still in their slit-trenches, "Charge, you bastards! Charge!"

Badger's conscience convinced him the exhortation unfairly marked him a coward. White hot anger surged through him. Suddenly the bayonet snapped into place. Determined to erase his imagined disgrace, he charged pell-mell past the Brigadier.

The exhortation also spurred every laggard into action. A hundred men were charging across the valley. The Japs had ceased firing as the men stormed uphill. The scuffing of boots and the panting lungs, lent a terrifying intensity to the Japs' pregnant silence.

Ahead of him, the leading elements were scrambling across a track barely five yards below the Pagoda, when the defenders swarmed from bunkers under houses. Jap officers brandishing two handed swords, their men with fixed bayonets, charged down into the attackers. In a banshee of Gurkhali war cries, Staffs bellows and screaming Japs, men were bayonetting, shooting, hacking, kicking each other.

Three Japs, bursting through the melee, charged down at Badger. He fired from the hip. His bullet, or someone else's, brought blood gushing from the leading Jap's forehead as he fell.

Instinctively, deftly working the rifle bolt, he fired twice again. The second Jap crumpled. The tip of the Jap's outflung bayonet pierced the shin of Badger's trousers. The third Jap lunged at his chest. Badger side-stepped and their bayonets clanged. His swift, powerful parry drove the Jap bayonet to the ground. Like a pole vaulter, the Jap's headlong velocity somersaulted him to Badger's left. Slewing to shoot the man, he pulled the trigger.

'CLICK'!

The Jap was on his back, rifle aimed at Badger's head, finger whitening on the trigger. In an aeon briefer than the blink of an eye, Badger cursed himself. He'd hammered into recruits, 'count your shots, always have a bullet up the spout!' He'd counted every shot. There were two cartridges still in his magazine. He'd forgotten to recharge the breech!

In that terrifying eternity, as he lunged his bayonet, his mind raced with the speed of light. Their eyes met. Under the comical pudding basin helmet, the almond eyes were ablaze with hatred. The Jap was an eye flicker from death, but contempt twisted his mouth. He had a western barbarian in his sights. This unflinching man in shoddy uniform, and ragged puttees, would neither give nor expect any quarter. In the cause of his god-Emperor, he would go to his ancestors with at least one barbarian to his credit. The Jap's gold filled mouth sneered. His finger continued to whiten on the trigger. Badger's bayonet flew at his neck. The Jap dodged and fired. The bullet whined past Badger's ear. In another swift motion his bayonet flashed in and out of the man's throat.

'Get the bayonet out as fast as it goes in', he had told recruits number less times, 'Don't listen to old soldiers telling you to plunge it in, and twist. It'll foul his equipment, uniform and innards. It's in! Out! On guard! Sharp as that!' Now he stood, bayonet outthrust. 'On guard'. Ready for the next assailant.

Panting, devoid of any emotion but malevolence, watching the gory, frothing gurgle of the man's dying gasp, he fired point blank into the man's forehead.

As he turned from the man, a warm dampness trickled down one shin, soaking into his puttees and dripping into his sock. The second Jap's bayonet must have gashed his leg. But another stain that ran from groin to ankle was bloodless.

"Jesus! I've pissed myself!" The ignominy of it fired his anger, vanquishing any further trace of nerves. His palms around the small of the butt, and rifle stock, were sweaty but free of their earlier trembling. He was past the crisis of fear. Certain, like all soldiers in the heat of battle, of his own immortality. Striding over the Jap he advanced uphill firing from the hip. Others would be hit, never him.

Dead and wounded were sprawled everywhere. Ahead, a Staffs lieutenant, in a blood soaked shirt, shot a Jap officer. The lieutenant dropped his revolver and snatched up the Jap's sword. His left arm had been sliced from the shoulder, and was hanging on by a scrap of flesh. With the sword in his other hand, he strode back into the thick of the fray, furiously slicing into any Jap within his path.

Calvert, his Chinese orderly and Irish groom, were slashing and shooting. In an area half the size of a soccer pitch, a couple of hundred men were in hand to hand combat. Steel clanged against steel, rifle butts crunched bone, Kukris clove through skulls, gunshots thwacked and whined. Wounded men shrieked and cursed.

Like a soulless robot, Badger parried a Jap bayonet. Crashed his butt against the man's jaw, shot him as he fell, and was instantly *en-garde* for the next comer. His psyche was somewhere above the battle, abstractedly witnessing his mortal limbs bayonetting, shooting, clubbing other mortals and gasping for breath between each assailant.

Then, suddenly, the Japs were breaking away. Dragging away any of their casualties within reach, they scurried up to the Pagoda.

But the battle was not over.

From the shelter of the Pagoda and houses they tossed grenades, and pinned down the attackers with sporadic small arms salvoes. The grenades curled through the air, spinning like infant rugby balls. Their detonations were ear-splitting but harmless as fire-crackers. Almost as harmless as the fractured English taunts the Japs hurled at them – 'You dirty hairy bastards'.'Give up Tommy'. 'You'll die like stuck pigs'.

Behind the scanty cover of rough earth and scrub, the British, replying with their more powerful grenades, steeled themselves for flight or fight.

Lying prone alongside a Jap corpse, his gory cheeks swarming with red ants, Badger fought back the nausea of funk as mechanically, he re-charged his magazine. He was down to his last 10 rounds and there were shouts that ammunition was running out.

The sun was already setting. The situation desperate. Telepathic alarm was beginning to fray their nerves. With the Japs still in possession of this dominant crest, the ill-fortified block was doomed. Throughout the afternoon Cochrane's planes had forestalled Jap re-inforcement of the hill. Their bombing and strafing, had kept the Jap garrison in the nearby village of Mawlu, pinned down. But the fast approaching night would put an end to the air sorties. Soon that garrison could be upon them.

Sensing that Calvert was not about to concede possession of the hill, Badger swivelled his head to locate his brigadier. There he was, just to the rear of the foremost Staffords, his moose shoulders slightly stooped, bayonetted rifle in hand. Whilst brazenly surveying the Jap positions, he was talking to two or three officers.

"Right!" He shouted loud enough for the Japs to hear, "We'll retreat as fast as possible in that direction." He pointed to the Jap positions, "Staffords right, Gurkhas left, when I say 'Now'!"

Badger's toes tensed against the earth, ready to spring into the uphill sprint.

"NOW!"

As if impelled by a starter's gun every able man, and some wounded, tore up and around the crest. Yelling wildly, hurling their last grenades as they ran, they charged around the Pagoda and houses. With Chindit bayonets and kukries almost at their throats, the Japs quit their cover. The attacker's yells changed to jubilant whoops. The defenders were scurrying down the reverse slope.

With Gurkhas and Staffords in hot pursuit, scores of Japs were fleeing downhill and across the hundred yards of paddy towards Henu. Behind the pursuers, Chindit 'odds and sods' set about a few resolute pockets of Japs. In the mass dementia of triumph and revenge, abandoning all caution, they stormed at bunkers and dugouts.

Twice, exultantly, Badger charged after Japs scrambling from perimeter dugouts. Twice, others beat him to it, shooting and then bayoneting the felled men. In this final assault he'd not accounted for a single Jap. In a fury of childish peeve, he bayoneted a corpse on a parapet.

A bunch of Chindits swept past him, bearing down on six Japs, the last enemy remnants, scrambling from two dugouts. Badger dropped on one knee and aimed at one of the Japs. Too late again. Other rifles cracked first and three contorting bodies dropped on the parados.

Scampering past the abandoned dugouts, he took up a kneeling stance among a group pot-shotting the three fleeing Japs. Steadily, as if 'snap-shooting' on a rifle-range, he shot at the rearmost man as, with Olympic speed, they zig-zagged down hill. At a hundred yards the leading two, still in full flight, vanished into scrub and hollow ground. Ten yards behind them, the third Jap spun like a top and fell. Getting back on his feet, he stumbled back uphill, grenade in his hand. Rifles cracked again. With his arms jerking heavenward, his spine arching, he dropped to the ground.

At least a dozen rifles had blazed at the fleeing men, but Badger was convinced it was his last two rounds that had sent the Jap to his ancestors.

Wandering back up to the Pagoda in search of ammunition, he took a bandolier from a wounded Stafford, and joined another man in a slit trench overlooking the Henu area, ready for any counter-attack. With his elbows on the parapet he filled his pipe and, over his cupped hands as he abortively drew on the match flame, he squinted at the Staffs and Gurkhas pushing through Henu. The tobacco was too wet with sweat to burn, his mouth was too dry to persevere. He stuffed the pipe back in his pocket, swilled his mouth from his water-bottle, spat out, and took a quick swig.

Badger had not eaten since breakfast. He was too gluttoned by excitement to need food, but the enervating heat and battle strain was dehydrating. The urge to drain off his water-bottle was almost irresistible. Only the faint hope that soon, somehow, there'd be an opportunity to brew tea persuaded him to conserve his water.

With a mixture of elation, and a horror that overrode his thirst, he watched the Japs being driven out of Henu. Elation that these reputedly invincible Japs – conquerors of the Orient – had been routed in their first brush with 77 Brigade. Horror at the flames belching from the British 'Life-Buoys' incinerating everything in their path. Back in India they'd gloated over these new flame throwers, with fuel tanks shaped like life-buoys. Joked about 'singed ah so's' and 'fried Jips and barbecued bollocks'.

Now the awesome flames, streaking like lightning through the dusk, questing for human flesh, seemed the ultimate barbarism. Debasing the British Army to the sub-human standards of the enemy. Revulsion bloated his stomach, and he was glad he was too far away to see if the flame-throwers were cremating any Japs.

An incipient invocation for God's mercy on any cornered Japs, was quashed by a rifle crack behind him. He spun round, rifle at the ready, to see an officer crumple to the ground with a bullet hole in the back of his head. A wounded Jap, having feigned death, was taking aim at another man's back. Before Badger could take aim, a nearby sergeant kicked the Jap's head in.

Watching swarms of flies gathering around the blood oozing from the man's split skull, and the yellow mucous dribbling from one ear, Badger vowed he'd never leave a Jap for dead until he'd made certain with a bullet or bayonet. Primeval reflex obliterated all civilised reasoning. Playing possum to kill his Emperor's foes needed great courage, but pagan lust for vengeance excised every vestige of Badger's Christian mercy.

Mentally screaming, "Bastards, burn the buggers! Fry the sods!" he swung back towards Henu. Now the Japs, under covering fire from the village of Mawlu, 800 yards away, were scurrying across the paddy beyond flame-thrower range.

§

In the brief Asian twilight, as the Staffords dug-in to meet any counter-attack, Badger trudged down Pagoda Hill with the Brigade HQ elements. The evening breeze clagged his sweat soaked shirt to his skin, but with the warm flush of victory still coursing through him, he scarcely felt the chilling contact.

Amidst swarming and zinging flies, medics were moving among the wounded. The severely wounded, on improvised litters, were being carried downhill. On the rough ground, weary stretcher bearers stumbled and cursed. Walking wounded, their bloody field dressings speckled with flies, shuffled or staggered ahead of the litters. Mike Calvert was stooping over the lieutenant with the severed arm. Officers were scavenging Jap corpses for documents. Down by the sunken road, a padre was ministering the mortally wounded at the dressing station.

The return over the ridge, back to that morning's rendezvous, was no silent single file trudge. Flushed with the relief of coming through physically unscathed, men dropped back or hurried forward to jabber with muckers. Garrulous as schoolboys on a holiday treat, they disguised their lacerated nerves with forced braggadocio.

As a comparative newcomer to this column, Badger plodded thoughtfully with the undemonstrative Hong Kong Volunteers, silently composing a letter to Barbara. She would be proud of him, so too would his father, when they read his account of the battle.

From behind and ahead of him, snatches of the bragging broke into his thoughts. '...huh! Japs, supermen? Ben, I've shit tougher lumps!...' '...Aye, Chalky,we went through the bastards like a dose of salts...' '...bandy legged buggers fled like rabbits with a ferret at their arses, didn't they Dusty..?' '...fair's fair Ben, they had a go at us...' '...come off it, Dusty, they're yellow as their skins...' '...wouldn't you run with Johnny Gurkha lopping off all those heads..?'

Badger couldn't recall seeing any heads lopped off. Skulls split, necks chopped, spouting blood – yes – but no decapitations, '...bet we killed a hundred or more' an Irish voice, '...best St. Patrick's foight I've ever had, so it was...' '...bloody idiot Paddy, it's not the seventeenth of March until to-morrow...' '...d'yer see that officer with the arm chopped off, laying about the Japs with a sword in his other hand...' '...that was Lieutenant Cairns of the Staffs...' '...deserves a medal he does...'

§

Morosely chewing on a 'K' ration Hershey bar, Badger strained his eyes through the black night. He still had another hour of sentry duty.

His Chinese companion, tapping his wrist watch to indicate their first hour was up, had just crawled off to waken his relief. They'd drawn the first watch for their section and, in order to stagger change-overs, one sentry of that shift did only one hour, the other did two. After that, it was two hours on and four hours off.

The night jungle played weird trick on the eyes. Especially on men newly awakened from sleep. Trees, bushes and foliage became mobile spectres, phantoms seemingly closing in, or sneaking across one's front. Ill-adjusted eyes could induce a pair of new sentries to open fire, revealing the bivouac to the Japs. The whole column would lose precious sleep 'standing- to'.

So sentry changing was staggered, one of each pair changing each hour. Badger, his mind restless and exultant with pride yet appalled by the day's slaughter, fermenting forebodings of the next battle, had opted for the first two hour stint.

As if by common consent, throughout the trudge back no one had spoken of British casualties. It was as though the merest hint of those casualties would have turned triumph into disaster. The reaction had set in at the bivouac, when the survivors mustered for roll call around their platoon commmanders.

"Adams"

"Sir!"

"Brown"

Silence

"I bags his rations." A comradely epitaph to forestall an unsoldierly sob.

Nearby a sobbing Gurkha, stumbling away from his platoon, had embraced a tree. A surrogate mother as incoherently, he mourned a lost comrade. Or brother?

"Davies"

"Sir!"

"Dixon"

"Sir!"

"Farrell"

Silence

Most of the absentees were strangers to Badger, but every silence had etched a death mask in his mind. Now, on sentry, as he lay brooding, chin cupped in his hands, eyes and ears straining for any human movement, the bowl of every tree was a corrupting death mask, eye sockets crimson with ants.

Tonight around their fires there had been no bantering. No pooling of 'K' rations for a chocolate 'duff' of crushed biscuits, Hershey bars, fruit bars, lime juice powder and instant coffee. No revelling in the enemy's rout, nor even any reviling of his slaughter of comrades. Muckers, in their pairs sat in doleful introspection, chain smoking their meagre cigarette rations.

The new sentry crawled alongside him. Parrot fashion Badger recited their field of fire, and the intersecting arcs of other posts but his mind was still on the Platoon briefing. Before the dusk 'stand-to' they'd been told that they had killed over forty Japs and wounded scores more. News of British casualties had been ominously vague. No man had pressed for details. They did not need to. They already 'knew' sixty comrades were dead or wounded. The very vagueness of the briefing merely confirmed the grim whispers of their own 'bush telegraph'.

The communal hardships of training, the disciplined silence of marches, and their almost total isolation from military and public communication media, had bred something like a telepathic information network throughout and between each column. Some ubiquitous Hermes harvested every slip of an officer's tongue, and eavesdropped every secret parley. Strategic appreciations and tactical intentions, supply priorities and casualty figures, reached every other rank almost as soon as any 'officers only' briefing broke up, and filled in the censured gaps in platoon briefings.

The dusk 'stand-to' had an almost tangible tenseness, that gripped their throats, stressed their sinews and fuelled their adrenalin ready for flight or fight. Sixty Chindit casualties – 25 percent of the assault force – in their first battle. A one in four chance of coming through the campaign unscathed? Previous 'stand-to's' were just routine chores, half hearted gestures to repel some nebulous enemy. This afternoon's savagery had put paid to their nonchalance. The enemy was now a fearsome reality. Real as their hearts now beating against the earth. Save for the rustling trees, the silence had been absolute. No hissed commands to silence gabbling muckers. No bored fidgeting with rattling weapons. Only absolute, pregnant silence.

It had been a silence that communicated every man's thoughts and fears. To-day had been no decisive Alamein. If this Block really imperilled the Jap supply lines, it would become an Asian Tobruk. A besieged citadel persistently bombarded and assaulted.

Badger did not doubt the strategic importance of the Block, but it would neutralise their hard won expertise as hit and run guerillas. The bush telegraph, humming that Calvert was taking Brigade HQ into the Block tomorrow, roused more anger than fear. Once in the Block, he'd not a snowball in hell's chance of getting back to his own column, back among his own muckers. And, above all, back to any of Barbara's letters that may have been air-dropped to his column.

Chapter Sixteen

Badger winced as the cigarette end singed his pubic hairs, scorching the flesh as gingerly he tugged a tick from the root of his penis. With an embarrassed grin at a passing Gurkha, he hitched up his trousers, squatted down on his pack, and took up his mug of steaming tea again.

Since dawn, for six hours under a blazing sun, with a working party, he had been packing earth into parachute containers and building them into protective walls around the dressing station and mule corral. His shirt was sweat soaked and the hot sweet tea had brought on a fresh outbreak of sweat on his spine and scalp. He swallowed a couple of salt tablets with a mouthful of water from his bottle, and cocked his ears at the outburst of gunfire from Bare Hill, the north east point of the Block.

Until yesterday, Badger was beginning wonder whether the Block was really a serious threat to the Japs supply line, and would have given scant attention to the firing.

In the six days since the Pagoda Hill battle, the Block had become a formidable redoubt. The nightly air drops of heavy machine guns and mortars, ammunition and barbed wire, picks and shovels, had festooned the trees with white parachute canopies. Mike had baptised it 'White City'. The southern perimeter had been pushed out to take in Henu, including a hill just east of, and higher than Pagoda Hill. This hill, now dubbed O.P. Hill, with its commanding view now housed the artillery observation post. Light planes repeatedly ferried casualties from a strip, alongside the railway, to

Broadway for evacuation by Dakota to India.

Until last night the Japs had attempted no more than small patrol sorties, mostly at night, inflicting negligible casualties, and scarcely interrupting the defenders' sleep let alone the collection of supply drops. Nor had the sporadic gunfire of their rarer daytime sallies held back the consolidation of defences.

Yesterday, as if White City was a trivial intrusion into their territory, a Jap squad from Mawlu had strolled across the open paddy, within a few hundred yards of the perimeter. Mortars and machine guns had killed five and wounded thirty more of them, for the loss of one Chindit killed and five wounded. Through it all working parties with only random squints at the skirmish, had continued stringing barbed wire and field telephone lines, roofing weapon pits with logs and laying mines.

Then, last night, the Japs had demolished any delusions about their tactical complacency. Their probing sallies had clearly, but erroneously, convinced them that the northern perimeter was the Block's weakest point. At the dusk 'stand-to' they had showered the area with grenades and mortars. Shouting 'Tik Hai Johnny' 'Cease fire' 'OK Bill' 'Stand down now', they had rushed the forward posts as the South Staffs defenders momentarily hesitated. Then it was close-quarter fighting, stabbing bayonets and slaughter with point blank shooting.

The overwhelming strength of the Japs breached the forward area, giving their leading elements a foothold between two South Staffs platoons. In extremis the Staffs had signalled for a 3inch mortar bombardment of their sector. Salvo after salvo of mortar shells, pre-targeted for just such a desperate contingency, whistling in high arcs, blasted the melee of friend and foe, electrifying earth and sky like lightning bolts.

Above the din of battle, the nightly procession of droning Dakotas had repeatedly swooped over the Block, parachuting their cargoes on to the airstrip.

Throughout the night, back in Brigade HQ defence lines, Badger with his rifle cocked, two fifty-round bandoliers and four primed grenades at his elbows on the parapet of his slit trench, had steeled himself for a Japanese breakthrough. Marvelling at the nerve of the Dakota pilots, he had waited with his cheek nestling the rifle butt, finger on the trigger, ready to snipe at any furtive silhouette. Calvert's orders had been unequivocal. Every man was to stay in his trench, no matter what happened. Anyone moving was to be instantly shot.

The ceaseless battle din, chattering machine guns, grenade blasts, defiant yells and shrieking wounded, fired his adrenalin with conflicting hope, fear and temptation. Hope that Mike would rescind his order, and commit them to the battle. Fear that he might do just that. Temptation to cower below the parapet, secure from the constant whine and ping of ricochets.

Moments became hours, before the battle crescendo degenerated to desultory fusillades. Above the hoarse, impatient cries for stretcher bearers, and moans of the wounded at the dressing station, in a re-entrant a hundred yards to his north, had come loud, almost demented, Jap jabberings.

A translation, by Japanese speaking Captain Ryan, had briefly cheered the garrison. The Japs, having lost all their officers, were arguing whether to retreat or resume the assault. But even as the news was telegraphed around the block, hopes of a Jap withdrawal had been put to flight by another determined assault. Yelling 'Banzai!', they had launched another assault on the same sector and had breached the defences. Again mortars had pounded the close-quarter embroilment. As captured documents were to reveal later that morning, the Japs' orders were to 'clear the block and take prisoners', and their fanatical soldiers had made fanatical efforts to do just that.

Before the dawn's first glimmer, the Japs had broken through to the dressing station area. Almost surrounded by the savage hand to hand battle, the blood soaked medical officers and padres, had serenely continued treating and comforting the multiplying wounded.

Two Jap light machine gun crews had gained a foothold behind the Staffs lines. Their distinctive woodpecker bursts had repulsed repeated attempts to dislodge them. With only the scrub-screened gun flashes as a target, Badger had abortively fired a score of rounds at the machine gun position, and had brought long bursts of fire on his own trench.

Then, throughout the morning, packing earth into the parachute containers, he had been plagued by the thought that maybe he could have, should have, crawled close enough to lob grenades on the machine gunners. Was it Mike's 'stay put' order, or self preservation that had held him back?

Just before first light, two commando platoons, with flame throwers, had wormed their way around to the west of the embattled sector. At dawn they had charged into the fray. In a whirlwind, no-quarter assault, flame-throwers blazing in their van, they pushed the Japs back slaughtering the resolute and driving all others out of the block.

Now, ears tuned to the Bare Hill gunfire, Badger fought off the urge to dive for cover. The working party sergeant had been summoned to Brigade HQ, and the other eleven men squatting with rifles between their knees, glanced furtively at each other. Hesitant, waiting for someone to take the lead and dive for cover.

The mopping-up shooting that had frequently punctuated the forenoon had, until now, been too brief to send working parties to ground. Amid the whine and ping of ricochets, working parties had carried on gathering in the supply drop and reinforcing the defence works, as other platoons ferreted out the enemy remnants. In treetops and on the ground, feigning death, resolute Japs lay in wait for opportunities to snipe at unwary Chindits, and the moppers-up took no chances. With bayonet and bullet, they made doubly sure every Jap body was dead before moving on. But those were sporadic volleys. The intensity of the Bare Hill outburst was unmistakably a pitched battle.

With a casualness that belied his trepidation, Badger packed away his mess tin. He wasn't in charge – there were two other corporals in the party – but someone had to take lead.

"Right, get your equipment on, and get to your platoon posts."

As he twisted to adjust his belt and pouches, he caught sight of the Brigadier and his Chinese batman, carrying a casualty into the dressing station twenty yards behind him.

"Hang on a sec. here comes the sergeant."

"Relax lads, the Brigade Major is coming over to have a word with you." The sergeant pointed to the slim figure strolling towards them.

"Settle yourselves down, chaps. That's only the Gurkhas mopping up." The major jerked his head towards Bare Hill, "It'll be like this seven days a week now, so don't get the wind up at every shot." Loss of sleep had etched deeper lines in his consumptive cheeks, but his eyes were bright with excitement, "I want an NCO and two men for a special patrol, any volunteers?"

"Yes, sir!" Badger's hand shot up like a child eager for a teacher's favour. Four British and two Chinese – Joe Tai and Robert Law – diffidently raised their hands.

"Are you a good map reader, corporal?"

"Yes, sir!" No point in false modesty when he wanted to prove his value as a patrol commander.

"Good. You'll have a Burma Rifles corporal with you. Pick your two men."

He hardly knew the four Britishers, so he chose Tai and Law. He never could memorise their full Chinese names. He'd shared cooking fires and sentry duties with the two Chinese. They were tireless marchers, resourceful, battle hardened and staunch pals. Some unspoken mutual antipathy, kept them apart from the other Hong Kong Volunteers, but Badger got on well with them.

"I'll brief you when the Burriff arrives. The rest of you will be guarding our four prisoners, making sure they don't commit hara-kiri before we fly them out..."

"Hara-kiri takes guts", some wag muttered.

"Oh, very droll", the sergeant growled. "Now shut your trap and listen to the major."

"I'll brief you as far as I can on last night's duffy. You can smoke if you wish." The major, motioning them to sit down paused whilst they settled down with their cigarettes or pipes. In a few terse sentences he sketched the night's battle. Three Jap infantry companies with two engineer companies, the equivalent of a British battalion, more than double the strength of the northern sector defenders, had put in the attack. There were sixty dead Japs inside the Block, scores more outside the perimeter, and God knows how many wounded they had carried away.

"I won't kid you that we got off lightly," he said solemnly, "You'll already know Colonel Richards of the Staffs bought it leading the dawn counter-attack, ten other officers were killed during the night, and a sniper got Major Jeffries this morning."

Officer casualties could not be fudged. The loss of any of them was too immediately obvious for any vacillating, and the major clearly realised that the bush telegraph had breached the HQ embargo on casualty roll details. To deflect their thoughts from the grimness of that roll, he hurriedly went on, "But we've done damn well. In one action I believe we've taken more prisoners, and captured more valuable Jap documents, than any other force has ever done. One of them is their adjutant. He told Captain Ryan the Jap command thought we'd be a walkover. He's disgusted with himself, but apparently not enough to commit hara-kiri. Apart from being knocked out by someone, he's unscathed. So much for their death before dishonour."

Badger's mind lingered on the casualties, and he only vaguely heard the next few sentences. There were at least thirty Chindit bodies awaiting burial, and forty wounded waiting for evacuation by light planes.

"....this afternoon Cochrane's chaps will be putting in an air-strike on the surrounding hills." The major looked intently at Badger, certain that the corporal had only been half listening, "Any questions?" Silence. "Corporal?"

"Who was the Brigadier carrying?"

"Paddy Dermody, his groom. Shot by a sniper. Brigadier killed the sniper with his revolver. Paddy's badly hurt, but he'll live. Anything else, corporal?"

"Can't we get some artillery flown in? Any news about 81 and 82 columns? What are the other Brigades doing, sir?"

"Oh, come now corporal, you're not so naive as to think I could broadcast details of other Brigades, even if I knew." The major's bright eyes bored into Badger's, perceiving there was more than naivity in the questions.

"No, sir, just ..." the sentence died in his throat.

"All I can tell you is, 16 Brigade are operating from the Aberdeen stronghold, 111 Brigade's columns landed at Broadway and Chowringhee and are concentrating south of us. As for 14 and 23 Brigade I have no information. Artillery?" He paused, his eyes trying read Badger's mind, "Yes... well perhaps we'll be constructing a strip for gliders and Dakotas to bring heavier guns in."

Badger's seeming naivity had wormed out confirmation of the ominous rumours. Bringing in artillery suggested the end to 77 Brigade's guerilla role. Gun batteries would not be brought in if White City was intended as a short-lived citadel. The other bloody brigades had been given the true Chindit roles.

"Are you with us, Corporal?"

"Sorry Sir... just dreaming what this special patrol is about." The lie was reinforced with an enquiring frown, "But what about 81 and 82 Columns, sir?"

"They're still operating around Broadway. Ah yes, you're a Kingsman. I suppose you've heard that many of those missing on the fly in to Broadway got back safely to Assam? They're now back with their columns."

"Yes, Sir, I had."

"Good, here comes your Burriff, Corporal Baw." The major beckoned the slightly built, femininely handsome Burmese corporal, to sit alongside Badger, "Before we get down to patrol details, I must tell you the Brigadier is proud of you all. Says the way you fought last night proves British troops will stand their ground when ordered to – regardless of the odds. OK sergeant, take your party off to relieve the prisoner's escort and now... Corporal!" He gave Badger an admonishing look, "kindly give me your undivided attention until I've finished briefing you..."

A brief volley of gunfire, followed by the booms of exploding mines, reverberated through the Block. The fighting on Bare Hill had died into silence some time ago, but some concealed pocket of Japs must have been have been flushed out, and been driven back through the perimeter minefield.

"You know," resumed the major as the echoes faded, "that there is an anti-British Burmese National Army, we call them the Burmese Traitor Army of course. Well, there's a Kachin from a village between the Nutmauk and Kauwkee chaungs, who claims the headman at a neighbouring village is whipping up support for them. Your job is to locate that village, and inform 81 and 82 Column..."

Badger could hardly believe his luck. He was cock-a-hoop, not only at the opportunity to get back to his battalion, but also because he'd volunteered for the patrol before he knew what its mission was. He hadn't a flicker of doubt he'd be allowed to remain with his muckers once he got there. And he could leave the Block with a clear conscience. Volunteering had been no cowardly wangle, he'd done so believing he would be only briefly away from White City.

With his enthusiasm whetted by the anticipated reunion, Badger calmed his fluttering heart-strings, and concentrated his mind on the major's briefing.

The Kachin informant, tracking the Brigade HQ's trail, had met up with a Burrif section at a pro-British village, an hour's march from White City, and was waiting there for the patrol. He didn't speak English; couldn't read a map, so a map reference couldn't be radio-ed to the King's. He was too frightened to be flown over the area in a light plane. In any case, he claimed the jungle there was too dense to distinguish the village from the air. The name of a village on any map of the Kachin territory, was an unreliable reference point. Kachin villages frequently moved, lock stock and barrel, and there were several pro-British villages around the Nutmauk and Kaukwee. Without a precise identification the King's might raid the wrong village, alienating friendly Kachins and alerting the rebels.

"...Apart from all that," the major went on, "God knows how trustworthy our informant is. Why did he not take the information to Broadway which is nearer to his village? He says he pretended to be anti-British and was sent to spy on the Block. If he had been seen going towards Broadway, he claimed that they would see through his pretence. Plausible perhaps, but he could be leading us into an ambush. We daren't risk sending a full patrol with an officer, even if we could spare one..."

"It could be a ploy to settle old scores, sir,"

"Yes Corporal, possibly that too – some tribal feud. But the Burriffs think that's very unlikely, don't they?" Baw gave an emphatic nod, and the major glanced at his watch.

Time was critical, he told them. They were to slip out around Bare Hill at dusk 'stand-to'. About two miles north east, guided by Baw, they would rendezvous with a detachment of Burriffs, disguised as Kachins, to pick up the informant. The five of them were then to march as far as they could before resting for the night. It would normally take a column three to five days to reach the area. They must locate the village, and rendezvous on the Kaukwee with 82 Column in three days at the most. According to the informant, the traitor with some henchmen intended to quit the village four days hence, on the 26th. They were to avoid contact with Jap patrols, and any villages en route. When they found the village they were to reconnoitre it without being seen, and then get to 82 Column as fast as they could. The map showed several villages on the route down to the Kaukwee rendezvous. If they couldn't bypass them without long detours, they were to say they were searching for any wounded left behind after last year's campaign.

"...Now, each of you memorise this map reference, that's your rendezvous with 82 Column. Corporal – pick up five day's rations per man; a map and a compass."

"And a watch, sir?" Hopefully. The major gave him a sharp, askance look and pointed to the wrist watches of the other three, "What for? You've got three already."

§

Sitting propped against a teak tree, contentedly puffing at his pipe, Badger could just make out the pole star blinking through the rustling forest roof. He was well pleased with the day's progress. His patrol had travelled faster and further than he had dared hope. *His* patrol. *His* men. He rolled the words in his mind. He – a corporal – commanding a tactically independent mission.

His three men, and the stocky Kachin, were curled under their blankets around the dying embers of their fire. Too exhilarated to sleep, he was standing sentry and at the moment he felt he could sit the night through without needing a relief.

Last night, after picking up the Kachin, they had pushed on for about five miles before bivouacking for the night. Today they had marched from dawn to dusk, with only a half hour mid-day break, through towering teaks. Spurred by determination to prove his professional competence, and the prospect of re-union with his own muckers, he had forced a brisk pace. The sun had blazed down from a virtually cloudless sky, but their route high above the steamy bamboo foothills had given them the benefit of a gentle breeze. He had chosen the high route for more important reasons than the breeze.

The foothills route would involve detours around, or noisy hacking through, bamboo thickets and would severely restrict their visibility. The teak route assured them the best going and all round visibility and he needed good visibility for his order of march.

From the first moment he was able to study the pock marked Kachin by the light of day, he was virtually certain the man was no BTA collaborator. A silver medallion, engraved with the valedictory appreciation of a District Commissioner, dangled from a heavy silver chain around his goitred neck. Heavy jade ear-rings distorted the lobes to Buddha-like droops. His dah, and 12 bore shot gun, were lovingly preserved relics from some pre-war government employment. His black head scarf, lungyi and jacket, were wefted with iridescent yellow and red stripes. This prosperous tribal father *must* be pro-British...

There was something chameleon about the man's features. Except for two silver capped upper incisors and a single black lower one, he was toothless. When he spoke or grinned he looked like a halfwit. At other times – with his thick lips closed – his keen nut-brown eyes, careworn cheeks and wispy goatee, gave him the aura of a genial and shrewd tribal sage.

Like most elderly hillmen, the stocky Kachin's bulging calves were puckered with knotted veins, and his powerful legs were congenitally bowed. Baw had introduced him as 'Ban The' something or other, and the patrol had instantly saddled him with the name 'Bandy'.

Bandy was no sycophant. He had met Badger's appraisal with the cool reciprocal scrutiny of a guileless peer. And, when Baw informed him of their intended route, his unquestioning assent had strengthened Badger's trust in his story. If he had any evil motive, he surely would have tried to influence their direction. Nevertheless, and as improbable as it seemed, Badger took the precaution of splitting the patrol in two.

He had assigned Bandy – and Baw dressed as a Kachin – as scouts with instructions to keep as far ahead of himself, Joe Tai and Robert Law, as the line of sight between the two parties permitted. Elderly as Bandy appeared to be, his pace had repeatedly forced the rear party to jog-trot to keep him within sight.

As he tapped out his pipe, a whisper of breeze wafted the fire embers into flame, and he strode over Joe to stamp it out.

"How far do you reckon we've got to go yet, corp?" Joe, pushing aside his blanket, raised himself on one elbow.

"I reckon we are more than half-way there. With luck we should be there early tomorrow afternoon. About 15 miles to go, if Bandy is not leading us on a wild goose chase. Now get some sleep. Its only four hours to first light, and we'll need every scrap of stamina to-morrow. Come what may, before nightfall we're going to get the gen to 82 Column."

Settling back against the tree, he told himself not only to get the gen to them, but hopefully to get news of any mail deliveries to Broadway. His eyes implored the heavens – please God, let there be a letter from Barbara waiting there.

§

It was noon when Baw and Bandy, halting at a half crouch, beckoned the rest of the party forward. The patrol had descended to the fringe of the teak line, overlooking a shallow, bamboo and scrub valley. Atop the opposite slope, through the swaying bamboo interstices, they could see the thatched roofs of a clutch of typical Kachin huts.

With emphatic replies to Baw's interrogation, and vigorous gestures, Bandy assured them that this was the right village, and described the tracks and village layout.

Reminding them that stealth was vital, Badger sent Joe to reconnoitre around one half the village, and Robert the other. With Baw translating Bandy's descriptions, he made a rough sketch of the village area on the back of his map. The two Chinese, returning as Badger finished the sketch verified its basic accuracy and within half an hour Bandy was leading them down into the Kaukwee valley

By mid-afternoon, the forced pace of the morning, sweating under their heavy packs, and the nerve-wracking tenseness of the surreptitious survey, had all but drained their vitality. Reluctantly Badger decided they must halt soon for a meal and a brew up, even if that meant they would not reach the rendezvous before night-fall.

"Baw, tell Bandy we're going to pull off the track for a meal."

With a delighted grin, the old Kachin muttered something to Baw and pointed down the track.

"He says this track goes past his village, Nutmauk, just further down. They will be honoured to give us a meal." Baw spoke with sing-song Asiatic intonation and mission school pedantry.

Badger thought for a moment.

"OK We'll take a chance." A detour would be a wasted effort. Unless they forcibly restrained Bandy, they could not stop him returning to his village. That would be a perverse reward for his services, and could forfeit his village's allegiance. If Bandy went alone the village would soon know the patrol's whereabouts.

"Tell him we accept... Wait a second." Realising their cover story would be futile once Bandy spoke to his kin, he pulled Baw to one side,. "Forget the cover story. They'll soon know it's false, and we'll lose their trust. Until we see which way the wind blows, go along with what he he tells them. He doesn't know the rendezvous, so keep mum about that. If we're pressed we'll say we're going direct to Broadway. At the first sign of trouble we'll slip away."

§

Nutmauk – eight stilted bamboo huts, an open sided shelter set around a small clearing and a solitary stunted tree – stood in a loop of the Nutmauk Chaung. In the neck of the loop, between the huts and the jungle fringe, was an acre of recently harvested paddy.

Waist deep in the crystal clear chaung, adolescent girls were bathing. Their saturated longyis, drawn skin-tight up to their armpits, betrayed every exciting line curve of their nubile torsos. As they paused in their ablutions, coquettishly taking in Badger's brazen stare, three older women drawing water in bamboo tubes, hissed some obvious rebukes at the girls, and brought a chorus of embarrassed giggles from the bathers.

Children, playing some form of hop-scotch in the dusty clearing, abandoned their game and, scuttling under the shelter, peeked shyly at the visitors from behind a teak framed loom. Under one of the huts, amidst scratting, squawking chickens, and rutting piglets, two toddlers squealed merrily and peep-po-ed at the patrol from behind a wicker basket.

A wizened man sitting cross legged with six others smoking cheroots near the tree, rose to his feet. The air of authority with which he motioned the others to stand up, marked him as the Thugyi. With what Badger guessed was a Buddhist welcome, the Thugyi dipped his head to his palms, held prayer-like in front of his chest. Badger solemnly returned the salutation and, in turn, the Thugyi clasped each of their right hands and forearm in a hearty greeting.

As Bandy talked to his Thugyi, the bathers scrambled from the chaung, wound dry lungyis over their wet ones, adroitly shimmied the soaking longyis down to their feet, and joined the knot of curious villagers gathering around the tree. After a few words with Baw, the Thugyi dispersed the women with some brief instruction and led his menfolk, including Bandy, and the patrol to the tree where two women hurriedly laid rush mats.

"He has sent for some rice beer." Baw, taking the lead, slipped off his equipment and beckoned the patrol to sit around the mats. "They are going to give us chicken broth and suckling pig."

A slender maiden and a plump matron, handed each man a bamboo mug, and filled them from long tubes of bamboo. The 'beer' was unlike anything Badger had seen or tasted. The warm, gruel-like liquid was tangy, thirst quenching and deceptively potent. In the twenty or so minutes before the food arrived, the Thugyi on one side of him, and a muscular villager on the other, twice directed the maiden to replenish Badger's mug.

The hot food, wrapped in banana leaves, was laid in the centre of the mats by the same two women. The maiden, kneeling between Badger and the Thugyi, leaned across the mats to fill an earthen basin for Badger. As she bent forward, her breasts strained her white cotton jacket. The stretching emphasised her exquisite waist, and tantalisingly tautened the longyi over her buttocks.

The 'beer' quickened Badger's loins, banishing his innate shyness of women. Baw was sitting on the other side of the Thugyi, and a furtive peek around told him they were too deep in conversation, and the others too pre-occupied filling their bowls, to look his way. His hand skimmed down the maiden's velvet shoulder. Through the thin lungyi, his fingers furrowed gently into the crevice of her bottom. With an anxious glance at the Thugyi, she straightened up and with careless grace, moved behind the old man and Baw. Over their heads, she flashed a startled look at Badger and nodded her chin indicatively at the back of the Thugyi's bowed head. It was an unmistakable warning gesture. The Thugyi must be her father, or even her grandfather, he told himself. He shot her a conspiratorial wink to hide his embarrassment and self reproach.

The aroma of the highly spiced broth whet his palate, but before anyone could take a mouthful, a Kachin boy trotted into the village. Panting up to the Thugyi, he gasped out something about "..Jarparnay..." that brought all the Kachins and Baw hurriedly to their feet. In seconds, without any apparent signal, villagers were scurrying away with all evidence of the meal.

"A Jap patrol is on the way from the next village." Baw translated, reaching for his rifle and equipment.

"How many?" Badger scooped up his rifle, and slung on his pack.

"About twelve." As Baw spoke, back up the track, with a flurry of beating wings and alarmed shrieks, flocks of birds soared into the sky.

"They will be here in five minutes!"

"Too many for us." Any less would also have been too many. His orders were to avoid Japs at all costs. And God knows what brutality they would inflict on the villagers if there was the merest hint of their harbouring British troops, "We'll bump into them if we use the track."

As if divining Badger's thoughts, the Thugyi, an appeal for urgency in his worried eyes, shoo-ed them towards the paddy. In the couple of minutes it took them to cross the paddy and hide in the bamboo thickets, the Kachin men with Bandy among them, were back around the tree, puffing their cheroots and nonchalantly chatting. Women were casually tending cooking fires, bringing up water, winnowing grain in huge rattan trays. One woman was working at the loom. Even the children were back, scratching out their hop-scotch pitch. The village was a canvas of rural routines.

The Jap officer, leading his men in double file, was tall and portly, with a Mussolini arrogance about the set of his head and shoulders. He marched with splayed legged, kipper footed strides, his baggy breeches accentuating his bowed legs. There was a spruceness about him that Badger had not seen in the Japs at White City. The peak of his cotton field cap was precisely squared over his eyes. His open necked bush jacket was snug fit, the lapels neatly overlapped by a white shirt collar. His polished sword belt and holster glistened as did, above his dusty ankles, his riding boots.

The soldiers were mirrors of their White City compatriots, short, wiry, hollow cheeked and shabbily clothed. All they had in common with the officer, was the uniformity of their unsoldierly buckled knees, and kipper-footed gait.

At the centre of the clearing the officer halted, and sent half of the patrol to search the huts. The remainder herded the villagers in a circle around him. In the centre of the circle, feet astride, arms akimbo, like an Asiatic Il-Duce, he slowly pivoted to receive the kow-tow of each villager.

Watching the searchers trotting from hut to hut, Badger wondered what spirit fuelled the fanatical courage of these ragged, scruffy malnourished rustics. No, they weren't just rustics. He knew well enough that the bulk of Japan's forces came from her teeming cities. Metropolitan dwellers, lured from urban penury, by some mystical feudalism, into Imperial army beggary.

"We had better get away now." Baw tugged insistently at Badger's sleeve and pointed to the Jap sentry posted at each end of the village.

"No, Baw, we'll stay here..." he hissed firmly, as he watched the women, kneeling at the replaced rush mats, pouring out the 'beer', and the Thugyi solicitously ushering the officer to a place beside them, "...he's being a bit ingratiating."

"Come on, let's get going while the going's good, and we've got the chance." The apostrophized colloquialism, and assertive tone, were out of character.

"What's put the wind up you Baw?" The hairs on

Badger's neck stiffened. Something more than those Japs had rattled the normally placid Burriff.

"You may have driven the Thugyi to betray us..." Baw swallowed hard.

"What the hell do you mean?" His eyes blazed at Baw.

"Feeling his wife!"

"His wife! Christ!" Badger's face went ashen, "He's old enough to be her bloody grandfather. How could I know! She hadn't a gold anklet."

"That is not a Kachin custom!" Baw muttered surlily,"It is south, in the Shan territory, that some tribeswomen wear them. A silver one for virgins, gold for wives."

"D'yer think he saw me?"

"If I did, he could have done. Kachins are ruthless with flirts."

"Did either of you two see me?" The Chinese shook their heads. "Let's hope he didn't, then." How outraged he'd have been if he'd seen a man do that to Barbara. What a bloody idiot he was. On the very brink of success he'd put their lives and mission in jeopardy. A chill of fear rippled down his spine. "We'll stay where we are for a bit, and chance it." He had to be sure of the Thugyi's loyalty. "They'll have to come across a hundred yards of paddy to get us. If they do, you three slip away, I'll give you covering fire."

The Chinese nodded, but there was a disapproving frown on Baw's brow, and he pointed across the paddy. The Jap officer and the Thugyi, now standing on the far edge of the paddy, were surveying the encompassing jungle. With legs astride, leaning on the hilt of his sword, the Jap's head followed the sweep of the Thugyi's hand.

Veins throbbed in Badger's throat as the Japs eyes paused on the patrol's position. Like a stuck gramophone needle, his mind repeatedly whispered 'the game's up' 'we've had it' 'the game's up'... Hardly daring to breath, let alone whisper, the other three started to squirm further back into the jungle, preparing themselves for flight.

"Psst" Throat taut, lips brick dry, Badger waved them to standfast, and pointed towards the village with his chin. The Jap and the Thugyi were returning to the mats, but the officer was shouting to the soldiers, directing them towards the paddy.

"Now what, Baw?" The Burriff's shrug said 'do not ask me, you're in charge'.

"Doesn't look like he's told them anything." More in hope than conviction, he watched the soldiers gathering around some women spreading another set of mats near the fringe of the paddy. "It looks like their officer has demanded they be fed before...."

"...Maybe the Thugyi's stalling so that we can get away."

"Maybe so, Joe, which means he's not given us away, yet." His hopes rose, "And he couldn't have seen me touching her up." He paused to watch the soldiers settle down around the new mats. At only a hundred yards range, with their rifles stacked in two tepee-like piles beyond arm's reach, they were tempting targets. He firmly quashed the incipient notion, "They're not daft, if they knew about us, they'd not give us time to get away."

"I still think we should get going now." Baw persisted, and this time Joe and Robert grunted in agreement.

"Not yet." Soldierly appraisal of the enemy was now overriding his fear, but he compromised in deference to the Burriff's entreaties, "As a precaution, you three move as far back as you can without losing sight of me. If I wave my panic map skedaddle as fast as you can. Don't stick together, separate and make for the rendezvous individually. You'd better take this." He passed the map with the sketch on to Baw, "If nothing happens, and the Japs leave the village, I'll wave my hat."

The fascination of observing the Japs tucking into the food and drink, shambling behind the huts to urinate, and of women trotting back and forth with victuals for the two sentries, robbed Badger of all sense of time and tension. Only when the officer eventually rose to his feet, did he notice his own limbs were stiff and cramped with tension.

The officer's high pitched command had an alcoholic slur, and brought his men scurrying into a double file facing the paddy. Getting ready to wave his panic map, Badger held his breath as three soldiers, at some angry shout from their officer, doubled towards the paddy. But at the fringe of the village they smartly turned left and, out of view from their comrades, accelerated to sprinting.

A suppressed guffaw of relief almost ruptured Badger's loins. The men, halting behind a hut, dropped their rifles. Waggling on heels and toes, as they cast off their equipment, they hastily shoved down their trousers in overdue response to nature's urging.

This was too amusing for the patrol to miss, and he beckoned the other three forward with his hat. There they were, three Japs, squatting like three gratified monkeys, oblivious of the giggling children peeking from beneath the hut, while their officer paced up and down the clearing.

A bellow from the officer abruptly terminated the ecstatic relief on their faces. Dressing on the run, still tucking in their shirt-tails, they caught up with their comrades as the last file disappeared up the track.

"There you are.." Changing his mind, Badger decided not to tempt fate by saying 'I knew they wouldn't betray us', "... next time anyone say's they're supermen remind 'em the Japs have got to shit the same way as any man."

It was a puerile over-reaction of relief. He must control his excitement, be more professional and phlegmatic, "Right lads, we'll give them ten minutes, then Baw can go and question the Thugyi."

§

At the edge of the village the Thugyi and Baw spoke for some moments before both of them beckoned Badger and the other two to come over.

"The Japs were on a routine policing patrol," Baw translated as they settled down again around the mats, "Boasted that Broadway and White City would soon be our graveyards. Let it slip that a Jap column with elephants was heading for Broadway. Promised them that British barbarians would never again rule over them, and soon their invincible Imperial Army would liberate their Indian brothers from the yoke of British oppression. The New Asia under the Japanese would bring them greater prosperity than they could ever dream of."

"Did he say anything about my doing... you know what?" Badger whispered as they settled down on the mats again.With a re-assurring head shake Baw continued translating. The Jap officer had not confined himself to propaganda. He had interrogated everyone, but not even the children had mentioned Badger's patrol. He had warned of executions for anyone helping the British, and promised handsome rewards for information and co-operation.

The Thugyi interrupted Baw with a nudge and few words.

"He's apologising. The Japs have drunk most of their beer. Oh yes..." Baw nodded at the broad grins on all the Kachin's faces, "They made the food extra spicy, no wonder some of them had belly-ache. They have saved a little for us – normally spiced of course."

"Thank him for us, and tell him we understand about the food and beer. The village has already been more than generous." He leaned aside as a woman, kneeling beside him, filled his mug for the second time, and another handed him a bowl of chicken broth. The Thugyi's wife was serving Robert and Joe, and when their eyes met for an instant, Badger blushed and took a long swallow of beer to disguise his embarrassment, "And Baw, you can tell them that the British are back to stay." He sounded like a pompous Victorian plenipotentiary.

With a deprecatory head-shake, the Thugyi brushed aside the translated thanks, and nodded his belief in the British re-occupation. Then going over to the largest hut, he pulled out a section from each of two corner posts. For the first time Badger noticed that this hut had triple supports at each corner, the other huts had only double corner posts.

Chuckling, the Thugyi pulled a tightly rolled wad of certificates and a tin of Nestle's condensed milk from one bamboo section, and two bottles of Haig whisky from the other and placed them on the mats.

"Great Scott!" Badger picked up the wad, "They're War Savings Certificates. There must be a thousand rupees worth."

With broad grins, the old man and his henchmen jabbered away and, while Baw translated, he doled out generous measures of whisky.

"When the District Officer made his monthly visit, before the Japs came, they had a big feast. He always brought a stock of whisky. The milk was for his morning tea." Baw briefly questioned the Thugyi, "He used to buy Saving Certificates from the Government Shroff when they went down to the Hopin market to trade crops and poultry for tools and metal ware. The villagers are all one family, they were saving for a plot near Moguang, so the kids can attend a mission school."

"Wish he'd shown us those before the Japs came. It would have saved us a lot of sweat." Badger took mouthful of the broth, and hastily washed it down with whisky.

The broth was cool but too fiercely spiced for his Lancashire palate. The neat whisky was bland by comparison. Robert, Joe and Baw were hungrily scooping up the broth with hardly a pause between mouthfuls. The Kachins watched with wry, not unsympathetic smiles as Badger gulped whisky between each miserly mouthful. By the time he had finished, long after the others had put down their empty bowls, the shadows were merging into purple dusk.

"We'd better get on our way." His head was fuzzy as he orientated his map, "We'll cross the Nutmauk here, and march on a compass bearing to the Kaukkwe Chaung." He traced the Kaukkwe with an unsteady finger. Following its meandering course would take hours. Cutting across it six times would get them to the rendezvous in half the time. "OK lads, packs on. We'll get our feet wet, but we'll take the shortest route."

They drained off their drinks, and the Thugyi and his men, rising to their feet, fell into a rough line to say farewell.

"Wish there was something I could give them, Baw. A sort token thanks for their hospitality, and esteem of their loyalty to the Crown." He whispered in a sort of alcoholic delusion of ambassadorial status.

"Your dah? The Thugyi has been looking wistfully at it all the time. Good tools are scarce, and Army issue tools are highly prized."

"I don't know about that... It's on my 1173." The dah was on his personal inventory, and the QM could deduct the cost of it plus – in that twisted Army logic – the cost of a replacement from his pay.

"I do not think they would stop your pay for giving it to

him. It would not be like losing it through neglect, or selling it for your own pocket..." Baw whispered, pedantic as ever.

"Mm..It would be like a goodwill gift to a tribal chief, and I *am* King George's representative." The grandeur of the notion seized his inebriated vanity. He would have witnesses to prove that – on behalf of the Crown – he had presented it to a loyal Thugyi. More likely he'd be commended for thoughtfulness than charged for its 'loss'. But he couldn't just hand it over, like a personal trinket. An occasion like this deserved some ceremony, some dignity, "OK, fall in line with me."

With Baw on his right, Joe and Robert to his left, facing the Thugyi and the elders, Badger unhitched the dah from his belt.

"It is with great pleasure that I present you with this dah, on behalf of ...er... the British Crown."

As Baw translated Badger stepped forward one pace with the dah horizontal, the hilt resting in one palm, the tip of the blade in the other, and bowed his head as the Thugyi took the dah. For a moment, the scene had the solemn formality of a court investiture, then the Kachins were chattering with applause. Bandy's face creased into that gummy half wit grin. The Thugyi's rheumy brown eyes shone with inexpressible delight, his head nodded half a dozen bows of thanks. His elders pressed around, nodding appreciatively as each thumbed the edge of the blade, and 'weighted' it for balance.

As the patrol made the final adjustments to their equipment, the Thugyi, bursting with gratitude for the dah, vigorously shook Badger's hand and, through Baw, pressed them to have one of his men as a guide. With the cocksureness beget of alcohol, Badger firmly but courteously rejected the offer.

Chapter Seventeen

Woodsmoke, tickling his nostrils, stirred Badger from sleep. As he raised his head from his pack, a pneumatic drill hammered his eyes – all four of them. With their heads pillowed on their packs, Baw to his right, Joe and Robert on the left, were still sleeping soundly. Through the dawn mist, and dozy stupor, he strained to focus his double vision eyes.

They were under a large derelict bamboo hut, on earth littered with chicken lime and cast off feathers. Between the uprights, on the other side of Baw, was a jumble of decaying wicker baskets. Outside, a few yards beyond the baskets, he could just make out a rifle stock hanging from the rotting shaft tips of a handcart.

For an instant sleep reclaimed him, but some obscure tocsin, rattling his brain, woke him with a stab of fear. There was a cleaning rod down the rifle stock, and a brass disc on the butt. Vaguely he made out a flower engraved on the disc. He blinked, rubbed his eyes, and blinked again. They were still there, and a steel helmet was hung on the muzzle. We don't have cleaning rods, nor steel helmets. The Imperial Chrysanthemum! The engraving was the mark of the Jap army!

Somewhere, beyond the wicker baskets, there was a jabbering of foreign tongues. Warily raising his throbbing head, he peered over the baskets, and swiftly dropped down again.

Fifty yards away, across an overgrown clearing that merged on both sides of the abandoned paddy, already sprouting bamboo, was a crescent of tumble-down huts. Cross-legged around a crackling fire, midway along the clearing, brown shirtless bodies were hunched over rice bowls.

Chopsticks! Fucking hell! They *are* Japs!

Without raising his head, he looked beyond the sleeping Chinese for an escape route. That's buggered it! Thirty yards away, through the shrubbery and elephant grass, screening that side of their shelter, he glimpsed a Jap setting up a machine-gun on what must be the banks of the Kaukkwe.

Rolling on to his stomach, he scanned each end of the hut. Beyond his head, the hut gave on to a wide stretch of calf high scrub, and a sentry was idly skimming stones into the chaung. No escape that way. Between the other end and the sanctuary of the jungle, lay a hundred yards of rough paddy. If there was a sentry that way, he was well concealed.

Flopping back in a cold sweat, clamping his hands to his throbbing brow, he wrestled against the incoherence of his befogged mind. What happened after they left Nutmauk?

Fuzzily, he recalled stumbling into the village last night. Dimly, he remembered elation flashing into anger, as they vainly searched in the dark for signs of 82 Column. Jesus, they'd busted their guts to get to the rendezvous in two days, and the bloody column was not there. In a fit of drunken pique he'd told the others to doss down under this hut, and stupidly posted no sentry.

What had happened to the column?

The awful truth hit him. He'd lost the way, not the column! Crossed the Kaukkwe too few times. Or too many?

When did the Japs arrive? Why hadn't they been discovered? What did it matter? All that mattered now was whether to fight, surrender, or flee. To fight was certain death. Jap imprisonment would be worse than death. If they fled, one or more of them might get away.

With one hand over Baw's mouth, he shook the Burrif awake, and pointed out the rifle, "Not a sound," he hissed, "don't stir, we're in a Jap camp."

Eyes wide with fear, Baw nodded his comprehension, and lay rigid. Swivelling round, Badger roused Joe with the same warning.

"Don't be..." Badger's vice-like hand crushed Joe's mouth. Horror blanched Joe's cheeks as his eyes sighted the rifle and helmet.

Robert was stirring. Joe, swiftly rolling over to him, clapped his hand over his comrade's mouth, and whispered in his ear.

For a long moment, the four of them lay in silence save for their fear-quickened respiration.

"What'll we do?" Badger, from one corner of his mouth whispered first to Baw, and then, from the other corner, to Robert.

"You are in charge, you got us into this," Baw muttered, side-mouthed.

Glumly, Joe shook his head.

Robert hissed something like "Da tiu mo!", that Badger knew was some vile, inceśtuous curse, and their four pairs of eyes focused on the clearing. A pair of puttee clad calves were padding towards the hut. Someone stealing up on them? Fear edged towards terror. Still on their backs, they levelled their rifles at the wicker baskets. Only a tissue of intuition held Badger back from panic. The Japs were still jabbering. They would not send just one man to investigate.

Ashen faced and tense lipped, they held their breath. The footsteps stopped near the hand-cart. Wiry hands claimed the helmet and rifle, and the legs padded off towards the machine-gun post.

"We have three choices." Whispering side-mouthed as he lowered his rifle, Badger brushed the beads of sweat from his brow with his forearm, "Give ourselves up, make a fight of it, or make for the jungle."

"What chance have we got of reaching the jungle?"

"I'll take it, Baw!" Joe's whisper was emphatic.

"I'd sooner die than let those barbarians take me." Robert tapped his rifle butt, "But I'll take more than one of them with me!"

Incredibly it struck Badger that in a film this would be bathos. Four dishevelled soldiers, terrified stooges, sprawled in chicken muck and fluff, distorting their mouths from side to side as they whispered to each other.

"OK we'll try for the jungle. Any objections?"

Joe and Baw shook their heads.

"Yes, let's make a dash for it", Robert whispered.

"That's just what we won't do!" Three pairs of astonished

eyes glared at Badger.

Sprinting from cover would instantly attract attention. A yell from the camp fire, would alert the machine gunner. He peeked over to the fire. The Japs were still squatting there, the only one facing the hut was still hunched over his rice-bowl. He turned his eyes towards the chaung. A Jap, lugging an ammunition box, was halfway to the machine-gun post. If luck was with them the gun was not yet loaded. Across the stubble, the sentry had abandoned his stone throwing and was strolling with his back towards them.

'When in doubt, be bold' was a Wingate doctrine. Right, they would be bold and walk out. The decision was a 'do or die' antidote for hopelessness. Like an elixir it rallied his nerves, and banished his despair.

Walking out quietly was their best chance of avoiding an immediate hue and cry. If they did not escape detection, their boldness might flounder the Japs for vital moments.

"Slip on your packs. We'll crawl to the end of the hut and walk out quietly, in single file, at ten yard intervals." Badger pointed to the camp fire. "We'll be in sight of them until we're halfway, then that hut will block their view. We'll be within the machine-gun arc all the way. And let's pray there's no sentry between us and the jungle."

Indian fashion they crawled to the end of the hut.

"Baw you go first, then Joe, then Robert. I'll bring up the rear." His matter of factness titillated his ego. "If they open fire go pell mell for the jungle. I'll do what I can to hold them up. One of you must get to the rendezvous." With an air of Victorian stoicism, he solemnly shook each of their hands, "Good luck! Off you go, Baw."

Baw, crawling out of the hut, momentarily stood under the eaves, glanced towards the fire, and with his rifle at the 'trail' strode through the paddy. As Robert followed Joe, Badger paused under the eaves to snatch a last look round. The machine-gunners, their backs towards him, had settled behind their weapon. The campfire group were still jabbering.

"Well, here goes," he told himself as he stepped forward, "Shit or bust."

The other three had lengthened their strides, and Baw was already forty yards ahead. Expecting a volley in his back at every step, Badger countered the urge to crouch and run by stiffening his spine. He marched after the others with parade ground erectness, but his spine was tingling, his mouth was arid, his teeth nipping his lips, and sweat smarting into his eyes.

When he was fifty yards from the village, an outburst of yells set the other three sprinting for the jungle. In a reflex action he spun around into kneeling aim, levelled his rifle at the machine gun, and took the first pressure on the trigger. With relief that almost brought tears, he saw the camp-fire group were hailing a newcomer leading a pack pony into the village.

How much longer could their luck hold? When he turned back towards the jungle, the others had already disappeared into the bamboo. Straightening up, he stepped forward, but this time the urge to run was irresistible. The others were safe. He could risk attracting attention now. With his pack and equipment pummelling his back and chest, he sprinted the rest of the way.

The others were lying a few yards into the thickets and stumbling past them, he sagged to his knees. With his rifle butt digging into the ground, he clung to the stock for support as he gasped for breath.

"Christ!.. A bloody bleeding miracle...We made it... Thank Jesus bloody Christ!" Not blasphemy, but a panting hosanna for their deliverance. He turned to Baw who was watching the paddy. "...Any of..the buggers..coming?"

Baw shook his head.

"Give us a couple of minutes Baw, and then follow us." Getting to his feet, he motioned the other two to follow him. "We'll wait for you a little further on. If the Japs move this way, don't open fire, just leg it after us."

§

"Bold as bloody brass! We walked out of that sodding Jap camp, as bold as brass." Badger had said when Baw first caught them up.

"Bold as brass," Baw now repeated, for the umpteenth time in the next ten minutes, "I can hardly believe it, Japs must have been deaf and blind."

Sitting on their packs, they garrulously relived the miracle of their escape. In the hollow of a bamboo glade buzzing with insects, less than half a mile from the village, the enormity of their boldness was so incomprehensible that the sanctuary of the hollow seemed a world – light years – from that perilously exposed paddy. It was as if only repetition *ad-nauseum* could convince them it wasn't just a nightmare, but that it had actually happened.

"Things like that just don't happen." Robert shook his head in disbelief, "Not even in Chinese folk tales."

"Would any of you believe it if you were not here." Joe stubbed out a half smoked cigarette, and with trembling fingers lit another, "But they say a 16 Brigade column came out of the jungle on to a track, and Japs a little further along just ignored them."

"I heard that, too, and after this morning it's easier to believe. What's more," Badger continued, "I won't be sceptical anymore about the tale of Billy and Alf Mullen any more."

The other three looked puzzled.

"Didn't you hear that one? Billy and Alf survived when their glider crashed. One evening they stumbled on a Jap patrol laughing and fooling around, whilst one of them was cooking his meal in a dixie. The lads had been wandering for days. Desperate with hunger, they crawled close to the fire, lifted the dixie with a long stick, and sneaked off with it while the Jap was talking to his mates."

"Fantastic! Unbelievable!" Baw paused for a moment as the Chinese gleefully slapped their knees, "If that really is true I would have liked to see that Jap's reaction when he found his meal had vanished.

"I bet he swears his mates pinched it." Badger swiped at a mosquito buzzing around his ear.

"I never really understood, until now, what officers mean when they say 'the jungle is neutral'." The Burriff swept the jungle with his eyes and outstretched arms, "Here we are, less than half a mile from the Japs. They cannot see or hear us, we cannot see or hear them. We only know they are there because we have seen them." He grinned at the obviousness, "You know what I mean. There could be Japs all around – as oblivious of us, as we are of them because the jungle's concealment is indiscriminate.

Likewise its malevolence is indiscriminate and..."

"Yes, we know what you mean, Baw." Badger envied Baw's high school English. It made him feel inferior, "We've no time for philosophising," was that the right word? "Packs on! Let's get moving." Getting to his feet he gave each of them a warning look, "Whatever you say, don't ever mention we were drunk."

Three pairs of accusing eyes said he was the only one drunk.

§

Less than ten minutes after leaving the hollow, they emerged from the jungle into a clearing in yet another loop of the Kaukkwe. On the far side of the chaung was a clutch of derelict huts.

From the opposite bank a Bren-gunner, training his sights on them, called the password, "Mandalay!"

"Peking!" Badger gave the counter word, and waded across to a sergeant who appeared from behind a clump of bamboo alongside the gunner.

"You're Dixon?" The sergeant, a scrawny, craggy faced scouser, without waiting for an answer beckoned Badger to follow him.

As the four of them followed the sergeant Baw, nudging Badger, cocked his chin at the huts. His meaning was clear and recriminating. 'You blundered Badger! This is the rendezvous, not that village last night.'

With a shamefaced 'anyone can make a mistake' look, Badger irately hissed, "None of you three thought so last night!"

In the centre of the village, Captain Coulthard, a blanket round his waist like an overlong kilt, bending over a steel mirror propped on a bush, was trimming his walrus moustache with nail scissors.

His trousers, soaked to the knees, were spread on the bush to dry.

"The recce patrol is here, sir."

"So soon! Right sarn't, tell the sarn't major would you." The captain, a rugged ex-Border Regiment ranker, whose face looked hewn from the granite of his native Cumbrian Fells, turned to face the patrol, "How come you're on this patrol, Dixon?" They'd been partners in the two man rubber dinghies, shooting the Betwa rapids during training, "You're 81 Column."

"On temporary detachment to Brigade HQ, sir." Briefly he explained the circumstances, "Sorry we were delayed, sir. Should have been here last night."

"You've done well to get here in just over two days, corporal. I didn't expect you until to-night at the earliest. With luck, we can get the job done to-day."

Badger was spreading his map on the ground when the sergeant-major arrived.

"Ah, Sarn't-major Thompson, come and listen to Dixon's report."

'Nat' Thompson, an ex-professional boxer who had coached the Battalion boxers and sparred with Badger, gave only a casual nod of recognition as he knelt alongside Coulthard. Sergeant Major Thompson a hard headed, pugnacious regular, had an 'old soldier's' contempt for youthful underlings. His caustic deprecation of their talents, more than fear of his sledge-hammer fists, imposed sycophantic obedience.

With occasional intervention from Baw, Badger described the BTA man's village. Then, with his eyes forbidding any interruption from Baw, he hesitantly admitted mistaking the rendezvous last night, and self-consciously recounted their flight from the Japs.

Even to himself, the story sounded like 'Boy's Own' fiction and he was not surprised by Nat's cynical whistle. Years of barrack room romancers, himself among them, had indoctrinated Nat with wariness of soldiers' veracity.

"It does sound far fetched," the captain, reading Nat's mind, looked intently and challengingly at Badger, then at Baw, Robert and Joe. "But it's too implausible to be bullshit, and there's four of them to vouch for it, and after the Mullins' escapade its not beyond belief, sarn't-major."

'Nat' gave a dubiously concurring shrug.

"Whether it is or not, we'll soon see." The captain pulled on his trousers, still wet from wading the chaung. "Leave one platoon here sarn't major. We'll take the other two platoons to see if we can catch those dozy Japs with their pants down. Then we'll have a go at that BTA bastard!"

"Are we going with you, sir?"

"No corporal, I'll take Baw and one of the Hongkong-ites. You and the other man are to make for Broadway. Major Gately with the rest of 82 Col. are here." He pointed to a spot on the map, just south east of the Stronghold. "Give him my compliments, tell him what we're doing and that I think the Japs may be recce-ing to attack on Broadway. I hope to rejoin the column in two days, that's the 27th."

§

"Thank you, corporal." Major Gately, heavily built and fleshy cheeked, with a pencil thin moustache, and a paratroop flash on his shoulder, had his headquarter bivouac under the only clump of trees in a large, otherwise shadeless clearing. The rest of the column, under the late afternoon sun, were bivouac-ed around the major in a defensive perimeter of fifty yard radius.

"Who are you going to attach him to?" With a dismissive hand flick, he turned to the adjutant at his side.

"The Commando Platoon, sir." The adjutant turned to Badger, "Report to Sergeant Aitchison over there."

§

"Where have you been skiving, corporal?" Joss Aitchison, dressing a festering bamboo slash on a soldier's leg, glanced up briefly at Badger.

"Just come from 'White City', sarge." While Joss was finishing off the dressing, Badger explained his absence from Broadway.

"OK, wacker, off you go to the MO" Then, weighing up Badger from his boots to his hat, Joss rapped, "Dixon, are you rostered for promotion?"

"Er.. no sarge." Bewildered and blank faced.

"The beard sonny, the beard!"

The lean, close cropped sergeant, was regimental from his hobnailed boots to his steel rimmed service spectacles. He could have been weaned on King's Regulations, and swaddled in Army Council circulars. Battalion Standing Orders were his Hymnal.

"Ah, yes, sarge." Comprehension dawned, and Badger stroked his jaw. His 'beard' was hardly a shadow. Only Pioneer Sergeants were allowed beards in the 'Kings'.

"Get it off, corporal, get it off, and get your haircut!"

"Yes, sarge." Blimey, a couple of hundred miles behind enemy lines, and he expects parade ground spruceness.

"The platoon commander's just gone to the column commander's briefing. Attach yourself to Corporal Holliday's section over there."

Badger started off towards the section.

"The beard first, wacker!" Joss pointed to the nearby stream.

§

"When the hell are we going join up with the rest of 77 Brigade!" In one form or another, the rhetorical question had been voiced half a dozen times as the section quizzed Badger around their camp fires. Throughout his first two hours with them, the section, consumed with awe and envy, had persistently quizzed Badger about White City.

82 Column's thirst for action had, so far, been rewarded with no more than wild goose trekking in search of rumoured Japs. To them White City was the stuff of legends. They were impatient for their own baptism of fire, fed up with being the Cinderellas of 77 Brigade. For Badger, when at last the 'stand-to' order broke them up, it was like deliverance from an inquisition. He was down for first sentry after 'stand-to' and there would be no more dredging up details of White City that night. Modest, and as altruistic as he strove to be, he was embarrassingly conscious he was being basked in the reflected audacity of Mike Calvert's force.

§

"Have you had any mail deliveries, wacker?" Crouched under their groundsheets, Badger almost had to shout to the sentry at his side to make himself heard above the hurricane of hailstones. Ball-bearings of ice, the size of golf balls, stinging their exposed flesh, bruising through the tropical clothing, had driven them on to the parapet of their flooding slit trench. Now in the bible black night, still half an hour from his next relief, icy pools chilled Badger's rump.

"Yes, had one from my judy two days ago."

"Expect there'll be one from my wife with 81 Column then." He silently prayed he would meet up with his own column soon. They must be holding Barbara's letters for him but, to blank off his dread foreboding there might not be even one, he changed the subject, "What happened to the Spits." When he passed around Broadway that morning, to join 82 Column, he'd seen several wrecked Spitfires.

"One crash landed, one was shot down in a dog-fight, three destroyed on the ground, then the last one was withdrawn to Assam, and bang went our immediate fighter cover."

"Bloody hell! What a loss."

Abruptly some omnipotent deity closed a heavenly sluice valve, and the storm ceased. After the drumming of hail, the plip-plopping of dripping foliage, and the distant grunts of some rutting predators, was barely noticeable as Badger's companion continued, "They did well though, corp, considering the odds. Cor! They must've heard our cheers in Blighty every time the Spits or Bofors shot down a Jap."

"How did they catch three on the ground? What about the radar?"

The sentry described the raids with a fusion of hearsay and eyewitness. In one of the first raids, thirty Jap planes had attacked Broadway. The Spitfires had shot down four, probably six, Japs – and the Bofor guns brought down another.

The bombing wounded three Gurkhas, damaged three light planes, set disabled gliders on fire, but, far worse than that, the radar warning sets were destroyed.

With graphically swishing arms, barely visible through the darkness, the sentry described the aerobatics. The outnumbered Spits had repeatedly swept low over the Stronghold, drawing their pursuers on to the Bofors.

"...those Bofors were bloody good, in all the raids they shot down at least six, maybe ten, Japs..."

A few days later, the Spits were scrambled several times without making contact with the enemy. Later that day, the replacement radar picked up aircraft a few miles off. The squadron leader and one other, wary of another false alarm, took off to recce. The Squadron Leader was shot down by Jap fighters. Jap bombers had then blasted the Stronghold and destroyed the Spitfires on the ground.

"Christ!" Badger muttered, "It might've been brave for just two to take off, but can't help thinking it was a tactical blunder. Was that the last raid?."

"No, a couple of day's after that the buggers blasted craters in the runway and damaged a lot of light planes. It snapped the nerves of a lot of light plane pilots and they refused to fly again."

"But those blokes have nerves of steel when they are flying."

"I suppose it's the opposite of us corporal, we're frightened in the the air, them on the ground. Anyway, a pep talk from Wingate and Alison, when they flew in for a look around, soon got them back to ferrying the wounded. In the next raid the Japs strafed the light planes, and one poor sod and the casualty he was evacuating, were killed taxi-ing down the runway."

Chapter Seventeen

"Well here I am, Fred, 27th. March, my wedding anniversary." Lying next to Holliday on Broadway's moonless, dew chilled air-strip, Badger wriggled his ankles to ease his cramp, "Every muscle stiff as a poker – except the only muscle that was stiff on my wedding night." Talking to Holliday somehow inhibited explicit army vulgarity.

Fred gave a commiserating tongue cluck. The slim, gentle voiced, draftee from the Warwick's, was the antithesis of a typical King's NCO. It was only two days since Badger had joined Holliday's section but already he had grown to respect, and envy, Fred's urbane nature and succinct orders. So much so that without a thought for his relative seniority, he had slipped easily into the role of the section's second in command.

Fifty yards behind them, the doors slammed shut. The last of that night's Dakotas had been loaded with the final White City casualties, ferried in by light planes in the afternoon.

It slewed on to the flight path.

§

Since last night's briefings, 82 Column's attention had been concentrated on the scent of a more immediate battle than White City. Kachins had reported five hundred Japs, with field guns, pack elephants and mules were crossing the Kaukkwe. At dawn this morning, a Major Astell, with a Burma Rifle patrol, had located them in bivouac, inflicted casualties on them and retired to warn Broadway.

All day reports and rumours had whetted 82 column's battle thirst. The Bofors were withdrawn from their weapon pits, around the airstrip, into the Stronghold. A fighting patrol of the Gurkhas was lying in ambush at the western end of the strip. The Japs were reported to be approaching from the south, then from the north. Hour by expectant hour, probabilities had become intoxicating certainties, invigorating their camaraderie, cementing the column's *esprit-de-corps*.

The King's, at last, could prove their worth to the rest of the Brigade. 82 Column was to conceal itself, ready to outflank the attackers. 81 Column, near the Irrawaddy was being recalled as soon as it could be contacted and, the radio net-work being what it was, it would be nightfall before they got the message. As the honour of being in action before 81 was relayed through the bush telegraph, successive sections had joined the parodied chorusing of 'Ye'll tak the high road...'

Oh I'll take the Bren gun and you take the tripod,
And I'll be in action afo...re you,
and if you get bloody shot,
Then I'll take the bleeding lot,
And I'll have your rations in the mo.orn..ing..

Their tails were in the air, and they had gone through the day outjesting each other with jingo-istic fervour. The seasoned warriors among them were too few to temper the column's contempt of the enemy. Their gusto reminded Badger of his own eagerness for action, before Pagoda Hill. With the cocky innocence of unblooded youth, they foresaw only the inevitable annihilation of enemy. It wasn't bravado but fearlessness, the blind ignorance of their own vulnerability to shot and shell. They had yet to experience the vulnerability that was the birth of fear, and the essence of courage. The coming battle, their baptism of fire, was a promise of regimental glory. The few battle-tested warriors had weathered the day's exuberance with indulgent 'you'll learn soon enough lads' smiles, 'glory is the *l* of gory'.

Late that afternoon, Colonel Rome had decided to risk bringing in the nightly flight of ammunition and stores. The wooded peninsula, encompassed by dense barbed wire and panjis, which formed the Stronghold, by now bristled with bunkers and slit-trenches. Jutting out a couple of hundred yards from the jungle, it gave an almost 180 degree view over thousands of square yards of the Broadway plain. A killing ground for the garrison's rifles, machine-guns, mortars and 25 pounder gun battery. But White City's claims on air supplies had taken priority, and the Stronghold needed to build up its ammunition reserves for what might be a long siege. Dakotas were also needed that night to evacuate that day's White City casualties.

§

For four hours since dusk, the section, with Joss Aitchison in charge, had lain in the dew-soaked turf in a defence picquet around the landing zone, and the slightest move to ease cramped limbs had brought the instant threat from Joss of a charge under '...Section 40 or 44 of the Army Act...'

Now, as the Dakota roared down the runway and soared over the jungle roof, ground crews, and a couple of jeeps, were racing back to the Stronghold.

"Just 22.30." A ground controller's call to someone, rang with relief as the runway lights were doused.

"On your feet! In single file!'" Joss barked, "Rifles at the trail. Right turn! Squad, to the Stronghold, double march!"

§

"....We commit this the body of our brother, Law Ping..." As Sergeant Joss intoned the burial service, two men lowered the body, wrapped in his blanket, into the shallow grave.

At the graveside, the section fidgeted in the carpet of dawn mist. Taut faced, their anxious eyes frequently swept the airstrip and surrounding jungle. An eerie stillness had settled over jungle and plain. No trees stirring, no monkey chatterings, no birds squawking, even the cicados were silent. But, somewhere out there, the

Japs would be re-grouping.

For once, Joss did not remind them that they were supposed to be at attention. Law's death had brought the realisation of their own vulnerability, brought home the fact that *they* were targets for bullets as well as the enemy. Their slit-trench, inside the Stronghold, was forty yards away, and they were impatient for that sanctuary. Their baptism of fire, negligible as it had been, had brought on the birth pangs of fear.

Glancing at them as he shovelled earth into the grave, Badger recalled the despondent, cowed Gurkhas, the morning after their night attack before the Pagoda Hill battle.

Law Ping! When the two of them had returned to Broadway – could it have been only three days ago – he had been attached to the Stronghold HQ. Last night, when they doubled into the Stronghold, he had joined the section in the only vacant slit-trench. Now he was dead. For three years he had fought the Japs – and the terrain – across half of Asia, only to be killed by a stray machine-gun burst. His discs said C of E, but did Chinese have different funeral rituals? Sorry Robert, it's the only way we know.

Joss jabbed a wooden Field Service cross into the mound, stepped two paces back and, with his rifle at a parade ground slope on his left shoulder, slapped the butt with his right hand in a salute.

§

Last night, less than ten-minutes after they had quit the runway, all hell had broken loose at its Western end. From then until first light, stuck in their slit-trench, they were little more than blind spectators, left to guess what was happening. Occasional bursts of fire had sprayed their area and they had fired wild volleys at anything they saw, heard or imagined outside the perimeter.

At first light, a Gurkha subadhar had led the remnants of his company back into the Stronghold. Gone was their habitual jauntiness; gone their moon-faced grins and repartee, as they trailed behind the subadhar. In stony silence, with grim faces and blank stares, they were unresponsive to cheers from the slit trench.

Then, with the dawn, the to and fro-ing ammunition parties, and HQ runners, had energized the jungle telegraph. Via the bunkers and slit trenches, spaced at little more than conversational distances, garbled piecemeal reports filtered round the garrison. The usually infallible jungle 'telegraph' was a jumble of fact and fiction.

There was word that a captured Nigerian Chindit had guided the Japs. Then it was a captured British Burrif, reportedly brought back to the Stronghold by the subadhar, who had led the Japs to Broadway. A company of Japs, bivouacked by the Kaukkwe, had been routed by a King's Own Lancaster's platoon, en-route from Broadway to join 111 Brigade. No, it was Major Astell and his Burriffs. The Japs were massing to the south. They were massing to the west. They were massing to the south and west.

As usual, grumbled the section, the Tommies are being kept in the dark, left to guessing and speculation, working themselves up on conjecture and 'scuttle-butt'. All that seemed certain now was that, as the roar of the last Dakota had faded away, the Japs had probed the Gurkha ambush. Shouting and banging tin-cans, they sought to draw fire and pin-point the Gurkhas' positions. Then they had advanced calling,'Thik hai, Johnny!' In Urdu,'We're Indians!' Then in English, 'Halt, right turn!' 'Charge!' But the Gurkhas would not be drawn. Only when the Japs were within bayonet thrust, had they revealed themselves. Then shouting, 'Nay thik hai! Jarparny wallahs!' they had charged into the enemy, yelling their terrifying warcry, 'Ayo Gurkhali!'.

Throughout the night, in savage, hand to hand, kukri and bayonet, rifle butt and pistol clashes, both sides gained ground, lost ground, regained and lost it. The Japs had caught and slaughtered stretcher bearers, and the wounded they were carrying. Over seventy Japs, including their Battalion commander, were dead. Scores were wounded. By dawn, when overwhelming numbers forced the Gurkhas to break contact, the Gurkha commander, Major Pickett had been killed, and fifty other Gurkhas were dead or wounded.

When word spread that the subadhar had vainly begged Colonel Rome for a platoon to re-inforce his survivors and recover Pickett's body, admiration for the Gurhkas had swelled to adoration. The Stronghold was the bait for the Japs and Rome was not going to distract them from this – depleting the garrison – by sallies outside its defenses. And the jungle telegraph buzzed...

'Japs already invested, in the Yanks light plane crew's and mechanic's perimeter bunkers, south of Joss and the section.'

Early in the night, a Jap force, stealing across the airstrip, had stormed the Yanks area, gaining a dangerous foothold in the perimeter defences. It had been the fusillades from this assault that had killed Law. The jungle telegraph throbbed the accusation that, at the first shots, the Yanks had quit their posts, and skulked behind the British and Gurkhas, while the Japs raided their cook-house and lodged machine-guns in their trenches.

§

Leaving the section back at their Stronghold slit trenches, after Law's burial, Joss marched off with his mucker to HQ for a briefing. Unlike the men trudging back from Pagoda Hill, they had neither performed, nor witnessed, any deeds to gabble about. Nor had they any roll call of fallen muckers to silence them with grief. They'd spent the night on the fringe of the battle, remote from its savagery. But they'd tasted real fear.

Sitting on the sandbagged parados and parapet, ready to dive for cover at the first shot, they garrulously reconstructed the night's battle. Yesterday's foolhardy oratory had gone. They were screening their lacerated nerves, and foundering egos, with animated cross-talk.

"Fucking, yellow Yanks!" The section railed as they waited for Joss to return from HQ "...Swaggering about, pinning up notices 'Chew Muckergee's beetle nuts!' and 'Kilroy was here!' Then they throw a blue funk at the first bloody shot". Castigation of the Yanks unified the section's fellowship and hid their own splintered morale.

"They may be scared rabbits on the ground," Badger conceded, "but God knows they're not in the air. They run the gauntlet of Jap fighters, in those slow, unarmed crates over hundreds of miles of mountains with our wounded, in the worst flying conditions in the world."

"Got to give 'em that", a Liverpool Irishman put in, "I don't mind admitting I was nervous in the gliders – and I'm shit scared here."

"Who isn't Mick!" chorused everyone but Badger.

"What about you, Badger," Mick challenged, "Were you scared at White City?"

"So scared I pissed myself in the first charge!" His eyes swept the section, daring anyone to snigger, "What's more I've been shit scared ever since!"

"Then how come you and the Chinaman lay on the parados all night?" To stress his disbelief, Mick pointed to bullet furrows on the parapet, and the punctured sandbags.

"That wasn't by choice, Mick, and you know it!" The slit-trench was too small for the whole section to stand in. Badger suppressed a shudder, remembering how close he'd come to screaming in terror as Law's torso had bucked convulsively with the bullets thumping into him, "Anyway, being afraid is nothing to be ashamed of, it doesn't mean you're a coward..."

Exploding grenades, Gurkhali yells and furious small arms fire around the light plane area, sent the section tumbling into the trench.

"Watch your front!" Sergeant Joss, returning at the double, threw himself down on the parados alongside Badger, "Have you checked the ammo, Holliday?"

"Corporal Dixon did. We've about 40 rounds each, six full Bren mags, and thirty grenades."

For long minutes, with ricochets whining above their heads, they scanned the airstrip. Fingers white on their triggers, expecting an assault any moment, they squeezed to their first pressure. But the battle died to sporadic shots and solitary Gurkhali yells.

"Right, stay watching your front while I brief you." Joss removed his spectacles to read his field note-book, "Strategic picture first. White City is still firmly astride the Japs supply line. Brigadier Calvert has taken the offensive and is attacking Mawlu. Number 50 Column commandos, from White City, are out blowing railway bridges. Jap casualties in the area run into hundreds. 16 Brigade have consolidated the Aberdeen strip, and are attacking Indaw. The Black Watch, from 14 Brigade, have landed at Aberdeen, and are harassing the Japs around Indaw and Wuntho. 111 Brigade are also operating down there. Morris Force from 77 Brigade is East of the Irrawaddy around Bhamo. Questions?"

"What about 23 Brigade and Merrill's Marauders?" Mick turned to face Joss.

"Watch your front, Private!" Joss barked, "23 Brigade's still in Assam, they'll garrison the Stronghold for the wet season, I suppose. Merrill's mob are still operating in the Kamaign valley, so the Japs are well stretched out and confused by the campaign. Right, now our tactical gen. The Japs got into the Yank's positions last night. That's the Gurkhas clearing them out." He nodded towards the light plane area, "Another lot have dug-in north of the perimeter..." The crump of mortars momentarily silenced him until his ears gauged their target, "That's them being bombed now."

Between salvoes, he told them that they had been ordered to back to the column, as soon as they could slip out. The Japs, he warned, have got snipers tied up trees, and the Gurkhas are sweeping the area for them. The best intelligence was that the attackers were a battalion strong with two field guns. Kachins had reported the Japs had a black guide, probably a West African. Gurkhas, on the perimeter defences last night, had reported that a detachment of Japs had marched boldly up to the wire calling, in English, 'OK Tommy, patrol coming in." The Gurkhas had blasted them with grenades and small arms.

"That's it." Joss put his glasses back on, "Probably a lot more Japs killed than have been counted. They've got coolies with them to recover the bodies. Leave one man on guard, corporal. Let the rest get something to eat. Be ready to move at a second's notice." Starting to rise, he added, "I'm going back to HQ for any last messages for the column."

Boom! The sergeant flung himself back down alongside Badger. The ranging shot from the Jap field gun whooshed overhead, and exploded behind the Stronghold. As the second shot exploded 25 yards short of the perimeter, the garrison's 25 pounders thundered in reply. In swift succession, the battery plastered the enemy gun positions with salvo after salvo. Before the slower Jap gunners could get the range, their guns were silenced.

For a full five minutes no one stirred. Then, confident of their success, the gunners let out wild cheers that were taken up by the whole garrison.

As Joss got to his feet an HQ runner trotted up to him.

"Colonel Rome is sending out a fighting patrol, sergeant." He panted, "You're to take the opportunity to slip out now whilst the Japs' attention is distracted," he handed over a note, " and give Major Gately this."

§

They found the column, in bivouac, around a stream in a densely wooded hollow. The platoon swarmed around Joss and the section, hungry for first hand details of the fighting that had only just been within earshot throughout the night. Their high spirits, eagerness to have a 'bash', reminded Badger of his own tingling impatience the night before Pagoda Hill. How craven he'd been at the first volley that next morning. Smugly he listened to their presumptive fearlessness. His ego would not credit any of them with being a whit less fearful than he had been. Well let them revel and vaunt, they'll be pissing themselves soon enough.

"Fires for half an hour." Within minutes of the relayed order, every man had his mess-tin balanced over hot smokeless flames. Hot tea was every Chindit's paramount nectar. They were as incurably addicted to steaming, sweet char as a dipsomaniac is to alcohol, and concentration on its preparation subordinated all other thoughts.

Badger dropped the customary spent matchstalk into his mess-tin. Watching it swirl in the water as its eddies gathered mites of dirt, he puzzled whether it truly prevented 'smoked' water, or cleansed it of foreign particles.

In the centre of the bivouac Major Gately, seated on a log, was gathering officers around him.

"You got back all right then, corporal." Captain Coulthard with a blanket around his waist again, was striding quickly past to join the gathering, and was beyond earshot before Badger could reply. Coulthard had just returned, a day late, from the Kaukkwe patrol.

His patrol had raided the BTA village, but there were no signs of the 'traitors' except for one who had scurried up the ladder into a basha. Nat Thompson had hauled him out, broke his right hand on the man's jaw, and had been put on the last Dakota last night. For three days, Captain Coulthard had chased the Japs that Badger's patrol had slept among, before ration shortages forced him to abandon the pursuit. Now, as he stood there, listening to the Major, his tightly drawn face and slumped shoulders, declared his utter weariness.

The major's voice rose a pitch or two. His words were inaudible beyond the knot of officers, but he was clearly rebuffing some objection. Every man's eyes focused on Jim. The other officers, grim faced, were dispersing to brief their men, but Jim remained facing Gately. His spine stiffened, the blanket lending his erectness an odd dignity. The communal telepathy, that hyperphysical courier, told the watchers that the Captain was smarting under some injustice.

Throwing up a salute, too perfect to be anything less than a demonstration of chagrin, Jim's trenchant parting to Gately carried beyond the dispersing officers, "I will see you when I get back, Major Gately!" The unequivocal threat sent a ripple of murmurs around the bivouac.

Ex-ranker Jim, one of nature's gentlemen, was a caring and good humoured officer. What had driven this usually imperturbable man – this veteran of Dunkirk and North Africa – to the brink of insubordination? The answer came with the platoon commanders' briefing.

A slim, fresh faced officer, gathering his three sections around him, called in Badger to replace a sick corporal, "Japs, in strength, are dug in just south west of the perimeter. We don't know their precise positions, but the orders," there was hint of censure in his tone, "are that time is too short for a recce..."

There goes one of Mike Calvert's cardinal tenets, Badger muttered to himself, thorough reconnaissance is a vital element for success.

"...Our orders are to drive out the Japs. At 1600 precisely, Captain Coulthard's three platoons, that includes us, will make a flanking attack to draw their fire. The remainder of the column, less HQ, will then assault their front and other flank." He paused as a soft whistle went round the group. So that's what had angered Captain Coulthard. He and his platoons, fatigued by their gruelling patrol, and barely rested, were being flung first into battle. In other circumstances the choice of Coulthard would have been ideal. With only one exception, he was the only battle hardened officer in the column. But to-day the humane course would have been to at least hold him and his men in reserve. So be it they must concentrate on the job ahead, "...So Corporal," he heard the officer icily repeating to claim his attention, "the dress will be battle order. Packs will be left at Column HQ. Make sure everyone has a hundred rounds and four grenades. Inter-communication between our group and the main body will be by walkie-talkie. Within our group it will be hand signals – NCOs will run through them to refresh your minds. We move off in 15 minutes."

§

A hundred yards below the rim of a sparsely timbered knoll, two platoons were signalled into a single extended line. Badger's section, with the rest of the third platoon, formed a second line. With barrack square deftness their bayonets clicked on to their rifle bosses. The Stronghold's desultory mortar salvoes on the area, had ceased long before they had reached the knoll, and the absence of any return fire from the Japs, had whetted their predictions of a 'walk-over'. Their derring-do perception of Jap opposition, was too nebulous to shake their cocksureness.

Captain Coulthard shook his walkie-talkie about his ear and, in disgust, handed the silent instrument to his orderly. Anxiously he looked at his watch. It was dead on 1600 hrs. He had to assume the main body were in position. If his platoons were to distract the Japs' attention from the main attack, he dare not delay his assault. A sweep of his bayonetted rifle signalled 'forward'.

With rifles at the high port, steady as an Aldershot field exercise, the lines advanced up the slope. The air was still and sultry with the threat of thunder. The boots, brushing through the scrub, and the intermittent screech of some distant brain-fever bird, seemed to emphasize the brooding muteness of all other life.

Among the sweat soaked backs of the first line the towering 'Tiny' Brown was edging forward of the rest. Directly ahead of Badger, two staunch muckers, the stocky Jack Lindo and wiry

Harry Winstanley, closing the gap between them after skirting opposite sides of a clump of bushes, exchanged re-assurring grins.

The front line, twenty yards ahead, were breasting the rim as Badger stepped around the bushes. Someone bellowed "Look out!" Instantly a hail of bullets scythed through the front rank. Tiny Brown, his spine bucking like an unbroken stallion, rolled backwards. Like dominoes a whole section crumpled to the ground. Stumbling forward through the withering fire, men shrieked in pain, and yelled in fury.

The second line leaped forward to merge with the now faltering front line. As on Pagoda Hill, fury carried Badger beyond fear. His psyche was again somewhere in the heavens, as he scrambled from bush to tree, and found cover behind a teak stump. But unlike Pagoda Hill the Japs would not be sallying out to meet them. They were too secure in log roofed bunkers, constructed from the trenches deserted by light plane crews. Furious machine guns and rifle fire, from their sandbagged loop-holes, relentlessly swept the attackers. Jim Coulthard, in full stride, suddenly crumpled within a pace of a bunker. Two men tumbled to earth behind him.

Men flung themselves down, squirming for what cover they could find – tree stumps, bushes, even tufts of grass. Standing in the murderous hail, urging his pinned-down men forward, the urbane Captain Hurst staggered and spun round. His once handsome face was a hideous mass of gory cheek and bone. In the clamour and carnage, the wounded were stumbling or crawling down the slope, others lay screaming where they fell.

The attackers' grenades were bursting harmlessly on the bunker roofs. Their frenzied Bren, and rifle fire, was ineffective in stemming the remorseless hail from the bunker loopholes.

Poking his rifle round to the right of the stump, Badger let off ten rapid rounds at the nearest bunker. As he rolled back to refill his magazine a man dropped beside him.

"Where the fuck's the main body?" The man spat frothy blood. His right arm was limp at his side, his chest was a bricky, foaming cavity.

"The buggers have got lost! Hold on, and we'll get you out, wacker." But Badger was speaking to a dead wacker.

The slaughter was achieving nothing but more slaughter, and men were warily edging back. Kipling claimed his thoughts as he pocketed one of the wacker's dog-tags.

If your officer's dead and the sergeants look white,
Remember it's ruin to run from a fight:
So take open order, lie down, and sit tight,
And wait for support like a soldier.
Wait, wait, wait like a soldier...'

Wait! Until every bugger's dead? Or someone's nerve breaks? If we don't get the signal to retreat, some buggers' nerves are going to break any second. One bugger, cutting and running now, will set off a wholesale panicked flight. And Badger was damned close to being that man!

But no one broke. Even as he steeled himself to resume firing, the retreat signal was relayed along the line. Able men, shuffling backwards, at the crouch, were giving covering fire for retreating wounded and their helpers. Badger lobbed two grenades in quick succession, and scrambled into the ragged line of shuffling, wild eyed men.

Slowly, the crouching line backed below the bunkers' sight-lines, and at some Jap officer's high pitched command, the Japs abruptly ceased firing. For a heart pounding instant, Badger was certain they were going to charge down on them. Taking to his heels, with the rest of the line, he scrambled downhill. But the Japs did not pursue them and in the gathering dusk, at the foot of the knoll, they met the main body .

Until the noise of the battle gave them their bearings, a detour around dense jungle had disoriented the main body. Now they were at the scene there was no rallying for a renewed assault. The element of surprise had gone. Night was closing in fast. There were a score of wounded to evacuate, and the dispirited babble of the retreating platoons shrivelled all resolve for resuming the action. But a flame-thrower was ordered forward, and the operator, 'Tricky' Williams, madly charged back up the silent hill.

"Bloody, fucking bastards!" He yelled as his life-buoy's roaring flames seared into the bunkers, "Bloody, fucking bastards!"

Shrieking human torches scuttled out of the bunkers.

Dumb with mesmerised horror, the main force watched the barbaric scourging of their enemies. The hideous sights and screams retched at their stomachs. Revulsion smothered any urge to rejoice at the flaming vengeance.

"Bloody, fucking bastards!" In minutes, the monstrous engine of fire ran out of fuel. Under a hail of Jap bullets Tricky snatched a Sten gun from a British corpse, "Bloody, fucking bastards!" He fired off the magazine at the bunkers. Still yelling, blood pouring from a neck wound, he loped back down the knoll.

No time for a recce they said! Now thirty Kingsmen were dead or wounded, and the enemy still held the field. Gathering their wounded the whole force, in sullen silence, trudged back to the column's bivouac.

Chapter Eighteen

"Stretcher party, halt! Fall out!... Five minutes rest." As Badger, and the the other three bearers, gently lowered their bamboo poled litter from their shoulders to the ground, he smiled wryly. If there had been a drill by numbers for it, in some barrack manual, Sergeant Joss would have ordered the litters to be lowered in synchronised precision.

The casualties, from yesterday's abortive assault, in the blanket troughs of their litters, lay in silence as bearers bent over to offer water, or to fan away insects. The walking wounded and escort spoke in whispers, apprehensive that the Japs may pounce on them at any second. Around them, the jungle was a hubbub of monkey chatter, buzzing insects, bird cries and the incessant shrill of cicadas.

The sun had not yet honed the mottled forest floor to sharp edged shadows, and the morning air was fresh, but the stretcher bearers were drenched in sweat, and the Stronghold was still a mile away. With four men to a stretcher, and wearing only skeleton order, their burdens were half that of their normal full marching order. But, the repeated raising and lowering of the litters from shoulder to waist high, manoeuvring them under branches and around trees, was exhausting work.

Contemplatively drawing on his pipe, Badger's eyes misted with sorrow and pride, as they had done last night at roll call. The muster had hit him harder than after Pagoda Hill. Every silence was a lost wacker.

"Brown!"
Silence.
"Deakin!"
Silence."
"Kneale?"
Silence.

It was Coleridge this time that stirred his emotions..

The many men, so beautiful!
And they all dead did lie:

They had been well and truly shaken by the Japs. Their nerves may have been shattered by yesterday's shambles, but their honour was intact. Before they quit the field Coulthard, and a dozen of their comrades, lay dead around the bunkers. And the murderous fire had not driven them back without their wounded.

It had been cold commons at the bivouac last night. No invigorating char. The column commander had decreed 'No fires' – they might reveal the bivouac to Japs. The order had added doom to their gloom. Fires would have raised their spirits, cocked a snoot at danger, pre-occupied them in creating novel recipes from 'K' ration contents. As it was, all through the night they'd skulked like trapped animals, ears attuned for any tell tale noise, their minds analysing every creak of a tree, every wild-life sound, that might materialise in a Jap attack.

Alongside Jack Lindo and Harry Winstanley last night, he'd supped cold bouillon and munched 'K' ration biscuits and cheese. Whispers that officers were having rum ration, had brought rebellious mutters of, 'Its fucking Them and Us as usual, and we're out in the fucking cold again'.

Jack could usually lift their spirits with a string of anecdotes about army stupidity, or Battalion characters. Last night even his chirpiness had turned to scathing condemnation of officers, "Bloody shambles – bloody fiasco." He had repeatedly muttered, "Johnny Duff.. Spike Deakin.. Coulthard.. Kneale.."

Badger, lacking self-conviction, had tried to argue that the main body's detour was unforeseeable. Harry, however, in his rural

Lancastrian drawl had vehemently retorted, "The officers ballsed it up from start to finish!'

"Take up stretchers! Let's get these men into the Stronghold"

§

Under a milky sky and hazy noon sun, in single file, with Sergeant Joss in the lead the erstwhile stretcher party and escort trooped out of the Stronghold. Their hearts were a little lighter, their pace more sprightly. The news they carried would raise the column's morale. A Chinese captain, captured and pressed into service as an interpreter by the Japs, had escaped into the Stronghold. He'd reported that the Japs had sustained over 200 casualties – over twenty were killed in the King's battle – and that a company of the Jap defenders, with scores of wounded, were retreating beyond the Kaukkwe.

Halfway across a hundred yards of open ground, between the Stronghold and the jungle edge, a single 25 pounder shot, booming the 'air raid' warning, sent them sprinting for the trees. The warning was short. As they reached cover, a Jap plane roaring through the Bofors ack-ack barrage, was showering the area with leaflets. Before the leaflets had floated to earth, the plane was spiralling in flames into the Kaukkwe hills.

"Grab 'em, Dixon!" Joss pointed to two leaflets, fluttering to earth at the jungle edge. Badger scooped them up and, as he dashed back into the trees, two more planes roared over.

"Jesus! Landmines!' someone cried as loaded parachutes dropped towards the Stronghold.

"Look out!" another man called.

A 'chute was yawing down less than a cricket pitch away. Hugging the earth, they braced themselves for the explosion. But there was only a muffled crump, and warily they looked up to see the canopy caught high in a tree. Acrid, grey smoke was pouring from the ruptured cradle.

"Gas!" Every throat cried in horror. Chindits carried no respirators. "The bastards!"

But the smoke changed to pale blue wisps, and had a familiar, pungent odour. Suddenly every man was laughing in hysterical relief.

"Cordite! Bloody cordite!" Joss pointed to the cartridge packets and machine gun belts tumbling from the swaying cradle. The impact had obviously detonated some of the ammunition. "The bleeding Japs are short of ammo and the planes missed the target. They don't have the knack of packing them right either."

Bofors were still pounding away. One of the planes, banking around for a second run, buffeted by the ack-ack barrage, erupted into flames. A figure baled out. His 'chute failed to open, and he dropped like a stone. The other plane high-tailed it for home. The Bofors ceased fire and, from the Stronghold, there was an almighty cheer as the flaming plane and its luckless pilot, plunged into the distant jungle.

"What's the leaflet say?"

Badger smoothed out one of the crudely printed sheets.

"British soldiers," he read, "you are trapped like fishes in a net. Give yourselves up to the honourable Japanese army before you are all killed. Come out unarmed and waving this paper and you will be well treated."

"Who are they fucking kidding!" Joss scoffed. To resounding guffaws he took the leaflet, wiped his trouser bum with it, and then tucked it carefully in his field notebook. "Half of them are across the Kaukkwe with their tails between their legs, the rest are short of ammunition – And they expect us to surrender!"

§

That night the column moved a few miles further from the Stronghold. There were fires, hot tea and meals concocted from everything in the 'K' rations. Mashes of biscuits, meat loaf, cheese, fruit bars, chocolate, everything except chewing gum and cigarettes, were stewed or baked in mess tins. Men pranced from fire to fire, performing vulgar antics, with leaflets Joss's men had gathered on their way back.

The reports from the Stronghold had lifted the column's spirits.

They had knocked the Japs harder than they had believed. They still groused about the shambles, and mourned their fallen comrades. But the knowledge that they had inflicted more than double their own casualties – and sent a company of them fleeing across the Kaukkwe – evaporated their despondency. Yesterday's assault became a topic of pride, not despair.

Their own wounded by now were back in India. This morning, under enemy fire, light planes had evacuated them from Broadway, and restored their respect for the Yanks.

To-night, the column's dwindling stocks of ammo and rations would be replenished by an air drop. To-morrow they would attack the Japs again. This time it would be different. This time they knew where the Japs were. This time, ahead of the assault, the bunkers would be pasted by Cochrane's Mustangs. This time the whole column, less signals and animal transport elements, would attack, and they would have a company of Gurkhas with them.

And, this time, they were burning for revenge.

§

In the dappled early morning jungle, the first wave of the column – and the Gurkha company – lay in an extended crescent fifty yards to the rear of the bunkers. Behind them Sergeant Joss's platoon formed the reserve line. Officers had their eyes glued on their watches. Every man hugged the ground, straining his ears for the first sound of approaching Mustangs. Only rustling leaves, and humming insects, stirred in the sinister, expectant hiatus.

Sergeant Joss, tapping his watch face, counted off the last ten seconds. Dead on time, mortar bombs from the Stronghold whooshed overhead, targeting the Jap positions with smoke. The Mustangs skimmed the tree tops. Their detonating bombs stunned the column's ears. The shock-waves thumped their stomachs. The blast showered them with dust. Each screaming bomb load seemed targeted on the column.

Whilst the air still vibrated from the last bomb load, the Mustangs roaring down, through the mushrooming debris, strafed the Japs with their guns.

With yells of 'Ayo Gurkhali!' and 'At 'em Kings' the first wave surged forward. Flame-throwers scorched everything ahead of them. The knoll seemed, to Badger, hardly more than a hump and

Bren guns from fixed positions, overlooking it, raked the bunkers. From the reserve line he watched the attackers sweep over the hump. Above the yells, the roar of flame-throwers and chattering Brens, there was no sound of any return fire, no screams of wounded. This time the front line, without faltering, swarmed over the bunkers.

Scenting victory, the reserve line – heedless of their role – sprang up as one man, and raced forward. Beyond the bunkers, the first wave were charging headlong down through the teak towards the the open Broadway plain. Sprinting past the bunkers, and the decomposing corpses of Japs killed in the first assault, Badger saw no sign of new British or Jap casualties. The Brens had ceased fire, and there were only sporadic volleys from the first wave. If there had been any Jap resistance it had been feeble. But there must have been some for further down, Bondano and another Chindit, lay sprawled in death.

The irony of it! Bondano killed, serving Britain, and his Italian born father a prisoner in a British internment camp.

At the jungle edge, the platoon commanders, chary of charging on to the Broadway clearing, halted the first wave, and the reserves merged into the hesitant line. Eight hundred yards across the clearing, Jap stragglers were disappearing into the jungle. Here and there, men were pot-shotting the stragglers. The halt was brief. They had the Japs on the run, fleeing like scared rabbits. The column's ego soared. In a ragged line, with no yells – no war cries – they jogged out of the trees.

For a few moments, only their panting lungs, and boots scuffing through the rough grass, blighted the silence. Then senior officers, at the rear, were commanding them to withdraw to the jungle. Most of the line halted, but a few bolder spirits, scorning the commands with two finger gestures, pushed forward. Louder, more imperative commands, brought them back to their wavering comrades, shambling back into the jungle.

In disgust bordering on fury, blinded by thwarted vengeance to the hazards of crossing eight hundred yards of open ground, 82 Column sullenly reformed into single file. Bondano and his mate had been dead less than ten minutes but, as the column filed back past them, their faces were already a revolting mass of red ants.

On the short march to the Stronghold, men vociferously vented their contempt for senior officers.

'Windy sods! They should have let us finish the bastards off.'

'Officers! I've shit better!'

'Stupid sods have given the Japs time to re-group.'

'The bastard Japs will dig in over there, and then the buggers will expect us to clear 'em out!"

The platoon commanders, tactfully deaf and poker faced, prudently refrained from rebuking the insubordinate gabbling.

§

There were fires again that night, and an extra 'K' ration packet all round. The column's mood was close on jubilance. Around their fires, men sang and joked. Prodigal muckers were treated to generous brews of char from the precious stocks of more provident comrades.

As they had passed through the Stronghold, after the morning assault, the repeated crescendos of huzzas from the Yank ground crews and British garrison lining the track, transformed their disgust to swaggering pride. Later in their bivouac, cleaning their weapons and refilling Bren magazines, they endlessly lauded the Mustang strike and blessed the commanders for ordering it. The sourness of the morning became approbation. The commanders would have been mad to allow them to pursue the Japs across eight hundred yards of open ground. Without a pre-emptive air strike and diversionary attack, they would have been slaughtered. They'd done all that was expected of them. The Stronghold and air-strip had been cleared of Japs. If the bastards were dug-in on the other side, the column would quickly see them off with the help of Cochrane's Mustangs. So afternoon trailed into dusk, and in high spirits they had brewed their char.

Now it was time to douse the fires, and the officers returned from their briefing with grim faces. The signallers had closed down their radios, but the jungle telegraph suddenly set the bivouac buzzing with rage. '

'Colonel Rome had personally led this morning's attack...

the King's had refused to chase the Japs across the clearing... Rome could not persuade them to continue the pursuit...'

Every section was a hubbub of enraged voices.

"Bloody lying bastards!"

"The fucking officers stopped us!"

"Colonel bloody Rome wasn't bloody well there!"

"If he was there, I never saw the sod!"

"Nor did I."

"Another cock-up. Blame the poor bloody King's!"

"Let's keep our hair on," some less sensitive soul urged, "Its only scuttle-butt. Just because we didn't see him doesn't mean he wasn't there. He's a good officer, and whether he was there or not, even an idiot wouldn't expect us to charge across hundreds of yards of open ground. What matters is we were ordered to withdraw....."

"Well some bugger's blaming us...."

"...Using us as a fucking excuse for another of their cock-ups.."

"What cock up? We cleared out the Japs..."

"...Bet some sodding officer forgot to order an air-strike and artillery barrage on the jungle to cover us across the airstrip..."

"Aye, and blamed us to cover his bleeding self.."

"Bet the report to India never mentions hundreds of yards of open ground."

Badger, puffing at his pipe, had up to that moment only felt irritated. Sitting in silence, he'd been puzzling how, where and why, such a malicious story had been dreamed up. The orders to withdraw were loud and clear. Everyone knew there were eight hundred yards of killing ground to cross. If someone had refused to pursue the Japs, he must have been senior enough for his reasoning to prevail against Rome's supposed orders. So, why should anyone want to blame that on the King's? The last speaker had flashed his irritation into anger.

A report of the attack *would* have been radio-ed to India. Some Stronghold wireless operator had leaked the report. If it was true, the false story would be enshrined in the history of the campaign. The King's would be damned to cover up another cock-up. **(Appendix 1)**

"The lying, hypocritical sods!"

"Who, Badger?"

"The Stronghold HQ officers!"

"That's quite enough, corporal!" An officer, sensing what had prompted the outburst, had strolled over, "There's worse news than bullshit rumour to concern you." There was distress rather than anger in his voice and eyes, "Everyone close up on the column HQ. Look sharp. Major Gately has some sad news to announce."

§

Gately's announcement purged the day's events from their minds. Wingate was dead! Killed in an air crash, on 24th. March, six days ago.

In a stunned silence, the major let the grim news sink in. Their champion – who had fought the bureaucratic hierarchy, and had won them the best weapons, rations, light planes to evacuate their casualties and their own special hospital in Assam – was no more. The Messiah, who had inspired and toughened them in India's jungles, dead! The caring commander, who'd had them dosed daily with vitamins, and nauseous shark liver oil, to combat the debilitation of India's endemic diseases, dead! Their dynamic leader, who had the ears of the mighty, like Churchill and Mountbatten, killed. Wingate, their general, the man who had demolished the myth of Japanese invincibility, DEAD!

"The new Chindit commander is..." The Major hesitated. Every man would have bet his life on it being Calvert, with Fergusson a runner up.

"...Brigadier – now Major General – Lentaigne, former commander of 111 Brigade and there will be no change in our role. That's all for now. Fall Out!"

For a moment the gathering stood in shocked silence. Lentaigne? An orthodox soldier, instead of Wingate disciples like Mike or Bernard Fergusson! With dismayed mutterings, they dispersed to their section areas.

"Lengtaigne's an old man!" One of Holliday's men grunted.

"He's at least forty..." To Laidlaw, a nineteen year old

Cumbrian, this was ancient.

"Maybe that's why they chose him." An equally young Scouser suggested, "He's got a good war record, a DSO. Better at using his brains, directing operations, than slogging it out in the jungle."

"Could be, but Mike's the best bloody officer we've got," another voice butted in, "the whole brigade would follow him to the gates of Hell!"

"We'd bloody well go through them, and spit in the devil's eye for Brigadier Calvert." Laidlaw always gave Mike his full title.

"Have any of you thought what could happen if Mike had been promoted," Badger said as muckers, in pairs, prepared their groundsheet and blanket beds, " Scottie might be made 77 Brigade commander. We'd lose him, and Dick Gately or someone else would take over the Battalion.."

"Nothing wrong with Gately," came a voice from under a blanket.

"No, but he hasn't got the Scottie flair and luck. Scottie's the best CO the Kings have ever had. Anyway it's done now." Badger slipped under the blankets alongside Laidlaw. The Cumbrian's previous mucker had been a battle casualty, and he'd paired off with Badger. As in everything else, Chindits slept in pairs for the extra benefit of two thicknesses of blankets – one groundsheet underneath and one over them to ward off dew, "We should be all right, Lentaigne's a Gurkha officer, and they are bloody good soldiers. Let's get some shut-eye, I'm on sentry in two hours. G'night."

The warmth of Laidlaw's body stirred his yearning for Barbara. If only the popular song were true, "...If you call I'll hear you, just close your eyes and I'll be there...'

Well perhaps. '...I'll see you in my dreams and hold you in my arms...' to-night.

Chapter Eighteen

The platoon briefings, the following morning, took some of the sting out of the malicious myth concerning their refusal to pursue the Japs.

Major Astell and his Burriffs, trailing the Japs, had reported that they were fleeing north over the Kaukke Hills. They had been badly mauled by the King's and Gurkhas, were dragging along hundreds of casualties, and were in no state to renew their attacks.

The Broadway strip and the Stronghold were back to normal. Kachins were trekking in to barter, the medics were treating their ailments and light planes were flying in and out unmolested. As April dragged towards May, any forebodings about the choice of Lengtaigne slowly withered. He seemed to be pushing ahead with all Wingate's plans. Save for the odd cancellation, due to bad weather, air supply services were undiminished, and the Chindit tactics faithfully pursued.

Mike Calvert was still astride the Japs' jugular vein. Bernard Fergusson had failed to take Indaw, but he was harassing the Jap lines of supply south of the Aberdeen stronghold, and had destroyed their main ammunition dumps. Morris, now the brigadier commanding Lentaigne's old brigade, was east of the Irrawaddy with 3 columns of 111 Brigade blocking the Bhamo-Myitkyina road. John Masters, with the other columns of 111 Brigade, was creating havoc to the Japs' supply lines along the Homalin-Banmauk road. 14 Brigade were harassing the Pinlebu-Nankin-Wuntho triangle. Scottie, with 81 Column of the Kings, was operating along the Irrawaddy around Bahmo. So over 6,000 square miles of mountain and jungle were invested with marauding Chindits.

With 82 Column, Badger roamed the Kaukkwe Hills. Trekking and counter trekking, they fruitlessly pursued rumours and reports of Jap detachments. Bent under back breaking packs and accoutrements, hacking through steamy bamboo jungle, they trudged up and stumbled down escarpments, to lay ambushes for an enemy who never appeared.

They raided villages which had victualled Japs with rice, chickens and pigs. Steeling their hearts, they cordoned off wailing women and sullen men, whilst their homes were put to the torch. Poor, peace loving hill folk caught between the devil and the deep blue sea. The iron laws of Kachin hospitality, and the fear of vicious punishment if they had failed to co-operate, left them no choice but to supply the Japs.

Then there were 'listening patrols' along the Kaukkwe Chaung, covering the approaches to Broadway – twenty four to forty eight nerve wracking hours, lying in fetid, sweltering bamboo thickets. No fires. No nerve-soothing hot tea. Just cold 'K' rations. Enveloped in a cacophony of jabbering monkeys and screeching birds, they lay for interminable hours hardly daring to whisper for fear of alerting Japs. The Japs never came, but with the imminence of the monsoon season, the rains frequently did.

Suddenly the wildlife would fall silent. A fresh breeze would sway the bamboo. Huge raindrops would splatter the leaves, and plop on to their hat brims. As they hurriedly wrapped cigarettes and matches in their bush hats, and stuffed the lot in their packs, the jungle would become a fearsome turmoil of wind, cracking trees and torrential rain. In swirling mud, they would cling to trees. The wind snatching open their groundsheets, drove the rain through their tropical clothes, uprooting trees and threatening to sweep them from their feet. In the aftermath, patrols sweltered in a torrid mist of vapourising foliage, and steaming clothing.

But there were days – usually on the eve of a supply drop – that were halcyon by comparison. Days when they relaxed under towering kanyin trees, their red or white blossoms overshadowing the the tallest teaks. Days when they would bivouac at mid-day.

Walking on air having dumped their monstrous packs, they would lay an 'L' pattern of beacons at the dropping zone, ready to be lit as soon as the supply planes were identified. Then for the rest of those warm afternoons they bathed in cool crystal streams, and yarned the time away with muckers, or squatted around Tony, awaiting their turn for a haircut. On these days they swapped tales of sweethearts and families, fantasized about meals to come – and brothel pleasures – after the campaign.

But events at White City were their main preoccupation. Round their fires they endlessly derided the Jap battle tactics, and lauded the tenacity of Calvert's embattled garrison.

The doggedness and exploits of White City defenders were the stuff of camp fire legends. There was the huge Nigerian Sergeant who – out of ammunition – had snatched up a heavy box full of grenades and swinging it by its rope handle, laid about the Japs with gusto. There were the tales of audacious Chindit officers tapping into the Jap telephone lines, and listening around the clock to the enemy's orders, battle reports and plans.

§

For fourteen days the eight Jap battalions, supported by artillery, aircraft and two tanks, had vainly assaulted White City. It was not their lack of courage that defeated them, but the stupidity of their commanders. Each attack had been almost identical in pattern and timing.

For an hour before dusk each day, the Japs pounded White City with artillery, mortar and aerial bombardment. Their 6-inch mortars hurled five feet by 6-inch missiles, that stove in bunker roofings, and flattened mature teak.

Incomprehensibly, there was always an hour's respite between the bombardment and a Jap assault. In that interval the defenders repaired their defences, had their hot char and a meal. Then a Jap assault would be heralded by wild yells. No diversionary tactics, just a concentrated frontal assault on one sector or another. The garrison's star shells would turn night into day. Suicide squads, each of three naked Japs, would be slaughtered as they attempted to breach the defence wire with Bangalore torpedoes – long tubes, packed with explosives. Then, throughout the night, repeated assaults would be driven back by withering hails of small arms fire and grenades.

Each dawn Japanese corpses were numbered in scores and the light planes ferried out all the Chindit wounded. In their remoteness from the 'White City' savagery, the King's gloated that pilots claimed they navigated to White City by the stink of Jap corpses.

§

At one of their late April bivouacs, the news broke that Mike, leading a strong force around the Jap rear, had sandwiched the attackers between White City and his force, and had put the Japs to flight. One party, taken by surprise while bathing, fled with Chindit bayonets lunging at their naked buttocks.

With news of the rout, and of a 'luxury drop' that night, the King's bivouac took on a festive air. Careless that the supply drop might not materialise, men pooled the last of their rations to cook 'exotic' mashes and puddings. They jigged and sang around their fires. They larked in a stream as they washed their clothes and – prancing nude – mimicked Japs with genitals in hand, fleeing before the prodding bayonets.

A 'luxury drop' meant tinned fruit, bread, tinned bacon, margarine and bully beef, as well as five days' 'K' rations. But, when it came that night, some parachutes drifted miles away. Others failed to open, splattering the ground with pineapple chunks, margarine and tinned meats. So it was only 3 days of rations per man, plus a one pound tin of bacon or bully beef, and a loaf for every dozen men. But as they gathered the supplies within reach, they took consolation in the 'pukka gen' Tony had spread that day.

The dapper barber was a vital relay in the jungle telegraph. Everyone in the column regularly sat under his clippers and scissors. With beguiling servility, and scouse cunning, he wormed titbits from his officer 'clients'. From chance remarks, subtle inferences and crafty 'kite flying' his 'pukka gen' disclosures could depress or boost the other ranks' expectations.

Today he had boosted their hopes. His gen was that 16 Brigade was on its way to Broadway to be flown out. The brass-hats were keeping their promise to fly the Chindits out before the monsoon set in. 16 Brigade being first in, were first out. 77 Brigade would be next. 111 Brigade would be laying a road and rail block south of White City. Mike Calvert would lift his block, and move north. Both King's columns, for one 'final' job, would rejoin the rest of 77 Brigade, and then be flown out.

Compared to the rest of 77 Brigade the King's columns, so far, through no fault of their own, had done little to justify their *raison d'etre*, only a battle at Broadway, and fruitless Jap chasing. But weeks of seemingly aimless trudging, sleep interrupted every night by sentry duties and/or storms, had blunted their enthusiasm. Despite daily dosages of Atebrin, fevers were beginning to erode their vitality. In this frame of mind, men clutched at any straws of comfort, and Tony's 'gen' dovetailed nicely with all they 'knew', had heard, and had wished for.

Wingate had set a maximum of ninety days campaigning. There were whispers that, within a month, Cochrane's Air Commando would be disbanded. That could only mean the ground campaign was coming to an end. The early rains were building up to monsoon frequency and magnitude. Air supplies would be thwarted, and General Mud would halt ground operations. Replacements, lately flown into Broadway had spoken of rest centres at Dehra Dun, being prepared for them. Lentaigne's recent conference with all the brigadiers, at Aberdeen, could have been only to programme the fly-out.

16 Brigade's leading elements had already been sighted a few days earlier, wearily trudging towards Broadway. For all their weariness, their bushy beards lent them a piratical fierceness.

"They look tough, sarge. Why can't we grow beards?"

"Because Private Hanning, you're in The King's. We are tough without breaking King's Regulations like that scruffy, weak chinned shower!".

In a couple of weeks they'd be following 16 Brigade, to live it up, on three month's back pay, in India's fleshpots. No more 'K' rations – which were designed for a week, or a fortnight at the most, in the field. Even a full day's supply left men short of hundreds of calories. As it was, more often than not, three day's rations had to be stretched to five or more. Soon they would be stuffing themselves with char and wads, mixed grills and apple pie, in cantonment canteens.

So mounting optimism, speculation, and wishful thinking became conviction. Everything pointed to their being flown out before the weather closed in, and serious malnourishment resulted.

§

The dawn air had been still but as they tucked into their breakfasts, the jungle had become a tumult of monkey chatter and bird cries. Now, as they stripped and cleaned their weapons in the lingering aroma of fried bacon, a breeze stirred the high teak tops.

"Fires out! Move off in 15 mins."

As if a signal for silence, all wildlife noise ceased.

"Pissing rain again!" men chorused.

"Or fucking Japs ready to attack!" a lone uttering voiced every man's fears.

Wild life silences had become omens of storm or battle. This time it was neither. For a moment or two the light faded and trees creaked in the wind. With almost tangible relief they watched the sun brighten the heavens and muckers, in pairs, hurried away to relieve themselves before yet another day of back-breaking trekking.

In a fold in the ground Badger hacked a shallow latrine trench, and was shaken to see, as he finished excreting, semen dripping from his penis. His knowledge of human biology was negligible. Some genital reservoir must be overstocked by protracted celibacy. Masturbation should relieve it. But when, where, was the essential privacy for that? The very intimacy of column life, sleeping in pairs, every action and bodily function under a mucker's shadow, proscribed privacy. He glanced over his shoulder at Laidlaw, on watch only yards away. Even at times like this he couldn't masturbate without detection and consequent ridicule. The MO might be able to give him something for it, that's if he could overcome the embarrassment of broaching the subject. An RC padre would know if this was a normal result of celibacy, but the column's diminutive Karen padre was Anglican like himself.

"Packs On!" The urgency of dressing, and mustering

with the section, pushed his anxiety into limbo.

§

"For God's sake Badger cheer up. As Captain Freeman told you, so you've had a raspberry from Gately. That's not the end of the world. In a couple of days it will be May, our last month in Burma, so cheer up."

"Perhaps I shouldn't have kept a breech cover on my rifle, but that was his petty final swipe, Fred."

In the late afternoon, bivouacked around an infant tributary of the Kaukkwe Chaung, the column was lazing away the last hour before 'stand-to'. Fires were already out, and as they dislodged ticks from their thighs and loins, with smouldering cigarettes, Badger had ceaselessly moaned to Holliday about Gately's injustice.

That morning he had been in charge of a section escorting the major and the adjutant to and from Broadway. When they returned the major had vehemently upbraided him. In a raging tirade he had called Badger slap-happy, incompetent, devoid of vigilance and unfit to be an NCO. White faced and trembling with anger, Badger standing at attention before the major and adjutant, had been brusquely silenced by one or the other whenever he sought to defend himself.

The more his mind churned over the Broadway trip, the more the unjustness of the major's outburst wracked him. Keeping the canvas breech cover on his rifle was not negligence, or lack of vigilance.He could tug open its press studs, discard it, aim and fire in one swift motion. Given the opportunity he could have demonstrated that. In any case, if it piqued the major so much why wasn't he told to take it off during the trip, instead of waiting until they had got back? Bet the sod didn't notice until he was bollocking me. Come to that, if the way I was handling the escort didn't suit him, why didn't he tell me when we were doing it.

"Fred, I had the escort in diamond formation all the way to Broadway, and back. The major and the adjutant on ponies, in the centre. Two men on point fifty yards ahead. Two men twenty yards out on each flank. Two men fifty yards to the rear. One man walking alongside the major, another alongside the opposite side of the adjutant. What more could he expect?"

Fred, engrossed in extracting ticks from a mucker's back, made no attempt to reply.

"We had bayonets fixed, rifles at the high port most of the way." Exasperatedly, "For Christ's sake! Broadway's over an hour's march. He ranted at me for carrying my rifle at the trail. In one breath bawled that I moved faster than the ponies – with the next said I sauntered like a mindless chimpanzee, heedless of possible ambushing from thickets... you can't move at the high port all that way, and at times I had to hack a path for the ponies... And, bloody hell, we had to move slowly enough... At anything more than a stroll we left the ponies behind. We did the same both ways, so why didn't the sod tell me before... Got you, you little bugger." He grimaced as he tugged another tick from his groin. "I'll take a bollocking without moaning – if I deserve it – but this one was so bleeding unfair..." Concentrating on finger combing his pubic hairs, for any other ticks, his voice trailed into silence. Finding none he put his shirt back on. "...Then the sod says, consider yourself reprimanded!" If it went on his conduct sheet, the reprimand would blight his promotion prospects, "Jesus bloody Christ! We'd never have got to Broadway and back if we'd scoured every tree and bush, every foot of the way. I think he's bloody windy without a whole column around him, and took it out on me just to relieve..."

"Corporal Dixon!" Sergeant Joss called as he passed by with Captain Freeman, their slender, scholarly platoon commander, "Report to me when we get back from checking the sentries."

What now? Joss might be a stickler for regulations, but he was also as obstinate as any shop steward in standing up for his men's rights. A 'reprimand' was a formal punishment, and a pre-requisite for it was a formal hearing. It would be typical of Joss to confront the adjutant and press for a formal disciplinary hearing.

Hitching up his trousers and tucking in his shirt, Badger envisaged Sergeant Joss reading out the charge from Army Form 252. '...you are charged under Section 40 (or was it 44?)... of the Army Act that whilst on active service on such and such date you were grossly negligent in that, as NCO in charge of Major Gately's escort....'

"Corporal Dixon! Over here, juldee!"

Slinging his rifle on his right shoulder, he doubled the twenty yards to where Joss, field book in hand, was sitting.

"It's not fair, sarge, is it?"

"What's not, corporal?" Joss looked puzzled.

"Why..." he tugged nervously on his rifle sling, "...the reprimand"

"That's not why you're here. But you got escort duty this morning because Major Gately wanted one of my best NCOs." That was an accolade coming from Joss, "Now we're told you were slap-happy..."

"I wasn't slap-happy!" Badger protested.

"You must have slouched along then, 'slap-happy, mindless of danger, devoid of vigilance' according to the major." The eyes, behind the steel framed lenses were challenging, inquisitorial.

"Sarge – ask any of the escort. We were on the ball all the time." Exasperatedly, plaintively, he scowled down at Joss, "He blew his top for fuck all! If I was as bad as he says why didn't the bugger tell me..."

"That's enough corporal!" The army creed was 'familiarity breeds contempt', and Dixon needed reminding he was not talking to one of his muckers.

"Sorry, sarge, but if I was so slap-happy, such a bad example, he should've ticked me off on the way out, not waited until we got back. I think he was too bloody scared of his own shadow to..."

"Count yourself lucky, corporal, that I didn't hear that." The stern tone was tempered by the flicker of a sympathetic smile.

"You'd have been on a 252 before you could bat an eye."

"OK sarge, even if it was all the major claims, he should've given me a chance to defend myself. Shouldn't he?"

"I'll take it up with Captain Freeman. But I called you over to tell you you're being sent back to 81 Column..."

"When sarge?" Joy and anger. He'd been yearning, praying to be back with his own muckers, and God willing, there'd be letters from Barbara there. But to be sent back under a cloud, would add insult to injury, "Why? What for?"

"Thought you'd be happy". With the ghost of a smile, he put Badger's mind at ease, "Nothing to do with the bollocking. Radio order this afternoon from 81 Column was unequivocal, 'Corporal Dixon to 81 first opportunity'. Your platoon commander must think a lot of you. I don't want to lose you." Compliments did not come easily to Joss, and avoiding eye contact, his voice dropped a few pitches, "You've got the makings of tip top NCO if you keep your nose clean."

"Thanks, sarge." His spirits soared. Captain Williams and Scottie must have a high opinion of him. It was unusual, if not unique, for a lowly corporal to be specifically requisitioned by name. If Gately transmitted the 'reprimand' to 81 Column, he'd get a fair hearing from Scottie. His absolute faith in that salved his wounded pride but deep inside, he knew resentment of Gateley's tirade would smoulder for years, "When do I go, sergeant?"

"Immediately after dawn 'stand-to'. 81 Column will be at the south east end of Broadway."

"Am I going alone?" An askance look. The anticipated reunion overrode any fear of travelling alone, but it would go against everything that had been drilled into him.

"No. There'll be a man from the Recce platoon with you. The Doc thinks he's got a grumbling appendix, and is sending him to Broadway for evacuation." In a rare show of fellowship the sergeant stood up and gripped Badger's hand, "That's all. Off you go. Good luck, corporal."

That night, hundreds of miles deep inside enemy territory, he felt at peace with the world. Lying alongside Laidlaw, hands behind his head, the day's injustice slipped into the catacombs of his mind. His eyes dreamily wandered up the tall, straight kanyin trunks past the lowest branches, sixty to eighty feet up, to settle on their restless canopies, massive violet silhouettes brushed by lilac grey clouds. To-morrow he would be with Jack, Ginger, Smudge and Terry.

He caught a glimpse of the moon, high and ivory in its last quarter. In a few hours the same moon would be over Barbara. He saw her – naked, ivory and pink in the fire-lit parlour. Stealthily, his hand groped for his stiffening penis. Laidlaw stirred, half turned and grunted. Mortification paralysed Badger's fingers. The *deja vu* vanished. Feigning restlessness with a low groan, he turned his back to his restive bed-mate, and dozed into the night fantasising about the first hours he had spent back with his wife. Her blurred image guiltily alternated with a procession of other loved ones. His mother, father, sister, and brothers, whose letters he seldom answered.

Chapter Nineteen

The mid-day fires were being doused when Badger arrived at 81 Column's bivouac and reported to the adjutant – a short, pompous, cynical man, forever brushing his bristling moustache with a forefinger.

"Captain Williams asked for you?" The adjutant's eyes swept Badger from boots to forehead, as though he was some flea ridden serf, "The Commando platoon is over there. To-morrow we're joining up with 82 Column. Presumably you can guide us to them."

"Yes, sir!"

With a limp wrist flip, the adjutant acknowledged Badger's departing salute.

§

"You know better than to expect me to comment about a senior officer's action, especially when I've only heard your side of the story." Nevertheless, Captain Williams had listened sympathetically to Badger's version of Major Gately's chastisement. With Sergeant Gregory, they were sitting around the cold ashes of the Captain's fire, "My guess is that we'll hear nothing more of it. Eh, sergeant?"

"That's right sir. Just treat it as a flea in the ear, corporal." Bob Gregory's blue eye winked reassuringly at Badger.

"If it does crop up again, I'll see you get a fair hearing."

The captain's tone, and lop-sided smile, was assurance it was no idle promise, "But you've got to bear in mind that, like all column commanders, Major Gately has a heavy burden of responsibility – four hundred lives on his shoulders."

"Thank you, sir." Only with great difficulty did he forebear from commenting that the major was not indispensable, and that the escort's lives had been at greater risk than the major's.

"So, once again, welcome back. Off you go, back to your section, and remember I want to hear all about your experiences at White City and the Broadway battle, before dusk 'stand-to'."

The captain and sergeant had welcomed him with warm hand shakes, but on his way to report to them, he had passed within twenty yards of his section, and to a man they had ignored him. He knew their game. There they were, Jack Ryan, Ginger, Smudge, Terry and the rest, circled around their dead fires, hunched over their mess-tins, all affecting to be pre-occupied in finishing off their meal. It was their plot to tease that he had not been missed.

Sauntering over to them, he dropped his pack between Scofield and Oughton, and without uttering a word, settled down on it. Not by the flicker of an eyelid did any of them acknowledge his presence. Badger played along with them. Lighting his pipe, he took out one of the leaflets from the Jap raid on Broadway, and feigned intense interest it.

It was the gentle, religious Scofield whose curiosity got the better of him first,"What's that, corp?" He held his hand out for it.

"Oh, just something the Japs dropped on Broadway." Instead of handing it to Scofield, he stuffed it back in a pocket.

All eyes were now on him.

"Bloody hell! Its him, back at last."

"So it is. The skiving bastard – been living the life of Riley at Broadway, while we've been marching hundreds of bloody miles, up and down the 'Waddy'."

"And who was going to march us all off our bleeding feet?"

"Badger, the dodger!" Every voice yelled.

Broad grins on every face, including Badger's, the mock insults were more eloquent than any back slapping greeting. Even a warmer welcome followed.

"Here you are, Badger, we saved this for you." Jack handed him a mess-tin of tea. Surreptitiously, they had kept a fire smouldering to keep it warm.

"And we kept this for you." Ginger tossed him a quarter pound tin of 'Coolie Cut'. There were few pipe smokers, and Ginger had purloined the tobacco for him from a luxury drop a couple of nights previously.

"Thanks, lads." For a few moments, to forestall disclosing the unmanly emotion that had brought a lump in his throat, he sipped at the tea. At that moment, the only place he would have been happier was in Barbara's arms, "Any letters for me?"

Someone murmured 'no', and shamming indifference to veil his bitter disappointment he said firmly, "I wasn't skiving at Broadway all the time."

"Oh, we've heard all about you holding White City single handed."

Wyles laughed, more in envy than derision.

"Yes, corp, what was it like?" Something akin to hero worship shone in Scofield's eyes.

"Don't encourage him!" Ginger playfully swiped Scofield's hat off, "He's big headed enough! Once he starts there'll be no stopping him."

"Shut up, Ginger!" Jack chided, "Go on Badger, we're all dying to hear about it."

"Some other time. Are you sure there were no letters for me?"

Every face went blank, every head shook in solemn precision. Too blank, too precise.

"Aw, cut it out! There must've been some."

"Put him out of his misery, for Gawd sake!" Jack urged, and Scofield handed him an envelope.

The letter inside was only a single page airgramme, postmarked Hull. But joy of joys it was from Barbara, and he turned his back on them to read it through misty eyes.

> My darling [She usually added 'husband' but his joyous mind barely noted the omission] I do hope you get this, as a letter from your unit arrived the other day,

saying you were engaged in operations that
made it impossible for you to write to me.
How, then, can they get this to you?
These airgrammes do not give enough space to
tell you all I want to do. So I must content myself
with telling you I Love and miss you.
I pray you are safe and well. I do hope you will
soon be able to write to me and, better still,
that you will soon be home.
Everyone here is terribly excited about the imminence
of a second front in Europe.
God bless and keep you safe.
Lots of Love.
Your bitterly lonesome Barbara,
[It was usually 'Your ever faithful wife', but the new style consumed him with pity. To be so lonesome, surrounded by all those men, must be the pinnacle of faithfulness]
P.S. Longer letter next week. xxxxx. '

Swallowing back a sob, he pushed the letter into a pocket and turned around again.

"Have a dekho of this." He handed the Japanese leaflet to Scofield, "I'll never forget the sight of Mike Calvert charging up Pagoda Hill..." To counter his heartache for Barbara's sufferance, he launched into an animated recital of his experiences since leaving 81 column.

§

"That's Clydeside." Strolling up to where Badger and Scofield were on sentry, Scottie pointed across the Moguang valley to the fires, dimly visible in the gathering dusk, "About five miles away, laddies."

Several thousand feet below them lay the single track railway and fair weather road. At dawn, the column would steal across the track to join 111 Brigade at a place code-named 'Clydeside', on the other side of the valley, for the jungle telegraph's prophesied last job.

Seven days ago, with Badger as a guide, 81 Column had rendezvoused with 82 Column and for a couple of days they had relaxed together as a battalion in the teak forest between the Kaukkwe and Broadway. The days had been pleasantly warm, but most nights they had been drenched by torrential rains.

Preparations for the closing down of Broadway, and its stockpiles, had provided them with five day's full scale rations, clothing and boot replacements. They had even been given the opportunity to send a letter home. Passing round a few pencil stubs provided by the signals section they had scribbled hasty notes on scraps from ration packets, field note books and even toilet paper.

Four days ago, leaving 82 Column to follow several days later, 81 Column, with three day's rations had started off on the gruelling ascent of the Gangaw mountains. 16 Brigade had been flown out. Broadway was being evacuated, lock stock and barrel. When Clydeside was consolidated, Mike's forces would close down White City, and join them to finish off this last job. The jungle telegraph prophecies were coming to fruition.

Impatient to get this last job over and done with, they had trudged up the bamboo foothills, and up teak escarpments and over crests that were always false. Once again it was backs bent, lungs gasping above compressed midriffs, sweat streaming from every pore and smarting into their eyes. As each day wore on, monotony increasingly fazed Badger's memory, and losing the thread of his silent poetry recital, the hour between halts seemed interminable. At mid morning and afternoon, it would be, 'two salt tablets and a sip of water per man'.

Now, bivouacked on a crest of the range, the air was chill with the threat of yet another storm. The sky was leaden grey, and rumbles of thunder repeatedly drowned the 'put-put' of the battery charger a few yards behind his sentry post. Twice on previous nights, storms had aborted supply drops. Rations were running short, and even with good weather their precipitous surroundings ruled out a drop to-night.

"What time is it please, sir?" Badger asked.

"Nearly 7 o'clock. Goodnight, laddies, keep your eyes skinned."

When the Colonel had strolled away, Badger nudged Scofield.

"Time for your relief. Go and wake him up."

Why the hell couldn't they issue one wrist-watch per section. He had nearly mentioned it to Scottie, but realised it would be senseless. There was no hope of vital food supplies, let alone hoping for wrist-watches. In any case, if Scottie agreed, the adjutant would have to draft the requisition to the Base, and the supercilious sod would come down on him like a ton of bricks, for not going 'through channels'.

With 82 Column he could generally borrow a private watch. In 81 Column there very few of those private possessions, and most of those had been ruined by rivers or storms. When he had rejoined 81, he had set up his first crude sundial – a small circle of twelve stones around a central stake – at his section's sentry post. It had brought loud guffaws, but it had worked well enough and whenever the forest roof was open to the sun, setting one out had become a routine chore.

In denser day-time locations, it was a matter of guessing the time, or repeatedly checking with any officer, or sergeant near at hand.

Night was a different matter. Moving a few yards could result in becoming hopelessly lost. For guide-lines the sections tied their toggle-ropes together, one end at the sentry post, the other made fast to the next relief's belt loops. For time-keeping, one of the dozen sentry posts would acquire a watch. Every hour, marked by a low whistle relayed from post to post, guide-lines would be jerked to rouse the relief.

To-night that system was impossible. The crest defied the cohesive deployment of platoons. Rugged ground and crevices dispersed sections, and with few places level enough to lie on, men settled down wherever they could find a piece of turf to squat on, and a rock to lean on.

"I could murder a drop of char." The relief sentry, smacking his lips, sat down alongside Badger, "You and you're bloody 'tinee'[7] ruined our last brew."

"Put a sock in it! Don't just blame me. It could've been anyone of us who did it... Christ!" An insect bite, or a barbed wire puncture on his shoulder, abraded by his pack straps was festering, and he could not resist scratching, "... *and* I could get flogged for pinching rations, like those blokes who got caught in 111 Brigade." To ease his conscience he told himself, as he scratched harder, it wasn't such a serious crime as theirs. After all, it was not as if he'd stolen it from muckers, like the men who were flogged.

The morning they had left 82 Column, their first halt had been close to a small compound of barbed wire, 6 feet high, enclosing stacks of bulging parachute containers. Small, one pound hum-bug striped cotton bags, swarming with ants, had spilled from one container. It could only be 'tinee' – sugar. Sugar was a prized char ingredient, and Badger had drawn his section's 'small straw' to steal some from the compound.

With the section bunched near one corner to cover him, he had wormed his way under the wire and brushing off the ants, stuffed two bags inside his shirt. In the far corner of the compound, was an open mail sack, bulging air letters.

"No fucking wonder letters are scarce – dumping them to rot!" He muttered as he squirmed back under the wire. Only the hisses of his section, urging him to get out fast, stopped him rummaging the sack. When one of them had suggested the dump might be some ploy, some tactic, to trick the Japs, Badger snapped, "Not bloody likely! What, a whole sack of letters, names, addresses, units! Jap intelligence would have a field day – you numbskull!"

They had saved the 'booty' until their official issue sugar had ran out, and to-night here had been no embargo on fires before 'stand-to', but tea was scarce. The section could muster only enough for four mess-tins. They had shared them out into their twelve tins, laced heavily from the pilfered bags. There was an instant explosion of spluttering.

"Salt! Bloody salt!"

"Our last char, buggered up!"

If Badger had not moved swiftly, he would have been drenched by the hot, polluted tea, aimed at him by his furious section. Only Scofield remained calm.

"Poetic justice, Badger," he had said quietly, dousing the fire with his salted tea.

§

"You're right Badger, we shouldn't 'ave taken it out on

you." The new sentry handed him a stick of 'K' ration Spearmint, "But it was a bloody waste of char. What do you reckon that compound was for Badger?"

"Might be a dump for something like Captain Musgrave-Wood's unit." Throughout the Gangaw ranges, the Captain[8] had built up a highly efficient network of Kachin spies, and saboteurs. As he spoke, it dawned on him that salt was a valuable trading commodity, and he wondered how long it would be before it was raided by some anti-British hillmen or – prized as it was – even by pro-British Kachins.

The thought triggered the recollection of villages put to the torch. It seemed so callous, so un-British. It went against the grain of all he had been brought up to believe – the paternalism of British rule, the chivalry of it forces. All those wretched, wailing women, sobbing children and gesticulating men, brusquely evicted from their humble shanties and penned by a British cordon while their homes were burnt to the ground. Even the great, gentle and humane Scottie had done it.

§

Two days after leaving 82 Column, they had cordoned off a village suspected of harbouring BTA men. The elders had vehemently denied any knowledge of the 'traitors'. At length, when brisk interrogation by Burriffs proved fruitless, Scottie had whispered something to a sergeant major. Then, loud enough to be heard above the encircled villager's jabber and whining, he ordered the sergeant major to seize the Thugyi and his wife, take them down into the forest, and shoot them.

In hushed shock and horror, the cordon had watched the victims being bundled by the sergeant major and two others, down the hill until they were lost from sight. The villagers, realising what was about to happen, fell into stunned silence. Moments later, a shot jerked every man in the cordon like a whiplash. A villager shrieked.

They braced themselves for the second shot. This couldn't be happening. A British officer – Scottie above all people – ordering the execution of civilians.

Then the second shot. All eyes were on Scottie. He was picking two more for execution! Badger wondered what *he* would have done if ordered to execute the people. Would he refuse? It surely wasn't a lawful order? A resurgence of jabbering arrested his thoughts. An elder was talking excitedly to the Burriffs. It seemed that every villager was pointing to the same hut. At last they were confessing, denouncing the 'traitor'! But what a cost for their breach of tribal loyalty!

A whistle and a shout from someone near Scottie and the sergeant major re-appeared. A wave of approbation, a surge of relief, swept the column. The Thugyi and his wife were walking back, sullen faced but unhurt. Good old Scottie! Wise old Scottie!

The 'traitor' and his kin had long absconded but judging by the Burriffs satisfied smiles, whatever they'd discovered in his house – before setting it on fire – convinced them that the villagers had not denounced an innocent absentee to save their own necks.

The village elders were firmly warned that the destruction of the culprit's hut, and 'mock' executions, were only a sample of what would happen in the event of future transgressions. Next time the entire village would be destroyed, and the executions would be for real.

With that, Scottie had led the column from the village.

Compared with the punishment meted out to other villages, Scottie's action had been lenient. But the more Badger reflected on it, the more the summary destruction of civilian homes distressed him. Punishing whole families, destroying their homes, all their goods and chattels, because one of them was an enemy, seemed a violation of justice. In his simplistic view, soldiers and spies were the enemy, not their children and womenfolk. The BTA weren't fighting for the Japs. This was *their* land. They were patriots, fighting against British domination. The far more brutal Japanese ravaging of pro-British tribes, was no excuse for the British punishment of BTA kin.

§

The battery charger spluttered into silence. The signallers cursed as they strove to re-start it. Once again he was glad he was not a signaller. They did not do sentry duty, but when he'd done his stint, he would get a few hours sleep. The signallers could be working well into the night and at dawn, they would hunched over their sets, before dismantling and packing up their equipment and loading their mules, while everyone else was leisurely sipping tea and smoking.

"Must be the worst job in the column," he said aloud as the charger coughed into life.

"Thank God for that!" a signaller cried in relief as the charger chugged into a steady 'put-put'.

"Penny for 'em, Badger," the sentry whispered.

"What?"

"Your thoughts. Dreaming of your missus again?"

"If I was dreaming of her they'd be worth a king's ransom, mucker."

Now the King's were going under the command of 111 Brigade, would the Field Post Office re-direct their mail? Barbara had promised a longer letter in a week. The thought reminded him that it was her birthday to-morrow, the 8th. of May. Each man had left the dates of next of kin birthdays and special anniversaries with the Assam Staff. If they had been sent off in time, or at all, the formal aerogramme's would be poor substitutes for personal greetings, but it would at least show Barbara that he had not forgotten her birthday.

Footnotes to Chapter Nineteen

Page 280 Note No.7 'Tinee' = Sugar
Page 282 Note No.8 Musgrave-Wood later to become 'Emwood' the Daily Mail cartoonist.

Chapter Twenty

At first light, under an oppressive slate grey overcast sky, 81 Column broke out from the thickets and lantana scrub into open paddy fields. The night trek had been a tense, precarious descent. Harness and weapons clattered and clanged, as men and mules stumbled and slithered down the trackless mountain. They had been sternly commanded to keep silent. Every muffled curse – every clang – had intensified the awareness of their long, snaking column's vulnerability.

They had waded the Namyin Chaung, a mile and a half back, before dawn, and in single file. Between protective picquets to their right and left, they had boldly crossed the road and rail track, now half a mile behind them.

Ahead of them, stretching half a mile north east to south west, the paddy had obviously been recently hacked into a crude air strip. Roughly levelled, the north east half was a few feet lower than the rest, and the step down between the two had been bulldozed into a humpy ramp. At both extremes, the split-level strip merged into shoulder high 'elephant' grass and thickets.

The airstrip was there, but where was the Clydeside Block? There were no defence works around the railway and road.

Half a mile ahead across the paddy, veiled in the sultry, wispy mist, was a wooded spur from the foothills of the Bumrawng Bum range. The 1000 yard long spur, a steep natural glacis, rising a couple of hundred feet to a ruggedly ridged crest, was broken by a re-entrant near each end, and a hillock just off the south west quarter.

From behind the spur, there was a rattle of musketry. To the north east, field guns flashed and boomed. High trajectory shells wooshed over, throwing up great gouts of earth on a northern slope. Despite the recent rain, the paddy was hard and finely crazed with dehydration. Anxious not to be caught in the open, the column's pace quickened. With the Commando Platoon at the tail end, Badger was almost trotting.

Then they saw them, files of men, lugging ammunition and coiled barbed wire up the steep spur. Halfway up, stripped to the waist, their sweating backs glistening in a brief shaft of sunlight, squads were stringing out barbed wire. A jeep loaded with barbed wire pitched and tossed, like a dinghy in a choppy sea, into a distant re-entrant.

By the time the Commando platoon reached the foot of the spur, the leading platoons were already deploying over the spine. At an order passed down from Scottie, the Commando Platoon split into two. The tall, owl-like, Captain Davidson and his sappers continued uphill. Captain Williams, with the two King's sections, were led by a Cameronian sergeant from 111 Brigade, to a depression near the foot of the hill.

"Ten minutes rest, then we're going down on the strip." With a salute and a smile, the captain dismissed the Cameronian.

"Carrying parties, sir?"

Behind him a water bottle gurgled, and Bob Gregory spun round. "Go easy on that water! We don't know what supplies are like yet."

"Yes, sergeant, working parties. The Cameronians, and King's Own Lancasters, have been here three days and haven't had more than a few hour's sleep – levelling the paddy, unloading planes and lugging stores about day and night, they must be about knackered. We've got to give them a break."

"Right, sir." Bob turned to Badger, "We'll carry rifles and a fifty round bandolier each... put your shirts back on!" Sheepishly, Wyles and Trott slipped their shirts on, "Even in this overcast – now the sun's well up – you're backs will blister before you know it... get all the packs and equipment stacked over there, corporal, and detail one man to to guard them."

The relief of moving without that terrible burden of packs and equipment, when they 'floated' back to the strip, gave way to depression. There was an air of impending doom about the place. The debris of two burnt out Dakotas lay at the southern end of the strip. Two other severely damaged Dakotas, with half a dozen wrecked gliders, were strung along the paddy edge.

Ammunition boxes, barbed wire and bales of stores, were piled at the foot of a steep, well worn path that wound uphill around boulders and rain fissures. To Badger, it seemed that every load destined for position around the top of that gruelling path, was assigned to his section, leaving the lesser hauls for 111 working parties.

Throughout the day, their snatched breathers at the foot of the hill with 111 Brigade working parties, deepened the sense of doom. In dribs and drabs, they pieced together 111 Brigade's story.

§

Before they had reached Clydeside, three days ago, fatigue had already sapped 111 Brigade's vitality. In army parlance, they were 'dragging themselves along on their chinstraps.' Bad luck had dogged it since it flew in, and incompetence – real and apparent – had all but bankrupted their trust in higher command. Only a frail strand of regimental pride was now holding them together, forcing each nerve and sinew to serve them when they had nothing in them, *Except the will which says to them: "Hold on!"*

Plans to land them at Broadway and Piccadilly, had been hastily changed with the eleventh hour abandonment of the latter. Half were deposited at Broadway, the other four columns at Chowringee, 70 miles away on the other side of the Irrawaddy. Two of the Chowringee columns, under Colonel Morris were to harry Japs near the Burma-China frontier. Banmauk, the concentration area for the rest of the split brigade, was over a hundred mile march over mountains from both Broadway and Chowringee.

The two remaining Chowringee columns had attempted to cross the half mile wide 'Waddy'. It had been a fiasco. Gliders, bringing in assault boats, landed half a mile off target. The boats, massive outboard motors, petrol and oil, had to be manhandled over rocks and sand dunes in the hot night, back to the crossing point. Outboard motors would not start. Others, petering out in midstream, were beached for fruitless overhauls. By dawn only two boats were serviceable.

Most mules could not be led, driven or cajoled beyond the water's edge. Others, coaxed in on the heels of the more amenable ponies, or by riders, turned back when the water reached their shoulders. Yet more, with their flailing hooves, swamped the boats attempting to tow them across, and dragged them back to shore.

In mid-afternoon, with only Brigade HQ, one column and a score of mules across, the operation was abandoned. The other column, with the bulk of the Brigade's mules, heavy weapons, radios and ammunition reserves, was ordered to join up with Morris's already two days march ahead.

A Brigade reduced from 8 to 5 widely dispersed columns before their campaign had started for real! It was incredible – to men who had not been there – that a river crossing, practiced to perfection so many times in India, could become such a fiasco.

Even more incredible, instead of a clearing, Brigade HQ had selected thick jungle for their first supply drop after the crossing. Flying conditions were good, but the jungle swallowed up nearly half their supplies, and it was three days rations instead of five.

After that, through despatch shortages or lost 'chutes, supply drops had seldom given them any more than 3 days rations for 5. One drop had brought them oil instead of petrol for the battery chargers. If the batteries failed they would be lost to India, and faced with starvation. But, for some daft reason, two or three days passed before they radio-ed for petrol. When, with failing batteries, they demanded fresh supplies, the rear base in Assam had replied, 'Your demand too late. Submit fresh demand for another date.' By then, unannounced, the Imphal base-station, threatened by the Jap thrust into India, had moved back to Sylhet and direct radio contact was lost. By a fluke, a quick witted 16 Brigade operator intercepted their desperate, fading transmissions, and relayed the signals to India.

For a fortnight, while 77 Brigade at White City were slaughtering and being slaughtered, 111 Brigade's columns, scattered over hundreds of miles of jungle and mountain, eschewed any contact with the Japs. The vaguest hint of an enemy presence, sent the Lentaigne's column scuttling. Once, in the middle of the night, they had fled from their bivouac because of a rumour of Japs in the area. The 'Japs' turned out to be four Burmese villagers.' This was not what Wingate had trained, toughened and inspired them to do. They were there to hunt and harass Japs, but they felt like the quarry instead of the hunters.

Days of back-breaking toil were wasted by last minute changes, indecision or misunderstood signals. They levelled glider and light plane strips that were never used. Other strips were badly sited, and wrecked the gliders or were aborted at the last minute by pilots.

Hours, sometimes days, of marching, were set to naught by disorientation, or searching for water. Bent under their crippling loads – all army possessions, and none of their own – men had despaired as 'U' turns brought the head of the long snaking columns back past the tail. A thing that had never happened to King's columns.

Until they rendezvoused with the Brigade HQ, the Lancasters and Cameronians, hacking their way through jungle – so dense at times that explosives were needed to clear a path – had been the butt of curt signals, urging them to get a move on. The Cameronians, having bumped into Japs, killed a score of them for three or four minor casualties of their own and had been rewarded by Lengtaigne's rebuking signal, 'Do not engage in unnecessary battles, advance to your objective.'

Like other 111 columns, it had generally been three day's rations stretched to five but when they reached the rendezvous, except for 'scraps' dropped from light planes, the Lancasters had been without food for four days. Then there were 'bloody rum issues after any day in the pissing rain – bloody officers for the use of only.'

The more 111 Brigade's men spoke of their experiences, the more their disillusion with Lengtaine's tactics – and their envy of Calvert's achievements – made itself felt.

In their first two weeks in Burma they had blown up a minor railway bridge, and the Japs had repaired it in a few days. A road they had been ordered to block turned out to be an overgrown disused cart track. The five columns had crossed different points of the Mandalay-Myitkyina rail track – the same track that Mike Calvert was grimly blocking – and save for that one bridge, they had left it intact!

Before he had been flown out to succeed Wingate, exhaustion had overcome Lengtaigne. In pity, more than resentment of their own terrible marching loads, they had watched their worn out Brigadier spend his last days with them riding a pony. Even flying him out had been a 'balls up.'

To fly him, and two stranded glider pilots out, a light plane strip had been laboriously cleared. The two planes, swooping to land from the wrong end, were warned off by a red Aldiss lamp and instead of circling around, gunned their engines and sped back to India. 'Some bugger got the signals wrong.' Another long march well into the night. Another strip to hack out next morning, and nearly another 'cocked up operation.'

Four tall trees stood at the approach end of the 200 yard strip and only minutes before the planes were due, someone realised that the planes would be too high to touch down before crashing into the jungle at the opposite end. Hastily laid explosive charges felled three of the trees, the fourth merely cracked. Two planes swooped down and were warned off with a red Verey flare. They circled round, and started down from the opposite end. From downwind, skimming the hundred feet high trees, then weaving and sideslipping, branches scraping their wing tips, they floated 150 yards and touched down to halt a few feet short of the unblown tree. '...bloody brave, those pilots... pulled some dim officer out of the shit...'

With the five columns concentrated in their operational area – Masters now in command – the emphasis of their lives changed. For two or three weeks, instead of monotonous, apparently aimless marches, dodging Japs, they became true Chindits. They moved stealthily to surprise the enemy – raiding his stockpiles, ambushing his transport and attacking him in his bases and bivouacs.

They had not got off scott free, but they had notched up Jap casualties at the rate of 10 to 1 of their own, and successful marauding had perked up their morale.

Then suddenly, they were back to slinking through the jungle and forest, heading for Aberdeen. Wishful thinking filled them with unbridled optimism. Wingate had said ninety days – they had done only forty – but the monsoon was imminent, and he'd also said they must be out before the rains. Five columns converging on Aberdeen, where there was no Jap activity, could only mean they were flying out.

The night before they reached Aberdeen was something of a gala bivouac that bolstered their expectations. Around huge fires, they feasted on luxury rations, saved for an occasion just as this. Tinned tomatoes, rice, bully beef and processed cheese, all went into their mess tins, and they sang and caroused around their blazing fires well into the night.

But Aberdeen was no 'Gateway to India'.

Masters, parading them there, bluntly disabused them of that notion, "Some of you" he told the hopeful, assembled troops, "think you are nearing the end of your strength. You are wrong. In the past months you have consumed the surplus energy you built up before coming into Burma. Now, you are down to scratch and from now on you will be drawing on your strength. You have not reached your reserves and will not do for some time. There is a big task still to do."

"Buggers led us up the garden path, didn't they Jock?"

After a day's rest, burdened with replenished ammunition and rations, they had headed north, crossing and re-crossing the meandering Meza river a score or more times. Two days, over rolling, afforested hills, before they hit 'the sodding mountains'.

"Am nae kidding, it was a glacier of bamboo leaves, two steps up and one step down."

The Jocks swore it was a hundred degrees in the shade. For two days – as they crawled and clutched their way up – the leading platoon clearing a path for the mules, had to be changed every half hour.

"Ah was never sae glad to see anything in ma life, as the Indawgyi Lake from the top of that mountain. It was mare bonny than Loch Lomond in the sunset."

"Aye, but the dafties had marched us 30 miles east to Aberdeen, then 30 miles north, when a diagonal from the start would've cut out miles and bypassed that mountain."

They had then sloshed through the marshes, and reed grass of the Indawgyi Valley, then slogged for days over the massive

Bumrawng range to reach Clydeside.

§

"Right me lucky lads, that's the lot for you. Get yourselves a quick breather, and get back to your positions." The Lancastrian quartermaster sergeant supervising the distribution of supplies, pointed to a stack of grenade boxes, "Take a few of these boxes with you, for to-night's fireworks."

Sitting on ammunition boxes, Badger handed a Lancaster corporal a few flakes of tobacco, and unbuttoned his shirt. The heat had gone out of the day, his sodden clothes and hat band were chilling his flesh. His back ached, and his inflamed shoulder itched. The sore was now a weeping ulcer. The MO had treated it with sulphanilamide powder, and his rifle sling had rubbed off the sweat soaked plaster.

"Phew. Ugh." As he contorted to scratch between his shoulder blades, sour sweat, sickly sweet suppuration and decaying sulphanilamide filled his nostrils, "What columns are here, mate?"

"Two Lancasters, two Cameronians, and yours." The corporal rolled the tobacco in a rupee note, lit the makeshift cigarette and drew deeply on it. His bare torso and arms were pock-marked with insect bites. His shoulders raw red, and peeled skin patches, "Every platoon has lost five or ten men, mostly sickness, and bloody Masters left a whole Gurkha column at Mokso Sakan on the Indawgyi Lake, as a rearguard!"

Mokso Sakan? Its very name had an evil ring about it. A whole column, days away over rugged mountains. For a rearguard? Three other columns of 111 Brigade, with Morris, their brigadier, still a hundred miles away east of the Irrawaddy. No 'floater' columns to strike the rear of enemy attackers! What had the strategists up their sleeves?

"What are we really here for?"

"Search me mate." His nails rasped vigorously through his matted beard. Lice? Badger was glad that was one source of irritation he was free from, "I'm a only a poor bloody footslogger, like yourself, they don't tell us owt. All I know is it's supposed to be a road block. Huh!" Spitting out a speck of tobacco, he glumly pointed across the strip, "Some block! The road and railway are a mile away. Only thing'll reach them is 25 pounders. The sooner we get them the better. The Japs 105's have been knocking ten sorts of shit out of us, night and morning, since we got here."

§

In Scottie's column, daily briefings were routine, and eagerly awaited sessions. At some convenient time and place, he would confer with platoon commanders, and they then briefed their men. 'Briefing' was a misnomer. As fully as strategic censorship permitted, platoon commanders first spelled out the current intelligence information, intention, method and administration pertaining to the columns' movements and assignments. That would be followed by the latest news of other Chindit columns; the 14th Army; European, Russian and Pacific theatres of war; and from Blighty.

To-night, their first in Clydeside, and out of contact with 81 Column HQ, Captain Williams had very little factual information to give them, "Dig in where we are, and wait for further orders!" 111's HQ Staff had nettled Captain Williams, and his unusually sharp tone hinted at his scorn for their 'locum' masters, "That's all I could get out of them..." Tongues around him clacked with disgust. He was fostering disrespect and hastily added, "...that's enough, remember they've got a lot on their plate." He paused, collected his thoughts, and decided it best not to mention he had vainly traipsed from post to post in an effort to locate elusive staff officers for instructions.

Jap artillery that morning, had inflicted casualties on 111 Brigade HQ and staff officers were busily transferring the command post, and main dressing station, to a less exposed site. Others were hurrying about co-ordinating fields of fire, checking perimeter wire, tallying the deployment of ammunition and mortars. Nonetheless, they should have organised an officers briefing.

All Williams had got, eventually, was, 'later, later, dig in where you are for now, before the shelling starts again'.

"We'll get a proper briefing tomorrow." Silently, the captain added, 'I hope to God we do', "Meanwhile, I can only tell you the scraps I picked up here and there. I'll stick to what I think is fact, without scuttle-butt. That means it will be historical – what happened here to date, and not any operational intentions or purpose."

Every morning and evening since the second day of the 'Block', he told them, Jap 105's had shelled it. With the usual yelling and screaming, the Japs had put in strong probing attacks, several times a night, usually on the north west sector. Two mornings ago in broad daylight, the gliders, carrying earth moving machinery and heavy plant, had come in. As they circled, Jap ack-ack guns had opened up on them. The first one crash dived half a mile away. None of the remaining four were hit, but all cracked up on the rugged, bumpy, split-level strip.

With only a bulldozer and a damaged grader, using picks and shovels, the paddy had been hacked into a rough runway, and that night the first two Dakotas had flown in. The ramp tore the undercarriage off the first, and on full throttle, without touching down, it had zoomed back to India. The other, carrying engineering equipment, landed and took off safely. No further aircraft had risked landing there until last night, when the ramp had been eased. One sheared off the runway, and burst into flames. Another, overshooting the strip, crashed into thickets. Japs got in among two being unloaded, and set one on fire. The other slammed its doors, roared down the runway, and crashed into the only undamaged one left.

"Any coming in to-night, sir?" Badger asked.

"I expect so, we desperately need artillery and..." The captain thought for a second, "a gunner major flew in last night with an advance party." Detailing casualties was not good for morale, but the jungle telegraph would be buzzing with this one soon enough, "He was killed this morning."

"Water point, sir?"

"Thanks for reminding me, sergeant. Over the ridge and down the other side, I'll show you in the morning. We can't go in the dark. The Dressing Station and Brigade HQ are in a northern re-entrant to our right rear..."

The thud and boom of 105's cut him short. Every man flattened himself against the earth. Thud, boom. The salvoes were bursting over the ridge, on the northern sector. Sheepishly they straightened up.

"I think the Brigade commander has ordered Colonel Scott to take out the rest of our column to hunt down those guns..." Thuds and booms cut the captain short again.

Huh, thought Badger, we don't even know whose commanding this place. He'd heard, but could not believe, that it was Masters. A major, with at least three lieutenant colonels under him? Never! But Masters must be good, he's a Gurkha.

"... Meanwhile, we're stuck here with orders to dig in. This is the weakest sector, but when we've dug the slit trenches we'll move out to that copse as a forward picquet." He pointed to a small clutch of trees on the other side of the runway, midway along its lower length, "If the Japs come that way in any strength, we'll just hold them up a little to give the command post time to reinforce this side of the hill. No digging in the copse. Don't want to leave the Japs ready made weapon pits when we beat it back here. We'll leave one Bren and two men here, to give us covering fire."

The Captain's initiative needed no explanation. Clydeside was no fortified stronghold. Its garrison, weapons, fortification resources, were still too meagre to encircle it with a substantial defensive perimeter. The east-north-west perimeter was surrounded by forest and dense lantana. Ideal for attackers to concentrate, and launch assaults. The steep southern slopes overlooked the runway and open paddy. Except for the copse, there was scant cover for any attackers for over half a mile.

The commander, whoever he was, was obviously banking on the Japs taking advantage of the forest, concentrating his resources on the east-north-west defences, leaving the runway side almost defenceless. The Jap commander must be thinking likewise. Every night he had attacked the northern perimeter, and had been savagely mauled. If he did not know now, he would soon realise that the southern slopes must be the weakest sector. It might be folly to British minds to attack across open country, but the Japs were fanatics, and the costly consequences of their northern assaults might make a southern attack across the airstrip an acceptable risk. The northern attacks could even be a ploy. Tempting the defenders to concentrate resources there, while he marshalled his forces for a surprise night assault across the strip.

"Dixon, take Oughton, four men and a Bren to the copse now. Set up fixed fields of fire, and lay out a few trip wire explosives forward of the copse. We'll join you when we've dug the trenches here."

Jack, Smudge, Terry and Scofield were already were on their feet stripping their webbing to skeleton order.

"What do you think our chances are of getting any mail now, sir?"

Williams derisively shook his head in gesture that said, 'silly question at a time like this'. A dozen tongues tittered.

"What Judy would write to a poverty stricken bastard like you," someone jibed, " with all those rich handsome Yanks knocking her off!"

"No, she's a Waaf," another taunted, "they're the officers' groundsheets."

Badger held his tongue. It was comradely baiting. He'd already made a fool of himself. Any retort would invite further ribbing. Barbara's virtue was too sacred to be bandied about, however good humouredly.

"Just ignore them, Badger," the reverential Scofield commiserated as they walked away, "Might be better if we get no mail. If the others got a letter and you don't, you'll have sinful thoughts about her."

He was right. Ignore them. They didn't know what real love was. He didn't need letters to keep their love alive.

No news was good news.

§

As Badger and Jack Ryan finished setting out the trip wires, there was a faint drone of aircraft and almost immediately came the thump-thump-thump of ack-ack guns. To the north, the thud and boom of 105s had given way to the clatter of small arms, the crack of grenades and the thumping of mortars.

When they hurried back to the copse, Oughton and the others were standing behind trees.

"Oughton! Get down on the ground!" How on earth did he get his stripes? Bloody high school prefect! Badger, still smarting at his own stupidity for asking about mail, had to re-assert his professional maturity by deriding Oughton's dim-witted deployment.

"What for?" Belligerently, "There's plenty of cover standing up."

"Because, Corporal," counting on his fingers, he growled, "one – best concealment; two – you make a smaller target; three – you see the enemy before they see you, silhouetted against the sky-line..."

"Anything wrong, Dixon?" The Captain arrived, with the remainder of the detachment as the runway lights snapped on.

"No, sir. Just settling firing positions." It was one thing to deride a colleague among colleagues, but it was not in Badger's nature show one up in front of an officer.

The overcast, moonless night was now a macabre carnival of colour and sound. The runway was a promenade of brilliant lights. To the north came the clattering of small arms, the crack and thud of mortars and machine guns stammering. Tracers criss-crossed the hill in glowing, deceptively graceful streams. Above them were brilliant electric blue flashes, thump-thumping ack-ack bursts. Verey flares – red, white and green – soared into the overcast, before floating leisurely to earth.

Behind the copse, Dakotas roared down the approach path with headlights blazing and wing lights winking. In breathtaking minutes, five planes tore along the strip, bounced violently at the ramp and screeched to a halt, before trundling to the unloading area.

For what seemed hours, the detachment strained their eyes towards the railway, blinking at the distant trees that mimicked humans in the gun flashes. The commotion of unloading seemed designed to entice Jap raiders. Aircraft doors slamming, controllers shouting directions, hustling working parties, flashing torches. Jeep engines labouring, wheels spinning, bouncing, ferrying ammunition from the planes into re-entrants. Gunners cursing, striving to control their 25 pounders and Bofors, rumbling and slewing down the aircraft ramps.

"Organised bloody chaos!" Badger snorted, to no one in

particular. It was admiration rather than censure, as in quick succession five planes revved up, taxied for take off against a flashing backdrop of ack-ack flak, and roared off back to India.

"Split them into three shifts sergeant – one on watch, two resting." Captain Williams peered at his watch, and, in a gun-flash, made out the time, "About seven hours to dawn. We'll do two hours on, four off, and all 'stand-to' for the last hour."

But there was little sleep for anyone. Throughout the night the battle over to the north raged to a crescendo, died to desultory firing, and flared up to a renewed crescendo. With every fresh outburst, men nodding off were jolted to tense wakefulness.

A little before dawn, the Jap infantry assault petered out and salvo after salvo of 105 shells thumped and thudded into the northern defences, covering their retreating comrades and the recovery of the wounded.

Their second night was a repeat performances. At dusk, for two hours, Jap artillery again pounded Clydeside. Again on the northern sector, there were hours of savage battle crescendos and brief lulls. The Dakotas roared in through the ack-ack flashes, and Captain Williams's detachment, still isolated from its roving column, picqueted the copse from dusk to dawn. But, at least at night, they were a cohesive unit, with a positive, comprehensible purpose for their vigil.

The second and third days were a hotch potch of tasks. They were the unattached 'odds and sods' typical of the army. Nobody's baby. Nobody's that is, other than any harassed officer who outranked Captain Williams and Shanghai-ed them for some chore. They hauled ammunition and supplies, from the strip up to the hard pressed Lancasters. They hauled slate grey corpses, from the Lancasters down to the strip for burial. They carried the severely wounded from the dressing station to the strip for light plane, or Dakota, evacuation. They were put to digging trenches across the north east end of the runway. After hacking away for hours, exposed to sporadic showers of shrapnel from Jap artillery bursts, a wiser officer saw the futility of trying to defend the strip and set them to lugging jerry cans of water up and over the steep spine, from the stream to the overworked dressing station.

The only thing they were certain of, as each day dawned, was that sometime in the day, two men from each of their two sections, would have the un-enviable job of running the gauntlet of snipers to fill the sections' water bottles and chagauls from the stream. Their only crumb of consolation was, that they worked without the burden of their torturing packs and free of constant abrasion. Badger's ulcerated shoulder became a healing scab. Throughout those days, he trawled for information from every weary, raw eyed Chindit he bumped into.

'Was Clydeside intended as a Block or not?'

'Your guess is as good as mine, mate.'

'What was happening over the northern sector?'

'The Lancasters are taking a bloody pasting every night. Bloody digging and wiring all day, bloody snipers potting at them.'

'Who is in command?

'Major Masters. Thinks this bloody place is a village cricket pitch.'

Men spoke in sardonic puns, of their trenches at 'silly point', and the night long battles at 'the deep'.

The third morning passed with still no briefing. They were still ignorant of Clydeside's operational purpose. Only through their roving tasks had they gradually pieced together its topography.

Clydeside was like a spreadeagled sway backed, pregnant sow, its belly lumpy with litter. The northern extremity – its left jowl – was 'the deep'. Its right jowl, the 'pavilion'. Eastward – along its ridged spine – was the 'umpire', 'bowler' and 'wicket'. At its tail was the 'keeper'. In 'mid on' – a re-entrant that formed its left armpit – was Brigade HQ and Main Dressing Station. The water point was below and between 'mid on', and 'square leg' was the re-entrant at its left hind hoof. 'Cover' and 'extra cover' lay in the curve of the right leg. 'Silly point' and 'point' were in the depression of the crook of its right hind leg. The hillock at the south west, was simply the 'Pimple'.

§

On that third morning, lugging water bottles and chagauls back from the water point Badger's sleep-hungry, and information-starved mind could not reconcile Clydeside with any Wingatian purpose. The lengthening periods of leaden, oppressive, overcast weariness and uncertainty compounded the air of doom that hung over the place. His confusion fostered a vague, gnawing presentiment that Chindit doctrines had been buried with their creator.

How could Clydeside deny the Japs passage through the Moguang Valley? It was too distant from the railway and road. What were they here for? True, each day the air force had bombed the railway, and since the 25 pounders arrived yesterday, they had shelled the valley several times. But were they really hindering the Jap's supply lines?

The jungle telegraph was buzzing that bombs and shells had cut the rail track in dozens of places, and that 25 pounders had destroyed an ammunition train. If the rail tracks and road had been breached in places, it *must* be wasted effort because the Japs seemed to have no difficulty in keeping their troops supplied. They must be shuttling supplies from breach to breach, or repairing them swiftly. How else could their artillery and infantry sustain their offensive.

The air force must be fully stretched making strikes against Jap ground forces, while dropping supplies to a penned-in garrison that could do little to supplement the aerial attacks. As well as shelling the valley, the gunners, with their limited supplies, had to duel with the Jap artillery. Every shell, every bullet, had to come in by air, and now that Cochrane's Air Commando had been disbanded, the Chindit requisitions had to compete with the demands of Slim's hard pressed Kohima and Imphal fronts.

If the intention was to cut off the Japs' supplies, wouldn't it be less costly and more rewarding to do it in true Chindit style? It was what they had been trained and equipped for. The style with which Wingate had first fired their imagination. Sorties from jungle hideouts, ambushing convoys, raiding supply dumps and blowing up roads and railways, a dozen times or more each night That was the true Wingatian way.

Strongholds were the only other static role in the Chindit book. Clydeside was certainly not a stronghold. It must be close to the Jap front line reserves. A Stronghold was supposed to be remote – an arsenal and a safe harbour for marauding columns. Like

Broadway, they needed to be inaccessible to all but men, pack animals and aircraft. Clydesdale was accessible to whatever artillery, armoured and infantry divisions the Japs wanted to throw at them. And there were no floating columns!

The column left at Mokso Sakan was too far away to strike at the rear or flanks of a Jap attack. And why (as Badger had heard and later seen for himself, as he passed Brigade HQ) had Major Masters sent all but about 25 mules back to Mokso Sakan? That was a fraction of the mules needed for a mobile Chindit brigade. Clydeside smelt of a static, odds-against battle to the last round and last bayonet. For what?

§

The sections were sitting in their depression at the side of the strip, eating cold rations when Badger returned with the water party.

"Thank you." Captain Williams took his chagaul and bottle from Badger, "Any snipers about corporal?"

"Not one, sir, thank the Lord."

"Right, get yourself a meal while I'm briefing you all."

After days of humiliating uncertainty, the buoyancy was back in the Captain's Welsh lilt, and there was a resolute gleam in his eyes, "At last, Brigade HQ have given us a definite role. In half an hour we're going up to take over part of 'the deep'. The Lancasters have had a tough couple of nights, and we are relieving one of their platoons." He avoided saying 'the remnants of a platoon', "The broader picture is that White City and Broadway have now been closed down, without the loss of a man or a gun.[Appendix 2] 77 Brigade moving north, will occupy the hills on the other side of the railway, ready to sweep down on the rear of the Japs if they attack us in strength...."

"Hurray!" The sections' bawls vented their relief.

"....Colonel Scott and the rest of our column are hunting out the Jap 105s. 82 Column should be joining us in a couple of days. 14 Brigade are coming over from Indawgyi as floaters. General Stilwell's forces, the Chinese, and Merrill's Marauders are driving the Japs back along the Kamaign-Myitkyina-Mogaung front. Clydeside will be held until they take Mogaung, hopefully by June 1st, and our job will be finished. We are now under Stilwell's command. General Lentaigne has moved Chindit HQ to his at Shadazup..."

"Good old Joe and Joe." Someone yelled.

The news brought grins all round. Joe Stilwell had a reputation as a tough, no nonsense fighting commander. Joe Lentaigne might be too old to march alongside his Chindits, but he was a seasoned soldier, and a Gurkha to boot. In their eyes the Chindits were in good hands. Clydeside might not be a good Block, but at least they now knew why they were here, and with all those forces pushing towards them holding it for a fortnight would be no great feat. Then, presumably, the two Joes would have them flown out.

"Right then, packs on. Let's get up to 'the deep' before the Jap opens up his evening barrage."

With resuscitated spirits, the sections filed after their captain chanting, 'We're here because we're here, because we're here, because old Joe's coming here...'

Footnote to Chapter Twenty

Page 289 Note No.9 The troops were not to know that Lentaigne was under strict orders to reach his operational area with maximum speed and concealment. Nevertheless he does appear to have been unduly cautious. After this incident he drafted a signal reporting that they had contacted strong Japanese patrols which Masters prevailed on him not to send. In his book *The Road Past Mandalay* Masters recalls that had Lentaigne insisted on sending the signal, he (Masters) intended to feign sick, fly out of Burma, and tell Wingate that he must come in himself to judge whether Joe was physically fit for the job.

Chapter Twenty-one

"No wonder those poor sods were shattered" Badger said, recalling the raw eyed, ashened faced Lancaster's after they had relieved them the previous night, "Four nights here like last night, is enough to snap the bravest man's nerve. I'd better get back to my hole, before the curtain goes up again."

Jack, Ginger, Smudge and Terry, hastily finishing their 'K' ration supper, gave him a swift 'two finger' farewell as he stepped from their trench. Dusk was less than an hour away and if last night and the tales of the Lancasters were any thing to go by, the Jap 105s and 'whizz-bang' mortars, would open up their evening pounding 'the deep' at any moment.

Badger felt guilty. His 'hole' was a trench deep enough to stand in – roofed over with stout logs. Theirs was not so much a trench as a shallow pit, less than thigh deep, with a rock hard base that would require a pneumatic drill to penetrate. The sandbagged parapet had been blasted to shreds during its previous occupancy, and each attempt to haul over felled trees had been blighted by sniper fusillades.

He hadn't taken his 'hole' because it offered greatest security, but because it was best placed to control the section. More than that, his was the 'strongpoint'. If the Japs got a foothold inside the perimeter, it would be his job to cover the section's retreat and hold out until a counter attack was mounted. His sections four positions were spread in a fifty yard arc, about five yards below the rugged crest. Twenty yards to his right Wyles and Trott, with the Bren, had a deep, well sandbagged pit that had previously housed a 3inch mortar section. Master's had now concentrated all Clydeside's eight 3inch mortars as a single battery under his HQ control.

Jack and Co. were ten yards to his left. Ten yards further left, Corporal Oughton and Johnson – a dour Yorkshire bricklayer – occupied a well dug slit trench. Bob Gregory's trench was only a couple of yards below the crest, directly above Oughton's and overlooking the other section's positions.

Last night, the Lancasters had barely staggered out of sight when the barrage started. Not intense by Western Front standards, but a steady thud, whine and thump of 105s. Along with the thwack, woosh and crump of 'whizz-bang' mortars they turned weapon pits into graves and devastated trees. For two hours they had cringed in their trenches, until the barrage had suddenly ceased, and in a fury, surmounting fear, they had fought off three determined assaults by yelling Japs. As the night-sky paled, and the jabbering Japs dragged away their dead, the 105s and 'whizz-bangs' had begun another two hour pounding of 'the deep'.

"Have you checked the wire, and booby traps, Dixon?" Captain Williams called over the parapet of his slit trench, just below the crest – slightly left-rear of Badger's position.

"Yes, sir. Still intact. Ryan and me replaced a couple of trip detonators that had gone off." Crouching at the entrance to his 'hole' Badger gave a quick look around. All chagauls under cover, no ammo reserves in the open, "There's a couple of dead Japs ten feet below our wire. We managed to snag a trip wire on one, sir."

"Good man. You'd better get under cover now, corporal".

The entrance to the 'hole' was a tight squeeze, a gap between the roof and the trench top. As he slid in feet first, he took a final look around the hill.

In the gathering gloom, the deepening shadows gave the splintered tree stumps and shell pocks a spooky, supernatural air. Around their trenches, the almost sheer slope had been trampled and blasted. It was barren of undergrowth. A belt of dense, thorny shrubbery, in front of their positions, added a natural barrier to the barbed wire, 20 feet below where the hill shelved into rolling timberland.

Thud, whine.

"Eyes down for a full house, off we go again!" Badger shouted to Jack, as the shell exploded on the reverse slope, and he slipped between Scofield and Jones at the parapet.

Standing at his loophole, guilt more than fear concerned him. They were secure from anything but a direct hit. His muckers were out there, flattening themselves in the earth of their trenches, vulnerable to the shrapnel and blast of near misses. During the day, to scotch any insinuations of cowardice, while he let them doze, he had risked snipers to fetch water and bring up ammunition. Between those jobs, he had joined them in their pit during desultory shelling, exchanging sporadic volleys with probing Japs.

Thud, whine, BOOM!

The roof timbers shook, splattering them with dirt. That was bloody close. He sent up a silent prayer for his muckers' safety. They were good lads, and for the rest of his life he knew he'd somehow feel responsible if anything happened to them.

"You all right!", he called.

"...cking bastards..!." It was all he heard above another thud and whine, but it was enough. They were OK. The whine whistled to a crump that hardly shook the ground. They would be grovelling at the bottom of their pit, desperate for revenge and sharing his thoughts, 'God, let's live through this barrage, and get at the bastards!"

During their days working down on the strip, they'd developed a certain indifference to shelling, comforting themselves with the old soldiers' platitude that you never hear the shell that will hit you. So, when you heard one you were relieved. Now, in this tight, targeted sector, the platitude was a poor sedative for belly quaking fear.

At every thud and thwack they cringed. Held their breath through the wooshes and whines. Jabbered blasphemies with relief when missiles crumped, and only the shock waves hit them. Then they waited, sweating out the hour long minutes, listening to the screams of the wounded, for the next salvo. Waiting as the thuds of 105s and thwacks of the 'whizz-bangs' grew more terrifying. Whines and wooshes gave force to the platitudes. An unheard salvo could have their names on it.

Hands clamped over their heads, flinching at every near miss, they prayed for the silences between salvoes to terminate in Jap yells that would signal the end of the murderous bombardment, and the launching of another suicidal ground assault. Then the garrisons Vickers guns, mortars, Brens and rifles would wreak vengeance on their besiegers.

In any longer-than-usual intervals, Badger fretted that his muckers would be tempted from their cover, meagre as it might be. Long intervals did not mean the barrage had ceased. Last night the Japs had been charging up almost as the last salvoes exploded.

Before last night, none of his muckers had fired a shot in anger at the Japs, or even seen one. Before he had re-joined them at Broadway they had trudged hundreds of miles fruitlessly chasing the enemy. They had picqueted the Clydeside copse, dry mouthed, wondering if their nerves would snap if the Japs swept across the strip.

But when their baptism of fire came, last night, white hot anger displaced fear. The yelling, screaming attackers, surging uphill, after that terrible barrage, had the defenders whooping with relief. Now they could hit back, 'Come on! You fucking yellow bastards!' In hysterical retaliation, they had rained down grenades and small arms fire on each wave of attackers. Please God, don't let that hysteria drive them to break cover prematurely to-night.

Thud, thwack! Whine, woosh.

To-night's barrage was not over. A 105 and 'whizz-bang' fired almost simultaneously.

BOOM! CURUMP! One behind them, one in front.

The flashes blinded them. The roof timbers convulsed, turf filling showered earth on them. Shrapnel tore into the sandbags. Debris rained through the loopholes and stung their cheeks.

A longer than usual silence. Had the barrage ceased? Or were the Japs tempting them to relax in order to catch them repairing damaged defences?

"Stay where you are!" The Captain bawled, "There'll be another hour of this."

In the pitch black 'hole' Badger felt the roof timbers, they seemed intact, but there were gaps in the turf filling. As he moved around, his foot clicked against something metal.

"That's buggered it!."

"What?" Jones, feeling around for a chagaul, brushed against Badger.

"The bacon." He pushed a battered can, hot with impregnated shrapnel, into Jones hand. The one pound tin of bacon he had been jealously conserving for the section, had been blasted from its parados storage point.

"You'll never live this down. Salt in our tea last week. Now no bacon. We should've had it this morning. But you said No..."

"Shut up, Jonesy. Its not my bleeding fault!"

Feeling around the floor, he found the loaf they had also been saving. It was now heavy with shrapnel and dirt. Jones was right.

They should have had bacon butties this morning.

They could not have fires in the open, but that morning he had brewed char for them in the confined 'hole', and they had pressed him to cook the bacon. The char, polluted by smoke, had been bitter and unpalatable. In the smoke-logged hole he had retched and his eyes had smarted, only to be twitted for wasting scarce water, precious tea and sugar. Huffily, he had refused to nurse the fire along to cook the bacon, they would have to wait until some better occasion, 'Smoke won't spoil bacon! Let's have it while we can!'

Now, near to sobbing, he slumped down on the floor with his back to the wall nursing the ruined loaf.

Thud! Whine. The 105 shell thumped into the reverse slope.

Then in quick succession two 'whizz-bang salvoes' crumped along the ridge. But Badger was more concerned about living through to-morrow's unpopularity, than living through to-night's barrage.

They would be edgy, fractious as tired infants, venting their anger at the least provocation. The lost bread and bacon would give them a common cause for that.

Jack would say nothing. But the stony look on his tough, street bruiser's face, would be more withering than any jibe. The lanky Ginger would spout a stream of ridiculing witticisms, that no mucker should let pass without some squelching response. But Badger was no match for Ginger's razor sharp taunting. Pulling rank to silence him, would invite greater ridicule. Smudge's simian nostril's would snort, pique would give his pugnacious jaw a more belligerent tilt and for days, every time he was given an order, he would splutter blasphemies. What of Terry? Terry was a bit of a mystery, a southerner, possibly a Londoner. He mucked in as good as the others but changed the subject, or drifted into sombre silence, whenever home life was broached. Terry's pale blue eyes never seemed to blink. He was as young as any of them, but his face had the gauntness of age. Still, he would make no bones about his disgust at the stupidity of not having had bacon butties that morning. Well, he was in for hot tongue and cold shoulder rations to-morrow.

A near miss, rocking the timbers, reverberated through the walls and brought him to his feet. The tempo of the barrage was intensifying. Like last night, the thuds and thwacks were coming in quick succesion. Now the thump-thump-thumping of ack-ack joined the din. The Japs were certainly not short of ammo.

Through the loopholes they could just see the Dakotas, headlights glaring, roaring through yellow ack-ack flashes, down the flight path.

"Blow this for a game of cricket! Major Masters ought to declare and let us bowl for a change..." The devout Scofield's jests to relieve tension always fell flat.

"Can't be long now, mucker." Badger put a reassuring arm around the little man's trembling shoulders, "Any moment now... Listen!"

The thumping of ack-ack and roar of aircraft was the only noise. For half a minute they listened, cocked rifles poking through the loopholes.

"Bingo! Here they come! Eyes down for the first line. Let them have it!"

Firing blindly, they poured rapid fire on the yelling invisible attackers. The Vicker's gunners, hammering away on fixed lines, swept the first wave with murderous bursts. Bom-bomming 3inch mortars blasted the lower slopes. Mortar flares were now lighting the pudding basin helmets, flashing on the circling, two-handed swords of officers urging them forward. The defenders' rapid rifle fire gave way to aimed volleys. Yelling mingled with shrieks of pain. Amid the din, Badger's ears picked up the stammering of a nearby Bren. Short bursts. Good! The schoolboys – Wyles and Trott, were doing their stuff.

With Jones, he dragged a box of grenades outside the 'hole'. Jack, Ginger, and Co. were already sprawled on their parapet hurling grenades, their grimy faces blanched by the flares were wild and demoniacal.

"Come on! Come on, you yellow bastards!" From behind the 'hole' he lobbed half a dozen grenades.

"Get 'em! Banglore torpedo, six o'clock!" Captain Williams called.

Rifle and Bren fire ripped into the four men torpedo squad, ten feet below the wire. The two forward Japs convulsed and lay still. The rear two, dropping the torpedo, shrieked in agony and dragged themselves on all fours downhill. A shower of grenades exploded the torpedo.

The assault was faltering in the face of the withering fire. Gaps in their stumbling ranks were not being filled. But a squad, with an officer in the lead surged forward, slashing wildly at the wire with sword and bayonets. A man threw himself on the wire, partially flattening it. In the act of stepping on the human bridge, the officer, throwing up his arms, fell back in a squealing heap. Two men rushed to drag him away. Trip wires detonated mines. Four men dematerialised in the blinding orange blast. Five survivors, dropping their rifles, stumbled downhill under a hail of small arms fire. Shrill Jap commands and whistles.

They'd had enough. For now.

"I'll check the wire, sir." Badger's tone was falsetto with elation. There was an erotic pulsing he'd not experienced since his wedding night, in his loins. The sensation had been increasing with every battle since Pagoda Hill, but now it was too intense to ignore. It was the same dry tongued, knee trembling and breathless titillation as the first time he had fumbled through an adolescent girl's blouse. Kill or be killed. A substitute for suppressed carnality? Professional fulfilment? Or a proxy for fear?

"Come on, Jack! We'll take a few grenades with us."

Indian fashion, they squirmed through the scrub and new shell pocks, down to the wire. The Dannert coils had rebounded into shape. All that was left of the human bridge, indistinguishable in the dark, was a mutilated limb and shreds of uniform snagged on the barbs. They could just make out that the booby trapped corpse, below the wire, had claimed at least one victim. Both bodies were a grisly, distorted heap.

Below them wounded Japs were moaning as comrades dragged them away. Badger and Jack each lobbed two grenades. Brilliant vermilion blasts lit the hill. Japs screamed. Jap machine guns raked the perimeter as they scrambled back to their positions.

§

Next morning, re-filling Bren magazines at the entrance to his 'hole'– under the oppressive, storm threatening sky – Badger brushed the sweat from his brow with a forearm, and called over to the Captain.

"Any idea how long they are going to keep us on 'the deep' sir?"

"None, corporal." Williams, sitting on his parapet, priming grenades smiled wryly, "We've had it rough, but we're all in one piece. The Lancaster's sectors have had dozens of casualties." He jerked his head to the positions flanking their own sector, "They've borne the brunt of every attack and bombardment, and need relieving more than we do."

"But we need sleep, too, sir! We were picquetting the copse every night..."

"Everybody in the Block needs sleep, Dixon!" At officers' briefings Williams had been tersely given the same answer. The compassionate Welshman was irritated that a loyal NCO like Dixon, could doubt that he had pressed for reliefs on his visits to Brigade HQ, "The Cameronians are patrolling all night. No one gets any sleep. And units not holding defence points, are lugging supplies and consolidating defences all day. So we'll have to get by with dozing when we can!" He gave Badger an appraising look, and his tone moderated, "It's not like you to complain. Grin and bear it a bit longer. The other columns will be here soon, then things will be easier."

The Japs had made three assaults before dawn, each more determined than the previous one. Mortar flares had again lit the heavens. Vickers guns had streaked the night with glowing red tracers. Brens and rifles had raked the hill, and grenades had rained down on the attackers. Ack-ack had thumped away at Dakotas, headlights blazing, ferrying in supplies. At dawn, for two hours, the 105s and 'whizz-bangs' had again pounded 'the deep'.

For an hour now the enemy artillery had been silent but just down the hill, above the drone of swarming insects, Japs were gabbling away as they dug in. Either they must have learned some lesson from White City or they were a different, craftier unit. Whenever they were repulsed at White City they had retreated far enough to be blasted by air-strikes and mortars, without endangering the defenders. Here they were sticking too close for any such bombardment.

In the stifling morning air, Padres were circulating among the raw eyed Lancasters muttering encouragement, pausing to sprinkle earth and mumble brief prayers over stoved-in bunkers and trenches that were now graves.

Thwack!

Williams ducked into his trench. A passing Lancaster's officer jumped in with him. Badger dived head first into his 'hole'. The blast seared across his calves, and stunned his ears. An avalanche of earth swept into the 'hole'. A dislodged roof log slammed his shoulder.

In the pitch blackness, Jones spluttered.

"Chee-riist! That's not cricket. Lobbing one over after the close of play!"

Badger felt Jones's dirt laden spit on his cheeks.

"Scofield! You all right?"

"Yes,corporal. Thank the good Lord!"

The avalanche had entombed them, blotting out every chink of daylight, sealing the entrance and every loophole. Badger squirmed round, and started scooping debris from the entrance.

Outside someone was calling, and scraping at the earth. A gleam of light!

"Corporal Dixon!" Bob Gregory, "Corporal Dixon! Jones! Scofield! You alright?"

"Yes, sarge!" Earth poured in, piling around his calves as

he scraped away. Bob's worried face appeared, "Jack and the others OK sarge?"

"Yes. But Williams has bought it."

§

Pounding a turf-sod into the last gap on the roof of the hole, Badger straightened up and gave a thumbs up to Bob as the sergeant, on his way to Masters' Command Post for the night's orders, doubled along the ridge at a half crouch.

After the random salvo that had killed the Captain that morning, 'the deep' had been quiet except for probing skirmishes, and pot shotting snipers. But, all that morning, the Mogaung valley had been a riot of noise. Flights of fighter-bombers, zooming at zero altitude, below cotton wool puffs of ack-ack, had bombarded the railway and road, and strafed the jungle. A procession of light planes, hedge-hopping to and from the strip, had ferried out the wounded. The 25 pounders had boomed away at suspected Jap artillery positions, and any transport movements in the valley.

Torrential rain had drenched the hill all afternoon, swirling bricky-yellow mud around Badger's boots as he dug up turfs, flooding the trenches. Now, as the last rays of the sinking sun shafted through the thinning overcast, a stiff breeze was stirring the undergrowth, and wobbling the marker on the Captain's grave.

The 'internment' service for the Captain and the Lancaster officer had been a brief, hurried sop to convention. The missile had eliminated the need for grave diggers. Only a few spadefuls of earth were needed to cover their hideously severed remains. Captain Mathews,[10] their little Karen padre, who would have been termed 'petite' had he been a woman, had braved snipers to reach 'the deep' that morning. His prayers had been almost indecently rushed Badger thought as he looked over at the marker. But what the hell! Why risk more lives for some conventional gesture. Any second another shell could have been on the way, and truth to tell, the whole detachment was anxious to get the thing over, and return to their funk holes.

The death of their platoon commander had one compensation for Badger. It had aborted any carping about the 'lost' bread and bacon.

When they heard about it Jack had cut their curses short, "Stow it! We've got more to worry about. There's a dead man there, and if we hang about in the open, cursing over spilt milk, there'll be a few more of us joining him!"

The evening barrage would be upon them again any moment now. Badger pushed the spade through the 'hole's' entrance and, with a self conscious salute at the marker, he followed the spade.

"That's another old soldier's myth buggered." He murmured, squeezing down between the squatting Scofield and Jones, "You never hear the one that's got your name on. Huh! Poor Williams heard his coming right enough. Living through all that barrage, and then copping it from a random shot."

"What's happening tonight, corporal?" Scofield asked, "Jones says Sergeant Gregory has gone to see Major Masters."

"Don't know. The Sergeant's gone to an officers' briefing, he's acting platoon commander until we get a replacement for Williams."

"Meizu" A voice croaked from below the barbed wire.

"That bastard's still alive!" Badger went to the loophole.

Since a noon skirmish they'd heard the cry a dozen times. At first it had been a clear strident appeal, now it was a barely audible gasp. Each cry had brought rifle volleys, Bren bursts and grenades down on the man. He must be lying 'dead' ground. A bloody sniper? If he was, he was a bloody good actor – really sounded as if he was dying. Playing on our Christian compassion. Take water down to him, and get a bullet in the head.

In the foreboding twilight, their ears for attuned for the first thud of the 105s, they sat silently for a few minutes.

"Meizu. Meizu."

"Water he wants! I'll give the sod something to shut him up!" With a grenade ready in his hand, Badger started to crawl out of the 'hole'.

"Don't, Badger." Scofield grasped his ankle, "Let the poor wretch be recovered by his own men." The unordained preacher sounded more concerned for the Jap's life than for the risk Badger was taking.

"Only putting him out of his misery!" Badger snapped as

he sat down again, “If he *is* wounded...”

Thwack! Woosh. The missile crumped well over the ridge. The barraged had started. He shuddered, and sent up a silent prayer of thanks for Scofield’s intervention.

Again the 105s and ‘whizz-bangs’ were thudding, thwacking, whining wooshing, thumping and crumping. Again the intervening silences stretched minutes into hours, and the silences became longer than last night. Were the Japs running short of ammo? Then, like previous nights, but seemingly sooner, the salvoes came over in a fast and furious procession.

“On your feet! This is it! They’ll be swarming up at us any moment.”

A momentary silence, and then the screaming yelling assault. Vickers hammering away. 3inch Mortar bombs crumping behind the attackers. Flares lighting the Jap’s pudding basin helmets. Rifles and Brens raking the surging ranks. Grenades bursting among them. He was on top of the hole again. Snap shooting. Lobbing grenades. Bawling at the yellow bastards! Again there was that groin trembling thrill. Blooding his bayonet on the sods would be orgasmic delirium.

But they were already retreating downhill.

§

“Right, Dixon,” Sergeant Gregory crawled beside him on top of the ‘hole’. The third Jap assault of the night had petered out into sporadic fusillades. The Japs, slowly withdrawing, were giving covering fire to comrades gathering their dead and wounded, “We are being relieved by a Lancaster’s squad who’ve had 48 hours in reserve. I’m going up to guide them in. Warn your lads to be ready for them. Don’t want them mistaking them for Japs.”

Sending Jones to warn Wyles and Trott, Badger crawled over to warn his other two posts, and scrambled back into his own ‘hole’. The hysteria that overwhelmed his fear, had died with the assault. His nerves were taut as piano wire again. All he wanted now was to keep under cover, and to quit ‘the deep’ in one piece.

“Can’t find them.” Jones squirmed into the ‘hole’.

“You effing fool!” Badger spat, “Get out there and find

them before the relief arrives!"

"Find 'em your bleeding self — if you're not too effing scared!"

"You couldn't find your way out of a bleeding paper bag, Jonesy!"

The insubordinate sod knows I'm scared. Wyles and Trott were only twenty yards away in a straight line, but undergrowth and boulders doubled the distance he would have to crawl. Now, when relief was imminent, it was more terrifying than sitting through another artillery barrage. Forty yards squirming in the hob black night, through thorny scrub, around boulders and shell pocks. Anything above a whisper to pin-point Wyles, might bring down a hail of bullets or grenades. But he had to do it, for the greatest fear of all was his fear of being proven a coward. He laid down his rifle, it might snag and clatter if he took it.

With a grenade in each hand made for the entrance, "Keep your ears tuned. Before you open fire on anyone, call out 'Dixon'. If the reply is not 'Badger' let 'em have it."

A pregnant silence had settled on the hill, and he had not crawled ten yards when he saw him. A thick, motionless Jap, silhouetted against the skyline. Five yards – or was it ten? – ahead and below him. Distances at night, and on a slope were deceptive. Was it the Jap who'd been crying for water? The Jap he'd had no mercy for? There'd be no mercy from this man whether it was him or not.

On his belly, cheek on left wrist, Badger felt he was squinting at death. A crouching Nemesis, rifle alert. The retribution of a brutal Empire embodied in one man, poised to avenge its massacred sons.

The grenades in Badger's hands were cold with sweat. Could he pull a pin out with his teeth, before the Jap fired. Dare he throw one? At this distance, it would kill them both.

Sweat coursed down his spine. Has the Jap seen him yet? Was he waiting for a move that would pin-point him? Was the Jap playing possum – as scared as *he* was – hoping I've not seen him yet?

To move anything but his eyes – and live – seemed impossible. Facing death he felt he should be beseeching the Lord's deliverance, praying for courage, making sacred vows of future goodliness in return for succour. Instead his mind, his eyes, were concentrating on the stars. His stars. The stars that would soon be over Barbara. Clearly, bitterly he now saw a full bosomed woman in a quiet English copse locked in a lover's arms. Stars were glistening in the sweat of their hands. The sweat of desire. Badger's were sweating with envy of deprived manliness, rather than death's imminence.

His woman! With a stranger, in a strange uniform! A thin cloud hovered over them. To him it was an apparition born of that grubby Bombay soothsayer. There, above, in the stars, she was yielding. He must not yield to screaming. He didn't want to see more, but he must see more. There, there beneath the Plough, her blouse was open. A soft, yet somehow granite like, breast naked to the night. Nippled by the cold North Star. Yielding... She was yielding. Welcoming the well-known caress. Another random, migrant cloud, rolled over her. A shadowy man, devouring her breasts, enveloped in her upthrust thighs.

A shooting star flashed across the heavens. Some other world disintegrating in God's universe.

The corner of his eye caught an almost imperceptible judder of the Jap's rifle. He edged a grenade to his mouth. Nothing to live for now. The metal split pin straightened in his teeth, 'Lord, don't give me cause to live!' His eyes strained to the heavens again.

There they still were! Swathed in cloud. A dark fusion of interlocked thighs.

The pin came away in his teeth. Bent double, he scrambled uphill and hurled the grenade.

The blast slapped his back as he flung himself down. Fragments whirred over his head. The grenade, like a starting gun, set Vickers stammering out streams of glowing tracers. Mortar flares lit the hill.

Where was the Jap?

"Bugger me!" He almost screamed in hysterical disbelief. Not a Jap but a half blasted tree, its single branch projecting like a rifle. The mortar flares dazzled out the heavens, and lying there, oblivious of what he had come to do, he panted blasphemies. He cursed God. Jesus. Gabriel. The Virgin Mary. And the soothsayer. They had fuelled his obsessive, unjustifiable jealousy.

There was no return fire from the Japs. The Vickers and mortars lapsed into silence. As the last flare drifted to earth, and only chaste stars lit the black velvet night, he warily raised himself on all fours. Where to? Wyles and Trott!

The undergrowth and earth cut into his knees like flintstones. Rising to a half crouch, he padded forward until the toe of his boot sank into a soft mound. A disintegrated sandbag.

Wyles and Trott, huddled together, were lying at the bottom of their pit. He called their names, in a whisper. No reply. They're dead. One of their feet stirred. He whispered again, and listened a moment. Asleep! The bloody idiots are asleep! The Japs could swarm through here unopposed. They deserve shooting!

Ice cold with anger, he stood on the parapet, and slipped the pin from his remaining grenade. The mothers' darlings had put hundreds of Chindit lives at risk. With only his hand holding the lever down, he backed away from the parapet, and drew back his arm to lob the grenade.

How could any bugger sleep through all that racket? The thought arrested his arm midway between waist and shoulder. His contempt for them as soldiers was ruling his reasoning. Men are responsible for the logical consequences of their actions. But if they were exhausted enough to sleep through shot and shell, it was not a consequence of their own action. The guilt lay with the actions of their masters.

Slipping the pin back into the grenade, he dropped into the pit, and savagely slapped the sleepers into wakefulness.

§

"You're too bloody soft. They could've got us all killed!" Jones growled venomously, as they trudged away from 'the deep', "You should've let them have it with the grenade. Aren't you even going to report them?"[11]

Badger shook his head.

"You're the only one I've told – or that I'm going to tell."

Only fear of ridicule had prevented him spilling out his heavenly visions, "You're sure I was gone less than ten minutes?"

"How many times! Yes! Nearer five. What's bugging you about that?"

Badger shrugged. Five, ten minutes to them, an imperishable eternity to him.

God, let there be a re-assurring letter from her soon!

Footnotes to Chapter Twenty-one

Page 312 Note No.10 Padre Mathews – now Arch Deacon Rangoon Cathedral.
Page 317 Note No.11 Over 40 years later Jones, a phlegmatic Midlander, still maintains that Badger *should* have killed Wyles and Trott (not their real names) or should at least have had them court-martialled.

Chapter Twenty-one

"Those are for the deep." The Lancaster's quartermaster-sergeant, pointed to a stack of ammunition boxes at the foot of the track.

"Let's have a breather first, sarge." The section had just come down to the strip from their fourth haul of supplies to 'the deep' that morning, "We were on the deep most of the night."

"Then you should know, they need all they can bloody well get for to-night. Where've they moved you to?"

"Three trenches at fine leg."

"Lucky buggers, the Japs are leaving the southern and western sectors alone." The quartermaster walked away a few yards, and took out a cigarette, "OK then, take a ten minute smoko."

They needed sleep not a smoke. The instant they flopped down, every man fell into a doze.

"Bloody hell-fire! On your feet! Juldee Juldee!"

Badger scrambled to his feet. His eyes filmed with sleep, the lids gluey, his neck a lather of sweat, such as only sultry tropical siestas, however brief, produce. It had been a brief nap. The quartermaster's cigarette was less than half smoked, and he was pointing it towards the east.

"Hell's bells!" Beyond the eastern extremity of the strip, through blurred eyes, he saw the cause of the quartemaster's alarm. A pall of black smoke, mushrooming above flaming thickets.

"The yellow fuckers are trying to cremate us." The quartermaster slung an ammunition box on to his shoulder, "Grab a box each and follow me to the deep. Then get back to your own positions."

As they climbed the hill the creeping fire crackled like machine guns and bamboo exploded like grenades. Smoke bombs from the garrison's mortars whizzed overhead, setting fire to the area behind the blaze where the Japs could be forming up.

Before they reached the crest, the heavens opened up. Torrential rain poured down on them. In minutes, the centuries old weather fissures were cataracts of mud. Coffee-like slurry swirled about their ankles.

The rain was a momentary Godsend. It doused the fires, but its intensity suggested it was more than a random squall. Leading the section to 'fine leg', Badger tried not to think of the train of consequences if this was the true onset of the monsoon. Living, fighting, trying to doze in waterlogged trenches. The strip too soggy to use. Aircraft weather bound. Light plane, Dakota, fighter bomber and supply drops curtailed. Rations, and above all ammunition shortages. What was the average supply drop – 9,000, 10,000, 11,000 pounds? In half a hour, the 3 inch mortar batteries alone could expend over 30,000 pounds. He was too weary for further mental arithmetic.

§

For nearly a week – at 'fine leg' – Gregory's men had been little more than spectators to the battles for Clydeside. But there were no quiet 'back areas' in Clydeside. No reserve lines for recuperation. Men could only be switched from sector to sector, and, at 'fine leg', they got no more sleep than those on 'the deep'. The Jap's assaults and artillery, still concentrating on 'the deep', left them unmolested. But, like the rest of the garrison, the barrages and assaults kept them 'standing to' most of the night.

During the day, they were back to being the 'odds and sods' again. There was always wire to be repaired and thickened up, huge coils of it to be hauled up from the strip. Ammo to be lugged up and over to the northern side. Wounded to be stretchered to the strip for evacuation. Corpses, stiff and slate grey, to be borne down to the evil smelling, fly ridden open-air mortuary, for registration and burial.

The monsoon rains were incessant. At best a hissing drizzle, at worst torrential downpours. The tracks were pernicious slurries, the trenches and weapon pits were knee deep quagmires. The tree-blasted 'deep' was a Flanders bog. Each downpour exposed bloodless fingers, limbs and battered scalps. Below the perimeter wire, the rotting corpses of Jap snipers, killed by Lancaster stalkers, hung from tree tops. The sickening sweetness of decaying flesh – Jap and British – polluted the air, fouling lungs with every breath and contaminating every mouthful of food.

The night attacks on 'the deep' were shorter, less determined, but tree top snipers made traversing along the north east slopes hazardous at any time. Snipers were even invested around the water point.

The dawn and dusk barrages were briefer, less intense, but desultory salvoes, throughout the day, from a battery of Jap 155mm's, was now adding to the 105s harassment. The batteries were constantly shifting, digging themselves deep in the jungle. The King's patrols searched vainly for them. Nothing the garrison threw at them seemed to have any effect. Not the 25 pounders, nor fighter bombers, swooping in whenever the rain eased off, to bombard the valley and hills.

For a few days, with the odds stacked against them, light planes braved the atrocious weather to evacuate casualties. The soggy strip was too perilous for Dakota landings, but at night sorties of them groaned through the gauntlet of storms and ack-ack to drop supplies.

In his waterlogged trench, one evening, listening to the roar of Dakotas, Badger told himself that the Japs were not the boneheads they thought they were. Their repeated, identical attacks on the same sector might seem foolish – but they had not wasted energy and resources to put the strip out of action. They had left that task to the weather. And below 'the deep' they were now dug so close that any mortar or aerial bombardment of their positions could wipe out the defenders as well.

In the few days of comparative lull in Jap assaults, the garrison husbanded its ammunition supplies and thickened up the defence works. It was also ominous. Time *and* weather were the Japs' allies. They must be biding their time, marshalling for an all out assault when the weather completely cut off the garrison's supplies. Time alone was the Chindit's hope. Time for 77 and 14 Brigades to close in on the attackers. Time for the advance of Stilwell's Chinese to draw off Jap reserves.

On their fourth or fifth afternoon at 'fine leg', Davidson – the sapper captain – briefed the platoon for a bridge demolition that night.

§

In parts, the Namkwin Chaung was chest deep, colder and deeper than the Namyung they had just left. The rocky bed made foothold treacherous, but the Commando Platoon was relishing the adventure.

After their defensive role it was exhilarating – almost a joy – to be away from their funk holes. For Badger an incipient fever, more than exhilaration, was warding off the chill of the river. He had been about to seek out an MO when the Royal Engineer captain turned up and, fever or no fever, he was not going to left out of this sortie. Time enough to see an MO to-morrow.

An hour ago, in the dark drizzly night, they had crossed the strip and slipped into the waist deep Namyung. Speechless and cautious, they had felt each step along the stony river to its confluence with the Namkwin. Crouching to chin deep, they had slunk through Jap detachments regrouping in the triangular confluence. Upstream, as they moved into Namkwin, Jap re-inforcements were noisily splashing across the chaung from the south east.

That morning Masters had decided, whatever the cost, the Japs must be forced back from their positions on 'the deep'. 3 inch mortars had bombarded the hill only five to ten yards below Chindit forward positions. Then the fighter-bombers had roared in. Mortars and Vickers poured down rapid fire as the bombs sent swathes of trees crashing. The hill had shuddered and convulsed. The noise reverberated and echoed round the hills, pulverising their ears and stunning their senses. Choking smoke and debris stung their eyes.

Miraculously the bombardment had caused no Chindit casualties, and the Jap survivors had retreated to lick their wounds in the triangular confluence of the chaungs Commando Platoon had just stolen through.

Now, in the starless night, with the Japs well behind them, stealth was less important than speed. They were striding boldly along with the current, towards the Namkwin rail bridge. If only for a few hours, they were true Chindits again, doing what they were trained for. With the tall, chubby cheeked, engineer officer and his sappers, they were out to blow up the bridge.

At the bridge they needed no instructions – they had practised such operations to a fine art in India. The bridge, a single rail track laid on steel girders, had a span of only about 20 yards. Small though it was, it was vital for Jap supplies, yet, to their delight, it was unguarded.

Whilst Davidson and his sappers laid the bridge charges, the Kingsmen set time-delayed charges 100 yards each side of the bridge, and picqueted the approaches. The bridge was over a mile from Clydeside, and the surrounding shell and bomb craters spoke of the near misses of repeated artillery and aerial attempts to destroy it.

Lying waiting for the three taps on the rail – the signal to withdraw – Badger and his picquet could clearly hear Japs gabbling and working around Namkwin station half a mile away. Steam was hissing from a stationary locomotive, and occasional flurries of sparks spouted from the chimney of its wood fuelled engine. He was pleased as Punch with himself. Here he was, with Japs a few hundred yards away, hundreds of Japs between them and Clydeside, not a tremble in his hands, not a nervous pang in his belly.

He felt like hugging himself. When the bridge blew up, the Japs probably would shunt down on the locomotive, or trundle along on one of those manually propelled trolleys, to investigate. With luck, as they inspected the damage, their trolley would be trapped between the bridge and track blown up by the delayed charges. What a bonus it would be if they came to investigate from each side, and were trapped on both sides. The secondary explosions would bring along more Japs. What an opportunity if this was a fighting patrol! Stop dreaming, you idiot, the sappers are too valuable to risk in close combat.

Tap, tap, tap! As they slipped back into the chaung, the red flare of a sapper's fuse sparked off 24 feet of safety fuse. 7 or 8 minutes to get clear!

At a loop in the chaung, a hundred yards upstream, they crouched against the bank. The explosion ripped the night with a brilliant crimson blast.

"Hang on here. If I'm not back in five minutes, get back to the Block as fast as you can." Captain Davidson waded back towards the bridge.

The clanking of locomotive wheels changed Badger's mood. Now all he wanted to do was to bolt from the scene, and the waiting seemed endless. But if Davidson didn't return soon, nothing would stop him, not Davidson's burly sapper sergeant, nor even Sergeant Gregory, from leading a volunteer squad to find the captain, even at the risk of a skirmish with the Japs.

"Splendid!" Davidson waded back into the loop, "Girders and tracks bent like bananas. It doesn't take long to throw a new bridge over a river like this from scratch, but it will take them days, maybe weeks, to cut away that tangle of wreckage before they can lay a new span. Come on, let's go."

They were entering the Namyung when the time delays detonated. A commotion of shrill yells, wild firing, the clanking to and fro and shunting of wheels followed the explosions. For a moment they stood listening to the panic-like disorder, and Badger wished he could have witnessed and pot-shotted the confused enemy.

Now the bridge had gone, the Japs would have a hard time ferrying supplies across the swollen Namkwin. For miles around the rail track the valley was flooded, and their wallowing rafts would be exposed to the strafing of marauding fighter-bombers.

Wading back along the Namyung, Badger could not rid himself of the gut suspicion that this had been their last true Chindit sortie. And how much more satisfying it would have been to have blown the bridge whilst a train was crossing.

§

Next morning, Badger took one look at the Dressing Station casualties and turned on his heels. He'd weather the fever until he met up with his Column's MO.

Last night's dusk barrage had pounded 'the deep' with unparalleled fury. The Lancaster's machine-gun positions had been wiped out, every man had been killed or wounded, or stunned to incoherence. The jungle telegraph put the Lancaster's casualties in the hundreds. In the nick of time to repel the Japs' first assault, the Cameronians had been rushed up to relieve the Lancaster survivors. Through the night, the Japs repeatedly stormed 'the deep', and were driven back by the the Cameronians. Twice they had penetrated the perimeter with Bangalore torpedos, and were blasted into eternity by 3inch mortars, bursting almost on the defender's parapets. On the threshold of dawn, to gather their dead and wounded, the Japs had made a last furious assault. At first light and in driving rain, Cameronian recce patrols had found the forest slopes as far away the Namkwin, deserted save for corpse-strewn streams, blood and flesh human remnants, and masses of discarded equipment.

Now, in the hissing rain scores of walking wounded, crudely bandaged with their own field dressings, were lolling against the Dressing Station's sandbag walls – soaking wet and ashen cheeked. Their bloody clothes and limbs streaked with chocolatey dye from their sopping dressings, they waited their turn for treatment, with only occasional groans and murmured curses.

Stretcher cases, blood seeping through their sodden bandages and flies swarming over their gory mutilations, lined the track down to the strip. Inside the station, raw eyed, blood-stained Medics were operating with the mechanical precision of robots. A direct hit had stoved in half the canvas and log roof.

In the debris a Padre was kneeling in prayer over the entombed dead.

§

"It's a bloody, bloody mess up there, sarge." Badger, returning from the Dressing Station, jerked a thumb towards the HQ re-entrant, and joined Bob Gregory sitting on the squelchy parapet of one of the 'fine leg' trenches, "The carnage on 'the deep' last night makes our battles there look like a picnic. And the poor bloody mules!" The sight had sickened him as he passed their 'pen' in the HQ re-entrant, "Poor buggers. Arses, backs, necks – the lot – gashed with shrapnel. Poor buggers, there they are, tethered, tucked up with voiceless pain, kicking and swishing their tails at flies. A couple of 'em dead, stiff legged, swollen, bloated."

"I know. I saw them when I was up at HQ this morning." Bob had got a one pound tin of corn beef from somewhere. The rest of the platoon were re-laying field telephone wires, and he was slicing the 'bully' to share out when they returned, "There's some garrum[12] char if you want it." He flicked a finger towards a mess tin on the embers of a fire, and cocked an ear at a sudden outburst of monkey chatter, "Hark at them!"

Every morning, at the same time, since they'd been at 'fine leg', there had been an identical outburst. On the first morning it had alarmed them. It was the only wild life noise they had heard since arriving at Clydeside. Their first reaction had been that approaching Japs had disturbed the monkeys, but none had appeared, and they realised it was just a wildlife 'dawn' chorus.

"Just what the doctor ordered, sarge." Badger sipped the tea. In steaming jungle, or cool mountains, there was no drink more luxurious, more satisfying, than a steaming mess-tin of strong, sweet Chindit char.

"We're now called Blackpool. 'More appropriate' says HQ with all the nightly illuminations and noise." The blue eye winked his disbelief.

"Huh! 'More appropriate'! Who do they think they're kidding, sarge?" He'd heard it at the Dressing station, and the jungle telegraph had already leaked the truth. Illuminations had little to do with the change of name. Some officer, in an *en-clair* radio transmission, had compromised the code-name, "Any other news, sarge?"

"Uh,uh! I'll tell you what I've already told the others. The rest of our column have come back for fresh supplies, and then they're going out again to find the Jap guns. Gately and 82

Column should arrive this morning. 81 Column's recce patrol have an outpost the other side of the strip to meet them."

"77 and 14 Brigades?"

"77 Brigade," Bob continued, were in the hills on the opposite side of the valley, re-equipping. Nothing definite had been heard from 14 Brigade, but Masters was certain they'd arrive any day. According to him they'd had thirteen days to cover the 120 miles to get here."

"They've had enough bloody time, sarge. Less than ten miles a day. What about Stilwell's mob?"

"The Marauders have taken Myitkyina, and the Chinese are still pushing down to Kamaign. That's all I have." [13]

"If they've got Myitkina, I bet we'll fly out from there."

Bob gave him a sceptical smile.

"Can I slip over to the Recce Platoon, sarge? I'd like to see Tiger Lyons."

"OK be back in an hour. We're on burial duties this afternoon."

§

The rain had stopped, and the sun broke through the overcast as Badger strode over the ramp in the runway. As at Broadway, the 'stick with a mucker' rule was universally disregarded as an unnecessary restriction in the heavily garrisoned territory. The hot tea had broken his fever. He was in a cold sweat, and the onset of 'malaria' blisters was tingling his lips. Yet he felt strangely at ease, as if he was strolling through an English park after a summer storm. A couple of Jap shells whined over, but with a disdain for danger that tickled his ego, he casually strolled on, rifle slung over his shoulder. If it was malaria, the fever would return. For the moment, the sweaty relief from it was euphoric.

Over the south west, a column was straggling across the paddy. 82 Column. He turned and hurried towards them. There was something disorderly, indisciplined about their formation, and it was only at half strength. Major Gately, on a pony behind the leading platoon, was grim faced. Each man's face was a sullen mask of humiliation and impotent rage.

Harry Winstanley was among them. Where was Jack Lindo? They were inseparable. Fred Holliday was there, but not Sergeant Joss.

"What happened, mucker?" Badger called to the rear files.

"Fucking ambush!" One of them shouted.

"Another sodding shambles!" Shouted another, "Half the column gone for a Burton!" [14]

Jack, Sergeant Joss and more than one hundred Kingsmen, lost? With his heart in his boots, Badger turned and headed for Tiger's outpost.

§

"...So that was it. Bloody weird wasn't it? I saw Barbara as clearly as I'm seeing you." Badger finished recounting his uncanny experience on 'the deep'.

"Come off it, Badger. You fell alseep, and had a bloody nightmare." Tiger scoffed. His section were deployed in a thicket, straddling a cart track wide enough for Jap armoured carriers to attack along, but the tubby Scouser was as relaxed as he had been back in the Bombay canteens, "I've told you before," he said in a forced exasperated, avuncular tone, "Barbara's sending you doolally. If you don't concentrate on what you're doing, you'll get shot up the arse one day."

"OK... don't believe me you bloody ignorant sceptic. So you know no more than I do about 82 Column being ambushed?"

Tiger shook his head, "I wouldn't like to be Gately with all that on his shoulders. Even if he wasn't to blame, he's sure to get a rocket, losing half a column."

Badger shrugged, and quashed the demon in his soul that wanted to rejoice at the major's plight. His 'bollocking' from Gately at Broadway, was still a festering canker. If Gately had been the only sufferer, he would have had no compunction about gloating. Even so, in his ignorance of the details, he was too vindictive to consider the cause of the debacle was anything but the major's timidness.

"I'd better be off, Tiger. Take care of yourself. Ta-ra. See you soon."

§

For two or three days after visiting Tiger, the evening barrages were desultory, and at night the Japs confined themselves to brief, probing patrols. The monsoon had well and truly set in. Fewer light planes were getting through, and only one supply Dakota had made the trip.

To Badger these were lost days. Wracked by fever, alternating with paroxysms of shivering, he was barely conscious of time, surroundings, or even the hissing rain. During the days, he laboured with the working parties in a stupor. At night, he huddled at the bottom of a waterlogged trench, wrapped in blanket and groudsheet. He curtly brushed aside the section's repeated urgings to report sick.

"Badger, you look like two penn'orth of death warmed up." One of them said, "Report sick, you idiot."

"I'm not being flown out before you lot." This was not gallantry. It was the knowledge that, compared with the sights he'd seen at the Dressing Station, his fever was too insignificant to bother medics with, and for the present there was no prospect of evacuation for anyone.

So the section scrounged a course of pills for him, from a medical orderly. Bob Gregory, on some HQ assignment or other, was away from them most of each day, and when he was with them, they concealed Badger's true state with insinuations that he was playing the 'old soldier' to avoid work.

Through ringing ears he dimly heard that Tiger had been wounded and flown out, and that Gately had also been sent back to India. His fevered mind barely registered the arrival of the 3/9th Gurkhas, their comrades of Broadway days. It was a sight that, normally, would have plucked his martial heartstrings, would have brought a lump to his throat. Nine hundred men, marching across the paddy, in two extended lines, as on an Aldershot Tattoo – their bush hats, tilted jauntily at the precise regimental angle and rifles at the trail. Even though carrying those monstrous packs through the slushy paddy, they were as erect as ramrods.

§

"This is it lads! Eyes down! Look in for a full house!" Badger called to others alongside him in their 'fine leg' trenches, "The poor bloody Gurkhas have had a real bashing this afternoon!"

The Japs had changed their tactics. Last night they had made probing attacks all round the perimeter. Whilst the attacks kept the weary defenders on their toes all night, forcing them to expend precious ammunition, convoys of Jap lorries carrying troops and hauling artillery, had been chugging into the valley.

The Gurkhas were deployed along the south west sector and on 'the pimple' – the knoll below the 'sow's' right hind hoof. At noon, Jap 105s and 77s had opened up on 'the pimple', and for four hours the Gurkhas had been pounded with hundreds of shells an hour. The wrecked aircraft and gliders were ablaze on the strip.

Now the barrage was creeping up the slopes, and Japs were pouring across the western half of the strip. The garrison's two Bofors on the strip, their barrels at maximum depression, were pomming away. Over open sights, British 25 pounders were madly thudding away. Chindit machine guns and rifles were sweeping the strip with withering fire. Mortar bombs were raining down on the massed attackers.

And still the Japs stormed forward.

Watching from 'fine leg', Badger winced as he nervously bit his fever scabbed lips. The Bofors were being overrun. The gun crews were racing back for the perimeter wire. 'The pimple' was swarming with Japs, pushing the battered Gurkha survivors into the 'silly point' sector. This was not a company, or even a battalion, assault. It had the hallmarks of a full scale divisonal attack, with all the artillery and support troops of a well founded and seasoned formation.

These were not the reckless troops of earlier assaults. They were purposeful, fearless, but not fanatical idiots. With disciplined swiftness, they were bringing up and digging in machine guns and mortars. Consolidating on 'the pimple', before pushing forward.

The lunacy of their ten days' pressure on 'the deep', had been more apparent than real. Their commander had induced the garrison to concentrate its strength there. Ravaging their stamina, eroding their ammunition supplies, whilst he marshalled sufficient strength to overwhelm the defenders. And he had chosen the right point to storm Blackpool. He was not squandering his troops on the natural glacis, east of 'the pimple'. He was pushing them at the gentler western slopes, and re-entrant, and keeping the worn out Lancasters, on 'the deep', occupied with holding attacks.

As dusk fell, the Cameronians, hurriedly switched from the northern slopes to counter attack 'the pimple', were slowly falling back under the withering fire from 'the pimple' to the 'silly point' trenches. Ahead of the attackers, a relentless Jap barrage was creeping yard by yard up the storm swept hills.

Block? The only thing blocked by Blackpool was the movement of its garrison. The Japs seemed to have unlimited supplies. No planes had landed at Blackpool for three days. Nor had there been any supply drops. Now, with the Japs dominating the strip, they would be entirely dependent on air-drops. Above all there could be no evacuation of the wounded.

In their trenches – ankle deep in mud – Bob Gregory's men, bracing themselves for the salvoes of the creeping barrage, suddenly breathed sighs of relief. Only both sides' machine guns, rifles and mortars, continued to hammer and blast the twilight.

The Jap artillery had ceased firing.

The artillery lull was a short lived respite. Within minutes, the whole of the northern perimeter was a bedlam of Jap yells, stuttering machine guns, rifle fire and bursting grenades. The Japs knew their business. They were keeping the defenders at full stretch, forestalling re-inforcing moves from one sector to another, whilst they brought forward more troops.

As they strove to hold back the Japs, men vent their fear cursing 14 and 77 Brigades.

"Where are the effing sods?"

"Sitting on their arses, brewing up somewhere!"

"Fucking 14 Brigade maybe, but not 77 Brigade. Some bugger's holding Mike Calvert back, otherwise he'd be here by now!"

Throughout the night, whilst the ferocious battle in and around 'the pimple' area raged without respite, the Japs held the rest of the perimeter defenders in their trenches with lightning assaults. Vickers and small arms rent the night incessantly, digging remorselessly into the garrison's ammunition reserves.

"Jesus Christ! If this goes on much longer, it will be Masters' last stand with bloody bayonets."

Badger reached in the ammo box at his feet, "About five bandoliers left, 250 rounds." He muttered to himself. The third holding attack had suddenly ceased. They had backed off too readily, and dawn could not be far off. Intuitively he knew the Jap artillery had only been re-siting its guns. Soon the barrage would open up again. His hand was still in the box when cannon flashes lit the heavens. 105s, 155s and 'whizz-bangs', firing almost simultaneously. The batteries were nearer now. Salvo upon salvo, thumped and thudded into the perimeter overlooking the strip. Echo upon echo reverberated around the mountains.

Badger's section were well above the barrage, but with heads down in their trenches. Like blind men at a cricket match listening to the thwack of bat and ball, they counted the salvoes.

"Fourteen!.. Fifteen!" They chorused.

Over three a minute, Badger judged. 180 an hour. How long could they keep it up? How long could the blokes on the lower slopes endure this pounding?

"18!"

"End of over." Some wag called, "Change ends!"

"...21! 22!"

"No ball!" A near miss showered them with debris.

"Ow'zat!" The wag called whenever the garrison's four 25 pounders or mortars retaliated with salvoes from their meagre reserves.

"...294!"

295 did not come. With dawn an hour gone, the lower slopes erupted with yells and small arms fire. Under the cover of intense machine gun fire from 'the Pimple', the Japs were rushing the lower slopes. A vicious hail of Cameronian and Gurkha small arms, and 3inch mortar bombs, ravaged the leading ranks. Banzai yells mixed with the screams of wounded. The Japs went to ground. The attack settled down to a static battle across 100 yards of 'no man's land'. Jap small arms and mortars raked the defences with a wild, rapid fire. The defenders, conserving their ammuntion, fired selectively, aiming their shots at positive targets.

§

At noon Badger 'drew the short straw' and went to fetch water. In grizzly, hissing rain he squelched warily up to the crest. The track was a quagmire, the fissures indiscernible and a misplaced step would put him knee deep into one.

Below him, the battle around 'the pimple' was dragging on. Desultory shelling was blasting up great gouts of slurried earth around the perimeter trenches. Padres, in teams, were rolling corpses into trenches and shell holes; there was neither labour nor time for burial niceties.

Across the strip, around the thickets skirting Namkwin Village, smoke from Japanese funeral pyres was billowing into the leaden sky.

As Badger stumbled down through the HQ re-entrant, the Dressing Station was thronged with casualties. Stretchers of mortally wounded, lining the track, were maimed beyond hope or help from the exhausted medics. Across the track, an officer was shooting mutilated mules with a pistol.

"Water, water everywhere..." He cursed as he lost his footing, and slithered on to his back into a mud swamped fissure. They were short of ammunition. Short of food. The only thing they were not short of was water. Undrinkable, muddy coffee cascades of it. Wind, rain, mud-slides and shell bursts had long ago swept away any groundsheets rigged to catch rainwater.

"Whoops, Joe what do you know!" A common, rhetorical greeting.

"Aah just got back from a Rodeo." Badger grinned up at the slim Kingsman helping him to his feet, "Hello Jack, where are you off to?" An unnecessary question. Jack had four chagauls strung over his shoulder.

"To catch the Mersey ferry, you idiot!" The tall, Douglas Fairbanks lookalike, with a fine baritone voice, was a popular turn at Battalion concerts. His rendering of 'Roses of Picardy' always brought roars of 'encore'.

"We're at 'fine leg'. Where are you Jack?"

"Halfway up, above 'silly point' and 'cover'. Scottie's just brought us back in. What's the latest gen on this bloody shambles?"

"According to the HQ officers, 77 and 14 Brigades are going to attack the Jap rear any moment."

All morning HQ officers, on morale boosting missions, had been dodging from post to post. Men, even officers, had listened in sullen disbelief to the sophistry.

"Well done, chaps. Keep it up. 14 and 77 Brigade will be here anytime now."

"Stilwell's Chinese Army will be relieving us before the week is out."

"Go easy on the ammo. We'll be getting a supply drop this afternoon..."

"That's all bullshit, Badger. They treat us like idiots. Why can't they tell us the bloody truth. Every bugger knows the other Brigades will never get here in time."

§

Ahead of the fallacies, the jungle telegraph had buzzed the hopeless truth. Mike Calvert's 77 Brigade had been without supplies for a week. The Namyung had flooded the valley, making it impossible for his Brigade to reach Blackpool without a fleet of boats. South Staffs, Lancashire Fusiliers and Gurkha patrols had repeatedly made determined sorties to find a way across. Individual officers – strong swimmers – had failed, and returned covered with leeches and requiring blood transfusions.

For days nothing had been heard of 14 Brigade.

Someone had lied. Stilwell had not captured Myitkyina. Merrill's Marauders had taken only an airstrip there. He was driving the Marauders into the ground. Less than half of their original 3000 were on their feet. They all had dysentery, so bad that they had cut the seats out of their trousers – and he was throwing them against the 3500 Japs holding Myitkyina.

Stilwell's Chinese were refusing to push on to Kamaign and Myitkyina. Yet Lentaigne was insisting that Blackpool be held until June 1st – six days away – to draw off the Japs from the immobile Chinese. And Stilwell – to cover his failure to get his Chinese forces moving – was publicly slandering the Chindits as 'Yellow-bellied Limeys' for not doing more to cut off Jap supplies. His sychophantic staff were fuelling his anglophobic ravings by debunking the difficulties of terrain and monsoon.

Joe Lentaigne, in the last few days, had become an object of thinly veiled contempt throughout Blackpool. He, and his planners, had set them tasks without regard to time, geography or weather. Wingate would, at least, have come to see things for himself. More probably, White City would never have been closed down and replaced by Blackpool, if he had been alive. To Lentaigne they were just pins on a map. He'd never even sent a staff officer to see what conditions were – let alone flown over the area himself.

And, while the garrison was fighting and dying, Stilwell and Lentaigne must be at each other's throats. Why else would Mountbatten have despatched Slim – from his hard pressed Kohima-Imphal front – to Shadazup to resolve the problems?

The jungle telegraph was also buzzing that platoons of the Lancasters, decimated and burnt out, were sullenly resisting any offensive tactics. They weren't openly mutinous – rebellion was beyond their last dregs of energy – and their weary officers had tactfully confined them to defensive roles.

§

Squelching through the HQ re-entrant, Badger nudged Jack and nodded towards where Masters, a re-assurring grin on his gaunt face, was handing a trembling Cameronian sergeant a cigarette.

" He's a cheery old card," grunted Badger to Jack, as they slogged through the mud, muck and rock, "But he's done for us all with his site for a Block'."

"Kipling again, Badger?"

"No, Sassoon. Misquoted."

The water point, a small sparsely wooded basin, fringed with knee high reeds, was an infant tributary of the Namyung.

"Fill yours first, Badger, I'll keep watch."

Crack! Thump! A sniper's rifle cracked again as Badger flattened himself in the undergrowth.

"Aargh!" Jack, both shoulders pouring blood, dragged himself through the reeds, to the cover of a tree bowl.

Badger started to crawl towards him, but Jack signalled him to flank around the sniper. His shoulders were too shattered to give covering fire, but he started to sing, softly at first, to hold the sniper's attention. Then, as more sniper's bullets thudded into the tree bowl, his voice rose defiantly to its old, beautiful richness.

"...Roses are shining in Picardy... In the hush of a silvery dew, Roses are flowering in Picardy.."

High in a tree, fifty yards away, the sniper's putteed legs with split-toed shoes were dangling over a forked branch. They were a good target, but Badger wanted better. He wanted a killing shot, not a wounding one.

"...But there's never a rose like you..."

Crawling slowly, Indian fashion, Badger's eyes never lost sight of the target, not even by a blink. Dry mouthed, alert for the slightest movement that might mean the sniper was shifting his aim to him, he wormed through the reeds.

"... And the roses will die with the summer time..."

On elbow and opposite knee, rifle across the crook of his arms, yard by painful yard, eyes glued to the puttees, he squirmed through the sodden undergrowth. There was his target. In clear profile, roped around the waist to the trunk, festooned with bandoliers and camouflaged with twigs and leaves. Badger pulled the rifle butt hard into his shoulder.

'Close the disengaged eye.' The ghost of a musketry instructor commanded, 'get the tip of the foresight in the centre of the v or u of the back sight'.

"Aim at his ear. Blow his brains out." He whispered to himself, "Be still my lungs!"

'... tip of the foresight on the centre of the target.'

"Steady rifle, Steady!"

'...with sights thus aligned, focus the aim.'

Pear drops of rain were trickling from the sniper's ear lobe.

"...But there's one rose that dies not in summer time..."

The Jap was taking aim again on Jack.

'take the first pressure. Stop breathing!' The ghostly instructor urged.

His fingers tightened around the small of the butt.

'Squeee—eze.'

"...Tis the rose that I keep in..." The voice was faltering, wheezy.

Crack! The Jap's head jerked back. His body slumped, and hung like a rag doll. Crack! His head jerked again. His rifle crashed down through the branches. Crack! His head jerked again.

"Bloody fool. Wasting ammo." The first shot had been enough.

Jack's song spluttered into a paroxysm of coughing.

"Hold on mucker." Scrambling back, Badger bent to lift Jack, "I'll give you a pick-a-back."

"Who yer kidding." Jack's chest was a crimson froth, his eyes bright, wide in a fixed sightless stare, "I'm done for... for my next number... 'Alice blue gown' ...Where's the pianist?.. What's wrong? No applause." His mind was back at some Battalion concert. Then a grin of recognition, "No more encores for me, eh, Badger." His blood soaked fingers snapped off one of his identity discs, and pushed it into Badger's hand, "Leave me here old son." Coughing and gasping, his hand, shakily, clumsy as a babe, wavered to his mouth, smearing his Fairbanks moustache with blood, "Try... get some... pawnee back ...to them."

"Sure, sure." Badger gently wiped the pale, blood streaked face with Jack's 'panic' scarf. What more could he say or do? "I'll stay with you mucker."

"Go!" Gasping, wheezing, he shook his head.

"I'll write to your folks..."

Jack shook his head again, "I'll be with 'em as soon as I close my eyes." A tranquil smile.

Embarrassment compounded grief. Jack's parents were long dead. And at Broadway, Jack, snuffing back tears, had hysterically torn a neighbour's letter to shreds. The letter, the only letter poor Jack had received, told him his wife and infant son had died of meningitis.

Jack's chin dropped on to his chest. Badger closed the sightless eyes, and dragged him a little way uphill, into a thicket. Tomorrow – if there was a tomorrow for anyone in Blackpool – he would bring down a spade. Bury him decently. For to-day a covering of leaf mould would have to do. He stuck Jack's bush hat on a bamboo stake as a marker, and folded his hands across the gory chest. Take off Jack's heavy gold wedding ring? For what? No-one to send it to. Did Barbara ever recover her engagement ring from Westerham? She must have done. Been to London enough times. Funny she'd not mentioned the ring since her first letters.

"Come to that, I've never asked her. Should've done. Should have." Hastily he filled the chaugals, and slung them, with his rifle and Jack's, over his shoulder, "Really should have. She'll think I don't value it much. Wasn't cheap. £9 including purchase tax. Two weeks' pay."

§

Later that afternoon Dakotas swept over from the west. On the ground, the Japs were pressing their attacks with renewed strength. Their ranks of fresh infantry were advancing rapidly across the strip. Their field guns, firing over open sights, from the south west extremity of the strip, the track where Tiger had had his outpost, were blasting the mid-level slopes.

Under a covering flight of American Lighning fighters, eight Dakotas, in line astern, roared over the advancing Japs. In blinding rain, they weaved and lurched through a furious barrage of ack-ack, cannon and machine-guns. Slipstreams swishing the tree tops, they skimmed the hill to identify the dropping zone.

Circling round, back through the barrage, they roared down the dropping path, crates parachuting from their open doors. But the Japs had pushed in the perimeter defences, and 'chutes were drifting into their lines.

"Christ!" Badger, mustered with his section as a carrying party near the ground controller, watched a Dakota's port engine explode in brilliant yellow flame. The plane, its remaining engine roaring, corksrewed to earth beyond 'the deep'. The following plane, still jettisoning supplies, banked frantically to avoid collision. Its entire cargo drifted into Jap hands.

Another plane yawed and pitched over the dropping path.

"He's saying he's sorry, if his drop is a bit off target," the ground radio operator shouted, "his rudder controls are shot away!"

Another plane, spewing petrol from a ruptured fuel tank and climbing sharply, scattered its cargo far and wide, as it soared for home.

In the rain and mud that gave every boot the weight of a ball and chain, they hauled in the supplies for distribution. The incredible gallantry of the flyers had brought them little to cheer about. Less than a quarter of one aicraft load had fallen to the defenders. Enough only for one meal per man, and ammunition for less than 24 hours. If 14 and 77 Brigades did not arrive before the morning, Blackpool was doomed. There would surely be no repeat of today's costly supply attempt. The jungle telegraph was already whispering that only four of the eight Dakotas reached their base.

"I'll never forget Queen Victoria's birthday after this." A Lancastrian quartermaster said as they collected their meagre supplies.

"Uh?" Badger looked blank.

"24th May today, sonny, Empire Day." He broke into song, "What is the meaning of Empire Day, Why do the cannon roar?"

Badger and half a dozen others joined in.

"Why does the cry 'God save the King' echo from shore to shore?"

82 days in Burma. At this rate, they would all be dead before they completed Wingate's promised 90 day stint.

"Well, he'd also said we're all going to die."

§

With dusk closing in, Scottie deployed 81 Column in a defence line, midway up the slopes overlooking the strip. Bob Gregory's 'odds and sods' were back with them. Below them, in the brief twilight, the Japs were now lodged in the 'silly point' re-entrant. In great strength they were hammering the Gurkha and Cameronian sectors with machine guns, mortars and cannon.

It was almost a one-sided battle. The attackers, with apparently limitless ammunition supplies, blazed away with incessant fury. The defenders, preserving their dwindling stocks, retaliated with small-arms fusillades and 3inch mortar volleys only when the Japs presented positive targets or attempted to rush the defences.

In a comparative lull, platoon commanders, in relays, mustered their men.

"Good news. Fifty of the missing men from 82 Column ambush have joined up with 77 Brigade." Their new platoon commander had the wiry frame of a jockey. He could be no older than Badger, but his face was as furrowed and careworn as an elderly grandfather. Lack of sleep and malnutrition was etching every face, and undermining resistance to diseases. Sickness, more than wounds, had depleted the column and it was a case of making one platoon from the remnants of two or more, "You've joined us just in time for a counter attack. At dawn, Captain Riley with two platoons, including us, is going to try and push the Japs out of 'silly point'. The rest of the Column – less the mule and signals sections – will be in close reserve behind us. The mule sections, or what's left of them, will be moving north into the hills." He looked round, knowing what he was going to say would sound laughable, "They'll be safer there until we secure Blackpool again."

So, thought Badger, we're going to abandon the place. The counter attack is a 'blind' – kidding the Japs that we've no intention of retreating.

"For tonight, we're to hold the southern mid-levels. If you can find dead ground for fires, you can brew up."

That's a bloody laugh. Brew up! What with? They'd run out of tea days ago.

§

At dawn, the column filed down the glutinous mud track, east of 'silly point'. In drizzle, indistinguishable from rising mist, the two platoons in arrow head formation, advanced slowly and warily into the re-entrant. Behind them the rest of the column at the foot of the track, in diamond formation, waited as reserve. Immediately ahead of them the re-entrant seemed deserted, but beyond their vision machine guns were stammering away, rifles were clattering and mortars were crumping.

Captain Riley – in the lead – burly but agile as a rugby winger, quickening their pace to a jog-trot, signalling to close ranks.

To Badger, dry mouthed, hands pouring with sweat round his bayoneted rifle, the re-entrant seemed like the jaws of death. If the

Japs came down behind them, they'd be locked in this canyon-like defile. But then – the time for fear was gone.

Seemingly from nowhere, a throng of Japs rose before them. Badger's psyche fled heavenwards. His genitals were siffening again.

"Roll on death! Let's get shagging the angels!" He yelled, shooting and working his bolt like an automaton.

Bayonets were clanging. Rifle butts were cracking against metal and bone. More Japs were charging down. Hemming them in on three sides.

Riley, towering over the pot-helmets, was furiously clubbing them with his carbine. Badger's butt crunched against a jaw. From the corner of his eye he saw Jack Ryan and Tony the barber, lunging wildly with their bayonets.

The butt of Riley's carbine snapped off as he felled a man. Now he was lashing out mightily with the barrel. Then they were falling back. The Japs pressing forward at them. A bayonet came at Badger's throat. Backing away, he parried it down with a mighty clout. The point jabbed his thigh. A screeching falsetto Jap command – and the Japs dropped back.

The Jap machine gunners, up at the re-entrant, were traversing round on to the platoons. In headlong flight, bullets raking their heels, the platoons fled from the re-entrant. Scottie, bringing up the reserves at the double, met them at the mouth of the re-entrant.

"One man killed, several slightly wounded... Japs in overwhelming strength... Futile to renew the action... Retire up the track!"

As they slogged back up the track, 105s, 155s and 'whizz-bang' mortars pounded the southern slopes. Japs were pushing forward behind the barrage.

Chindit gunners were lugging their 25 pounder breech blocks, to bury them where the Japs would be unlikely to find them. Halfway up the steep, treacherous glacier of mud, Captain Davidson and his sappers were hastily laying booby traps. Down near 'silly point', a Gurkha lieutenant hammering away with a Vickers, was holding back a surge of Japs.

Step by perilous step, in ragged lines, men were stumbling up the slimy glacis to 'the spine'. Orders for a general retreat, if any had been issued, were superfluous. The alternative was to be overrun, and hopelessly butchered by the enemy mass.

Crump! CRUU-UMP! The barrage was creeping closer. A blast thrust Badger, the last man in the column, to his knees. Scrambling up he cast a fearful, backward look.

Captain Davidson and his sappers were dead. The Vickers, at 'silly point', had run out of ammo. The lieutenant[15] and his Gurkhas, in a despairing final foray, were hurling grenades at the advancing Japs.

Below the 'spine', Scottie, wearing a dead gunner's helmet, had a picquet of a dozen men, and was calmly directing the retreating men up to a Cameronian rearguard on the crest. As Badger stumbled past Scottie, the tail end of his Column had already passed over the crest.

Over the crest, sloughing down into the Brigade HQ re-entrant, he weaved through medics marshalling stretcher parties. Four ponies, carrying badly maimed men, were being coaxed down the track. Vickers guns and 3inch mortars were being loaded on to the ten remaining mules.

A medical orderly, noticing Badger's blood splotched trouser leg, handed him an adhesive dressing. By the time he'd stuck the dressing over the superficial bayonet wound, 81 Column was out of sight.

There was only one track out of the Block. From all quarters of the perimeter, platoons burdened with 2inch mortars, picks, shovels, and their personal arms and equipment, were staggering towards the track.

Below the Dressing Station, men were tipping the dead – from blanket litters – down from the track into the mud and brush. A mortar bomb thudded into stretcher party, killing the two bearers and strewing limbs on the track.

Further down, stretcher parties – many of them wounded themselves – were laying down improvised litters of mutilated casualties at the side of the track. Masters and the Senior MO, grave faced, were surveying hideous human wrecks. Twenty gory, frothy messes. Men with no legs. Men without chests and shoulders. Men with bloody cavities where their bellies once were. And men without faces. Shells and bombs were whining and bursting, thick and fast, along the ridge above them. With a despairing nod, Masters headed back up to the Cameronian rearguard.

It was plain what he meant, but it was sickening mercy. Slithering down the churned up track to water point, Badger counted the carbine cracks. 5, 10, 15, 16, 17, 18, then no more. Two must have gone to their Maker before the *coup de grace*.

The drizzle had stopped, but it was no relief. The vaporising jungle was keeping him saturated, spreading the bloodstain down his trouser leg – but it was only a nick. The throbbing was nothing. Nothing compared to the suffering of the poor wretches back there.

At the water point, Jack's mound was swarming with ants. He swiped them off with his entrenching tool, shovelled a few inches of mud over the slate grey, black blooded, remains and replaced the bamboo marker.

Picking up a stone, as he crossed the water point, he hurled it at the sniper's body, still dangling like a rag doll from the tree top.

"If I had a grenade I'd blow you to smithereens. You bastard!"

The mud churned track followed the water course, down towards the Namkwin, below 'the deep'. He was well behind the column, but resisted the urge to hurry. Warily, he followed the track scanning every tree top for snipers, until he came to a fork. Which way? He listened for a moment. Nothing but the distant crump of shells, and the whine of ricochets.

To the right, the track cut through tall reeds. To the left it slipped down into a shallow nullah, a natural drainage ditch feeding the water course. Along the nullah, was a British body. Face down, hands clutching tufts of shrubs atop the nullah bank, as though in a last desperate effort to climb out, he had given up the ghost .

From down the right fork, Badger thought he could hear muffled voices and the clinking of equipment. Might be a Jap ambush. Or the column?

Which way? Make up your bloody mind. Had the dead man walked into an ambush? Or dropped out of the column going that way?

Almost imperceptibly the body stirred. Or was it just the shrubs yielding? No! The head twitched!

Striding down into the nullah, he rolled the body over, and gulped back vomit. A drenched shell dressing, stiff with blackened blood had slipped from the man's face. His lower left jaw had been torn off. That side of his face was a viscid mash. Splintered bone and bluey flesh. The pelvis was a gory pulp of bone and entrail. The man's eyes flickered with recognition. The right cheek quivered as he strove to speak.

"Billy, little Billy!" Choking back nausea, Badger stooped to catch the words, but they were only incoherent grunts.

For all his wounds, Billy's coarse, gorilla-like face was still recognisable, 'You make Frankenstein look like a lily – Billy' was a common taunt, and the little man would just grin inanely. Poor, little Billy, the butt of every prankster in the Battalion. Too clumsy. Too slow witted for any duty except permanent sanitary orderly. Yet the little man was one of the best marksmen in the Battalion. That, alone, had got him through recruit training and had kept him from being chucked out of the army.

The casualty tag, around his neck, registered only his face wound, and a morphia dose, about two hours ago. He must have copped the pelvis packet as he came over the ridge. Must have the heart of a lion to get this far.

"Can you put your arms round my neck, mucker?" He crouched to raise Billy's shoulders.

Billy's cheek twitched again, "Clurk, clurr." His hand wavered over Badger's rifle butt, and shook his head.

"Come on try!"

One feeble hand pushed Badger back, the other pulled on the rifle butt, "Sh..magh." The pale blue eyes were bright, beseeching swift relief from pain.

"Can't leave you here. Japs'll be on our tail."

The hand tugged the rifle again. Billy vomitted with the effort. Poor sod would be dead soon. But the Japs might be here sooner. What would those bastards do to him? He couldn't leave Billy for their sport. What else could he do? Couldn't even give him a drink with that wound.

He shuddered, remembering the eighteen carbine cracks.

Could he? Should he? Dare he? Had he the guts to do what Billy plainly wanted him to do?

Billy was wiggling his trigger finger in front of his eyes.

"Sorry Bill, can't do it." He let Billy's shoulders drop gently back to earth, and stood up, "I'll go and find an MO"

As he moved away, Billy feebly, vainly, tried to grasp the rifle and placing his hands in prayer, groaned, "Plu... perp."

"No Billy! No! I won't do it!" But he couldn't leave Billy to die alone, in such demonic pain and in such a hell hole.

Ten yards away, Badger turned and aimed. The sights quivered. Tears blurred his focus. Billy's eyes were fixed on him, without a flicker, "Turn away Billy. O God. Turn away," He whispered into his sweating fingers, around the small of the butt. But the eyes were unflinching. He pulled the butt more firmly into his shoulder. Got to be as steady as those eyes. Do it. First time, clean and instant. He choked back a slobber of funk.

Heart or head? Billy's lids, as if in sleep, drooped over the bright, wide eyes as the tip of his foresight traversed them. The right temple. Steady. Second pressure! The foresight quivered. He eased off the trigger, dropping down to a kneeling aim and brushing away sweat and tears with his forearm. Tugging the butt hard into his shoulder, he took the first pressure. Steady.

"Thank bloody God!" As he eased to second pressure, Billy, with one agonised heave, crumpled down the bank to a muddy death.

"Jesus, bloody Christ! I was nearly a fucking murderer!"

Smashing his rifle into the ground, he slumped on both knees, sobbing into his hands. God! How must that MO feel?

Somewhere towards Blackpool, a single shot rang out. A rifle! Not a carbine! Some other mucker dispatching a mortally wounded comrade.

Hurriedly, he dragged Billy up the nullah bank, clear of the mud, pocketed one of the dog tags, and threw Billy's groundsheet over him.

Sniffing back his sobs, wiping away tears with the backs of his hands, he warily moved upstream.

The nullah was barely shoulder deep and, with all rivers in full spate he was suprised the water barely covered his boots. But it was clear and swift flowing. If the rain came on again there would be a flash flood. The banks were dense scrub and bamboo. He had to get out of it soon. A short way up, the nullah ended at a corner of rough rectangle of open paddy. On one knee, he took in the lie of the land.

To his left was forested hillside. To his right the paddy dog-legged down beyond his vision, into a valley. The water course and track ran diagonally across the clearing, skirting a clutch of dilapidated bashas in the centre. About a hundred yards ahead, at the opposite corner, the stream cut through two knee-high boulders. Beyond the boulders, the track climbed into teak forested hills.

Badger started towards the forest at his left. Then, with exquisite relief, saw Scottie, sitting on one of the boulders. Good old Scottie! He must have been last out of Blackpool, yet miraculously, he was here, ahead of the main body. With the steel helmet rakishly tilted on his head, chewing gum, he looked as if he was just taking a breather during a peaceful Sunday outing. Masters and the rest must have lost their way.

Ryan, Ginger and the rest of his own section – as a rearguard picquet – were lying across the stream and track. Rifles and Bren cocked, anxiously scanning the clearing.

He trotted up to Scottie and saluted.

"Got delayed at the dressing station, sir." He pointed to his blood splotched trouser leg, "Only a nick though."

Scottie, with a sympathetic grin, waved him to join the picquet and, as he flopped down behind a boulder, someone called, "Here they come!"

From the nullah, a ragged crocodile of men was trudging across the paddy. Men burdened with picks, shovels, mortar and machine gun parts. Wounded dragging other wounded. Stretcher bearers stumbling over the decaying paddy bunds. A few mules – men slumped over their withers.

As they neared the bashas, mortar bombs rained down on the lower slopes of the paddy. Machine guns raked the bunds. Everything was falling short of the now scampering men. But down below the bashas, there were screams of pain. Another part of the Brigade, coming up from the valley, was scattering under the murderous fire. Men were cowering behind the crumbling bunds. Stretcher parties were jettisoning their litters.

Jesus! The Japs had been around the right fork of the track from the water point. Billy! Poor dimwit Billy had saved him from that hell. But for seeing him, he'd have taken the right fork, and been down there!

The mortar barrage was creeping up the dog-leg. Now the bombs were bursting among the column from the nullah. The machine gun fire was whining too high and wide, but salvo upon salvo of mortar bombs was bursting among both parties. A mule reared over, pinning its wounded rider under its shattered flanks. A stretcher casualty and his two bearers disintegrated in an orange flash and black smoke.

The stretcher parties could only move at a stumbling trot over the rough ground. From their boulders the section cursed at terror stricken bearers dumping their wounded, and 'hurrahed' at the gallantry of others who snatched up and stumbled with the litters towards the picquet.

Impotent to help, the section could only watch and fume at the carnage. The section was down to its last few rounds of ammo, but even with inexhaustible stocks covering fire was out of the question. The Japs were too well down in the dead ground of the valley for it to be effective. Their own men would be caught in the cross fire.

Men and mules – wounded and unwounded – limped, crawled or dashed past the bashas. Men screamed in the beaten zone of bullets and bombs. The machine guns waned into sporadic bursts. The mortar barrage dwindled to desultory salvoes.

As the gasping, fear ridden men staggered past the boulders, the heavens opened up. In the torrential rain Scottie, unruffled as ever, marshalled them into an orderly file. With a re-assuring pat on the back here, an encouraging word there, he led them up the steaming teak hill.

At a snail's pace they moved up the single file track. Higher up, in places, it was too steep for anything but hands and knees scrambling. Every hesitation – men or mule stumbling, wounded men balked by some obstacle, stretcher parties pausing for breath – brought snarls from the shaken men. Short machine gun bursts were whining overhead, and they were fearful that the Japs were on their heels, "Get a bloody move on!"

"Its some dozy bugger in front of me!"

"*You're* all right, Jack, you're in the fucking lifeboat!"

"Shit in it, mate! There's a bloke here with both arms in slings!"

From somewhere above, a pony, ripped by bullets, crashed down the slope, scattering the men milling around the bottom of the track.

When at last the tail end of the column disappeared up the trail, the utter loneliness of his picquet filled Badger with the desperate urge to abandon their position, and head after them. Crouched behind a boulder, he pulled his glistening groundsheet more tightly around his shoulders, and glanced at the others, waiting for the anticipated rush of pursuing foe. Crouching or lying with rifles and a Bren at the ready, they were grim and white faced but there were no signs of the gut trembling, cut and run funk that Badger felt. Jack Ryan, tucked behind a clump of shrubs on the right flank of the line, gently chewing gum, seemed impervious to the rain or fear. Shame overcame Badger's urge to flee, and he settled down to wait for the Japs.

Footnotes to Chapter Twenty-one

Page 328 Note No.12 'Garrum' = Hot.
Page 329 Note No.13 Some historians charitably record Stilwell's boast to the world, his government, and his superiors that his forces had captured Myitkina in May as premature. It was in fact an outright lie to cover his bungling and his unjustifiable deprecation of the Chindits' fighting qualities.
Page 330 Note No.14 82 Column were ambushed whilst crossing the Moguang Valley. Rightly or wrongly Major Gately, leading the Column, pushed on to Clydeside, leaving half of his command to fight it out. After a confused battle the survivors retreated into the hills and eventually joined up with the Lancahire Fusiliers of 77 Brigade. Major Gately later distinguished himself in Malaya and was killed in action.
Page 342 Note No.14 Wm. Smylie, post-war journalist on the South China Morning post

Chapter Twenty-two

Before he had struck off up into the teak Scottie's orders, as usual, had been simple and direct. They were to hold the position until Major Masters brought up the rest of the Brigade, or until Scottie came back for them. If the Japs attacked they were to hold on until he reinforced them. The next rendezvous would be the junction of a track and chaung, map ref. 227105, about two miles north.

Where the hell *was* Masters? They were only about a mile from Blackpool. It must be well past noon. Three or four hours since he had trudged across the water point. Over an hour since Scottie had left. Except for the occasional, distant clatter of small arms fire, there had been no sign of enemy activity. Certainly not enough to account for Master's being held up. The Japs must be biding their time, in order to catch them as they crossed the paddy.

The section were restless, repeatedly fidgeting their arms and legs, fighting off tiredness and hunger. More than once, Badger's eyes had drooped, and his head plopped against the wet boulder.

"Badger!" Scofield pointed towards the nullah.

Instantly, their rifles came up to the aiming position. The groundsheet flapped around Badger's foresight and stock.

"Bloody useless!" He tore it off.

In the veil of driving rain, the figures filing out of the nullah could have been Japs. Squinting along the sights, Badger breathed a sigh of relief.

"Relax, they're ours."

Relax? Any second now the Japs would open fire.

Standing up he waved frantically, trying to direct them into the forest to their left. Still they came on through the paddy. Any moment now, all hell would break loose.

Down behind the boulder, he braced himself for the barrage as the leaders trotted past the bashas. But there was only the hiss of rain. The panting of lungs, and the thudding of boots. Loudest of all was the lub dub of his heart, as the leading files reached the boulders.

The long mixture of men, Cameronians, Lancasters, Gurkhas, Gunners and Sappers, hurried past them up into the steaming teak.

"What kept you, Jock?" Badger called to a Cameronian, pausing to adjust the Bren slung over his shirtless shoulder.

"Yon daftie took the bluddy wrong way." Panting heavily, he pointed to the head of the column, "We had tae double back on oorsel!"

Masters, at the rear of the column, marched with a Jap officer's sword in one hand, carbine in the other, kukri and pistol bouncing on his mud smeared trouser seat. As the leading files pushed up the hill, the column concertina'd into a shuffling line, and Masters sank down on one of the boulders.

"Who are you?" He took a deep, weary breath that arched his back, "King's?" Another deep breath, "Colonel Scott ahead?"

"Corporal Dixon sir. Colonel Scott's gone to map reference 227105, sir."

Masters ran his fingers over tired eyes, and studied his map. The man was dead on his feet, yet Badger could feel no pity for him. His cricket pitch battlefield, his Block – that blocked nothing but true Chindit marauding – had put them all in these desperate straits.

"Bring up the rear, corporal." A wan smile, another deep breath and a limp pat on Badger's shoulder, "Well done. Well done." He stretched, put the map away and trudged past the shuffling men.

§

The hill was was a maze of streams and criss-crossing tracks, but there was no mistaking the right route to the rendezvous. The couple of thousand men ahead had churned it to a glutinous slurry. As Badger's section trudged, slipped, fought for footing and clawed uphill, men were slumped on the side of the track, gathering their energy for another effort.

When, at last they breasted a crest, the track took them across open paddy into a wide pebbly nullah. Dakotas were swooping over. Circling to drop supplies on Blackpool!

'Too bloody late mates!'

Men swarmed back into the clearing, wildly waving their orange 'panic maps'. Three planes roared over, jettisoning their cargoes over Blackpool. The fourth waggled its wings, banked sharply and tossed out a stream of parachuted containers. The supplies floated on to the paddy. Cheers echoed through the hills.

The cheers turned to groans and curses as the containers were torn open. Shells, mortar bombs, shovels, picks, petrol! Two cases of rations for two thousand men! No small arms ammo!

§

At the rendezvous – a wooded plateau, half a mile up the nullah – Scottie had posted defence picquets covering the chaung, and ringing the plateau. The ground was a quagmire. In the gathering dusk men sloshed from group to group, searching for their own units.

There was no briefing that night, only mouth to mouth messages, embellished with wishful speculation and half truths. Only two things seemed certain, they were heading for Mokso Sakan and Blackpool was three miles – and an age – behind them.

The battle for Blackpool was over. The only battle before them was to keep their eyes open when their turn came for sentry duty. If they could get to Mokso Sakan their war would be over. They'd done their bit. Shot their bolt. None of them would ever be fit for battle again.

Huddled under their sodden blankets, for the first time in weeks they were free from bombs, shells and bullets. For the first night in weeks, dawn held the certainty of life. Pursuing Japs could not move through this rugged terrain of ridges and chaungs at night, let alone mount a cohesive suprise attack. By dawn they'd be on their way again, and the Japs couldn't move as fast as Chindits.

To-morrow, so the rumours ran, the Gurhka columns left at Mokso Sakan, would meet them with rations and medical stores. The Jocks and Lancasters scoffed at the optimists who had dreamed up – or believed – that one. They'd been this way before. In better weather than this, it had taken them three or four days to get from Mokso to Blackpool.

Meals for the unwounded were a couple of biscuits and half of a four ounce tin of meat or cheese, between two. Anything above that was pooled for the wounded.

A crack of thunder awoke Badger with a start. He grabbed for his rifle, thinking he was back in Blackpool. The rain was sheeting down, a torrent of icy bodkins. He lay there, shivering against the shivering Scofield with water lapping over their legs. And hunger held back further sleep. Funny in Blackpool, scarce as rations got, he never felt hungry. Battle staved off hunger? Now he begrudged the wounded their meagre extras.

In the centre of the bivouac, the dog-tired medics were moving among the wounded. Two hundred men who somehow, limping, crawling, slouched on mules, or slumped in the troughs of blanket litters, had clung to the the last shreds of life and hope throughout the agonising day. The groans and squeals, as medics moved some injured limb, barely audible above the dinning rain, had liitle impact on Badger's self interest. There's no pain in the world worse than the pain you feel yourself – and his hunger was pain. He sucked sullenly on his unlit pipe. He couldn't even have a smoke, his tobacco was sodden. What sort of a cook was Barbara? She'd never made him a meal. Could she cook steak and kidney pudding as good as her mother? Those farmhouse meals were... ah so deliciously filling. And the sweet tea, from that big brown pot, hot as hell and strong as the devil.

§

'...Smokin' my pipe on the mountings
sniffin' the mornin'-cool
I walks in my old brown gaiters
along o' my old brown mule...'

Badger gently tugged the lead rain, to coax Daisy round over a fallen tree across the precipitous track.

§

Yesterday – the second day out of Blackpool – Daisy's doting master had slipped from her back. For two days, with a shattered thigh, he had slumped over her mane, whispering to her between stifled groans. Then it was all too much for him, "Sod this for a game of soldiers." He had moaned as Badger bent over him, "Take over Daisy." He was dead before the MO could get to him, and the rear files were urging them to get a move on.

Badger had clicked his tongue, but Daisy had refused to move.

"Come on, old girl, get moving."

Daisy had walked a few steps, and stopped again.

"Get a bleeding move on up there!"

"What's up with yer!" yelled the rear files.

"Giddyup! Daisy, you stubborn sod!" Daisy had moved forward, and stopped again.

"What's up with you!" Daisy had moved forward again, "Good girl, nothing to be afraid of."

For once they were only on a gentle gradient but the instant he stopped speaking, Daisy had stopped. He had tugged hard at the lead rein. Daisy remained stock still, "Blast you Daisy! Come on!"

The mule moved forward and stopped, and it had dawned on Badger that, when they were on the march, the dead muleteer had talked ceaselessly to her. That's it keep talking to her! There was a nauseous limit to repetitions of 'Come on, you old bugger' and such like, so soon he had resorted to spouting Kipling's 'Barrack Room Ballads'.

At first he had recited in a self-conscious *sotto voce* monotone, afraid of becoming a laughing stock. But within a few verses he was reciting in full voice, trudging with grim faced men, mud wrenching at their boots. In that procession of misery, men needed every ounce of energy just to drag one foot in front of the other. Bent with fatigue, engrossed in their own self-preservation, they were oblivious to the bathos of a mud-smirched soldier soliloquizing alongside a mule that could not even 'eeh-aw'.

Whatever the obstacles, however perilous the track, however treacherous it was underfoot, as long as he was speaking Daisy had moved steadily forward. Soon it seemed she was nodding her head in rhythm to his metre. Whenever he had got round to 'The Widow of Windsor', she seem to step out more briskly, especially when he substituted 'poor buggers' for 'poor beggers'.

§

'...There's a wheel on the Horn's o' the Mornin,
an' a wheel on the edge o' the Pit,
An' a drop into nothin' beneath you
as straight as a beggar can spit...'

"Steady Daisy, steady!" She was now carrying a Cameronian sergeant with a leg splinted from ankle to hip, and she was losing her footing on rocks below the swirling mud.

'...With the sweat runnin' out o' shirt-sleeves...'

The poetry was carrying him through the monotony and despair. Endless rain and mud. Nothing, except his brain, seemed impervious to the sodding rain. It even penetrated condoms, their official purpose – storing sticks of Nobel's 108 explosives – long overtaken by events. Men now kept their matches and fags in them, and wore them on their limp penis's to guard against leeches.

The slimy slugs got everywhere. Slim as boot laces, they wriggled in everywhere. Through boot lace holes, puttees, threadbare trousers, and up shirt sleeves. Too wet to feel blood trickling down your flesh, the first sign was the blood splotching your clothes. By then they were tenacious great black snails, removable only by the application of a burning fag end, or a pinch of salt.

To-day was another yesterday. And to-morrow would probably be the same. Mud clutching your ankles. Slogging up into the clouds, then squelching down into a valley. Fighting for balance with every step. Mules and ponies floundering, down on their haunches, their forelegs ploughing through the mud, colliding into the animals and men in front of them.

The mountain ridges and knolls were a tortuous trail of timeless suffering and despair. Men clinging to the belts of the men in front. Men hobbling with wounded comrades clinging around their necks, their dressings filthy with mud and blood. Stretcher parties stumbling. Grunting.

They had scant rations and ammunition, but with soggy blankets in their sodden packs, the webbing straps were as punishing as ever. The flesh of their shoulders, softened by constant soaking, was raw from pack straps and rifle slings.

Their horizons were mud caked boots and swishing mule tails. As they topped each crest, there was the heart breaking view of yet another rain drenched valley and mountain to be crossed.

To-night would be another waterlogged nightmare. A couple of biscuits, half a tin of meat or cheese – if he was lucky – and a dilution of lime juice crystals or soup powder.

'...You may hide in the caves,
they'll be only your graves,
but you can't get away from the guns!'

"Let's have Barbara's favourite now, eh Daisy."

'The Border Cattle Thief' wasn't one Badger liked, but it would bring back that summer evening when, caught in a thunder storm, they had cuddled together in a Scarborough park shelter, out quoting each other with lesser known poems.

'O, woe is me for the merry life,
I led beyond the bar,
And treble woe for my winsome wife
That weeps at Shalimar,'

"...Now how does the next verse go? Oh God, Daisy I hope I get a letter at Mokso Sakan. Ah yes!..."

'They've taken away my long jezail,
My shield and sabre fine..."

"Listen!" The Cameronian dragged himself upright in the

saddle.

"What?" The rain had eased off and Badger's ears were attuned only to the creak of saddlery, the squash of boots and the croaking of the wounded. He was silent for a moment and Daisy tugged him to a halt.

"Birds!" The Cameronian slumped back down on to Daisy's neck.

For the first time in weeks, the forest was alive with bird calls and monkey screams. A Sambhur stag belled, ringing and echoing from the valley behind them. They were not startled cries, more like applause for the misty yellow sun, now peeping above the purple rims of yesterday's mountains. Ahead the leading files – breasting another ridge – were wreathed in leaden clouds, and there was cheering. There was another sound too. Axes thwacking into trees.

"Get a move on!" A man behind slapped Daisy's flanks and as Badger resumed his recitation, a ripple of optimism quickened the column's pace.

'...And heaved me into the Central Jail,
for lifting of the kine...'

Over the ridge this time, there was no valley, just a few hundred yards of scrubby depression. Beyond it, another steep escarpment, and the head of the column was already milling round its base.

Badger's heart sank to his boots. Then he saw them. Not 14 Brigade, but huge damson black Nigerians, a battalion of the 3rd West African Rifles. Jolly faced black men, taking over the stretchers. Others were lopping trees and bamboo – beds for the wounded and sick.

They were among friends at last. The sight of the huge grinning Nigerians dissolved all anger at the failure of these Africans and 14 Brigade to come to the aid of Blackpool. They'd not been sitting on their backsides. They'd been battling terrain and weather, hacking through mountainous jungle, gaining only a few miles each day. And they had built a 'staircase' of logs and bamboo down the escarpment.

Dusk was still hours away, but they bivouaced in the jungle, around the foot of the prodigious stairway, gathering strength for to-morrow's climb through the clouds, and up to the pass into the Indawgyi Valley. The ground was another lake of slurry, but the wounded, at least, were above it in rudimentary bamboo beds constructed by the Nigerians.

The Nigerians were short of food themselves and what little they could spare went to the wounded. For the rest – at most – it was two biscuits, and a sachet of soup powder or lime juice. The clouds had closed over again yet in the drizzle and mud, men somehow got fires going for soup or just to chat around.

Inside the screen of Nigerian picquets and relieved of sentry duties, free from shelling and mortaring, the ignominy of defeat gave way to optimism. Their deliverance became a triumphant outmanoeuvring of the overwhelming Jap force. To-morrow they would be at Mokso Sakan, and the jungle telegraph was buzzing that flying boats had been ordered to the Indawgyi Lake, to evacuate the wounded and sick. For the rest, the end of their ninety day stint was in sight. Even officers were letting slip expectations of the signal to march out any day now.

Beside their dying fire Badger and Scofield squatted together, sharing a blanket round their shoulders. With his mucker's dozing head lolling on his shoulder Badger pondered their escape from Blackpool. Why hadn't the Japs pursued them? They were fresher than them. Did they think we were drawing them into a trap? Nonsense. Was it because they knew we were a spent force? Knew we were in no fit state to harass their supplies any more? Perhaps. In these mountains we were no threat to them. We couldn't get supplies. Like us, they could only move in slow snaking columns. They couldn't collect their troops for a concentrated attack. They'd lost hundreds of men driving us out of Blackpool, and chasing us would be a drain on their forces facing Stilwell. That could be it! Their commanders must have thought the retreat could be a tactic, tempting them to waste time and strength, pursuing a decoying force. They were too wily for that bait. Whatever the reason, Badger could sleep in peace tonight, and not even the mud and rain would keep him awake.

§

Next day at the top of the stairway, Badger slumped face down at the side of the track. Too exhausted to remove his pack, he lay there, lungs heaving, gasping. Every nerve, every ligament and every muscle in his legs trembling uncontrollably. Daisy stood for a moment, her forelegs quivering, hang-headed, nostrils flaring against the earth. Then her legs buckled, and she collapsed on all fours. Further along, the track was lined with sprawling, exhausted men. Further along still, the leading files were staggering to their feet, and queueing for rations.

When, at length, Badger rolled on to his back, Daisy was already back on her feet munching at shrubbery. The giant damson cheeked men were trooping past with stretcher cases, or pic-a-backing wounded. He watched with admiration and envy the effortless ease with which these men, grinning from ear to ear, carried the wounded up the stairway, handed them over to medics waiting at a cluster of newly built bashas and trotted back down again.

A team of muleteers gathering mules and ponies, led Daisy behind the bashas as stiff legged, aching in every muscle, Badger fell in behind Scofield in the ration line.

The stairway had been a slow, painful climb, and he had lost track of time. All he knew was that it was now late afternoon, and they had set off at dawn.

After only ten steps, he had wished the way up was a muddy track. They'd been conditioned to that and, treacherous as they were, at least they snaked around the contours. Every hairpin loop held a hope that the summit was around the next bend. The stairway was as straight as a Roman road, hemmed in on both sides by dense jungle, its summit somewhere above the cloud ceiling.

The risers and treads had been built for fit giants. For exhausted men of lesser stature it was a demoniac obstacle course. The risers were almost knee high. Each step had meant raising a knee waist high, straining backwards, both hands on the knee, a jerk to get the ascending foot on the tread, and lugging up the other foot to join it. For Daisy, it had been a case of lunging her forelegs two steps up, and a lurch to tuck her hind legs on the tread below. With the Cameronian sergeant on her back she had baulked at the first step, and two Nigerians had relieved her of the burden with seemingly effortless ease and carried him to the top. At each footfall, the logs and bamboo shoring groaned and creaked under the impact of boots and hooves, but it held firm.

He had started off reciting 'Mandalay', but by twenty steps up he had no breath for it. All he had been able to gasp was, "Up again, girl!" at each step. At 150, he had lost count of the steps and high above, the head of the column was still climbing into the clouds. Up ahead, even the lanky Ginger was finding it hard going. Behind him, the diminutive Karen padre had looked as though he could do with a helping shoulder under his buttocks to gain each tread.

Gurkhas, from Mokso Sakan, had brought up a string of mules loaded with rations, but there was only enough for one meal per man. Badger collected his, and strolled to the end of the pass. Seven or eight crow flight miles away, and a couple of thousand feet below veiled in drizzle, he could just make out the Indawgyi Lake. From this distance it seemed more an inland sea than a lake. The track down looked precipitous and rugged. He had a momentary tinge of vertigo, and hobbled back along the track, grateful that they would be bivouacing here for the night and not attempting to move down in the gathering dusk.

Round their fires that night, scoffing their sole ration packet, prudence was thrown to the winds. They were too buoyed up with tales of plenty at the lake to-morrow to give a passing thought, even to saving a biscuit. Faith in Lengtaigne was not quite dead. He'd send in supplies by flying boats and Dakotas.

Hot char would have turned the meagre meal into a feast, but there was none. While they supped their soup or lime juice there were envious moans about rum rations that never seemed to materialise for the rank and file.

"Be thankful for small mercies." Badger consoled himself, as he dropped off to sleep alongside Scofield, "I suppose rank deserves some privileges, and if they could only bring up one meal per man, couldn't expect them to lug up rum rations for everyone as well."

§

On the retreat the long snaking column had been a haphazard collection of units. Cameronians, Lancasters, Kings and Gurhkas interspersed with each other, trudging along in any order. In the marshes between Mokso and the lake, having sorted themselves out into column bivouacs, 81 Column was concentrated around a deserted village two or three miles east of the lake. From the first evening Scottie resumed his daily briefing sessions.

They were told that 77 Brigade was moving to join Stilwell's Chinese in an attack on Moguang. The Chinese were pushing the Japs out of Kamaign. The Marauders, Morris Force and another Chinese Division were attacking Myitkyina. The West African column they had met above Mokso, were going to hold that pass. 14 Brigade and the rest of the West African Brigade were operating ten to twenty miles south of the lake. Snuffy Lockett, leading a column of the Leicesters, had driven the Japs from the Kyunsalai Pass, seizing their vital medical stores, and securing the Indawgyi Valley from attack from the south. The mere mention of Lockett brought broad grins to their faces. Other ranks affectionately called the dedicated Wingatian 'Scruffy'. He affected the same shabby appearance as his 'Master', even to wearing a sun-helmet instead of a bush hat. The Gurhkas, who had been at Mokso during the Blackpool battles, were patrolling west and north. So with 14 Brigade to the south, Nigerians in the mountains to the east, and Gurkhas west and north, the Lake area was a safe harbour for them to rest in.

Worldwide news was scanty. In apparent desperation, Hitler had launched flying bombs on London. The Germans were being rolled back by the Russians from the Baltic to the Black Sea. The Americans had re-captured the Marshall Islands and were sweeping onto the Mariannas. In New Guinea, the Aussies were pushing back the Japs. In northern Burma and Assam, General Slim's 14th Army had beaten off the attacks on Kohima and were counter-attacking along the whole front.

The growing ascendancy of the Allies over the Axis Powers were of little cheer to the debilitated men around the Lake. They felt they were forsaken elements of a forgotten army in an obscure, God forsaken valley. The jungle telegraph was soon fleshing out their officers' skeleton briefing.

Time around the lake dragged without distinction of days or dates. The Cameronians held a service of thanksgiving for their deliverance and around the gathering of these descendents of Scottish Covenanters, at the four corners of the compass, sentries knelt at the alert just as their forebears had done at every church service since the seventeenth century, when the Established Church outlawed their Presbyterian faith. Their padre spoke of the hand of God having been with them. They had been defeated, but not in spirit. Each man had done his best... and could give thanks for the preservation of his own life, knowing he had done his duty. They must realise the debt to the Commanders for their leadership.

A derisive groan rippled through the congregation, and the padre turned abruptly to the remembrance of the dead and comrades in captivity.

The Kings held their service in more common style. At an altar, made of bamboo by their Burriffs, with a blanket altar cloth, the tiny Karen padre spoke not of thanksgiving – nor of any debt to commanders for bringing them through the ordeal. His sermon sought to uplift their heart, with 'If God be with us, who can be against us, what have we to fear, my dear comrades...' And they sang 'O God our help' with a vigour that raised their hopes of His intercession in their distress.

In a small clearing, Jack Masters gave a talk to the NCOs, in groups. On a bamboo easel he had set up a blackboard, obtained from God knows where. In formal Staff College style, he gave a post mortem account of the Blackpool battles. The orders, he told them, had been to establish a 'permanent' road and rail block north of Hopin and south of Mogaung. So at last we know, thought Badger, it was supposed to be a block. Master's emphasised *permanent* seemed to convey that he, personally, considered such blocks a contravention of Chindit principles.

He had chosen the site after personal reconnaissance. It was not ideal, but bearing in mind it would be closer to the Jap front lines than White City where the enemy artillery and infantry reserves could be turned on to them, it gave the optimum combination of fields of fire, observation, protection from shells and bombs, water supplies and airfield. Whilst it did not straddle the road and railway like White City, he stressed at length that nightly patrols by Cameronians had pin pointed road and rail targets. Subsequent shelling by the 25 pounders had, before the final battles, destroyed bridges, blown up a train, and stopped all but a trickle of enemy road and rail traffic.

On the blackboard he demonstrated the intention of 14 Brigade and the West African from west, and 77 Brigade from the south, to sweep down on the attackers. Weather and terrain had beaten that effort, but the bitter edge to his words hinted he felt they could have made greater efforts to come to his aid.

The rest was a résumé of the savage assaults leading to the final attack across the strip. It was all history now. They were being told what they already knew. To what purpose? Masters defending, justifying his actions? In the sultry clearing Badger's concentration wandered, his eyes drooped. Then he shook himself. Master's was saying something about the Japs breaking through a 3/9th Gurkha platoon on 'the pimple'.

He had called them 'Garhwarlis'[16] in a tone implying they were a cut or two below his idea of Gurkhas. Badger bridled. These were the Gurkhas he'd fought alongside at Broadway. These were the men he recalled seeing, through fever blurred eyes, marching into Blackpool in 'Review Order'. They were on the weakest part of the perimeter, and the Japs had attacked it in overwhelming strength.

It smacked of Masters unfairly pinning the root cause of Blackpool's fall on the 3/9th's doorstep. Any Tommy could see Blackpool was doomed from the start by its proximity to Jap front line reserves. When White City was solidly blocking Jap supplies, why close it down and set another – closer to their forward echelons? Joe Stilwell ordered it to relieve Jap pressure on the Myitkina-Kamaign front. Him, and his bloody staff, had criminally disregarded the inadequacy of Chindit weaponry and the bloody, bloody weather.

Masters outlined his orders for the withdrawal. How successfully they had broken contact. How the well disciplined retreat.

'More by luck, than discipline...' Badger added silently, remembering the confusion of routes; the carnage as men scurried across that clearing; the abject fear on men's faces, blanched cheeks and fixed wide eyes. The deafness of some to comrades' cries for help. The sacrifice of others, killed as they aided wounded muckers. The 18 carbine cracks. Little Billy's pleading eyes haunted his nights. Badger was haunted by the fact that he had almost murdered Billy. Perhaps Billy might have endured a less painful death if Badger had found a medic. A medic who would have administered a carbine bullet!

"...You can now say you've been in a major engagement..."

The words seemed patronising. They did not need to be told that. Chindit *raison d'etre* was mobility, not pitched battles like Blackpool. The generals had culpably disregarded this. When Masters wound up, complimenting them on their courage and warning that the campaign was not yet over, there were lukewarm cheers, and half hearted clapping.

As they dispersed, the honking of bull-frogs seemed to lend a derisive echo to the applause and Badger could not escape the feeling that the talk had been a valiant attempt to justify the squandering of Chindit potentiality. The toil-worn Masters had endeavoured to present a scenario of a great victory being snatched from 111 Brigade's grasp. The target times for 14 and 77 Brigades to reach Blackpool had been over optmistic. His faint praise of Stilwell's and Lentaigne's objectives damned them for their ignorance of ground and weather conditions. It seemed to indicate Masters' professional confidence in them was at breaking point.

Above the waist high reeds and knee deep bog that bordered the lake – wherever it was little more than squelchy underfoot – bashas sprang up for a Casualty Clearing Station, Brigade and columns' HQ's, and wireless posts. Muckers built two man shelters of bamboo frames roofed with banana leaves, for themselves. At night in hissing rain they lay rigid, dozing fitfully, surrounded by honking bull frogs and zzinging mosquitos, fearing any sudden movement would dislodge the flimsy roofing and drench them.

By day, they hauled sick and wounded to the swampy patch that served as a light plane strip. The planes buzzed in and out in a continuous procession, braving the driving rain and 150 miles of turbulent mountain squalls. But there were never enough flights. Chindits no longer had their own air arm. Other formations also had claims on air force resources. Weather and terrain had wrecked many light planes and too few remained to meet the mounting demands of the whole of the Burma theatre. At dusk when the last flight had left, a despondent file of stretcher borne and walking wounded would slush back through the marshes to the bashas, praying for places on to-morrow's flights.

The lake was no land of plenty.

Whenever the leaden cloud ceiling permitted, supply dropping Dakotas swept across the tree tops, jettisoning their cargoes. These too, were never enough to feed the encamped columns. Lentaigne was giving priority to re-arming them, weapons and equipment cutting into the weight and space for rations. There were times too, when the valley was bathed in brilliant sunshine yet the Dakotas did not come, and men cursed the 'base wallahs', not knowing that the Assam air strips were weather bound.

To Base, 'Why no sorties to-day?'

From Base, 'Regret sorties aborted due to weather.'

The jungle telegraph buzzed with 'leaked' signals. Mike Calvert's, from over the Moguang hills, '...Column's out of rations eight days. For God's sake tell air force to pull its finger out. Weather suitable. It is the air force which is wet...'

S.O.S. from West Africans to the south, 'No supply drop for eleven days.'

Then, when all rations were exhausted at the lake, their desperate signals brought the brusque reply from base, 'Quite realise your plight, but famine not confined to your Brigade.'

Column commanders called for ex-butchers, and Animal Transport officers selected the mules for slaughter. Only the largest and healthiest animals were the safest and best option and for 81 Column, that included Daisy. Watching her being led behind the altar to be shot, her tail swishing gently and vigorously nodding insects from her trusting brown eyes, Badger had only a tinge of sorrow. Anything deeper could only be hypocrisy. If the big, docile, de-vocalised creature understood English and could speak she'd be the most erudite beast in creation. But she was just meat on the hoof, and his fleeting compassion was no match for his hunger.

The section had liver that night, whether it was Daisy's they cared not. It was food. They boiled it for hours with the core of banana bushes. Even then, the core was tasteless, rubbery as raw leeks, and the meat was tough as leather. The broth however, was delicious and for the first time in weeks, they slept with full stomachs.

On the lake, the Brigade's RAF officers' HQ laid out a landing 'path' of wooden floats decked with parachute strips, for the flying boats. Sappers built jetties and rafts to ferry wounded to the flying boat anchorages. Two or three days later two ungainly Sunderlands, christened Gert and Daisy,[17] and designed for anti-submarine patrols, made the first hazardous flight. Lumbering over 200 miles of mountains, they droned down through the Indawgyi valley, over the heads of the Japs around Kamaign, to skim to the anchorage.

The huge planes brought in medical supplies, outboard motors, fuel, assault boats, engineering stores and some rations, before flying off with the wounded. At times the lake was whipped into giant waves and with prayers in their throats, they watched as a Sunderland perilously rocked and buffeted as it put down or took off. And there were days when especially foul weather, at the lake or their base, aborted their sorties.

With each flight, Gert and Daisy each carried off forty to fifty wounded, depending on the ratio of stretcher to walking cases, but sickness was outstripping evacuation sorties. Worn out bodies succumbed to afflictions that, in their robust days, would have been brushed off. Minor scratches swiftly became septic, followed by terminal fever. Mild malaria and dystentery turned men into helpless wrecks. The exertion of gathering in supplies, or brief patrols, brought on chills that swifly developed into pneumonia. Burial parties were almost a routine chore.

Soon, the Medical Officers' opinion of wholesale unfitness was no secret. They would have no truck with malingerers, but had collectively warned Masters that 'a high proportion of troops were on the threshold of death from exhaustion, undernourishment, exposure and strain'. The troops optimistically reasoned that the High Command dare not ignore this, and must surely be arranging to get everyone out. Gert's and Daisy's first sorties brought another ripple of optimistic speculation. They calculated – and argued – about the carrying capacity of the Sunderlands, and how many sorties were neccesary to fly them all out.

The ripple was ephemeral. The lake was to be no embarkation port for India. The jungle telegraph was soon buzzing with Shadazup's imperative instruction, 'Essential re-equipping to be carried out with all possible speed.' Each supply drop brought them sacks of boots, clothing and cases of weapons.

If they *were* going out, it would be by Shanks's pony, fighting their way through Jap territory!

For hours, officers hung around the radio bashas, expectant of the order to 'march out', and came away with glum faces and bitter mutterings. Shadazup, scoffing off medical opinions, were repeatedly demanding, 'Re-equipment and evacuation [of casualties] must be carried out at all speed.'

With foul mouthed bitterness, the troops openly castigated Stilwell and Lentaigne.

'The fuckers should come and see for themselves...'

'They've fucked up all Wingate's plans. He would have come in to see us...'

'We wouldn't have got into this bleeding shambles if he'd lived!'

'If the bastards think the MO's are exaggerating, why don't they send a new medical team?'

'We're just sodding pins on their maps. They sit in their cushy offices – scoffing grub, shuffling map pins – while we bloody starve.'

§

"Thanks, sir." Badger, at the Casualty basha one morning, took the pills for his diarrhoea from the MO's orderly, "Any news when we're getting out, sir?"

The MO gave a despairing shrug, as he directed the orderly to dress a festering sore on Badger's forearm, "To quote Chesterton, corporal," he said with a wry smile, "They have given us into the hands of new unhappy lords, Lords without anger and honour, who dare not carry swords. They fight by shuffling papers; they have bright dead alien eyes; they look at our labour and laughter as a tired man looks at flies..." Breaking off to beckon in the next man, he added, "There's something to occupy your poetic ardor – make a parody of it."

The gloomy forebodings drew column officers and other ranks closer together in common umbrage. Marching and fighting together, enduring the same privations, they had worn out their bodies and souls at the bidding of remote generals. Now those generals, scorning their fatigue, were welshing on the promise to get them out in 90 days.

With the united umbrage, officers were less circumspect in their chatting, and the jungle telegraph babbled with revelations.

'Lentaigne never had any liking for Chindit tactics.'

'Lengtaigne despised Wingate and his theories.'

'Even when he took command he was declaiming that White City and Broadway would fall within 48 hours.

'Brigadier Tulloch was a dedicated Wingatian, and look what Lengtaigne did to him. Slim made Tulloch second in command of the Chindits. Lengtaigne brought in Brigadier Alexander, another Gurkha mate, and shuffled Tulloch to admin work.'

'And look at Stilwell, he's wangled his son and son-in-law on to his staff. Sacks anyone who's not an arse-crawler.'

Stilwell was still bragging to the world that his Marauders and his Chinese had taken Myitkina. Yet it was still in Jap hands, and he held only the rudimentary airstrip. The Marauders had been virtually annhilated by battle casualties and disease, but he was still broadcasting they were going fine and attacking the enemy, while the yellow Limeys were sitting on their 'asses'.

'The butcher is lying through his teeth. He's Shanghied hundreds of US Army engineers from road construction and called them Marauders.'

'His 30,000 Chinese outnumbered the Jap garrison by 10 to 1, and the untrained engineers had broken under a Jap counter-attack.'

It was now common knowledge that Stilwell was complaining to Mountbatten that the Chindits – notably Morris Force – were disobeying his orders to carry on advancing. The information was scrappy but what little the men at the lake heard was enough to fire the hatred of their Anglo-phobic master and his nepotistic staff.

After more than two months harassing the Jap supply routes along the mountainous Burma-China frontier, Morris Force had been ordered down to 'secure' two Irrawaddy villages on the eastern outskirts of Myitkina. Shadazup had told them the villages were lightly held.

Still believing Myitkina was in Stilwell's hands, they had made three assaults on Waingmaw, which dominated the ferry crossing. Each time they had penetrated its defences, killing a couple of hundred Japs, but had been driven back by the overwhelming enemy strength.

Meagre though the information was, the men at the lake knew what Stilwell seemed blind and deaf to. Morris Force was too lightly armed for pitched battles and must, like them, be at the limit of their endurance.

There were rumours too, that Stilwell had refused Slim's offer to fly the 36 British Division into the Myitkina strip.

'Covering up his bloody balls up...'

'After his bragging, he don't want the Britsh pulling his chestnuts out of the fire, and stealing his thunder.'

Mogaung was another of Stilwell's frenetic demands on Chindit resources. The Jap occupation of Burma had cut off all supply routes to China, except by air over the Himalaya 'Hump' which could only feed a trickle of war material to Chiang Kai-shek's forces. To re-open a land route to China, US Army engineers had the task of driving a road, and pipe-line, from Ledo on the Burma-Assam border, through the Hukwang Valley, to Moguang then along the railway to Myitkina.

Now, with his 'triumphant' forces bunkered by Jap tenacity at Myitkina, and Chiang Kai-shek holding back the Chinese troops north of the Mogaung River, Stilwell was frantically ordering the Chindits to attack Moguang to take the pressure off Myitkina.

Lengtaigne was 'a bloody man of straw' to let Stilwell send in Morris Force to do what his 30,000 troops – with massive artillery support – had failed to do, and be brow beaten into keeping the Chindits in the field when they were 'dying on their feet'.

They were mutinous, but mutiny was beyond them. Front line troops could desert – take refuge in some safe back area – until they were herded into some equally safe penal compound. Threats of penal retribution were not staving off rebellion by 111 Brigade. Nothing could be a fraction as punitive as their current conditions. They were hundreds of miles inside enemy territory. Where could they flee to? Who could they mutiny against? Their own officers, in the same boat and sharing the same hardships were their vital link for supplies, however meagre. Without men like Scottie holding them together, they would become a lost rabble in the jungle.

So the days ground on. Master's decimated columns replaced their tattered uniforms and boots, built up their weaponry and with mutinous rantings, prepared for the worst. They abandoned hope of imminent deliverance from their privations.

Daisy took out over 100 casualties in 3 flights before being severely damaged at her mooring base on the Brahmaputra. Gert, in 10 flights evacuated nearly 400 before she was recalled for submarine patrols. The resourceful Yanks fitted floats to light planes to fly casualties to the lake from other brigades. But with the loss of the Sunderlands, weather restrictions, and the more urgent demands of 77 Brigade, the hospital bashas were bursting at the seams with sick cases.

Every signal from Moguang was grim. 77 Brigade were meeting stiff opposition. The Chinese they were supposed to be helping were sitting in the hills. And after ten days at the lake, the official briefing confirmed the jungle telegraph's forebodings. Stiwell had ordered 111, 14 and the West African Brigades to advance on Moguang from the west, over the 4,000 feet Bumrawng Bum mountains.

"...81 Column will start out at first light to-morrow, 10th. June. First job of 111 Brigade and us will be to secure Lakhren, about 20 miles north of the lake..."

"What about the wounded and sick, sir?" Badger was worried about Jack. Everyone in his section had dysentary or a fever – or both – but the stalwart Jack Ryan had a much more deathly and hollow eyed look than the rest.

"Ah, yes. Well... Kamaign is now held by the Chinese, and the sappers are organising a fleet of rafts to ferry casualties there. Casualties will be evacuated from here or Lakhren, whichever is nearest."

"Where do I get a ticket?" Someone called above the cynical cheers.

"There's other good news too, lads." The briefing officer, affecting an enigmatic grin, paused for them to settle into silence, "Allied troops landed in Normandy yesterday. The second front has opened up at last."

"Fuck the second front." A rich Scouse voice, "Churchill wants to get some of those fucking Allied troops out here!"

The officer could only smile in sympathy.

"Why don't they fly in 23 Brigade?" Another Scouser, "They've done fuck all yet. Bill Slim offered to fly in 36 Division. Why not fly in 23 to relieve us poor sods?"

23 Brigade was the only Chindit brigade not yet flown in, and the firm belief was that it was being held in immediate readiness as a reserve and relief force.

"That's out, chaps." The officer shrugged forlornly, "General Slim has collared 23 Brigade for the Kohima front." The news inflamed their sense of being forgotten, expendable troops, "All right, all right, simmer down!" He called above the angry mutterings, "They've not been sitting on their arses, they've had some hard front line fighting. Now, back to tomorrow's move. There'll be four day's rations per man. You'll all have a hundred rounds of 303, four grenades, and six magazines per Bren gun. Right, get back to your bashas and get yourselves organised for moving out to-morrow. Lentaigne's order of the day is 'You are Chindits. You can take it and make it.' The newspapers are calling us 'the toughest of the tough'. He's promised this will be our last task."

"Yeah! That one's got whiskers on!"

As Badger settled down alongside Scofield, listening to the rain drumming on the banana leaves, he was sure that if Vinegar Joe Stilwell, or Lentaigne – or even Slim – had come within sight of most of the men of 81 Column that night, they wouldn't have lived to see the dawn.

As on most nights, since Pagoda Hill, he prayed silently for enough strength to get through the next day, and asked, 'Dear Lord, guard and keep my family safe wherever they may be, and especially help my devoted wife through the burden of our separation.' Unfailingly, as he mutely ended with the Lord's Prayer, apparitions of the Bombay soothsayer, and his bizarre hallucinations on their last night on 'the deep' marred the thrilling vision of Barbara, naked in the firelight.

Why did he persist in distrusting her so much? There had been some letters at the lake – from his dad, sister, and even a copy of 'Men Only' from one of his brothers, but nothing from her. Now, going back into the mountains, it would probably be weeks before the next mail reached them. They had been allowed to send a letter out and as he dropped off to sleep, he worried that his scrappy, mildly carping note would upset her.

Footnotes to Chapter Twenty-one

Page 362 Note No.16 Garhwali was conquered by the Gurkhas during the Napelese Wars of the late 18th Century, and until the 1939-45 War Garwhali Regiments were distinct from Gurkha rifle Regiments although they wore similar uniforms and were equipped with kukris. In the 1914-18 War Garwhali battalions performed with outstanding elan and a Garwhali Brigade won three of the five VCs awarded to Indians in France.

In 1930 during the fierce rioting in Peshawar, a Garhwali battalion on internal security duties was attacked by hostile Pathans using clubs and bricks. They were forbidden to retaliate. The following day two platoons refused to resume their duties and after a Court of Enquiry the NCOs of the platoon were sentenced to various terms of imprisonment. The remainder of the men were dismissed. (see *A Matter of Honour* by Philip Mason, published Jonathan Cape, 1974.)

The recruiting distinction between Gurkhas and Garhwalis seems to have disappeared by 1940, so perhaps a legacy of the 1930 'mutiny' was that officers of 'true' Gurkha units resented Garhwalis being looked upon as Gurkhas – and Masters was a Gurkha zealot, a jealous custodian of their traditions and honour.

Page 365 Note No.17 Named after the music hall characters, two blousy comic charladies – Gert and Daisy – played by Elsie and Doris Waters.

Chapter Twenty-two

"Packs On!"

Badger felt like a superannuated war horse, pricking its ears and pawing the ground, as some distant trumpet summoned the old thrills of 'The Charge'. He slipped on his equipment and, humming 'Onward Christian Soldiers', led his section into the column forming up on the squelchy track.

It was another grizzly, rain soaked dawn but he was light hearted and eager to get away from the depressive, fever ridden lake. After a mess-tin of steaming char and a full 'K' ration packet for breakfast, Badger had broken wind without soiling his trousers for the first time in days. His new boots were a snug fit, and he was looking forward to a 'good leg stretch'.

With the lake on its left, the long snaking column shuffled off along the narrow foothills track to Lakhren. When, an hour later, they halted for their first ten minute rest, Badger had long lost his light heartedness. The track was just higher than the marsh and reeds, and the mud was barely ankle deep, but it was thick and glutinous, dragging at their boots. Bamboo enclosed it like a Stygian tunnel, impervious to any breeze, and corking in the stifling heat. Time and again, as the leading platoons slashed through overgrown thickets, the following files crumped into each other.

They were carrying no more than at the outset of the campaign, but their saturated burdens seemed to be double the weight. Rifle slings and pack straps scourged their shoulders. Socks slipped down their boots, crimping in abrasive ribs around the ankles. Salty trickles stung their eyes.

By mid-day, the accumulated weariness of months had taken its toll on Badger's faculties. He lost the thread and mixed up the verses of his Barrack Room Ballads, and dragged one mud loaded boot in front of the other in an amnesiac stupor.

At their hourly halts, there was nowhere off the track to squat. They stood, hunched over their rifle muzzles, or bowed over thumb-sticks. At night, they hacked spaces in the bamboo to sleep in soaking undergrowth. Sleeping or walking, mosquitoes plagued their exposed flesh and avaricious leeches gorged like vampires on their blood.

On the fourth day, a fusillade of Bren and rifle fire from the advance platoon brought the column a startled, apprehensive halt.

"Ambush!"

There was no way around the flank without slashing through the bamboo. And slashing was too noisy for any suprise counter attack. But even as they cocked their rifles, the firing stopped and the column trudged forward.

Half a mile ahead they traipsed through Lakhren. Four days to cover twenty or so crow flight miles, and all that was here were two or three small derelict bashas and a track, crossing theirs, winding uphill.

Around the bashas were the emaciated corpses of a dozen Japs, some of them the long dead victims of starvation, others still oozing blood from the recent gunfire.

After that night's bivouac just uphill of Lakhren, with Scott's column in the lead they were, once again, trekking up into the cloud shrouded peaks heading for Padigahtawng.

'About eight miles. Two day's slog at the most, lads. Then we'll rest for a couple of days, and take a supply drop.'

But those eight miles were up an almost sheer mountain. Up 3000 feet – down 1,000 – and up another 1,000. For most of the way leading platoons had to slash a path through dense jungle and needed relieving every half hour. The ground underfoot was glassy with decaying leaf mould. At best it was three paces up and one down – at worst it was one foot forward and one down on the knees.

The slow, halting progress had some compensations. Men weakened by malaria, or dysentery, could flop on the side of the track, take a short rest, and soon catch up with their section without too great an effort.

Just before dusk, the first day out from Lakhren as they settled in to bivouac, they were mustered for a column briefing.

"It seems at last, men, we have made world headlines."

With exaggerated solemnity, the briefing officer held up a page from a message pad.

"From the BBC World Service : 'In Burma, troops of the 3 Indian Division [cover name for the Chindits] have captured the important communication centre of Lakhren..."

Hysterical laughter drowned the next words. Important communication centre! A mud track and a couple huts.

'Our privy is Buckingham Palace compared to that!'

'Yeah, but what about that bloody great railway station.'

'And all those tarts waving from the windows'

'Liverpool pubs have got nothing on Lakhren, there's two on every corner.'

'Can I 'ave a ten days leave at Lakhren sir.'

'Yeah Betty Grable is on at the Lakhren Roxy, let's all go!'

'King'll give us'n a special medal for capturing it!'

'Naw, they'll give us the VD Cross with syphilis cluster for all those knocking shops.'

"All right, all right! Quieten down. Lakhren will be a rear base and staging post for evacuation of casualties. If any of you fall out, make your way down there. Let me warn you though, unless you've one foot in the grave the medics will boot you back to us, *tout suite..!*"

Badger only vaguely heard the next few sentences. A relapse of fever was fogging his mind, and he was fretting about the ailing Jack Ryan's whereabouts. With the loss of the sappers at Blackpool and re-distribution to even-out casualty losses, the Commando Platoon had been merged with the Recce Platoon. Even then the 'new' platoon was half strength, and Corporal Oughton, Wyles, and Trott had been detached to strengthen another depleted section. But where was Jack? He'd been detached for work around the lake and had not returned to the section. Had he been scheduled for evacuation or – ill as he was – in a following column. He shuddered and shrugged himself back to the present.

"...West African and 14 Brigades are advancing along the southern side of Bumrawng above Blackpool. News from 77 Brigade is scarce. They are still meeting fierce opposition but they've taken the eastern outskirts. Bladet Force are being dropped to help..."

"Good oh! Fry the bastards." A Scouser bawled. Bladets were demolition and flame thrower specialists, all trained parachutists.

"...The Chinese should be there soon. General Stilwell is still battling for Myitkina. The Allied armies are making good progress in France on a wide front. Rome has been occupied by the Americans. In the Pacific the Yanks have taken Saipan. Jerry is still lobbing flying bombs on London, but they don't seem to be causing a great deal of concern. That's it for now. Fires out in half an hour. We move out at first light, Recce Platoon will lead off first."

§

Three days out of Lakhren, in driving rain, the columns straggled into bivouacs around Padigahtawng. The village consisted of ten or twelve large bamboo huts on stilts. It lay astride a web of boggy tracks which meandered along the rugged contours, or zig-zagged down to the ten miles of open country between the foothills and Moguang. A handful of villagers, mostly men and elderly women, standing on hut steps greeted them with broad, thick lipped grins. All other villagers had decamped to the lower slopes to escape the misery of ceaseless rain and wind. The monsoon season had put a stop to work on the quagmire patches of paddy, hacked from the jungle around the village.

Brigade HQ and Signals' units established their 'offices' in vacant huts. Muckers fashioned bamboo shelters for themselves. A working party marked out a dropping zone on the paddy. Even the most frugal had all but exhausted the four day's rations they had when, seven or eight days earlier, they had set out from the lake. For anguished hours, they listened for the drone of Dakotas. The afternoon seemed to be racing towards dusk, and night would abort the sortie.

Then their spirits rose and they were yelling wildly as if they expected the droaning Dakota, searching for them in the mist, to hear them. The Kachins, in wide eyed wonder, watched their frantic yelling and excited gesticulation at the sky as a single Dakota dropping through the clouds, skimmed the trees on its recognition run.

It was only one plane. Three 'K' ration packets, one day's rations per man, but it was something. Surely there would be more planes to-morrow, now they knew where they were. But the meagreness of the rations was swept to the back of Badger's mind – there was a bag of mail for 81 Column.

He was sitting by their shelter when Scofield returned with the section's mail. If he had gone himself and there'd been none for him, he was certain he'd not have been able to hold back the tears.

"Nothing for me. Two for you, corp. Air letter from your wife – and a card from Tiger Lyons. He's in convalescent hospital, doing fine."

"Cheeky sod! Reading my mail!" Shamming indignation, to hide his childlike joy, he scowled and snatched the card and letter.

He was impatient to read Barbara's letter but he wanted to savour it in privacy. Scofield's gentle brown eyes were on his, waiting expectantly for snippets of news from home.

"That's poetic!" Stuffing the letter in his pocket, he grinned as he read the card, "There Tiger was, at Blackpool, telling me if I didn't keep my mind on the job I'd get shot up the arse. Then he gets wounded in the backside. Wait 'til I see him again, I'll rib him rotten. He says Jack Lindo, Kelly and Sergeant Vasey were wounded at Moguang but are doing well. Must tell Jack's mucker, Winstanley – haven't seen him for a bit."

As he spoke, he fought back the irritation of Scofield's attentiveness. He wanted to get into Barbara's letter. Why doesn't he push off and do something.

"Do us a favour mucker, we've got enough for one brew, stir up the fire and make some char."

With Scofield crouching over the fire, fanning it with his hat, Badger took out the blue air-letter. The British post mark was obscured by heavier Field Post Office marks, and there was something dismaying about the crumpled letter. No SWALK. His addresss was smudged. Too old and little for rain stains. Tears? The writing was shaky, not her usual uniformly sloped hand. Her address on the back was c/o Sgt. M. O'Connor, ATS, at some Anti-Aircraft Battery near Portsmouth. His fingers and heart trembled as he tore it open.

It was dated over two months ago and typewritten.

> 'My dearest Badger,
> I am sorry, but there is no painless was of telling you this.'

His heart thudded against his ribs. His stomach quaked. The soothsayer, and the vision on 'the deep' flitted across his moistening eyes. He knew what was coming, and had to force back the rage that was urging him to tear the letter to shreds, so he would never see the confession that would tear his heart strings.

> 'I am pregnant. Believe me, dear kind Badger, I would give anything in theworld to undo what I have done. I won't torture you with the sordid detailsexcept to say it happened about 3 months ago, after an officers' mess party.
> I'm not trying minimise my guilt, but I was drunk, and please, please try to understand it was the drink on top of two terrible years of pent up chastity, and not the man's attraction. I hardly knew him, and he has been posted away, and I have not seen him since.
> It was truly my one and only indiscretion. Can you ever forgive this one stupid loveless sin.'

He blinked away his tears. '...one and only indiscretion.' There was something phoney about that. Why 'indiscretion' and not 'one and only unfaithfulness?' Covering up other times when she had got away with it? There was something evasive about her whole story. She never would let drink get the better of her. Never submit to a hole-in-the-corner fumble, let alone go the whole hog. Unless she was infatuated with the bastard, then she couldn't have hardly known him.

His eyes took in the rest of the letter in mist veiled bitterness. Something about not having told her parents... had left the RAF... write to her c/o Mary. He did not even take in the last lines.

'Your broken hearted,
still loving wife,
Barbara.
xxxxx'

"Tea up! Where you going, corp?"

Badger was thrashing through the bamboo into the jungle. It was not like him to flout the rules and go off alone.

"Hang on, I'll come with you."

"Stay where you are! I'll be back in a mo!"

Out of Scofield's sight, he fell to his knees, violently pummelling the ground. He knew only too well the tyrannical strain of enforced chastity. If it truly was a drunken, loveless romp with someone she hardly knew, he thought he could live with that and forgive her. It would cancel out his own loveles romps in the Bombay brothels. But he could not believe her faithlessnes was a 'one and only indiscretion'. He was numb to the bruising, and the splashing mud, as his fists pounded the ground. The conviction that she had found love with another man was shredding his heart and convulsing his guts with wild jealousy.

"The bloody stupid bitch!" Panting into the earth, "Why did she wait so long to tell me." If she'd told him as soon as she knew he would have still been in India. He could have seen the Welfare Officer. Maybe got compassionate repatriation. Straightened things out with her, face to face. Here, in this God forgotten place, he could do nothing. Couldn't even unburden himself to anyone, not even the padre, without reflecting the humiliation of her infidelity on himself.

§

"What's the blooming matter with you, corp? Was it that blinking letter?" 'Blinking' and 'blooming' were the vilest words the gentle Scofield ever uttered, "You've hardly spoken a civil word for three days, and you've volunteered for every blooming patrol and ambush."

"For God's sake Scofield, put a sock in it. I've told you a hundred times a day, that letter's none of your bleeding business."

They were sitting around their fire, warming their feet, and trying to dry off their boots and socks before the dusk Stand-to. 'Trench feet' was now adding to the miseries of relapsing fever, dysentery, and the endless rain.

For three days, Badger had sought to numb his tortured emotions with physical exhaustion. He'd been curtly officious and martinet with the section. They had put up with it because, knowing Badger, they appreciated he must be going through some emotional purgatory. Today, 81 Column had slogged the six or seven miles from Padigahtawng to occupy Pahok, another village of half a dozen huts – a boggy depression in the mountains.

"It *is* our business corp – when you behave as though you've got a death wish, and you're dragging us with you." Scofield irately poked the fire with his bayonet, "You're not just being blooming careless, you're deliberately taking risks. This afternoon you charged down on this blinking village like a wild man, shouting, 'Roll on death, lets get...' well you know what, '...the angels'. If the Japs had put up any resistance we'd all be dead."

Scofield was right of course, but Badger remained silent. They hadn't known how many Japs there were when they'd charged across the paddy patch. In the event there had only been a dozen on the other side of the village, and they had fled hell for leather into the Moguang Valley without a shot being fired.

For the time being, their advance towards Mogaung had ceded priority to clearing and securing the hills overlooking the railway valley. For three days they had slogged, ankle deep in mud, searching out Japs in villages with strange names. Ngusharawng, Hkamutyang, and Pyidaw. There seemed to be pockets of Japs everywhere, and usually it had been a case of chasing them down the hills. The only show of resistance had been yesterday, when they bumped into fifty or sixty Japs occupying a small crest. It had been a brief battle with no Chindit casualties.The Japs had fled, dragging away their casualties into the jungle.

"And what about yesterday morning. You stuck your blinking neck out, pinching fodder from the mule lines – under the adjutant's nose."

§

From the first night, thickening cloud had blotted out the sky over Padigahtawng. Dakotas droning over each day had failed to locate the dropping zone, and flown on elsewhere. For two days the only food they'd had, was a handful of rice for each section, bartered from the Kachins by the Burriffs for parachute silk. After dawn Stand-to yesterday, fantasising about future breakfasts, the lip-smacking mention of porridge had triggered the suggestion that atta for the mules was a form of oatmeal. The few bags of fodder were under a HQ hut and Badger had curtly elected himself to 'nick' some – and to hell with the risk of being caught.

He had crawled under the hut, filled his hat with atta, and was sneaking away when the top step creaked. He had turned to see the adjutant, opening a 'K' ration packet on the top step. For a micro second their eyes had met but the adjutant, affecting not to see him, had turned back into the hut.

"The supercilious sod always looks at – and treats – Tommies as if we're pox infected serfs." He had muttered to himself, "The bugger never seems to be short of rations. Let him dare charge me for stealing food, when he's got plenty."

§

"It wasn't bad porridge though Badger, was it?" Scofield asked deferentially, trying to break through his mucker's untypical moroseness, "Good idea of yours to sweeten it with Dextrose tablets."

"Filled a hole anyway," Badger grunted as he dabbed his feet with his 'panic-map'. Mud working its way into their boots, and the friction of socks on skin softened by perpetual soaking had worn their soles and heels to raw, red flesh.

Damn the medical hierarchy in India, Badger cursed under his breath as he thought of their reply to the Columns' recent requeat for gum boots. 'Rubber boots not advisable for Trench feet. Best treatment is to keep feet and socks dry at all times.'

Masters's rumoured reply had sent a brief spark of cheer through the columns' gloom. 'ONE – kindly arrange for rain to stop falling. TWO – please turn mud into dry land. THREE – please terminate the war so that we can build huts and stay in them. FOUR – am confident cases of foot rot will then materially decrease.'

The signal rebounded with threats of court-martial for gross insubordination, and had brought derisive hoots throughout the bivouacs.

Badger eased on his socks and boots, and prayed for miraculous healing before to-morrow's operations. At dawn Scottie's column was under orders to capture Mla, three miles east. Then march three miles south to take and secure Hkamutyang. Then five miles down into the Moguang Valley to set up an ambush, and blow the railway south of Sahmaw.

The evening's briefing had been confined solely to local operations. A Chinese battalion had, at last, reached Moguang to help Mike Calvert – his brigade was now advancing against stiff opposition. 111 Brigade, with 14 and the West African Brigades were to get on with clearing the Moguang Valley, and link up with the Chinese in the Indawgyi Valley. Stilwell's HQ claimed that the Chinese, pushing down from Kamaign, were within a few miles of Lakhren.

But no one believed Stilwell's signals anymore.

Chapter Twenty-three

"Damn! Thought it was too bloody good to be true." Badger snorted to Ginger Slater, as they scouted ahead of the column. The rain had stopped sometime during the night, the air had freshened, and since then the overcast had been thinning out. The mud had still wrenched at their boots as they had marched to Mla but for once, they had set out in dry clothes and their only damp parts up to now, were their armpits, the backs of their rotting shirts, and their ankles and feet.

Mla had turned out to be a cluster of vacant huts. A trio of 'caretaking' villagers had told them that the Japs had quit two days ago, but there was a detachment still at Hkamutyang.

Now, with Mla two miles behind them and Hkyamutang a mile ahead, the sky was blackening and drizzle was sweeping the hillside. Badger slipped his groundsheet on as a cape. He might sweat a bit more but his blanket, dried over the early morning fire was in his pack, and he wanted to keep it dry.

The track cut through dense bamboo thickets and with the rain now sheeting down, he trudged round a bend twenty yards ahead of Ginger and Scofield. Beyond the bend the track ran across a scrubby clearing about the size of a football pitch.

"Japs!" Sinking down to kneeling aim, he hissed the warning.

A hundred yards ahead, a single Jap turned on his heels and bolted for the cover of the jungle.

"Bugger it!" The groudsheet tangled with the stock as he

brought the rifle butt to his shoulder. Furiously he tore it off, ripping button holes and only managed to get off one shot as the Jap disappeared into the bamboo. Flinging the groundsheet into the jungle, vowing never to carry such a useless encumbrance again, he waved Ginger and Scofield to his side.

With a platoon in extended order behind them, they warily crossed into the jungle. Here and there were splotches of blood, but no sign of the Jap. The search was brief. Getting to Hkaymutyang was now more vital than anything else, as the shot, or the fleeing man, could have alerted any Japs there.

From the clearing the track cut through half a mile of bamboo thickets, before suddenly giving way again to scrubby hillside. A hundred yards below, the scrub dipped sharply into a dog-legged depression. Beyond the depression, rolling hillside, patchworked with paddy plots, swept down into the rain veiled Moguang Valley.

A single large hut, perched on the rim of the depression, was all that could be seen of habitation. But when the column, in pincer formation reached it, even that was deserted.

Scottie, deploying the column in extended order along the rim, searched the hillside with his binoculars and mustered the officers around himself.

Lying prone alongside Ginger in the saturated scrub, Badger could only guess what Scottie was discussing. He could now see the full extent of the depression. To his right, beyond the hut, it petered out at the jungle edge. Two hundred yards to his left, it flattened out to a shelf of paddy and a clutch of small huts. A Kachin couple and two children were squatting on the steps of one hut. The track they had come along followed the depression to the huts before snaking downhill another two hundred yards into a bamboo jungle. So this was Hkamuytang. Half a dozen deserted huts, and an acre or so of neglected paddy. It was too much to hope that all the villages, between here and Sahmaw, would be as easily 'captured'.

Scottie was sweeping the distant valley with an index finger, describing the lie of the land. A thousand or so feet below, they would have to cross a couple of miles of open country to reach Sahmaw. Ten miles of it when they advanced on Moguang. The town was out of sight, but the distant rumble of guns was evidence enough that the battle for it was still raging, and that the rear areas must be packed with Jap reserves. It would be a tough enough venture for a regular division, with artillery and all its supporting arms. For the exhausted, lightly armed Chindits it would be sheer bloody murder. More than a skirmish would exhaust their ammunition and would fail to distract the Japs enough to be of any help to 77 Brigade. They couldn't dig in and wait for supplies. Even if the weather permitted, the enemy action would fend off the Dakotas.

Scottie's conference broke up, and an officer walked over to Badger, "The Colonel's decided not to push on to Sahmaw. We're returning to Padigahtawng. Your section will remain here as a rearguard for an half an hour. We will rest halfway and wait for you. If the Japs turn up we'll hear the firing and come back at the double. We'll leave you another man with a Bren, "Any questions, corporal?"

"No, sir."

"Us again! We always get the shitty end of the stick." Someone moaned as the column moved off.

"Shut up grousing." Badger snarled, "Spread out. Check the Bren gun."

"D'yer think I'm bloody stupid," the new Bren gunner, riled at having to stay behind, growled, "I've already checked it! Don't need the likes of you to tell me my job."

"Not so much lip." Badger snapped officiously, "Check it again!"

"About time you stopped being so shirty, Badger." Ginger grunted as the man checked the Bren, "You're a corporal not a general. We've not had a civil word out of you for days. We were all bloody good muckers until you got that letter. Now if anyone speaks to you, you just grunt or blow your top. If you've got wife trouble, you can't do anything about it until we get out. So snap out of it."

"Let me be, for Christ's sake." Sullen faced, he squirmed a yard or so further away from Ginger and for about ten minutes no one spoke. Life was miserable enough without his irascibility, and he wished he could obliterate the anguish that was gnawing his heart strings, and get back to the old chumminess that had carried them through so many privations.

"I've got to have a tom tit." Smudge Smith scrambled down the depression, hastily dragging off his equipment and undoing his trousers.

As Smudge squatted down Scofield, giving a slow whistle, pointed up the track to the shelf. A pot-helmeted Jap, strolling up to the Kachins, prodded the man's stomach with his rifle. The two children had their heads buried in the woman's longyi.

"Hold it!" Badger hissed as the Bren and rifles were aimed, "Don't want to hit the Kachins if we can help it, and he might be a scout. Let's see if any are following him."

The Kachin obviously knew where the section were, but he was agitatedly pointing in the opposite direction.

"God bless him!" Badger said under his breath, "Ah! Thought so."

The Jap turned round and waved his rifle. The Kachin family raced up into some thickets. A dozen Japs started uphill from the jungle below.

"Ho-o-old it!"

Too late. The Bren gun stuttered a short burst and jammed. Rifles cracked. The single Jap jerked, doubled up, and fled down the track. The Bren opened up again, and the rest of the Japs scurried back into the jungle.

"Cease fire!" Badger ordered and then glared at the Bren gunner, "You blithering..."

His castigation of the man was cut off by whoops of laughter, and loud guffaws. Smudge, doing a straddle leg hop, was scrambling up the slope. With one hand he was dragging his pack, equipment and rifle – with the other he was struggling to pull up his trousers. His penis and testicles were bouncing out of the 'v' of his unbuttoned flies, and half his milk white buttocks were sagging over his lop-sided waist band.

For the first time in days, Badger's sullen face gave way to a smile, "Dingle dangle, lads!" He was choking back tears of laughter and contrition, "All together..."

They all chorused with him, "Never let your dingle dangle in the dirt. Always keep your dingle covered by your shirt!"

With a satisfied grin Ginger winked at him, and Smudge was grinning broadly as he tucked away his genitals. Badger was 'one of the lads' again. Brooding about Barbara was pointless torment. Let her do the stewing and fretting. The brief comedy would be retold round their fires, and embroidered with each telling.

"Quiet, lads!" Finger on his lips, and nodding at some thickets, Badger pulled the pin from a grenade.

Someone – more than one – was thrashing towards them. The Kachin family broke out of the jungle close to their left, terror written on their faces. Badger lobbed the grenade, and their rifles and Bren raked the thickets. But there was no return fire. Either the Japs were not following the Kachins, or they had turned tail.

"All right corporal?" An officer, with a platoon at his heels, panted up to the section.

While Badger explained what had happened, a Burriff spoke to the Kachins and with the children skipping at his side, led them from the clearing along the Column's tracks.

"Give us five minutes, corporal," the officer said as the Burriff and the Kachins disappeared, "then if it's all clear, follow us. The Column's resting half a mile up the track."

It was more like ten minutes before they were able to move off after the officer. First one, then another had to slip down into the depression to relieve themselves. As Badger squatted, with Scofield on guard behind him, a wry smile creased his face. Even dysentery had its compensations. For days he'd been so loose that he didn't have to strain. It had been straining at Broadway that first forced out his semen, and he had not expelled even a drip since Blackpool.

§

The Column was already trudging into Padigahtawng when they caught it up. In the middle of the column were seven scarecrows of men in a tattered mixture of uniforms and Kachin clothing. They were chatting excitedly to the files in front of them, and to a dozen or so Kachins ambling along with them.

"Who are they, mate?"

"Six Gurkhas, and a BOR. The Kachins have been hiding

them from the Japs." A man at the rear of the column replied, "Some of 'em got left behind from Wingate's show last year, some escaped from POW camps."

Among the Kachins was a heavily pregnant woman, and the reminder of Barbara's pregnancy set the canker of anguish searing and tearing at Badger's guts. He knew he'd never be free from that gnawing, pit-of-the-guts bitterness.

"Bugger the two timing Bitch!"

"What d'yer say?" The man in front slewed his head round, and all but stumbled into the man in front of him.

"Nothing mucker, just thinking aloud." Love was a tyranny, a paranoia of tormented possessiveness. If she *was* a flirt he could believe her story – but she wasn't. He knew, as sure as he was dragging his feet through this bloody mud, that she had given herself in love. It was this – more than the copulation – that was salting his wound.

London, July 1944

Chapter Twenty-four

Barbara was glad to be in the fresh air, out of that smelly boarding house. It was a pleasant July morning as she strolled along Euston Road, towards Tottenham Court Road. This time of the morning the tube would be bursting at the seams with commuters and the three mile or so stroll from King's Cross to South Audley Street, would give her time to rehearse her enquiries. She was convinced it would be an acrimonious confrontation if Mrs. Brodie was there. She would be as tactful as she could but she had to prepare herself to parry any rancour, and to face up to any rebuff. What can you expect when you tell a wife you're her husband's pregnant mistress, and you've lost contact with him?

Twice, in the two years since their first week-end together in Hull, Brodie had brought her to London. How different this visit was to the other times. Then, they had stayed each time in a sumptuous Kensington hotel.

Last August, on the rebound from Brodie after another of their flaming rows, Barbara had spent five days and nights at the Ritz with Caleb. The ever generous, lanky Virginan horse breeder had taken her shopping at Harrod's. The fawning and purring sales assistants, calling her 'Modom', had pressed her to accept the hall-marked silver lighter that the greying-haired Colonel was offering to her as a keepsake.

And then there had been theatres, night-clubs, museums, all night parties. Now, alone and almost penniless, she was reduced to the damp, semi-basement of a squalid boarding house.

Euston Road was a congestion of vehicles. Nippy military jeeps, brashly zig zagging between taxis monopolised by American servicemen. Bunches of crowded buses, sandwiched between shambling horse-drawn delivery vans and carts. Strings of cyclists swerved and weaved through the rumbling profusion.

The pavements were a bustling mass of humanity. Men and women in all forms of Allied uniforms, British, American, Polish, Free French, Czech and Commonwealth hurrying to or from main line stations. A crocodile of children, hand in hand in pairs, was shuffling into St. Pancras station. Evacuees, labels on their coats and gas-mask boxes strung around their necks, clutched carrier bags and bulging school satchels. Some weeping, some excitedly chatting. Sorely tried teachers, or mothers, remonstrating them with dire, impotent threats to 'keep quiet and keep together – or else'. A repeat of 1939, but this time to safeguard them from Hitler's flying bombs.

Despondent beyond tears, Barbara watched mothers dabbing their eyes as, after a snatched hug, they nudged their offsprings into the hands of the registration women. What a cruel world to be bringing any child into – let alone her unwanted bairn.

As she turned into Tottenham Court Road, the entire throng – as if by Olympian command – halted in its tracks. All eyes trained on the heavens. Traffic jolted to a halt with a cacophany of tooting horns, and drivers pointed skywards.

With eyes watered by the sun, Barbara watched a demoniacal, flaming missile roar across the sky. Abruptly, beyond the frame of the Tottenham Court Road roof tops, the roar ceased. A brief and deathly silence. An ear splitting Boom! The explosion terminated the holy hush, and the figures instantly sprang to life. The movements resumed as if there had been no interruption.

The Normandy landings were less than a month old, but the high hopes and optimism of 'D' day had been dispelled by the loosing of Hitler's secret weapon, the rocket bombs on Britain. War weary Britons, and especially Londoners were, once again under bombardment. This time it was not squadrons of bombers. At all hours of the day or night, usually in advance of any warning sirens, flying bombs with flaming exhausts, roared through the sky. Already they were being scornfully dubbed ‘doodle bugs’. But Barbara saw it as a misnomer, British cynicism, belittling their terrifying flights and horrendous destruction. There was nothing doodling about them. Whenever they scorched the sky, taxis hooted warnings and pedestrians halted in mid pace, praying that the flame wouldn't die over their heads and plunge it to awesome detonation in their midst.

Crossing into Oxford Street she glanced her reflection in a shop window, and knotted the belt of her Burberry even tighter round her thickened waist. How could she hanker for – still love – that brute Leslie after he'd done this to her and then taken flight.

With a bitter, angry snigger at the heavens she snatched off her velour hat and shook out her hair. Quickening her pace, for no reason other than inner rage, she threaded and hustled her way along the crowded pavements. She should have had done with the bastard last year, after she vainly waited two hours for him at The Bell. What an Easter that had turned out to be. What a scene when he turned up at her quarters, next morning. No apology. Just some cock and bull story about being kept in the Control Tower all night. Bloody liar! He'd had a WAAF in his quarters most of the night.

She brushed blindly through a strolling couple, lost in the memory of that flaming row. White hot anger had surged through her. Friends and colleagues had poked their heads out of windows, as they slanged each other on her billet doorstep. After that vicious row, he had effrontery to expect her to spend that leave with him in the Lake district, as they'd originally planned. Sending him packing, had brought its rewards. Spending that leave at her parents' home and meeting Stefan, had given her a memorable fling.

Billeted at her parent's home the Polish officer had charmed the family with his old world chivalry, and fascinated them with his accent.

Irately Barbara tried to blink Stefan away, but he was still there. Would she never be free of that delightful wantonness? Here she was perversly savouring the immorality that had wrecked her life.

"Hi sugar! Where're you heading?" Two US soldiers were hurrying after her, and she realised she had been muttering aloud.

With a 'get lost' wave, she dodged into the subway lavatories at Oxford Circus. Spending her penny, eyes tightly closed, she tried to erase the memory of Stefan. The familiar longings were coursing through her. He was stealing into her bedroom. His wiry body pinning her to the mattress. Fingers snatching open her pyjamas. Startled from sleep, she had fought against his rape. She could, have screamed and wakened her parents. But her satanic hunger had been whetted. Desire had overwhelmed resistance, and they had feverishly stripped each other. Seven nights of surreptitious "fokking". Six days deceiving her parents. Feigning indifference during the day to Stefan, and wishing the hours away between their nightly romps.

She'd really had liked Stefan but when that fair skinned, cornflower blue eyed lover had left her parents' home, he'd slipped into the limbo of her past. She disliked – hated – Brodie, why couldn't she have done the same with him? Why the hell did she take up with him again after that Easter row?

Back on Oxford Street, she stalked haughtily past the two US soldiers, who were now handing packs of Camel cigarettes to two ATS girls outside a tobacconists. She needed cigarettes but the sign in in the cracked window, proclaiming 'Positively No Cigarettes To-day' meant she'd have to try elsewhere. One of the girls, seeing her hesitate to read the sign, caught Barbara's sleeve.

"Here mum, you can have one of my packs." Brushing aside Barbara's offer to pay, she added, "That's alright duck they've cost me nowt." Winking, as the foursome strolled into Regent Street, the girl called over her shoulder, "So far, anyway."

Walking on along Oxford Street, glancing in shop windows, diagonally braced with anti-shatter wires or parcel tape, Barbara thought that, before the war, she could have spent hours dreamily window shopping along a street such as this. Nowadays, the windows that were not completely shuttered, were sparsely filled. Wartime austerity had degenerated into national penury.

The meagre displays of crockery offered no more than could be bought in any village shop. All made of identical thick, plain white china. Squat crudely-moulded cups, and equally crude saucers.

Putting on her velour, and adjusting it in a window reflection, she grimaced at a display of utility furniture. Serviceable maybe, but depressingly inelegant. Only three designs to choose from. You couldn't even have an upholstered three piece suite. Worse, she gave her reflection a wan smile, unless you were a newly wed or bombed out, you couldn't get a docket to buy a single stick of furniture. Idly totting up the units required for each piece, she calculated that the permitted 30 units would get you three dining chairs, a table, a fireside chair, a wardrobe and a bed, but no sideboard or dressing table. You could not even have an easy chair – in lieu of any other piece – because manufacture of them was prohibited.

That's one problem she didn't have. She really must overcome these mind-blocking distractions, and get her stall set out for the imminent confrontation. The thought of meeting Mrs. Brodie, the imminent closeness of it, instantly parched her throat.

Turning abruptly from the window, she collided with a pram loaded with raspberries and plums.

"Er, missus, no queue jumping." The youthful street trader was doing a roaring trade. Even with plums at '...two bob a pound and rasps one and a tanner a half...' people, bunched around the pram, were jostling each other for his extortionate goods. Looking cheekily at Barbara, as she backed out of the crowd, he called after her, "...sell you this bleeding pram for a tenner missus, arter this lot's gone."

Hurrying away from the trader, she turned into a side street, found a sandwich bar in a back area of Bond Street, and bought a cup of tea.

With a Camel cigarette in her mouth, she rummaged through her handbag for the slim silver lighter Caleb had given her. Dear honest Caleb. He'd made no secret about missing his lovely 'statesides' wife. Made it clear from the start that their time together at the Ritz was purely a 'no strings attached' *affaire*.

Weatherless, bitter sweet visions of their time together flooded back. Light hearted 'Somewhere over the rainbow' days, romantic 'Nightingale in Berkeley Square' nights.

She found the lighter tucked in her newly acquired civilian ration book. The green, expectant mother's book was a constant, distressing reminder to her of the ignominy of her discharge from the service. None of the officers had openly maligned her. But the instantly silenced chatter of so called friends, whenever she'd came within earshot, exposed their hypocrisy. They were all sanctimonious sods. All that is except dear Mary.

With the ration book in her lap, drawing deeply on the cigarette, her mind remorselessly dragged her back in time. Back over the raptures and sufferings of her on and off relationship with Brodie. The nostalgia of Caleb's unfailing solicitousness, mingled wth the memory of the vituperative row with Brodie.

What were they thinking of, picking that vainglorious sod Brodie as an aide to the top air force brass for the Anglo-American Quebec conference last August? The unmitigated pompousness of Leslie when, with new squadron leader's insignia, he squired her round when he came down for that pre-conference briefing at the Air Ministry. How could she have basked in the reflected esteem of such a prig?

She'd been bloody daft to take him back after that August afternoon in their Kensington suite. The fury in his eyes when he had unexpectedly walked in, just as she was picking up the letter and the official looking postcard from the bottom of the wardrobe. She hadn't had time to read them. Hadn't intended to. All she'd had time to see, before he viciously snatched them from her, was the South Audley Street address embossed on the letter, and a Red Cross symbol on the postcard. Her's were the only clothes in the wardrobe at the time. It was obvious they'd slipped from his pocket *before* he went out. But still he had accused of going through his belongings. Called her a lying cow! Grilled her about what she'd seen!

Later that afternoon, when he'd calmed down a little and told her to be ready to go out in half an hour, she'd refused to do so until he apologised. His refusal to apologise had aggravated the tension. Her outburst of recriminations climaxed with her screaming, in the crudest expletives, about his 'bits on the side'.

Reflectively now, sipping her tea, she rubbed her cheek. She could still feel the sting as his clout reeled her against the wall, and, in the crudest language she had ever heard, he'd told her to get out of his life. When, calling his bluff, she'd telephoned for a taxi, the sod had made no effort to stop her.

How humiliated she had felt, that evening, asking for a room at the Regent Palace Hotel. Unaccompanied women, especially with no luggage other than a vanity case, and no advance reservation, were undesirables in hotels overburdened with pleasure seeking service-men. Only when she produced her RAF record book did the wary receptionist allocate her a room, "...only for to-night and payment in advance...'

Later in the cocktail bar, Caleb, with his 'hail fellow well met' American open-heartedness, had charmed her out of her misery. Thinking about it, she absently lit another cigarette. It seemed incredible that to somehow spite Brodie in absentia, she could have agreed so readily, to move in with Caleb at the Ritz for the remaining five days of her leave.

After all that, she was back with Brodie within a month of his return from Quebec. Bloody fool that she was. Rushing to his hospital bed when he'd pranged his M.G. and was on the critical list. Soaking in his contrite pleas, trusting his pious pledges of love, when he was doped with pain-killers. Endlessly commiserating with him, when he was convalescing, about his permanent limp, and his wrecked beyond repair M.G. Then those months of slipping away together at every possible opportunity. Until the bombshell of her pregnancy.

She never had understood why he had been so furious that afternoon in Kensington. Except on her second visit to the hospital, when he blamed it on the stress and tension of preparing for that conference, they'd never mentioned it again.

Well, it was all water under the bridge.

Now she had to steel herself to confront his wife.

Chapter Twenty-five

Standing nervously in front of the red brick Georgian porch, Barbara could not summon the courage to pull the polished brass bell knob. For the past half hour, she'd walked up and down the opposite side of South Audley Street, rehearsing her enquiry. She'd convinced herself that it would be an acrimonious confrontation. She had steeled herself to cross over to the stately house but her resolve had wilted and, as she turned to walk away, the door opened and she froze in her shoes.

"What can I do for you, young lady?" The tall, corpulent be-medalled general's eye twinkled as he brushed his bristling, grey moustache.

"Excuse me, sir," She had to fight the constriction in her throat to sound casual, "I'm trying to trace a Squadron Leader Brodie."

The general looked non-plussed, bewildered.

"Er, this is Khyber House?"

"That it is, me dear." His kindly eyes swept Barbara's swollen figure, "But you won't find him here."

"This is the address he gave me." She lied.

"Oh, he did, did he?" His brows shot up in astonishment.

"What's the damn fellah up to now." Gruffly, and with a tinge of admonition, "Hope that damn reprobate's not a friend of yours, young lady. Uh, squadron leader now is he? Damn fellah!"

Barbara felt the colour draining from her cheeks before his shrewd gaze. Her lips mouthed a reply, but her voice was silent.

"Don't be frightened I'm not going to eat you." Standing aside, he motioned her to step indoors, "I'm off out me dear, but me daughter is in the drawing room. She might be able to help you. Go along, second door on the left." As Barbara hesitantly walked up the hall, he called, "Pru! There's a young woman to see you. Looking for Brodie. In a bit of trouble I should think. Bye! See you to-night!"

The high ceiling of the drawing room was huge. Its bare walls and floor, except for a tiger skin rug in front of the Adam fireplace, lent it the atmosphere of a deserted ball-room. The only furnishings in the room were two shabby, brown hide armchairs, a matching Chesterfield sofa and coffee table, set around the rug. The only splash of colour was a vase of flowers in the empty fireplace.

At the rear of the room, shafts of dust laden sunlight were streaming through the French windows. At the other end a fair haired woman, in a finely tailored khaki FANY uniform, was feather dusting the faded blue velvet curtains of the small street window.

"Do come in – have a chair – be with you in a sec." Her 'jolly hockey stick' voice was pure Rodean and Girton. Her chubby face had the typical peaches and cream complexion of a 'Tatler' debutante. Her hair was swept up into a neatly plaited bun, on the crown of her head.

"Sorry for intruding like this." Bearing her weight on her toes to deaden the clack of her heels on the parquet floor added to Barbara's sense of intrusion.

Nervously perching on the edge of one of the chairs, she glanced wistfully at the woman's 'V' shaped back. Only her cheeks were chubby. Brodie's hands, she thought, must easily have spanned the a tiny waist cinched by the tunic belt. The legs, as she walked over to the sofa, had an enviable feline gracefulness that, even in khaki lisle stockings, lent her ankles a sensual elegance.

"So, you're looking for Leslie Brodie?" The woman's lively hazel eyes momentarily focused on Barbara's thickened waist, then compassionately settled on her visitor's strained face, "His? Miss, ah Mrs..." Her dimpled chin gestured at Barbara's waist.

"Barbara Dixon." Dodging the marital disclosure, and the woman's pitying eyes, she unknotted the belt of her Burberry.

"Yes, I'm afraid its... he is the father."

"But why come here?" There was no hint of shock, only puzzlement, in the woman's knitted brows.

"I'm afraid I lied to the general. Leslie didn't give me this address..."

"Oh, that was daddie, but I still don't see why you are here."

"I remembered this address from a letter he carried, Mrs..."

"Miss. Sorry I'm Pru – Prudence really – but of course everyone calls me Pru, and I prefer that. So that's how you got it." Watching the dawning of comprehension in Pru's eyes, Barbara's mind flashed back to the letter and the Red Cross post card Leslie had snatched from her in their Kensington Hotel room.

"He said his wife lived in London, so I'm here." She nodded at Pru's uniform, "Said she was a FANY"

"Ah. So you think I'm Mrs. Brodie?" Pru leaned back in the sofa and eyed Barbara suspicously, defensively.

"And you're not married to him?" Abstractedly Barbara toyed with the wedding ring that, since her pregancy became obvious, had been back on her finger. What was this woman's connection with Brodie then? He was obviously no stranger to Pru and her father.

"No, of course not!" Smirking, scornful, "So if you've come here for revenge – to break up a marriage – you've come to the wrong place, my girl!"

"Nothing of the sort!" Anger flushed her cheeks, and her fists clenched, "True, I came to see his wife, but he told me you... or whoever she is, were separated and going to get a divorce. All I want is to get in touch with him. Revenge won't help me!"

"You poor, trusting soul." The tone was sympathetic. The smirk had given way to a commiserating smile, "It'll be no consolation to you, but I was besotted by him once. Was even going to marry him. So now he's gone to ground has he?"

Barbara acknowledged the sympathy with a rueful nod. Haltingly at first, she spoke of her affair with Brodie. Then, as Pru's sisterly probing gained her confidence, the whole story tumbled out.

Last February, when her pregnancy was still in doubt, she'd

caught the MO watching her intently. Her breasts had been prickly and, sitting at her desk, she was unconsciously rubbing them through her shirt with the inside of her wrists. Abstractedly she demonstrated the action to Pru.

Pru nodded, "Yes, I've heard that's a first sign of incipient pregnancy. I suppose then he tipped off Brodie?"

"I think so, but Leslie never mentioned it. When I broke the news to him, he promised to stick by me whatever happened, and persuaded the MO to give me some liquid extract of Ergot."

She shuddered at the recollection. The high dosage had violently, but vainly, contracted her uterus. Later, Mary had poured glasses of gin and ground nutmeg into her, and dunked her alternately in steaming hot and freezing baths.

After missing two periods, Mary had taken her to a back street doctor in Hull. Stumbling out her tale to Pru, she shuddered again with revulsion. The weasel man, after probing inside her, had unneccesarily, lingeringly, palpated her breasts. She had suffered his lechering hands in the hope he would agree to do an abortion. Then, when she had replied to his questions in clinical nursing terms, and mentioned the Ergot, he had become brusqely professional. He had ordered Mary to get her out of his surgery, and not to try compromising a doctor again.

"A week later Brodie disappeared, and I've not seen him since."

"So, you think the senior commanders spirited him away, hoping to avert a scandal?"

Barbara nodded forlornly. Prudence, hands in her hip pockets, walked across the rug to lean against the Adam mantlepiece.

"Sorry, I can only offer you a sherry." Her hands gestured round the sparsely furnished room, "We sent everything down to our Wiltshire place, for the duration – for safety. Daddie and I stay here alone and always eat out. We've a couple of cots in the wine cellar."

"Thank you, no. But do you mind if I smoke?" Barbara had almost chain smoked through the distress of the last five months.

"Not at all, have one of these." Pru flipped open a gold cigarette case, "You've not even heard from him since?"

"No." Barbara inhaled deeply, as Prudence held the flame of her gold lighter to her cigarette, then smiled sardonically, "I've tried everything. Oh they all put on a show of sympathy, 'Sorry, regulations and all that. We aren't allowed to disclose officers' whereabouts, but let us have a letter. We'll see it's forwarded to him'. All that rot. I've written a dozen, and he hasn't replied." She stared down morosely at her nicotined fingers, the skin roughened by pumice stone attempts to remove the staining, "I heard a whisper that he was at the Air Ministry, and hung around there for a couple of day's in the hope of seeing him. I even made enquiries at the Australian High Commission. Same old stone-walling."

"You poor thing." Prudence clicked her tongue and shook her head, "He really is a cad."

"He isn't married then?"

"Oh, he's married alright, but not to me." Returning to the sofa, Pru stared astutely at Barbara as if considering how much she should confide to this stranger, "I'd better tell you." Frowning thoughtfully, she blew smoke rings to the ceiling for a few moments, "He told me he was a widower – wife died just before the war. Daddie never trusted him, but I wouldn't listen. Thought it was just because he was afraid that wedding a 'colonial' – as he calls all Aussies, Canadians and the like - would be marrying beneath me, and couldn't bear the thought of my emigrating *apres le guerre*." Kicking off her shoes, she tucked her ankles underneath her thighs, "He was right of course. He saw Brodie going into the Savoy arm in arm with Joyce.."

"Ah!" Barbara's brows knotted questioningly, "The Hon. Joyce, the Wren?"

"She's an old college chum. Anyway daddie didn't tell me at the time. He might look Blimpish, but he's a wily old bird, and checked out Leslie on the old boy network. Found his wife is still alive..."

"In Australia?"

"No. She's an American." The voice was trenchant, but it was manifested by disdain for Brodie, not his wife's nationality, "She's in the American Red Cross. A prisoner of war. Captured in Bataan."

"The lying ..." Words failed Barbara as the reason for his fury, last August, hit her. The postcard must have been a Red Cross POW notification.

"There isn't a word vile enough, my dear. Naturally I called the wedding off. Daddie, bless him, got all my love letters back..."

"But what about the one I saw? With this address on?" If her own plight hadn't long since exhausted her tears, her eyes would have moistened with compassion.

"Ah, that couldn't have been a love letter." Pru lips stretched in a cynical grin, "I checked them all before burning them. The one you saw must have been my demand for the return of £200."

"You loaned him £200?" Her brows shot up in astonishment. It was a small fortune, nearly a year's pay, "For what?"

"To buy an M.G. – fool that I was. Never got the money back." Getting to her feet she said, "None of this is helping you. I'll make some tea whilst I put my thinking cogs to work." Putting her cigarette case on the occasional table, she added, "Help yourself if you feel like another.

§

The teapot was hallmarked silver, but the sugar basin and cups, without handles, were the same crude china Barbara had seen the shops.

"Milk?" Pru had the milk bottle poised over the cups. Barbara nodded.

"Help yourself to sugar." Genteelly stirring her tea, Pru thoughtfully studied her visitor's finely drawn face, "Before I make any effort to help you, Barbara, I must be sure of two things. First, do you mind if I tell Daddie, in strict confidence of course, all that you've told me?"

"Not at all, if you think it will help." She wondered how the general could help, "And the other thing?"

"If we find him, are you out for revenge, blackmail? Because if you are, I'm not going to get involved."

"No I'm not after anything like that, I promise." With

guileless eyes she held Pru's, "But there are pactical things to be settled. Maternity costs, the child's maintenance. I won't be able to work and look after a baby. I've no place of my own. Can't go home to my parents – daren't tell them. Then there'll be the birth registration formalities.

It wasn't the entire truth. There would be revenge. If Brodie wasn't man enough to live up to his responsibilities, there'd be no life for either him or her. Covertly she squeezed her handbag weighted by the pearl handled .22 that Caleb had given her for safe custody until he returned to England. He'd been culling his personal belongings, parcelling them to send to the States and wouldn't include the gun because of the risk of customs examination. Foolish Caleb had been an Embassy aide, a safe post, but had, after persistent applications, secured a combatant posting to Italy.

"Your parents don't know? Aren't you living with them?"

"No, I've not been home since it started to show." She patted her stomach, "I rented an apartment in Hull." She wasn't going to tell Pru that she only had a bed-sitter in a cheap lodging house.

"You are married?" Eyes on Barbara's wedding ring." Where's he? Does he know?"

"He's in Burma. I wrote to tell him about two months ago."

"Oh, my God. Poor chap. What a ghastly thing to learn about when you're thousands of miles away. What was his reaction?"

"I Don't know." What badger decided to do about her was the least of her troubles. The real worry was what the 'Dear John' would do to the self confidence – the frail ego – of that innocent lad, "Don't know whether he even received the letter." Her lips trembled, "Or – God forbid – if he's still alive."

"Two months, and you haven't heard from him!" Pru put her cup swiftly on the table, and looked askance, scèptically, at Barbara.

"All I've had are these." She took an aerogramme from her bag, and handed it to Pru.

As Pru read it Barbara visualised every word, every comma, of the brief stereotype aerogramme.

Dear *Madam*

IT IS PROBABLE THAT YOU WILL NOT RECEIVE ANY LETTERS FROM YOUR *Husband* NUMBER 02574677 RANK *CPL* NAME *DIXON, A.* FOR SOME TIME TO COME. THIS DOES NOT MEAN THAT HE IS UNWELL. FOR THE PRESENT HOWEVER THE TYPE OF OPERATIONS IN WHICH HE IS TAKING PART MAKE IT IMPOSSIBLE FOR HIM TO WRITE TO YOU, BUT HE WILL AS SOON AS HE CAN.

PLEASE HOWEVER GO ON WRITING TO HIM, AS YOUR LETTERS WILL GREATLY CHEER HIM, AND PLEASE ASK HIS RELATIVES AND FRIENDS TO WRITE TOO. IF YOU USE HIS NORMAL POSTAL ADDRESS, YOUR LETTERS WILL BE DELIVERED.

UNTIL HE CAN WRITE TO YOU HIMSELF, A LETTER SIMILAR TO THIS WILL BE SENT TO YOU ONCE A MONTH.

CAPTAIN

"Cheer him indeed! Even the 'Dear Johns'?" Pru's eyes were as rebuking as her words, as she handed the letter back, "How long have been receiving these?"

"Since March."

"Nearly five months! There he is involved in some dangerous work, in some God forsaken land, and you send him a 'Dear John'. Why didn't you wait until the operations, whatever they are, are over. That aerogramme was virtually pleading you to keep up his morale."

"I know. Perhaps I should have waited. It was a cowardly way, but not for the reason you apparently think." The self-reproach in Barbara's tone brought a soothing pat on her knee from Pru, "You can't imagine how awful it was keeping it bottled up inside me. Tossing and turning through nightmares of Apocalyptic retribution. Days of melancholy dilemma – to write or not to write. I'd have preferred to tell him personally. Faced up to the brunt of his anger, got it over and done with, in one fell swoop. But I fretted that he might come back maimed. Imagine a broken man coming home, his future pinned on the loving wife he expected to be waiting for him, only to find a stranger with a child. What would we do then?" Her tongue ran around her trembling lips, "Then it was, 'what if he was killed?' The fear that he might be. And God forgive me, I began to hope that he would be. I can't honestly say I love him, but that doesn't mean I don't feel anything for him. Men like him are the salt of the earth. It was his class that won the Empire, for the upper classes to rule over."

The tongue wet her lips again, as she looked meaningfully at Pru, "That made my mind up. The 'Dear John' quashed any motive for wishing him dead. That's what I meant by cowardly. Salving my conscience if something did happen to him."

"It was cruel of me criticise you." Pru had accepted the jibe at her class with an indulgent nod, "I'm sorry, but I was so shocked at the callousness of keeping men isolated for so long. Anyway what is he in? Some damned secret service? Odd he can get your letters, but you can't get his." With a puzzled frown she added, "I suppose they parachute them in, but if they can't get letters out – what do they do with the wounded."

"God only knows, it puzzles me too. He wrote, when they were training, that they were Special Force." She wrinkled her brow, trying to recall some other designation, "Chindits. That's it, Wingate's Chindits."

"That's irony for you." Pru handed her another cigarette, took one herself, and fanned the fresh smoke away from her face, "Daddie told me those operations were planned in Quebec. Brodie behind the scenes, your husband in firing line. Pity Wingate was killed, Daddie says he was hated by the top brass, but worshipped by his troops. Beat the Japs hands down at their own game."

"Badger – my husband – said his battalion would follow Wingate into hell. Now I think of it, even Brodie was full of praise for him. 'A Pom with fire in his belly' he called him."

"You surely didn't tell your husband the whole truth?" The hazel eyes pleaded for a negative answer, "You know... about loving Brodie – having a long affair with him?"

"No, of course not. Rightly, or wrongly, I persuaded myself it would be kinder to let him think it was a drunken moment of madness. A once only, inebriated hole-in-the corner snogging, with a man I hardly knew."

"I'm sure you did the right thing. Bad enough for him to be told you're pregnant, even more shattering to be told you'd loved and slept with another man. Especially when he isn't able to vent his wrath on you, nor confront the other man."

Meditatively staring into Barbara's eyes, Pru handed her another cup of tea, "Look, I'm not promising anything, but maybe Daddie can run him to earth through the old boy network. How can I get in touch with you? What's your hotel telephone number?"

"I don't know, there are no 'phones in the rooms." It was true. If there was any telephone at all, it must be in the proprietor's private parlour. She didn't want this upper class woman to know she was staying in a tatty boarding house, "It's not very private receiving calls in the reception area." There was no such area, "Can I 'phone you?"

"Yes, all right." Prudence froze in the act of taking a pad out of her tunic pocket.

Both women's eyes were fixed on the ceiling. White faced, they listened to the VROOM, like the open exhausts of half a dozen motor-cycles, passing overhead. For what seemed an age, they sat motionless, ears cocked for an explosion that never came.

"More than one, I think, this time. Relax Barbara, they've overshot London, or been knocked off course by a Spitfire." With a sigh of relief, she scribbled on the note-pad. "Those Spit pilots are wizard. Saw one the other day tip a doodle bug off course with his wing tips." Handing the note to Barbara she said, "Ring me at this number about 1600 hrs. each day and I'll let you know if we've had any luck. It's the Duke of York's HQ Chelsea. Make sure you ask for that extension." Passing the pad to Barbara she added, "Write your hotel address, just in case I need it."

Barbara scibbled the name and the address of the non-descript King's Cross boarding house and handed the pad back.

§

Barbara pulled aside the basement's dingy net curtains. The pavement was just below eye level, and she stared forlornly along the glistening street. The rain had stopped, and there were azure patches in the grey-black overcast of the double summertime twilight.

Except for a woman carrying a baby and with two school children in tow, the street was deserted. The children, trotting behind the woman, each held a handle of a bulging shopping bag. Two Thermos flasks were poking out of the bag, and she guessed they were making for the tube station for a night's refuge from the doodle bugs.

A taxi drew up across the street, and her heart skipped a beat. But it wasn't Brodie. With a despondent sigh she watched a woman pay off the taxi, and turned from the window.

Would Brodie keep his word this time? He was already an hour overdue. Half of her was terrified by what she may be driven to do if he came. The other half was anguished, nauseous, by what she would force herself to do if he didn't come.

The gas fire was guttering, a sure sign that the the coin box needed another contribution. It was early July but, even with the fire, the semi-basement room seemed like an ice-box. As she crouched to put another shilling in the box, one hand on the damp mottled wallpaper to steady her ponderous body, the slimy paper slipped under hand, almost throwing her off balance.

Plopping down in the rickety basket chair, she clutched the Burberry tightly over her swollen stomach.

What had she come to? She'd no more tears to shed. She couldn't even vent her misery by wailing 'what have I done to deserve this!' She knew damn well what she'd done to deserve it. Drained of remorse, gazing with unseeing eyes at the chipped wash-basin and verdigris taps, she brooded about her immorality. Remorse would neither undo the past, nor restore her future happiness – even if she could feel truly contrite.

For there to be any future at all, if Brodie turned up, he had to agree to share her burden. If he wouldn't, both of their futures would be measured in hours. If he didn't show up, she would end her own future at mid-night.

God, how depressingly different this visit to London was from the other times. Twisting an empty cigarette packet in her hands, a chain smoking spectre of Caleb flickered around the broken clay elements of the fire. Dear, dead Caleb. What a luxurious haven that regency furnished suite had been. How they'd waltzed along the richly carpeted Ritz corridors that dawn, humming 'Two sleepy people', oblivious of the page boys laying freshly polished shoes outside each room.

Now here she was, almost penniless, absolutely friendless and cigarette-less in crummy lodgings. Her Driffield quarter had been a palace compared to this gloomy room. Just looking at the grubby quilt and lumpy mattress on the truckle bed made her feel itchy.

Her vanity case was on the bed. Her only pair of shoes were drying by the fire, and the cracked linoleum floor chilled her feet as she padded over. She had chain smoked through the last three months. She had no apetite, but there was a cellophane wrapped sandwich in the case. It was no substitute for her nicotine hunger, but eating would take her mind off cigarettes for a while.

Back in the chair, munching the sandwich, she mulled over that afternoon's telephone call to Prudence. The general had worked fast. In two days, he'd found out what she had been trying to find out for months.

"Don't know how he did it," Pru had said. "Not only has he run Brodie to earth, he also made him promise to see you. Not too soon either. Leslie's due to leave for New Guinea to-morrow."

Wheels within bloody wheels, Barbara almost screamed to the ceiling. Someone had been pulling more strings to spirit him further out of her reach. Anyway, according to Pru, he should have been here an hour ago. He could not have got lost. The place was not difficult to find, and she'd have seen him if he had walked up the street.

When she had hurried back after the 'phone call, her bladder was bursting, but the chubby landlady in a pinafore of bleached flour sacks, had waylaid her. The chatty cockney, leg-o-mutton arms folded across her mantle-shelf bosom, was in the lobby looking up at three men and two women, who were halfway up the stairs.

"Shime ain't it, duck," she flicked her chin at the stairs. "Mr. Dobson, him in the black trilby, just buried 'is mum. Heart attack they say, only fifty. Broken heart more like it. If you arsks me she pined away for her old man. He parssed away last year. Married thirty years, so they said. Strangers, never seen 'em afore. The expectant one's 'is wife. Other three's her mum, dad and brother. They're Channel Islanders. Escaped to England jest afore the Jerries invaded it. Work in the docks. Had a council house in somewhere in East 'Am 'til it was 'it by a doodle bug last week. They're going to move up north next week. Best out 'er London with these doodle bugs about. Wish we could..."

Fidgetting from one foot to another, Barbara had no alternative, short of being downright rude, but to listen to the woman's tales of the Blitz.

"...me and my old man used to sleep in the cellar. Your room before my old man – clever wiv his hands 'e is – did it up and made it cosy. A'course any guests were welcome to bring down their bedding, and join us when the Jerries came over. Yes we made 'em comfy, gave 'em tea and sarnies. Didn't charge 'em. Well anyone 'rarnd 'ere will tell you we looks after our guests, duck..."

The nearest w.c. was on the first floor, and Barbara gazed longingly up the staircase. Please God don't let it be occupied. In the distress that only a pregnant woman experiences, Barbara oh'd and ah'd and vainly tried to cut short the woman's ramblings with repeated, "excuse me, must go..." pleas. The sickening reek of boiling cabbage was adding to her distress.

"...if these 'orrible doodle bugs don't stop, me and my old man will 'ave to move back into your room. A'course if you're still 'ere we'll find you another room. We're not the sort to throw you into the street for our own ends. Two more buzzed over s'arternoon. D'ja hear 'em? Sounded like they hit Holloway and Camden."

Barbara could hold herself in check no longer,

"Sorry, bursting to pee."

She brushed passed the woman and, halfway up the stairs, heard the woman call, "Gawd bless me love, you should 'ave said so." Then, in awed tones, "The one that hit the Guards' Chapel, Wellington Barracks, the other day, killed 200 while they were at prayers... poor buggers."

The wooden lavatory seat was split in two and the coconut matting reeked of stale male urine

Back in the basement, washing the sandwich down with tap water, she shuddered at the thought that she'd soon have go up there again.

Anxiously she peered again into the street. It was still deserted, and soon she would have to put up the black-out shutters. For a few minutes, she restlessly padded about the small room and then, fully clothed, lay on the bed.

"If only I had someone close like dear Mary, to talk to." Closing her eyes, she relived Mary's compasionate hug when she'd first told the Irish girl of her pregnancy. Dear, supportive Mary. Nobody could have done more to help her terminate the pregnancy. Now she was with her battery, in some restricted south coast district.

Footsteps on the stairs jolted her bolt upright. Her stomach tensed as she contrived a poker-faced welcome.

But it wasn't Brodie.

"You in there missus?" The landlord rapped on the door, "Time you had the black out up."

"Yes, all right, I'll put them up now." Bet he has a cigarette. Never seen him without a fag in his mouth, dropping ash on that scruffy white muffler round his scraggy neck, "Excuse me," she called out, "could you let me have some cigarettes, I'll pay you."

"Got 10 Kensitas upstairs, I'll get 'em." The voice was unusually chummy, "You can get me a packet to-morrow, dear."

Hearing him almost running up and down the stairs, she guessed at what he hoped to see when he brought in the cigarettes.

With a cursory knock, he sidled into the room. His expectant grin instantly vanished when he saw she was fully dressed, and had her coat on. Swollen as she was, she was still attractive enough to turn most men's heads, and she'd caught this cockney sparrow of a man ogling her on dozens of occasions.

"You goin' out, dear?" More than a hint of chagrin, then hopefully, "Nice pub near Copenhagen Street I could show yer."

"Thank you. It's very kind of you, but I'm waiting in for a ...for my husband."

"Yer can't have him staying 'ere." Officiously, "An we've no vacant double rooms."

"Oh no, it'll only be a short visit. He's on duty. Thank you again for the cigarettes, I'll get you a packet tomorow morning."

Giving the landlord an appreciative smile, she held the door open for him. He opened his mouth to say something, changed his mind, and eyed her suspiciously as he backed out of the room.

It was still light enough to see the whole length of the Edwardian street and before she put up the hardboard shutters, she glanced hopefully along the deserted pavements.

Sat in the chair, toasting her feet in front of the fire, she took her silver lighter from her handbag, lit a cigarette and threw the bag towards the bed. It missed and slipped to the floor spilling most of its contents. Lipsticks, a comb, compact, ration book and and air-mail letter, lay around the pearl handled .22 automatic. Stuffing everything, except the letter, back in the bag she returned to the chair, and blindly stared at the note clipped to the letter.

She knew every word of that poignant note. It had arrived the day after she had sent the 'Dear John'. With tear filled eyes, she had read it scores of times before, fruitlessly seeking comfort from the knowledge that her own suffering was minor compared to that of thousands of other women.

Dear Sergeant Dixon,

Your letter, enclosed, was re-directed to me by the US Army mail service, after my wonderful husband was killed on 21st.January, whilst leading his men in the assault across the Rapido, (Italy).

I do not know who you are, or what your association with Caleb was, because I refuse to open your letter, but the handwriting suggests you are a woman.

We had twenty wonderfully happy years together. He was the most adorable, caring husband, and worshipping father to our two sons and daughter, and a highly repected member of this community. Frankly, I suspect the contents of your letter might sully my wonderful memories of him, and what my eyes do not see my heart will not grieve. His memory will aways be pure for me and I give thanks to our dear Lord for blessing me with Caleb's love.

I am not putting my address on this letter. If I have misjudged you, forgive me, but I don't want any replies. You see, if I have not misjudged you it is unlikely I will ever hear from you, and this way, whatever your relationship was, I can believe there was nothing improper between you. You do see what I mean. Leave me in blissful ignorance, please.

Yours truly,

N.----

What a blessing she'd put 'Sgt. B. Dixon' and not 'Mrs' above her Driffield address on the back of the air-letter. It was little more than a 'thank you' for the parcel of oranges that, somehow, Caleb had sent her through the US Army PX, but any wife, 'reading between the lines', would have realised the endearing terms signified much more than a platonic relationship. Caleb's wife could have destroyed the letter, but the poor grieving woman had obviously been determined to prove she had not read the letter.

She lit another cigarette from the stub of the previous one, slipped on her shoes, shoved the letters back in her bag, and put the automatic in her Burberry pocket. She could put off another visit to the insanitary w.c. no longer and with no lock on the door, Brodie – or anyone – could walk in and find the gun in her bag.

On the way back down to her room, she stealthily opened the front door and surveyed the street. She was suprised that it was still light enough to see both ends of the street. Two special constables, with casually measured tread, were patrolling along the pavements in opposite directions, probably looking – prematurely she thought – for 'blackout' infringements. Still no sign of Brodie.

Back in her room, she paced about the cramped basement, shoulders slumped, one hand deep in the gun pocket, cigarette in the other. She had smoked two, or three more, when she heard voices in the lobby overhead. Her heart skipped a beat. Her stomach tensed. There was no mistaking Leslie's baritone. Swiftly stubbing out the cigarette, and hastily fanning smoke heavenward, she pressed an ear to the door.

"Darn here sir, foller me please, careful sir, the lino's torn." The ferret of a landlord was clearly awed by the newcomer. She could imagine him forelocking Leslie, all the way down the stairs.

"Are you there, missus?" Unctuously, gently tapping the door. Like a 5 star hotelier he annouced, "Squadron Leader Brodie wishes to see yer."

Nervously combing her fingers through her hair, and tugging creases from her coat, she backed up to the window.

"Come in."

Leslie, leaning on a walking stick, limped in. The landlord, hand on the knob of the open door and cigarette in his mouth, slyly glanced over at Barbara, then servilely looked up at Leslie.

"Thank you, we won't be long. I'll show the Squadron Leader out." Barbara's dismissive tone was lost on the fawning ferret.

"If you'd told me yer husband's a real war hero, I'd 'ave given you the best room." Squaring his bony shoulders, he snatched off his greasy cap, as if suddenly remembering his manners, "Nothing too good for our lads in blue. Wanted to be one myself. Too young for the 14/18 lot – Chest too bad for this." He forced a croupy cough that sprinkled cigarette ash on to his muffler, "Like a cup of tea, sir?"

Leslie shook his head, and gestured the landlord out with a flick of his stick. The top of his cap brushed the low ceiling and leaning heavily on his stick with both hands, Leslie's eyes briefly met hers, and swept her figure.

"Late as usual. Typical of you." She had to steel herself to be curt. The months since they last met had aged him. His face was paler, the lean cheeks were almost gaunt, and there were grey strands in the the black hair at his temples. Only the arrogance still in his eyes, and his indolent stance, held her from rushing into his arms.

"Well, I'm here now!" Belligerently, "You should know better than to expect me to be punctual." He shifted the weight on his feet, and squinted meaningfully at the chair.

"That stick won't get you any pity here." Leaving him standing, she sat in the chair and looked coldly up at him, "You don't need it." Scoffingly, "Haven't needed it since you finished convalescence." Her knowledge of him, rather than her medical experience told her it was an affectation. An ice-breaker when chatting up a woman. A conversation piece. A pity enticer.

"So now you're an orthopaedic specialist!" Signalling towards the bed with his stick, his limped over to it, "Don't mind if I sit, do you."

"If you must." Same presumptious Brodie. His limp was so patently exaggerated, that she had difficulty in suppressing a snicker.

"I suppose you are after a war disability pension." The set of his jaw, and the defensively downcast his eyes told her she'd struck a raw nerve. It would not be stretching the truth too far to claim it an 'on duty' injury. If he had not drunk so much that night – after the Group briefing at Leconfield – he might not have wrecked the car, and himself, driving back to Driffield.

Studiously avoiding her eyes, he probed a crack in the lino with his stick.

"Now you've got me here, what do want?"

"Need you ask?" Barbara dug her fingers in her swollen tummy, "I want to know what you're going to do about this!"

Still with his eyes on the point of his stick, he muttered, "Why should I do anything? Even if you do have friends in high places."

"What do you mean by that?"

"Aw, c'mon, we both know I'm only here now because your Air Vice-Marshal friend threatened me with half a dozen courts-martial charges." For the first time since he came into the room, he quirked that brow, and the fully opened eye challenged her repudiating glare, "Blackmailed him in bed, did you?"

"I don't know any damned Vice-Marshal!" Her outraged eyes held his, determined to outstare him, "Don't be so bloody stupid. No man, let alone a Vice-Marshal, would want to take a woman as far gone as me to bed?"

"Someone pulled some effing strings, and you must have been behind it!" Leslie's eyes opened in a disbelieving, interrogating stare, "Who then?"

"Never mind that." Still holding his stare, Barbara unbuttoned her coat, "What are you going to do about this." Patting her bulging tummy, "You were going to stand by me, whatever happened. Remember? Then you slink away, like a thief in the night!"

"I didn't bloody slink away." Shamefaced, outstared, his eyes wandered down, "It was an emergency posting. Back to ops. No time to tell you."

That accounted for his strained look. There had been hints that the deal to spirit him away from Driffield, involved a return to bomber operations, and it looked as if it had shattered his nerves.

"You know I can't marry you. Knew from the start. Knew the risks you were taking." His stick poked a hole in the rotten lino.

"Emergency posting! Even if that were true, which it isn't, you could have written, answered my letters. Yes, I knew the risks!" Scoffing, head back, her bitter laugh flickered the gas mantle flame, "But I took them because I thought you loved me. Took them because of your promises at Hull. Remember?" Where was the power over men she thought she'd discovered then? She who was going to be a mistress over men, "I was going to be the ultimate Mrs. Brodie. You were going to get a divorce!"

"Well, thing's have changed. You took things on accepting that they might."

"How have they changed? Who are you shacked up with now?"

"No one. The wife and I have agreed to give it another go together. As soon as the FANY release her."

"You're a sodding liar!"

The conviction of her vehement assertion jolted him upright. His knuckles tensed, whitening on his stick handle, "If you were a man, I'd belt you for calling me that!

"That didn't stop you in Kensington! And you are a liar." She taunted, "You couldn't have agreed anything with her. She's no FANY, she's not even in England..."

"What the hell..."

"....she's a Japanese P.O.W!"

"Where'd did you get that beaut of a rumour from?" The blanched cheeks betrayed the absurdity of the wounded innocence in his tone, "Your bloody Vice-Marshal accomplice?"

"I've told you I don't know any Vice-Marshal!" Barbara's hands thumped her knees in exasperated emphasis, "But don't waste your breath denying it. Pru told..."

"So that's how you found me!" Comprehension set his head nodding, and contorted his mouth in an odious sneer, "Snooping again, you bitch. So that vindictive cow got 'daddie' to pressurise the Vice-Marshal."

"Obviously."

"All right, I lied. But it doesn't alter a bloody thing. I'm still married." Thoughtfully, for a few seconds, he tapped the stick against the floor. Then, chin on his hands, he looked smugly across at her, "Even if I wanted to, I couldn't get a divorce whilst she is a POW. So what do you want, money?"

"Among other things, yes. At least until I can support two

of us. No one is likely to give me a permanent, decently paid job, until the child is old enough for nursery school." Pensively sucking in a corner of her bottom lip, and absently nipping it between her teeth, her troubled eyes pleaded for his aid, "Then there's the birth certificate to consider, and I have to rent somewhere to live."

"You forget – there's no proof that its mine." Softly, without conviction, but it was gasoline on the fuse of her strained temper. Her pent up wrath erupted into wild, outraged fury. She flung her bag at him. It missed him by a sliver. Her ashtray followed it.

"You fucking, fucking bastard!" The ashtray crashed into his shoulder, "You know fucking well it's yours!" Her foot viciously kicked the stick from his hands. Wild eyed, she vainly looked for something near at hand to hit him with. Both of them reached for the stick. He beat her to it, and breathless, she slumped back in the chair.

"OK. OK. Simmer down." He held his hands up, palms towards her, gesturing 'pax'. "I'm not denying its mine. It's not born yet, anything can happen. You know yourself, tests can't prove paternity conclusively, but they can prove who is not the father. So you've nothing to fear. We can have the tests, if and when it's born. If they don't eliminate me, I'll make you whatever allowance I can afford." The brow quirked at her, seeking her acquiescence, "You can't ask for fairer than that, now can you Barbara?"

"Fobbing me off." Barbara spoke calmly, menacingly, as digging her hand in her pocket she stood up, "Tomorrow you'll skip off to the other side of the world, and I'll never hear from you again. That's not good enough for me."

"What the hell?"

The automatic, even in her quivering hand, could not miss his head across such a short distance.

"Put that bloody thing away! Lets get down to something more concrete, something you can trust."

Barbara's green eyes were polar cold, unblinking as she transfixed his. Mesmerised, he watched the knuckle grow bloodless with compression. His cheeks paled, a nerve in his temple twitched.

"They'll hang you." Hoarsely.

"They won't, I'm going to follow you to hell." Coolly. No

trace of nerves now.

She started towards him and froze. Vroom. VROOM. Both pairs of eyes fastened on the ceiling. Both heads cocked their ears heavenwards.

All but her mind was petrified. She couldn't let the rocket cheat her. *She* had to be the instrument of retribution, not Hitler. Desperately she willed life into her hand, but the trigger finger was dead to her command.

VROOM. V R O O M. V R O O M.

Swishing. Now silence. Except for a creaking floor board as her balance wavered.

The dazzling crimsom flash blinded their eyes, seared their lungs. The cataclysmic detonation pulverised the foundations. Like rag dolls, they were hurled upwards in a vortex of violently disintegrating masonry and splintering timber.

§

"All accounted for?" The special constable, dodging a plume of water from the shattered main, stumbled up the mound of debris.

"We'll never know, guv." The leader of the rescue squad, his boiler suit smothered in dust, waved a hand indicatively up and down the devastated street. A moonscape of rubble and craters. Lonely brick chimney stacks pointing accusingly and defiantly at the dawn sky, "They're nearly all boarding houses. No way of telling how many were indoors when it hit."

"The girls have asked if they can go back to their depot." The special constable pointed to the end of the street, where two women were sitting on the running board of an ambulance.

"Just waiting for 'Arry." The leader took off his steel helmet, rubbed his grime streaked face with the back of his sleeve, and gestured his scuffed boot at a cavity in the debris, "He's tunnelling into the basement. We're packing up then." Pulling a dusty pipe from his overalls, he tapped it against his heel, "Bin here six 'ours. I've sent the rest of the squad for some breakfast. Can't be anyone else alive under this lot. What's the count so far?"

"15 dead, in the mortuary, and I think about 22 detained in hospital." The constable shook his head sagely, "It's a miracle there's not more. Over fifty treated for shock and abrasions, and discharged."

The leader sucked the match flame into the bowl of his pipe, coughed, hawked, and spat out dust drenched phlegm.

"Here he comes. Anything 'Arry?"

"No one in the cellar, far as I can see, guv." Blinking in the sunlight, Harry, pushing out a battered vanity case, and a dark blue officer's cap, squirmed his brick grimed body out of the cavity, "If there was any poor souls in there, they must have been blown up into the ground floor. These might help identification." He slapped the cap against his trouser, sending up a suffocating cloud of dust.

"Hey! Steady on 'Arry!" The rescue leader, hastily stumbling clear of the choking cloud, almost lost his balance as he reached for the vanity case.

"Must be the dead Aussie officer's." Turning the cap over, the constable looked thoughtfully at the other two men, "Name inside, L.F. Brodie. Gawd knows why an officer was staying in this dump. Let's see what the case can tell us. Pair of knickers, a bra, cosmetics, couple of letters. Ah, ration book, name of Mrs. Dixon, pregnant poor sod. Not a married couple then. Can't make out the address, somewhere in Hull." He recorded the finds and cap in his note book and, as he picked his way down the debris called, "Must have been a new lodger, poor lass. Three of them in the morgue were pregnant, the bag must be one of theirs."

Kachin Hills, July/August 1944.

Chapter Twenty-six

As Scottie's column moved once again into bivouac in the quagmire of Padigahtawng, a haggard procession of walking sick and wounded was limping, slipping, and slithering down the glutinous red mud track to Lakhren. In the mountains and jungles, elusiveness was the Chindits' greatest strength. The Japs knew that Chindits could hit, run, and vanish in the jungle vastness and were wily enough not to expend resources chasing them. Instead, they had hemmed the columns in with a chain of strongpoints around the northern, eastern and southern foothills. The treacherous track, down to Lakhren, was the only undisputed evacuation route for the wounded and sick.

In the cascading rain, men too disabled by malaria, violent dysentery, pneumonia, typhus and a dozen other afflictions, to make the trek to Lakhren unaided, lay in make-shift 'hospital' shelters. Dog-tired medics, mud-smirched and frustrated by lack of drugs and clinical resources, had little but compassionate words and their caring hands, to nurse men through their pain.

In the boggy, storm swept slough of sludge, squirming colonies of slimy black leeches and swarms of zizzing mosquitos, 'fit' men were plodding to and from patrols, plagued with foot rot, septic jungle sores and intermittent fevers.

In 81 Column's absence, families of Kachins – seeking medical treatment and sanctuary from Jap reprisals, had trooped into Padigahtawng and were encamped around a hut set aside as a 'hospital' for them. They had been unstinting in their hospitality and aid to Chindits. Because of this loyalty, some of their women had been mutilated by Jap bayonets. Though their wounded and sick were another burden on the scarce medical resources, they could not now be denied succour and protection.

In the late afternoon, as a mule was being slaughtered to feed the sick and wounded, Dakotas droning above the leaden clouds brought the men to their feet, cheering and desperately scanning the overcast. But the drone faded to a throb before being lost in the moaning wind and hissing rain. Another day without rations. Either the planes could not locate the dropping zone, or they were destined for some other – more favoured – column.

No rations, but there were no fire restrictions. In the gathering gloom, the chattering around crackling bonfires gave way to a sort of holy hush. A British officer and two Burriffs were pushing a wizened Kachin, his hands bound behind him, down the hill below Brigade HQ hut. One, two shots! A smattering of callous Kachin cheers joined the echoes.

"Poor man, God rest his soul, and their consciences." Scofield closed his eyes in silent reverence.

"Why pity the sod? The bloody traitor deserves it. Masters had no choice. He couldn't let anyone get away with betraying Kachins to the Japs." Badger was trying to convince himself, as much as Scofield, that the man's summary execution was just.

The Thugyi of a nearby village and three elders, who had brought the man in had among other aid, provided guides for Cameronian patrols. They swore the executed man had informed the Japs. The Japs had crucified the Thugyi's wife, and bayoneted to death six villagers including his eldest son.

"Think of it. ." From a condom, Badger charged his pipe with the last of his tobacco, lit it with a burning twig, and puffed reflectively for a few moments, "...If the Kachins were lying, just wanted to settle a grudge, they could have done him in themselves. No, they wanted a lawful end. And Masters represents British justice to them."

"Maybe," Scofield said dubiously. Loosening his puttees, he took off his boots and socks, hung them on his bayonet, and held them over the fire to dry.

§

The frequency of jungle telegraph transmissions were always directly proportional to a column's proximity to Brigade HQ. At Padigahtawng 81 Column was barely beyond earshot of it. For two days as they rested between patrols, huddled around their bonfires, the bivouac buzzed eavesdroppings, embroidered with alternately gloomy predictions and optimistic speculation.

The sick and wounded at the Indawgyi Lake numbered 450. Men were dying of malaria, dysentery, jaundice and starvation. They had no medical supplies, and were living on meagre catches of fish. The brighter 'gen' was that the flying boats had resumed evacuation sorties. Then, it was whispered that down in Lakhren, 'hundreds' of casualtes were piling up. No, some others opined, they were being steadily evacuated by rafts, down river to Kamaign.

'A Cameronian patrol over sixty strong yesterday, had only four men fit for patrol this morning.'

'The Lancasters were down to twenty five per cent strength.'

'Their commander had reported even those few were unfit for further duties.'

'They've been sent down to Lakhren, lucky buggers!'

'Scottie's told Masters that all men in 81 Column were in worse condition than the survivors he led out from last year's campaign.'

'Scottie wanted a five hundred bomber raid on the railway valley, before he would lead men down there.'

'Good old Scottie. And the King's officers were refusing to lead an advance into the valley.'

'They would go, if ordered, as PRIVATES, but not as OFFICERS.'

They listened, spread and interpreted the 'scuttle-butt' with a sort of perverse, ignoble gratification and wishful clichés.

'Things cannot get worse, so they must get better.'

'The darkest hour's before dawn – things can only get brighter'

They argued the number of days they had been in Burma. Wrangled about the nutritional deficiency of 'K' rations, and their weight losses.

'A hundred and ten days.'

'Naw, nearer a hundred and twenty.'

'Twenty days more than Wingate promised'

'Bet yer a pound to a piece of shit, its thirty'

'Well, whatever it is. 'K' rations are meant to keep you going only for ten days.'

'Yes, bet they are a thousand calories a day less than we should have'

'Look at me, skin and bones. Must've lost twenty pounds'

'Me ribs are like me mam's scrubbing board. Bet I've lost three stone'

'When I get out of here, I'll never eat another bit of American processed cheese or meat loaf'.

It was oh, so rational to them that the order to 'march out' could only be days away. They were starving, their shirts were rotting on their backs, most of them had foot rot, all of them had endured at least one bout of malaria and dysentery. They were too worn down to be kept in the field. Even the most heartless general could be in no doubt about that now, and must soon order them back to India.

§

Late on the morning of their third day back at Padigahtawng, the clouds thinned out, the rain stopped, and the hazy sun broiled the hills into a steam bath.

"Was he a friend of yours, corporal?" The adjutant asked Badger, as he led the burial party uphill from the grave. For two or three days, around the clock, medics had fought desperately to pull the young Kingsman through. This morning he had succumbed to meningitis, pleurisy and dysentery.

"Hardly knew him, sir." Looking back at the lonely mound in the trough of a depression below Brigade HQ hut, he could not suppress his rancour, " Bloody Stilwell and Lentaigne! Never would have happened if Wingate had lived. Poor kid would have been out of Burma with the rest of us long ago. They murdered him and a lot more, keeping us in after the rains started..."

It was a measure of the wholesale dissaffection of the Column's officers that the adjutant, that supercilious god-head of battalion discipline, merely reacted with a vacuous smile, and dismissed the party with a flick of his hand. Weeks ago, Badger have would been lucky to escape with a stream of vituperative rebukes.

"Listen!" Scofield pointed skywards as they trooped to their bivouác, " Planes!"

The drone of aircraft rose to a roar. A Dakota breaking through the thin clouds skimmed perilously low over the hill. Banking sharply, exhausts stirring the tree tops, it jettisoned a string of parachutes before roaring back into the clouds. Three or four planes followed. Line astern they made several circuits. Surrounded by hills, shrouded in clouds, they had only fleeting glimpses of their target, and the 'chutes dropped wide of the zone. It was deperately risky flying. The gathering of the supplies would be exhausting, but they promised the end of famine, and the airmens' gallantry brought wild cheering as each circuit dropped more loads.

§

In a late afternoon downpour, with twelve 'K' rations – four days supply – and three days supply of tea, powdered milk and sugar in their packs, 81 Column trudged out of Padigahtawng to Pahok. It was only a few miles, but the slush dragged at their feet and their sodden packs were heavy with rations and damp belongings. Badger's pack held the 'luxury' issue for his section. A loaf, a pound tin of bully beef and a tin of peaches. His foot rot made every step agony. A relapse of malaria was stiffening his limbs, and burning his eyes. Until supplies had ran out last week they had been on three anti-malarial pills a day but, in any case, they seemed to have long lost their prophylactic potency.

Through his threadbare trousers the slap, slap of his entrenching tool had broken the scabs of jungle sores on his buttocks. At the first halt he slipped it off, and chucked it into the jungle. He'd not need it again. The day had brought other cheer besides food. Mike Calvert's lads had captured Moguang. This, and the fact that the

Dakotas seemed to have dropped little ammunition, could only mean one thing – the campaign was over. Scottie's depleted column was on the way to bivouac for a few days, at Pahok. Once there, so they had been told, platoons in rotation would only have to do 'standing patrols' at a small chaung below the village. There would be no restrictions on fires.

"Packs on!"

The last miles were an excruiating hobble for Badger. He dropped further back with every teeth-gritting minute, and Scofield already had a fire blazing when he limped into Pahok. But the pain faded as he stripped off his boots and socks, and doled out the 'luxuries'. In buoyant mood around roaring fires, they toasted bread on their bayonet points and baked a 'duff' of bully beef, processed pork loaf, cheese and crushed biscuits. As they topped off their 'feast' with peaches and sweet, steaming char, the MO and his orderly strolled over. Their crude chatter about their anticipated whoring in Bombay's fleshpots faded into embarrassed silence. Raw feet and weeping jungle sores were painted with gentian violet. Pills were doled out for dysentery. The MO sounded Badger's chest, peered into his eyes and took his temperature.

"Your temperature is 99.6. Looks like mild Malaria again, corporal. Take two of these tonight, two in the morning." 'Doc' Pritchard's commiserating eyes, in the care-lined face, spoke of his impotence to do more than dispense a few pills, "If you feel worse tomorrow, we'll see about sending you back to Padigahtawng. Goodnight lads."

"Thank you, sir, I'll be all right." A murmur more of hope than conviction.

"Don't waste pity on him, Doc. He's a born skiver." Ginger called as the MO moved on to the next fire.

Badger playfully swatted Ginger with his hat, and they were back swapping ardent fancies. They had over four month's back pay to squander in Bombay's brothels, massage joints and cafes. In the sheeting rain and moaning wind, they fantasized about mixed grills, hot arsed bints, apple pie and custard. They were so inured to their rain sodden life that even Badger, wracked by malarial rigors, gave the prospect of dry, comfortable beds only fleeting thought. Gluttony and women dominated all else. Barbara's letter had released him from the constraints of fidelity. He was as boastfully bawdy as the rest in conjuring up night long orgies.

When, eventually, he lay down alongside Scofield, he was too consumed by anticipated debauchery to pray. With fevered genitals that owed nothing to his malaria, he dozed into sleep, savouring the thrill of a faceless, naked whore. His fingers rolling her nipples. Hand working its way, through dense black hair, to part the moist cleft in the crotch of copper thighs. Good for the goose – Good for the gander. Bugger Barbara! The thought of her with another man, stiffened his penis with perverted pleasure.

At the dawn Stand-to the jungle telegraph brought another dent in their buoyancy. The BBC was broadcasing that General Stilwell's Chinese-American forces had captured Moguang.

'The lying bastard! The nearest Yanks are at Myitkina and Stiwell's not taken that yet.'

'No Chinese got to Moguang until Mike Calvert had the Japs on the run.'

'The only Yanks there were bloody wonderful fighter-bomber, and light plane pilots."

Later that day news of Mike's casualty figures reached their ears and were spoken of in holy whispers. Over 1,000 killed, wounded and sick. Less than 800 men left, and 500 of those 'dying on their feet'.

Towards dusk, as Badger and his section returned from their 'standing patrol' stint on the chaung, news of Mike Calvert's signal to Stilwell sent a babble of sardonic banter through the embittered columns, 'Moguang having been taken by Chinese, 77 Brigade is proceeding to take Umbrage. Map reference...' According to the jungle telegraph, Stilwell's staff were tearing their hair out, trying to pin-point Umbrage.

The evening briefing buried the Column's buoyancy and plunged them into a quagmire of despondency, grimmer than the mud itself.

"...The Japs are strongly dug in on the crown of Point 2171, about four miles south and a thousand feet higher than Pahok, dominating the the Moguang Valley." As his eyes swept the circle of expectant faces, the briefing officer's face was taut, strained with the dismaying instructions he had to pass on, "111

Brigade has been ordered to capture it, put a holding force on it, clear the valley to the east, and join up with the Chinese pushing down from Kamaign..."

"Effing bloody hell!" A tear choking sob among groans of despair.

"Like hell as like! That cunt Stilwell wants us to do the job for his flaming Chinks again!" A bolder, rebellious soul.

"Stilwell boasted he would take Myitkina and Moguang before the rains." Someone called and spat out, "Now the bugger is telling us to do what his sodding Chinks won't do! Someone should tell bloody Lentaigne to take a fucking running jump at Stilwell – SIR. "

"All right, all right! That's enough from you!" The officer glared, and thrust a threatening finger at the man, "The 3/4th Gurkhas will put in the assault at first light to-morrow. The 3/9th Gurkhas will be first reserves. Our column will remain here, at Pahok, to secure their rear. What's left of the Cameronians and Lancasters will screen Padigahtawng with patrols. 14 Brigade will be coming up from the south to join us. So buck up. The sooner this last job is done, the sooner we get out. Shouldn't take us more than a couple of days. Any questions?"

Sullen silence except for a muffled, "Last job! How bloody many times have we been told that?"

"Right, back to your fires chaps. Stand-to in fifteen minutes."

§

The 'couple of days' dragged on to a nightmare fortnight. Days of patrols, probing the slopes and dislodging Jap picquets slipped into weeks. Few battle casualties, but the sick toll was accelerating. Order of battle nomenclature ceased to have meaning in relation to the effective fighting strength of units. Columns were down from about 400 to around 200 men. At the lower end of the scale, sections were down from 10 or 12 to 6 or 7 men. Gurkha units, operating in traditional battalion formation, had lost more than 25% of their manpower. Nor were these depleted establishments an indication of physical condition of personnel. Exhaustion was so universally deep that rest periods brought no significant amelioration. The endurance, range and effectiveness, of patrols diminished each day. More and more, patrols shambled back to their bivouacs before completing their missions. In conventional warfare, the entire force would have been consigned to field hospitals for treatment, or to reserve area camps for recuperation.

Then there was two days 'rest' in soggy bivouacs. Taking supply drops – lean on rations, heavy on ammunition – for an over optimistic plan to dislodge the Japs from the summit of Point 2171. Point 2171, a sort of truncated cone, overlooking the Moguang Valley, and surmounted by a hillock in the truncated plane. The summit was accessible only via a steep, yard wide defile from a shelf hundreds of feet, and a mile below. The Japs were also entrenched on the shelf.

Slashing up vestigial tracks, scrambling up rocky rain fissures in the densest jungle 111 Brigade had ever met, the 3/4th Gurkhas stumbled into withering fire from the shelf. The Brigade's mortars briefly pounded the Japs. God only knew when the next supplies would be dropped. Every round of ammo had to be jealously husbanded.

In scattered files, on the sheer slopes below the shelf, the Gurhkas struggled for footholds in the mud and boulders. For the pinned down leading men, it was one hand clinging to a tree, a shrub, a rock, and one hand shooting. A concerted charge was impossible.

Jap re-inforcements crept down from the crest. More machine guns sweeping the forward Gurkha ranks. Jap mortar bombs, whining and crumping into the rear ranks. Wounded screaming.

Forward movement halted, but the leading files clung to their positions, while Gurkha support platoons pushed around the flanks. Nearly an hour of slashing, hacking through bamboo and scrub, ankle deep in mud. Then they were on the shelf, yelling 'Ayo Gurkhali'. Rifles, Brens, machine guns clattering, grenades bursting.

Dusk was closing in. The Japs, fighting disciplined rearguard action, were only yard by costly yard being being driven up the steep declivity. With Jap artillery now shelling the shelf, the 3/9th Gurkhas were pushed through the 3/4th. For close support, Scottie and his 81 King's Column, scrambled to the rim of the shelf.

Behind the 3/9th, the Japs counter attacked through a re-entrant on to the shelf. Rifles and automatics blazing from all quarters. 81 Column scrambled up, but the Gurkhas had driven off the counter attack. A score of Jap corpses were being given the *coup de grace* and being searched for documents.

Around the shelf rim 81 Column lay through the night. Under the sporadic clatter of small arms, mortar bursts and whining ricochets, Badger and his section shivered in the ceaseless rain. It was nothing compared with the hell of Blackpool, but there they could vent their fear in retaliation. Here they could only lie in miserable impotence.

To Badger, the fighting up the defile had a Biblical ring. Some character holding some pass with the jaw bone of an ass. Only this jaw bone was a brace of Jap machine guns, clacking away like hysterical woodpeckers.

He lost count of the hours, vainly trying to re-call the character and place. All that came back to him was a Sunday school class, sitting in a semi circle on the floor around the teacher's chair. Her legs were wide spread. Plump, leprosy white thighs above her black, woollen stocking tops. She'd caught him staring up at her baggy white bloomers. He smiled at the memory, stroking his cheek where all those years ago, she had landed a stinging clout. He had told his parents the bruise was the result of a school yard scuffle. It was the only time he'd ever lied to them and even now, he felt more guilty about that than the misdemeanour. Who was that character? Who was he slaying? The answer was in the caverns of his mind, still tantalisingly just beyond re-call when before dawn, the column crept from the ridge.

"Quiet as possible now." Mouth to mouth, the orders were passed, "A company of the 3/9th are leading a flanking move. 81 Column will follow in close support. Move quietly – Japs mustn't see or hear us."

For what seemed hours, they followed the lower contours to the foot of another hill. When the going was good Badger found himself pacing to the tormenting rhythm, 'Who held a pass with the jaw bone of an ass? Who held the pass with the jaw bone of an ass?' Scofield would know of course. Asking him would be like cheating himself. He wanted the satisfaction of working it out for himself. But mostly the going was rugged, and he lost concentration on the quotation, squiggling through thickets, mud sucking at his boots, clambering along rocky gullies.

When dawn paled the sky, they paused for breath at the foot of a thickly wooded escarpment. High above, in the drizzling rain the spine curved up to a ledge just below the truncated plane of 2171.

"Samson!" Badger snapped his fingers as the rear files of the Gurkhas disappeared uphill.

"What?" Scofield shot a perplexed look at Badger.

"Samson. It was Samson who held the pass against the Israelites with the jaw bone of an ass."

"Not so loud, Badger. It was the Philistines he slew, and he was on a rock, not in a pass."

Badger dismissed the correction with a shrug. His version was the best analogy.

An officer nudged his arm, "Off you go, corporal. Your section lead off. Follow the Gurkhas."

They had shivered through the night. Now, as they climbed, sweat was stinging their eyes, dripping from their chins, drenching their shirts and soaking their crotches.

Back over at 2171 as they clambered through the dense, fetid jungle, the fight up the defile was hotting up. Machine guns and mortars were concentrating the Jap's attention on that single file front.

If they'd had sight of the sun, it would have been at its noon zenith when they gasped on to the spine. Over six hours to cover a couple of miles.

Ahead, as they lay getting their breath back, the spine rose in a series of densely wooded ridges, to the truncated plane of 2171, two hundred feet above. Halfway up the spine, the Gurkhas were fanning into extended order. Major Blaker, their company commander, through a walkie-talkie was notifying the Brigade HQ that they were in position for the assault.

The classically handsome Major was something of an idol to the King's. From their Broadway days, he had always been in the forefront of any action, fearless, indestructible and inspiring. With him leading, the assault could not fail this time.

Seconds after Blaker finished with the walkie-talkie, the Brigade's mortars and machine guns from the shelf, were blasting the crown of 2171. The Gurkhas started forward, slowly, quietly up the spine. The Kings in single file, slipped into a narrow defile that rose steeply towards 2171.

"Check your weapons. Fix bayonets." The order was whispered down the line.

Then, above them, the 'Ayo Gurkhali' war cries, and the murderous hail of Jap machine guns. The Brigade's Barrage had not distracted the Japs

"Oh! Christ!" Badger, digging his nails into the soil, pressed his body hard against the bank. So hard a rib cracked. No not a rib! Damn! It's my pipe. Ah well, no tobacco left anyway. The Japs had not been caught 'off-guard'. Their machine guns were scything the undergrowth. Thumping the earth, like torrential hail.

The war cries gave way to the shrieking of wounded Gurkhas. He could only guess what was happening. The charge had collapsed. The Gurkhas had dived for cover. They were crawling up through scrub and bamboo. Major Blaker was yelling.

"Come on! Come on 'C' Company!"

War cries again. More wild, more demoniacal. Now Jap yells and shrieks.

"On your feet, Kings! Follow 'em up!"

Scottie and his men swept from the defile. The only noise now, was the threshing of their boots, the hiss of rain, the moans of the wounded and solitary rifle shots. The Gurkhas had taken 2171.

Pot-helmeted figures were racing, full tilt, downhill. Corpses lay among the trees, crumpled in dug outs and slumped over machine guns. Their shabby uniforms and ragged puttees lending a touch of pathos to their gory, contorted bodies.

In a depression, just below the truncated rim, the indestructible Blaker, his stomach a bloody mass from a machine gun burst, lay dead among the dead and wounded Gurkhas. A moist eyed Gurkha subahdar, in faltering English told them that Blaker sahib charged forward alone, was shot in the stomach. He collapsed and sat against a tree, and shouted 'Come on, 'C' Company. I'm going to die. Take the position.' His men fell on the enemy in a wild, unstoppable charge.[Appendix 3]

Chapter Twenty-seven

"Hope it doesn't rain again to-day, Badger." Scofield said with a crooked smile. "It's St. Swithin's Day, we'll have 40 days and nights of it, if it does." One of Scofield's rare flashes of drollery.

"Bloody Job's comforter!" He flicked a pebble which Scofield dodged as he poked his tongue at Badger.

For once they'd had a dry night, but black clouds were already rolling over the crown of 2171, 300 feet above. The 15th of July, six days since Major Blaker's death. Four sleepless days and nights, consolidating the 2171's defences and repulsing Jap attacks. Last night the Gurkhas had relieved them, and now they were in reserve, bivouacked on a rugged outcropping halfway up the rocky defile to 2171.

Masters' HQ, and the dressing station, were down on the shelf that had cost them dear in the initial assault.

Fires were prohibited and their boots and socks, off for the first time in a week, were hopefully hung up to dry on scrub and rocks. Badger's fever had receded, but his feet were a smarting mass of pink flesh. Soon they'd be moving down to the shelf to haul up supplies, and boots would have to go on again. The prospect made him wince more than the gentian violet he was dabbing on them. A steady procession of battle casualties were limping, or being carried, down to the dressing station shelf.

On the crown, it was Blackpool scaled down to a diameter less than the length of a soccer pitch. Scaled down too, in savagery.

The Japs had kept up an around the clock harassment of desultory artillery shelling and mortar bombing. Their attacks were mostly probing, seeking the defender's weak points. Brief assaults that a few Bren, and mortar bursts, put to flight before they reached the wire.

Between assaults, the tension was almost as crippling as bullets or shells. A few feet down, the ground was rock hard and in their shallow trenches, their nerves were kept taut as piano wire by the thud and crump of missiles. The Japs, dug in below the crown, augmented their artillery and heavy mortar torment with knee mortars. Every few minutes a sharp click, a shrill whistle and thump. In that small area every shell, every mortar bomb, vibrated every trench. The Japs, from safe positions, in 'dead' ground, were intent on wearing them down, denying them sleep. Tempting them them to retaliate, to divulge their strength, and waste precious ammunition whilst they built up their forces for an all out attack.

For the troops not holding the crown, it was Blackpool all over again, only worse. Supply drops on 2171 were impossible, and mule trains were hauling supplies, heavy on ammuntion, weapon parts and defence material, but lean on rations from Padigahtawng and Pahok to the shelf.

Dakotas were getting through to Padigahtawng just often enough to keep the guns fed, and the troops on the starvation threshold. From the shelf men had to lug the loads to the crown. Two hours each trip. Lugging ammunition and defence stores up that steep, rocky and muddy defile.

Holding on. Waiting for bloody 14 Brigade. Where the hell were they? There had not been a whisper of them since 2171 was taken.[18]

The remnants of 111 Brigade, and the King's 81 Column, were resigned to a hopeless 'expect the worst and you won't be disappointed' philosophy. Marching out was seldom mentioned, for fear of tempting the opposite from fate. Myitkina had still not fallen, and Stilwell had ordered Mike Calvert's battered brigade to advance towards it. Mike had cheekily signalled back, 'I have only 300 men all told. Do you want me to form the King's Royal Staffordshire Gurkha Fusiliers?' Since then, nothing had been heard of his brigade, and Stilwell's sycophants were branding the

Chindits 'cowards – yellow deserters'. They had 'walked off the field of battle' and should all be courts-martialled.

"July 14th." Badger mumbled to Scofield as the order came to move down to pick up supplies, "One hundred and thirty days behind enemy lines. JEEZE!" His face screwed in pain as he eased on his boots, "Over fifty days of sodding rain and mud, and no end in sight yet mucker."

"Why don't you ask the MO to send you down to Lahkren?"

"Don't talk so daft. If the MO sent everyone down who had bad feet there'd be hardly a man left here. Anyway, I'd never make it on my own feet, and nobody's going to carry me. No, I'll stick with the column."

Lahkren was a gruelling two or three day trek for fit men, for Badger it would be more like five. If the jungle telegraph were to be believed, for the past fortnight power driven rafts had been ferrying casualties from the lake and Lahkren down river to Kamaign. But, with hundreds of men in worse straits than him, he could see his feet being healed before he got a place on one of them. Then, like many others, he would be declared fit to climb back to 2171.

Got to give it to the sappers though, they had got a 'real' navy going. Bamboo platforms lashed over five assault boats, with real latrines, and canopies, powered by outboard motors. A flotilla of ten, flying outsize union flags, with names like 'Dreadnought', 'Ark Royal', 'Valiant', 'Vanguard', 'Renown' and 'Revenge'. Impudently plying the Indawgyi River, each evacuated thirty odd walking casualties, or a dozen stretcher cases, on each trip, under the Jap noses.

No, Badger told himself again, as he hobbled up from the shelf with a case of grenades, I'll take my chances with the column. That power behind the Chinese throne, Madame Chiang Kai-shek, had demanded they hold 2171 until 'her' armies got there. They were supposed to have been there by 'breakfast' two days ago, but no one believed they'd ever get there. So it was a probability, bordering on certainty, that in a couple of days 81 Column would be back on the crown, relieving the Gurkhas. Stuck in a slit trench, with no walking, would be the lesser of two evils.

§

A week later, back on their rocky outcropping, two days after their second stint on the summit, Masters ordered that every man be medically examined the following afternoon.

In the gathering dusk, and chilling drizzle, hunched over their tin of meat loaf, or processed cheesed – their only meal of the day – officers and men vehemently cursed Stilwell and Lentaigne. If Masters was ordering medicals, it was a pound to a pinch of shit, that Shadazup had another 'job' in mind for anyone who could stand on his feet.

At Pahok, Padigahtawng and a dozen other places around 2171, stripped to the waist in pouring rain, contemptuous men were auscultated, probed and questioned by the humiliated MOs.

"How many times have you had malaria, corporal?"

"About three times, sir." Badger slipped his rotting shirt back on.

"Dysentery, diarrhoea?"

"Had it on and off since Blackpool, sir."

"Your feet are still very bad?"

"Yes, sir. Not the only one, sir." He gave a depreciatory shrug. They had scabbed over a little on the summit, but after lugging supplies up, yesterday and this morning, they were once again raw and weeping.

"Righto, young fellow, off you go and get them painted again." 'Doc' Pritchard was only a few years older than most of his 'patients', but he was as revered as a compassionate and devoted father. He carried his pack like them, and was tireless in caring for the wounded and sick. Through night after night he would nurse casualties, shoulder his pack in the morning and trudge with the column, often dropping back treat casualties, and usher along the weak and lame.

§

Less than 120 men, the jungle telegraph whispered that evening – 120 men out of a couple of thousand – fit for further action.

"At Blackpool, 111 Brigade with the Kings, must have been what?" Scofield paused to calculate as they lay under their sodden blanket, "Over three and a half thousand strong. Badger?"

"I reckon so."

"They can't keep us in after that, can they?"

"I wouldn't put any money on that, with those inhuman sods at Shadazup. Especially after what we've got coming tomorrow."

Jap artillery and mortars were keeping up their harassment of 2171 and hard on the shocking medical figures, had come the shattering instruction that Scottie's column – regardless of their condition – were to once again relieve the Gurkhas on the summit, next morning.

"What're the blinking Chinese and 14 Brigade doing?"

"God only knows! Let's try and get some sleep." Badger pulled the blanket over his head, trying to deaden the noise of mortars, and the thunder rumbling around the summit.

§

On their third night back on the summit, thin clouds veiled the moon. Lying prone in the shallow trench with Scofield, Badger had only to raise his head to peer over the parapet. If he *did* still have his entrenching tool, it would have been of little use. A few feet below the surface, the ground on 2171 was solid rock.

Ten yards to his right the heads of Terry, Ginger and Trott, were frozen profiles on their parapet. Until he had been wounded this morning and sent down to Pahok, Jones – the stoical soft spoken Midlander – had shared Bob Gregory's trench, ten yards to Badger's left.

Twenty yards in front, Wyles and Smudge were on 'listening watch' in a scooped out hollow, close to the perimeter wire. Since Blackpool he never put Wyles and Trott on sentry together. Why couldn't it have been one of those dreamy sods that had copped it, instead of a good mucker like Jones? Soon Bob would signal him to relieve one of them, and he was dreading another stint out there. For two hours at a time, around the clock for the last three days, two men per section, staggering their change-overs, had the task of lying silently, in similar hollows around the small plateau, listening for Jap movements. Two hours with their noses almost on the perimeter wire. No overhead protection from shrapnel. Two nerve wracking, speechless hours within whispering distance of the Japs. Hearing every discharge click of the Jap knee mortars. Nipping your lips as the missiles whistled over. Ears tuned for a stealthy scuffing, or rustling of undergrowth, that warned of the forward movement of the enemy. Limbs tensed for flight back to the slit trenches. And, through it all, the zizzing of mosquitos.

Oughton and Johnson were replacing casualties in another section. Jack Ryan should by now, he fervently hoped, be recuperating in India. With only seven men and himself the listening duty came round every eight hours, but other sections were worse off and none of his lads had been killed – so far.

The wind moaned restlessly through the trees, but every man was deaf to it. Their brittle nerves attuned their ears only for the click and whirr of knee mortars, and the crack and whine of shells. Between showers, even the delayed plop of raindrops was spine jerking. Silence between salvoes was more terrifying than all else. Every night, between each dusk and dawn bombardment, the Japs had put in three or four increasingly determined attacks. Shouting and banging cans they had flung themselves at the wire.

Driven to the threshold of dementia by the Japs' unchallenged mortaring and shelling, the attacks brought deliverance from their bridled fears. Retaliation numbed their senses to the enemy guns and missiles. With frenetic yells, and a wild extravagance of ammunition, each attack had been driven back by a withering hail of small arms and mortar fire. In the gun flashes of tonight's first attack he had glimpsed Tony, the dapper barber, charging forward and screaming with rage, firing a Bren from the hip and driving back a Bangalore torpedo squad from the wire.

They could not hold out against many more attacks. Casualties were not heavy but ammunition was running out fast. Earlier recce patrols had found that the Japs were lodged across the defile leading down to Brigade HQ, cutting off the supply and evacuation route. Where the hell were 14 Brigade and Madam Chiang's promised army?

Now, with dawn a couple of hours off as Badger steeled himself to relieve Wyles, a rustle behind spun him round, grenade in hand.

"Pass it on. 111 Brigade is withdrawing towards Kamaign." An officer, crawling from Bob's trench, whispered to him, "We're breaking contact, and making for Moguang. In five minutes follow the platoon on your right. If we get split up make for Pahok. And for Christ's sake no noise. Crawl if you must, but don't disturb even a pebble."

In some places, it was literally a case of crawling. The track was pitted with mortar and shell craters, and obliterated by landslips blasted from central hillock. Somewhere under the piled up earth, shells and mortars had entombed comrades, including Captains Henry and Thomas. Tough, down to earth war-time officers, the idols not only of their own platoons but also of every man in the battalion. Limping through the loose earth, Badger felt he was desecrating sacred ground. In the nerve wracking hush, he crossed himself in penance.

It was Blackpool all over again. But this time in the black of night, encircled by Jap picquets, they were shuffling down a trackless jungle escarpment. Above them, the Jap dawn barrage started blasting the crown. Soon they would charge up and meet no resistance. Then what? The Japs had let them get away with it at Blackpool. Would they let them get away with it this time?

A man in front stumbled, his rifle bounced and clattered downhill. He could almost feel every man biting their lips, stifling curses.

By God and by guess, they eluded the ring of picquets and when dawn paled the sky, were picking their way down the rugged reverse side of the same hill they had climbed for Major Blaker's flanking assault. Above them they heard the clatter of automatics, and yells. The Japs were making their dawn assault on the now deserted 2171.

Footnote to Chapter Twenty-seven

Page 431 Note No.18 The West African and 14 brigades were having enough troubles of their own, fighting weather and terrain as well as battling with Japs north east and south west of 2171. The West Africans were down to less than half strength. 14 Brigade were no better off – in fact their Black Watch columns were down to about 50 fit men.

PART 4

The Kachin Hills/Dehra Dun, August 1944.
London, July 1944.

"Because I Live, Ye Shall Live Also "
John, 14 v.19.

There are things of which I may not speak;
There are dreams that cannot die;
There are thoughts that make
the strong heart weak
And bring a pallor to the
cheek,
And a mist into the eye

Longfellow

§

Chapter Twenty-eight

A jab in the ribs jolted Badger awake. Someone dragged back the collapsed canopy of the hammock. Four figures, dark with the early morning sun over their shoulders, stood above him. The rifle muzzle of a man straddling his legs, was a foot from his nose. The other three had rifles slung over their shoulders.

Blinking to adjust to the light he made out their high, Oriental cheek bones, and almond Asian eyes. Japs! Last night, ready for death, he had given up the ghost. Now he wanted to scream for his life. In desperation, he reached for a grenade alongside the hammock. A canvas boot pinned his hand to the ground. His belly writhed. His throat croaked.

The man astride him jabbered something that sounded like "Ying kok yan, yick wack, may kok yan?"

Badger's lips were rigid, his throat paralysed with fear.

The man said it again, "Ying kok yan, yick may kok yan?"

Badger's frightened eyes flicked from one to another of the men. There was something different about their rifles. No imperial chrysanthemum on the butts. Korean auxiliaries? But they had calf length canvas jungle boots, not split toed plimsolls. No puttees.The uniforms were darker, greener, heavier drill than any Japs he'd seen. Their cotton field caps were different, squarer, bigger peaks.

The questioner lowered his rifle, and groped out Badger's identity discs. He made no attempt to read them. A glance at the fibre tags told them he was British. Americans had metal tags.

"Ying kok yan!" A broad grin creased his squab nosed face, and two of them hauled lifted Badger to his feet, "No Yankee!"

Now he saw that, though they had high cheek bones, they were more moon-faced than the sharp featured Japs. Southern Chinese! Suddenly he guessed 'Ying kok yan' meant 'Englishman'. 'May kok yan' must mean 'American'.

Relieved at his good fortune Badger slapped each one on the shoulder, and vigorously pumped each of their hands.

"Dixon, I'm Dixon." Excitedly, he poked his chest. "King's Regiment, Wingate."

Uncomprehending, they grinned back. One of them gave him a cigarette and lit it for him.

"Me Dixon." He poked his chest again.

"You?" He tapped each one on the chest.

This time they nodded.

"Ah, Dickson." The man with rifle tapped his own chest. "Chung"

"Li" said another.

"Wong Lap"

"Wong Sun"

Handshakes and grins again all round as they squatted in a circle, puffing their cigarettes. The Chinese put two thumbs up, and gave approving grins, when he mentioned Wingate again. But they grimaced sourly, and gave vigorous thumbs down when he spoke of Chiang Kai-shek and Stilwell.

Badger's fever had lifted, but his head felt like a hollow, vacuous dome. His own words seemed to echo in the base of his skull. As he struggled to recall the odd Cantonese words he'd picked up from the Hong Kong Volunteers, he noticed for the first time that morning that his bare feet were throbbing.

"Kwai lo!" He tapped his chest, suddenly remembering what Robert and Joe had often teased him with.

The Chinese rocked on their heels, roaring with laughter.

"Yes. You twirps, kwai lo!" He wiggled his forefingers above his forehead, like horns, showing them he knew it meant foreign devil, and they laughed loudly again.

By sign language – patting his head, stomach and feet – he got them to understand he had fallen out of the column last night. From their mimicking of pack laden soldiers, their gestures at the hill where the two officers – Dick and John – had given their final waves, and by gestures at the ashes of his fire he gathered they had seen the column in bivouac last night.

Then, after heated squabbling amongst themselves, Wong Lap, who seemed to be their leader, indicated they would take him to the column.

Chung plastered Badger's feet with black, tarry ointment and smeared Tiger Balm around his nostrils and neck. Li gave him two doughy, minced meat dumplings. Watching him eat them, they smoked a second round of cigarettes and resumed their arguing in a more muted vein. Badger had the impression they were not at all keen to take him to the Column.

When they stubbed out their cigarettes, Wong Lap snapped out some instructions. Chung gave Badger a pair of white cotton socks to put on. Wong Lap took up the hammock and Badger's boots. Chung shouldered Badger's pack and rifle. Li and Wong Sun each took one of his arms around their shoulders.

With Badger's feet barely taking any of his weight, they jog trotted through the morning, stopping only at the rim of each hill to change pairs of bearers.

By mid morning the day was heavy and oppressive, the sun hidden by leaden clouds. The Chinese, loping along in an easy rhythmic pace, showed no sign faltering. About noon, halting suddenly atop a teak timbered crest, they handed him his pack, rifle and boots, and pointed down the hill.

Along a dirt track, that led on to a pot holed tarmac road, at the foot of the hill, the Column was resting.

From some reason the Chinese did not want to be seen with him. They backed quickly from the crest, and he hobbled a few steps after them to thank them with handshakes. He had nothing worthy of their help to reward them, but he offered them Tony's lighter as a keepsake, and motioned Wong Lap to keep the hammock. They refused the lighter, nodded thanks for the hammock and trotted away without a backward glance.

Hobbling downhill, Badger concluded they must be deserters. He would not breathe a word about them to anyone – but he would give thanks to God for their help every night for the rest of his life.

The column was already moving off when he reached the tail enders. Doc Pritchard, gathering the lame and the sick, handed him a water bottle.

"Well done, corporal. Have a good swig." He said with a sympathetic smile, and a fatherly hand on his shoulder, "Better put those back on." He pointed to the boots strung around Badger's neck, "Only a few miles to go, but it's metalled road from now on. Stick it out, we'll be in Moguang in less than an hour."

"There the bugger is at last! Come to see us now it's all over." The man in front of Badger, was pointing to a tall, stooping man strolling towards the Column.

Lentaigne! For the first time, 81 Column were seeing one of the men who had been the butt of their curses. Beneath his crumpled red banded cap, his face was grimly wrinkled. Etched with tension. The eyes behind steel rimmed spectacles were tired. Lifeless. The man that any of them – without the slightest compunction any time in the last two months – might have shot, reminded Badger of an ashes and sackcloth penitent as with despairing shrugs and gestures, he spoke to Scottie and some officers. Now that the danger and privations were behind them, emnity of the man almost dissolved into pity. It *would* have dissolved into pity, if the man had possessed the common touch just to pass along the column. A smile, and a "Well done, lads", would have done it. But Lengtaigne did not. And the enmity would smoulder for years.

After months of muddy vestigial tracks, the tarmac was a pleasure to march on and the column stepped out lively. They were survivors. Danger and hardships were behind them. Their packs were light, their spirits rising. Someone struck up with 'O'Reilly's Daughter'.

As I was sitting by O'Reilly's fire,
Drinking Reilly's gin and water:
Suddenly a thought came into my head:
I'd like to shag O'Reilly's daughter.

The column bawled out the chorus.

Titty-i-i, titty-i-i,
Titty-i-i the one-eyed Reilly,
Jig-a-jig jig, frig a little pig,
Jig-a-jig jig, tres bon.

Halfway through the song, they met the British 36 Division, flown into Myitkina airstrip, streaming out of Moguang. Motorised artillery, scout cars, ammunition lorries, mobile field kitchens, jeeps and – AMBULANCES! Fresh faced infantry in 'skeleton' equipment, their packs piled on 15 cwt. platoon trucks. Good naturedly, the passing troops joshed each other.

"Has yer mammy changed your nappies this morning?" A Scouse Kingsman called, "God help us, if you lot are on our side"

"What took yer so long?" Another Scouser.

"Queen Victoria's bloody funeral!" A passing infantry-man yelled, and made a two finger gesture.

"Has Mafeking been relieved yet, mucker?" From 81 Column.

"Yeah! And Kaiser Bill's dead. And they've abolished horse trams in Blighty!"

"Get off yer bleeding knees! The Japs'll be in Tokyo before you lot catch 'em."

Suddenly the column was whistling the Regimental March, 'Here's to the maiden of bashful fifteen, And here's to the widow of fifty...' Their shoulders squared, and even Badger's hobble had improved to a limp, as they entered the outskirts of Moguang.

The town was desolate, a landscape of devastated buildings, completely devoid of inhabitants. Other than passing troops, the only souls in sight were the Kachins with the pregnant woman, settling themselves around the shell torn railway station. It needed no stretch of the mind to imagine the savagery of the fighting that had taken place.

"Thoughtless bloody Base wallahs," Badger grumbled to Scofield, as Scottie mustered the column around him in a cratered orchard, behind the rubble of what had been a substantial bungalow, "They could at least have had a field kitchen waiting for us. Not even a dixie of hot char for us"

To-night, Scottie told them, they would bed down in Moguang. To-morrow morning they would travel by Jeep railway to emplane at the Myitkina airstrip for India. After a few days in a transit camp – at Dibrugah in Assam – for de-lousing, re-clothing and a decent rest, they would travel by train to Dehra Dun. For to-night, the QM had managed to get enough tea, sugar and powdered milk for them all to have a good brew up.

Loud cheers!

As Scottie outlined the following morning's arrangements, Badger's thoughts wandered to that Sunday evening five months earlier, when the Battalion, eight hundred strong, fit and fired with enthusiasm, had climbed into the gliders. Now they were down to a couple of hundred gaunt survivors, their vigour as limp as their rotted clothing. Every man looked like two-pennorth of death, warmed up.

"...So you can have a good rest tonight laddies, no 'stand-to' no sentry duty – and you more than deserve it." Scottie was concluding, "No one could have done more, or better, than you. Wingate would have been proud of you. In years to come, when you're having a pint or two, you'll be proud to say you were a Chindit. Have a good night."

"Three cheers for Colonel Scott!"

Moguang rang with cheer upon cheer.

§

"What's the date today, mate?"

"August third." The Yank, checking them off as they clambered aboard the Dakota, glanced at his clip-board, "Yup, bud. All day."

It was late afternoon, the cloud ceiling was thin, and the six Dakotas dispersed over the rough airfield, shimmered with heat refractions. That morning, with their feet dangling over the flat bed trucks, drawn by Jeeps with flanged wheels, they had sung and whistled through a host of bawdy ditties, for thirty miles along the railway from Moguang to the airstrip. Weeks ago, thirty miles could have meant a week's gruelling march. They had covered it in less than two hours.

They were really bound for India at last. In the overwhelming relief of survival, the soothing balm of retrospection was already hazing the horrors and privations, mellowing Badger's hatred of senior commanders, and gilding his pride in the Chindit's doggedness. It seemed like the tales he had heard of childbirth. Women, in the agony of labour, screaming, 'Never again!' Then the joy of safe delivery, the pain forgotten, and soon the yen for another child.

He was a veteran now. The word tickled his ego. He rolled the word round his tongue. Veteran. And a Chindit veteran at that! He would have a damn good leave. Maybe he'd get a compassionate furlough to England.

Whatever it was that the Chinese had pasted on his feet had dried the weeping skin into scales, and Doc Pritchard had assurred him that they were not gangrenous. They would be fine after a few days treatment. Badger had also, at last, plucked up the courage to mention the loss of semen to the Doc. The MO, after probing his prostate, had assurred him that their was nothing sinister to worry about, but he would arrange a thorough check up for him when they got to Dehra Dun. Diarrhoea was still plaguing him, but most of the others had that, and he'd get himself fit for next year's campaign. He could take pride in doing what he'd vowed to do. He'd marched out with his section. Comradeship, deeper than most men would ever share, had brought them all through. Well, not quite. Jack Ryan had been evacuated – it worried him that he could not recall when or where – and Jones had been wounded, but all the section had come through alive.

That morning they had heard – at last – that Myitkina had been captured two days ago, over two months after Stilwell had declared to the world that he had done so. The remnants of Morris Force – fifty men out of the original force of some 1,350 – had flown out two weeks ago. 14 Brigade had not got through to reinforce 2171 because they were now battling to take Taungni, and then were under orders to re-capture 2171. Poor sods.

Mike Calvert – with the survivors of 77 Brigade – was back in India.

As the Dakota's engines roared to life, Badger exchanged affectionate grins with Ginger, and in the euphoria of survival turned his mind to how he would reply to Barbara.

> My dear wife
>
> For you are still my wife. I cannot truthfully say your letter was a bolt from the blue, for some time, probably by the jealous telepathy of my love for you, I have had...

How should he put it?

> ...a presentiment that a woman as beautiful as you, living among so many attractive men, would be tempted beyond human endurance. What hurts is that you left it so late to tell me, and I find it incredible that this could happen on your only 'infidelity'. It's not so much the act, but the thought that you could love him more than me. Were you hoping an abortion would get you out of trouble? Or that I might be killed and never know...'

No. No! That's all wrong. Start again. He tried three or four more times, and did not get beyond the first sentence. Let it stew, let it hatch until the time was right to actually put pen to paper. He'd find the right words then. The right words to forgive her, without grinding her nose in the gutter.

§

At his trestle desk in the Dehra Dun Orderly Office, the Rear Base Adjutant leaned back in his chair, with his fingers laced across his bald scalp.

Everything was ready. Charpoys, mosquito nets, the canteens, mess rooms. The dhurzee had taken on two cousins, and had increased his treadle sewing machines from 1 to 3 – to cope with the rush to buy walking out clobber – and he had stocked up with Elgin towels and cotton sheets from Cawnpore. The QM had bales of new blankets ready for issue but even in this climate, sheets were a 'luxury' the army wouldn't provide – for hygiene and comfort, the lads would be rushing to buy two or three pairs apiece from the dhurzee. The cook-houses had been stocked with dairy produce and meat from the Italian POW Farm. Mail had been sorted into Companies for distribution.

The trucks, bringing what was left of the 1st Battalion from the railway station, would be here in the next half hour and he had just made his final inspection of the barracks. The Band and Drums were formed up, a quarter of a mile outside the main gates. The sergeant in charge of the main gate guard had his men on top form, ready to turn out.

The 'March-In' would be a grand, heart stirring sight. The lads, dismounting from the trucks, would form up behind the band. With sloped arms, bayonets fixed they would march in to 'Here's to the maiden of bashful fifteen'. The guard would 'turn out' and 'Present Arms' in salute to returning warriors.

But it would be a sad 'homecoming' for one young fellow. He glanced at an air mail letter – and an official cable - on his desk. Weighted by a paper knife it was rustling under the desk fan.

An ex-ranker, after 21 years with the regiment, the adjutant had retired just before the war and settled in India with his Anglo-Indian wife. At the outbreak of war, he had wangled his way back into the battalion. Regimental to his core, his affected gruff, rough cut diamond image, hid an avuncular solicitude for young Kingsmen. How was he going to break the news to Dixon? Should he get the Padre to do it? Would that be dodging a heart wrenching duty?

His spectacles, as he pulled them from his breast pocket, snagged in the pin of his World War I and Long Service medal bar.

"No thanks, Moti." He waved away the mug of tea – brought in by a grizzled officers' mess bearer – and took up the letter once more.

Dated a fortnight earlier, it was addressed :

The Adjutant/Wefare Officer. 1st. Bttn. Kings Regt. BFPO 1, India.

The letter been on his desk for a couple of days. He would tell the lad himself, in the privacy of his office, where the initial shock could be absorbed out of the eyesight of his muckers. He read silently.

> *Sir*
> *Please forgive me for writing to you direct, instead of through official channels, whatever they might be in this*

case.
A few days ago I found out that my very dear friend, Mrs. Barbara Dixon, the wife of Corporal A. Dixon of your battalion, has been killed in a flying bomb raid, this month, God rest her soul.
I have sent a letter of condolences to her parents, (I do not know the address of Cpl. Dixon's parents) and yesterday I received a most distressing reply that they had not been informed of her death. So I am presuming her husband does not yet know about it.
I do not know Cpl. Dixon, and I do not think a letter out the blue from a stranger would be a decent way to break such sad news to him. Would you please arrange for a chaplain, or welfare officer to do it.
I have verified her death with the [name snipped out by censor] *Borough Town Hall, and the local police.*
If Coporal Dixon wishes to write to me, I will be pleased to give him whatever additional details I can.
Thanking you in anticipation of your sympathetic disposal of this matter.

Yours obediently,
M. O'Connor, (Sgt. A.T.S.)

The Adjutant had telegraphed the War Office for confirmation. With a long, sad sigh he slipped the letter back under the paper knife, along with the War Office's confirmatory cable.

London, July 1944

Chapter Twenty-nine

Barbara forced open her heavy eyes. Soft warm fingers were on her right wrist. For some hours, in a dry mouthed stupor, she had been vaguely aware of anti-septic odours and rustling aprons. She was also conscious that her left arm was constricted and throbbing. Her left leg was unnaturally rigid, and her jaw was aching.

She felt herself slipping back into a stupor, and her eyes lazily wandered around the room. There seemed to be a dozen beds lining the opposite wall of the ward. To her right, there was a white bedside locker, and four or five more beds. To her left, another locker and more beds. In a dreamlike way she seemed to be suspended in time. She had seen this all before. But where, when? Her drowsy mind began to register differences. Last time, nurses, in their starched white aprons and navy frocks, were creeping about, drawing the curtains over the windows between each bed. Now, the nurses were bustling about the ward, in brilliant sunlight, their bonnets bobbing like delicate china cups. Vaguely she recalled being on a stretcher, and that the the clock over the double doors at the right end of the ward, had said 9.30. Now it was only 8.15.

Must've been last night.

"Ah, you're awake my dear." A strangely familiar, middle aged Jewish looking woman, her iron grey hair tightly swept back in a bun and dark eyes peeping over gold framed half lenses, was checking her pulse.

"I don't suppose you remember seeing me last night." She smiled ruefully, "You were too drowsy from the anaesthetic to take anything in when I popped in to check you. I'm Doctor Jacobs."

That's why she's familiar. Barbara dimly recalled seeing the doctor, sometime before, as though through the wrong end of a misty telescope.

"You're a very, very, lucky young woman." The doctor gently laid Barbara's hand down on the sheet, "It's a miracle you and baby are still alive." She flicked a thermometer vigorously, and smiled down again, "Keep this under your tongue a minute. You have a complicated fracture of the leg. Your left shoulder was dislocated, and lacerated, and there's a nasty gash on your head. Lie still!" She snapped as Babara's hand moved to feel her scalp, "You have a friar's pate where we had to stitch it. Ah, good, your temperature is down a little."

Putting the thermometer in a jar of antiseptic on the bedside locker, she stood, with her hands deep in the pockets of her white overall, looking thoughtfully at Barbara.

"Your face is not a pretty sight." She said at length, "You have bruises everywhere. It will take a few weeks, but as far as we can tell you should make a complete recovery. And baby is unharmed." .

Sitting down on the edge of the bed, she took Barbara's right hand in hers, and tenderly squeezed it.

"That's the good news, my dear." She paused, choosing her words carefully, "The rest is bad – very bad – and I'm afraid, dear, there is no painless way of telling you this..."

'...No painless way..' Why was this twitching her memory, '...No painless way...' Where had she used that phrase. Ah! A fleeting vision of Badger seared Barbara's conscience.

"...your husband was killed..."

"Killed? Dead, shot?" Barbara stammered. She suddenly remembered pointing the gun, "I didn't really mean to..."

"Not shot, dear. The flying bomb. Your husband, parents and brother. Your whole family killed. I'm terribly sorry."

"Husband?.. Parents?.. Brother?" She repeated. Dazed and perplexed. Somewhere in the canyons of her mind, she knew this could not be. Had her parents and brother been there?

Absently she noticed that a nurse, hovering behind the doctor, was holding a shabby patent leather handbag.

"The funerals have all been arranged by the Borough Council. The Women's Voluntary Service have ordered a wreath on your behalf. The card for it is on your locker. When you've written it, Sister will see that they get..."

"But it's not right, only Leslie was..." Her voice trailed into silence. Something was dreadfully wrong. There had only been Brodie with her. How could her parents and brother be involved? She closed her eyes, trying to recall the moments before the vroom.

"You're bound to be confused, you were badly concussed." Dr. Jacobs patted Barbara's hand as she rose from the bed, "I'll pop back later. When you've had a little more rest, Mrs. Dobson."

"But I'm not Mrs..." She cut the protest short. Where had she heard the name Dobson? She kept her eyes shut, for fear the doctor could see through them into her mind.

"What my dear?" Doctor Jacobs took the handbag from the nurse, and placed it on the locker.

"Oh, nothing. Must be still dopey with the anaesthetic." The boarding house. The Dobsons on the stairs. Five of them. All dead. An embryonic notion was forming in the concussed labyrinth of her mind.

"Just rest my dear. Would you like nurse to bring you something to drink? Tea?"

Still with eyes closed, Barbara nodded, and fretfully plucked at the cotton theatre gown, as the nurse went for the tea.

"I'm sorry, my dear, the only thing they brought in with you was your handbag. Your clothes were in shreds.The Red Cross ladies will be round soon with a nightie and some underclothes for you. I'll pop in later. Bye."

Something was teasing, exciting her with the promise of a new life. When the nurse brought the tea she feigned sleep. For an hour – perhaps more – she lay still, sorting out her thoughts, delving for snags in her plans. If the Council were arranging the funeral, Mrs. Dobson could have no relatives alive. At least, none in England. The Channel Isles were still under Nazi occupation. Close friends?

Unlikely. The Dobsons, lodging in that boarding house, never had any visitors.

Identity Card? Ration Book?

When she was certain no nurses were hovering around, she reached for the shabby handbag from the locker.

It was better than she hoped. A Green Ration Book and a National Identity Card, in the name of Betty Dobson. What a godsend that identity cards did not have photographs. The initials were same as her own.

Looking at her face, in Betty Dobson's compact mirror, she saw that her face and neck were bluey-yellow with bruises, her eyes bloodshot. Her hair was shorn around a bulky, blood stained Elasto-plast on the crown of her head. For an instant, as she rummaged in the handbag and found two or three dog-eared family snapshots, conscience threatened her scheming. But the prospect of a new life was too inviting to be thwarted by conscience. After all, she would be harming nobody.

She fished out a pencil from the bag, and reached for the black bordered card. For a few moments, she tapped the pencil against her teeth, and then boldy wrote, 'For a loved husband, mother, father and brother. You will live always with me. R.I.P. Evermore your B.' The words triggered a Bible phrase, and she added, 'Because I live Ye also live'. Well, she had not lied. She had not written 'For my beloved husband, father...'

Her child would be born into her new life. There'd be no stigma of illegitimacy on the birth certificate. Her own disgrace, the whole of her past, expugned, buried with the Dobsons. She would not even contact Mary. No one would ever know her other than as the widowed Betty Dobson. She might be eligible for some sort of government grant. A widows pension?

If only she'd not written that 'Dear John'.

Badger would have grieved for her 'death', and lovingly remembered her.

Now his memories would be full of bitterness for a faithless wife.

Appendix 1

The following extract from Page 131 of Shelford Bidwell's well researched book *The Chindit War*, indicates that the official records blame the King's for the failure to pursue the Japanese.

Rome now sensed that Wakayuma (the Japanese commander) was ripe for a counter-stroke, so he summoned the outlying column of the King's Regiment (82 Column) and ordered it to be ready to attack on the morning of the 30th. That night the Japanese attacked again but not with the same spirit, and once more they were beaten off.

Rome was now to encounter a communication difficulty that was to bedevil all Chindit operations involving the coordination of widely separated columns throughout the campaign. The radio network was designed to work 'up and down', and lateral links were unreliable. Thus a message to an outlying column only a few miles away often had to be passed to brigade headquarters or right back to India for retransmission: Gaitley [sic] *received the message, but was not able to tell Rome he had just fought a company of Japanese and was in some disarray.*

However, he sent part of his rifle company under Captain Coulthart [sic] *to Broadway, who duly attacked from the west up to the stronghold wire, only to be badly cut up by Japanese, who had stealthily occupied air raid trenches dug outside the perimeter by light aircraft pilots (against orders). Coultart* [sic], *a good and brave officer was killed. The attack failed and Rome pulled the King's inside the stronghold...*

This account is not entirely accurate. Captain Coulthard's assault took place in the afternoon of the 28th not the 30th March, and was the first contact 82 Column had with the Japanese at Broadway; if the column was in 'some disarray' it was after Coulthard's assault. Moreover, Rome did not pull the King's inside the stronghold. The survivors of the assault retired back to the column's bivouac outside Broadway. In fact Rome gave permission for the King's to withdraw a few miles from Broadway for a supply drop. Shelford Bidwell goes on.

On the 31st. Rome called in the Air Commando, and mounted a strong attack to follow up the strike, using a company of Gurkhas and the group of King's, whose attack he led personally. The Gurkhas soon over-ran their objective. In fact the Japanese fled, but the King's had been badly shaken in their two [sic] *previous encounters having lost, besides Captain Coultart* [sic], *some thirty six killed and wounded. Nothing Rome could do would persuade them to follow up. 'They saturated the jungle with bullets and made a lot of noise, all sound and fury and not much else.'*

Michael Calvert's account of this attack, in *Prisoners Of Hope*, Corgi Books, reads

The enemy was at first severely mauled from the air, but there was a bit of a time lag before our attack went in, with the result that when our troops reached the enemy they found only minor opposition: the main body retreating in disorder and leaving much equipment behind. 82 Column, although ordered to pursue, were slow in reorganising, and the enemy got away. The commander of 82 Column had tried to command his column from behind as taught in military text-books. This is quite hopeless, and always leads to lost opportunities and lack of control. A commander must place himself where he himself can influence the battle at short notice; otherwise he is nothing but a military commentator.

It must be remembered that Shelford Bidwell's account is based on incomplete war diaries, and, since Brigadier Calvert was embattled at White City at the time, his account is based on reports from the Broadway HQ.

There was no time lag. Immediately the air strike ceased the King's and Gurkhas charged forward with bayonets and kukris, and both forces, not just the latter, over-ran the Japanese positions. The author remembers this as clearly as if it was yesterday, and when he and his section broke into the open plain, other sections were jog trotting well ahead, a few of them, heading for a log 50 yards into the plain, when they were ordered back.

Mike Calvert's account clearly puts the 82 Column commander (Gately), not Rome, in charge of the assault and responsible for the failure to pursue the enemy. Colonel Rome may well have participated in the attack, and he was a distinctive figure with a red pugaree around his bush hat, but the first sight the author, or any of his comrades, had of him that morning was when he welcomed them back into the stronghold.

Whoever was in command, it was not as Shelford Bidwell reports, because the King's had been badly shaken by previous casualties, that they did not 'follow up'. The troops were, in the modern vernacular, too 'hyped up' and in 'full cry' for Japanese blood to need any urging forward. Nor was it that they were 'slow in reorganising'. No reorganising was necessary since forward movement was merely continuation of the initial assault. In sum it was not that nothing 'would persuade them to follow up' but that one or other of the commanders firmly ordered the King's to break off the pursuit.

§

The Japanese never attacked, or even approached Broadway, after 31st March, and it became a peace harbour and trading centre until it closed down over a month later. A disgraceful postscript to the 'Battle of Broadway' is that no attempt was made to decently inter the bodies of 82 Column's fallen comrades, although there were no pressing operational problems to prevent this. When the author returned to Broadway – with a Graves Registration Unit some nine months later – their skeletons. in rotted uniforms lay just where they had fallen, except for some disturbance by predatory animals. Someone had collected their weapons and most of their identity discs were missing. Identification, for their eventual headstones was, therefore, largely a matter of recalling their physique and their precise location at the moment they were killed. To this day the author is plagued with guilt that some of his identification may have been faulty, and the headstones at their last resting place may bear the wrong names.

Appendix 2

Michael Calvert strongly opposed the 'replacement' of White City by another 'block', especially as Blackpool would be so close to the enemies front line. In *Prisoners of Hope* pp 163-164, he gives his reasons.

...Immediately behind the a front there is divisional and corps artillery. Behind that are reserves of infantry and artillery and much ammunition close at hand. Then there is a gap in which for many hundreds of miles, perhaps, there are practically no troops at all. ...Now that gap is the best area for attacking the enemy's line of communication. If you get closer to the front you meet his reserves, who without much movement and inconvenience can be set upon you. Ground commanders who have limited vision are always trying to get guerrilla or airborne or penetration forces mixed up just behind the enemy's front. This does no good as they are then easily destroyed. At Blackpool, the artillery [Japanese] *was already present, and had hardly to make any move to start its bombardment – whereas at White City, which was about the right distance behind the lines, the enemy had to form a base, build up his artillery, and generally redeploy new forces, all the time being harassed and weakenedby our lighter force. On a long single line of communication it does not matter where one breaks it any more than where one breaks an oil pipe line or a railway line. In fact, the further away from his main centres one breaks it, the better. Any railwayman would much prefer to mend a bridge close to a large junction where he has his engineers, his material, his reconnaissance parties etc., and where he does not have to make new administrative arrangements for the feeding of his labour force...*

...So one can sum up. It is always wrong to direct forces operating behind the enemy's line in co-operation with the direct offensive of a major force, too close to the enemy's main force. It will always pay greater dividends if the penetrating force cuts the enemy's communications many miles behind the enemy's own reserves. He (the enemy) must then either move his reserves away from the main battle to free his communication, or draw troops from elsewhere, both of which can be easily resisted....

Shelford Bidwell records Calvert's chagrin on this subject in pp 224-

226 of *The Chindit War*.

Calvert was by no means so cooperative or complaisant. He felt (as many of his young men felt, and feel to this day) that White City could have been held indefinitely, and that it was disgraceful to surrender what had been captured with so much sacrifice. He had been contemptuous at what was, in his eyes, the passive, defensive policy which accompanied the evacuation [of White City], and furious when he had been foiled in an attempt to borrow Lockett's column for an attack on the Japanese, concocted between the two 'old Chindits' in the old, independent, buccaneering Chindit style. Moreover his amour-propre was understandably bruised. Under Wingate he had always been consulted and the two had regularly discussed plans and tactics, and Wingate came to him, in the field. Now he was summarily given his orders by signal, and his two freshest battalions had been equally summarily removed from him [The King's and 3/9th Gurkhas assigned to 111 Brigade], *together with Vaughan's Nigerians, for whom he had formed a high regard* [35 Column of the West African Brigade had been involved in White City battles]. *He was then invited to express an opinion on the state of his troops. By mid-May he had lost thirty eight officers (the Gurkhas alone had ten British officers killed in action) and 592 rank and file killed, wounded or evacuated sick, and the drain of sick was increasing. All three commanding officers agreed their columns badly needed rest. There was first a half-promise of evacuation, but shortly after came an order to stay in. This did nothing to soothe Calvert's black mood.*

As regards the new plan Calvert objected, and with some reason, that he was being given an unsound position – a 'death-trap' was the term he used, and he was not a nervous commander – wedged between the mountain wall and the Namyin River, facing Blackpool with the Japanese behind him. His signals to Lentaigne went from argumentative to abrasive to insubordinate. ('I was getting too big for my boots,' he admitted thirty four years later.)

As Shelford Bidwell goes on to point out, Calvert was very tired at the time, he had malaria and was suffering from depression which often follows release from stress. He thrived on danger and was a romantic. For him, like so many men who had volunteered for special forces, battle was a test of manhood – like sport – with a noble aim. *'Working with Stilwell was all very well, but how much more inspir-*

ing was Wingate's call to liberate Burma and restore it to the British Empire.'

Wingate's death had hit all Chindits hard, but for Calvert it was a grievous personal loss. Now he was gone, Calvert was convinced that Wingate's plans were being flung aside and his master's *'vision betrayed'*. Moreover, hard-fought actions under the new order meant Calvert would have to send men into battle, instead of always leading them.

Lentaigne had little stomach for personal confrontations, but he eventually summoned Calvert to meet him at Broadway where, Shelford Bidwell records, *'...Lentaigne's natural kindliness came to the fore...'* After patiently explaining that, with the Fourteenth Army engaged in a crucial struggle with the Japanese, there were no reserves to relieve Calverts brigade, and the way to prove Wingate's ideas was to help Stilwell secure Moguang and Myikyina. He is said to have added that he did not want to lose Calvert, but he would relieve him of his command if his antagonism persisted. Ultimately Lentaigne's *'tact and firmness'* in Shelford Bidwell's words, *'prevailed. Calvert came to his senses and the commander of Special Force was relieved that he had not been forced to dismiss his ablest and most aggressive brigadier.'*

What should not be glossed over, is that the abandonment of White City, the debacle of Blackpool, and Calvert's battle of attrition at Moguang, were deplorable concessions to Stilwell's self-interest and aggrandizement. To make good his failure to maintain the aggressive momentum of his Chinese divisions, his floundering strategy pitilessly sacrificed the Chindits' superb mobility

Appendix 3

Some accounts state that Major Blaker and his dead comrades were rolled over the edge into the jungle and that three months later a Graves Registration Unit found them, bamboos six feet tall, growing among and through them. This is only partly true. Once 2171 had been consolidated they were buried and the spot marked with a knee high bamboo cross. The Graves Registration Unit reached 2171 nine months later, not three months later. The Unit spent two or three days searching, often on hands and knees in the undergrowth, for fallen comrades and recovering them for interment in a military cemetery, but could not find Major Blaker and his Gurkhas. Reluctantly, it was decided to abandon the search and move on to other battlefields the following day. At dawn the next morning, the author, lying in his blanket and blinking the sleep from his eyes, caught sight of a bamboo trunk gilded by the early sun. About nine feet up was the 'cross tree' lashed with vine. Major Blaker's marker had taken root.

There were no bamboos growing through the bodies.